Homecoming

VOLUME TWO

PAMELA YAYE

Essence Bestselling Author

ADRIANNE BYRD

Hollington Homecoming

VOLUME TWO

HARLEQUIN® KIMANI ARABESQUE®

HOLLINGTON HOMECOMING, VOLUME TWO

ISBN-13: 978-0-373-09132-4

Copyright © 2013 by Harlequin Books S.A.

This edition published September 2013

The publisher acknowledges the copyright
holders of the individual works as follows:

PASSION OVERTIME
Copyright © 2009 by Pamela Yaye

TENDER TO HIS TOUCH
Copyright © 2009 by Adrianne Byrd

**Coventry
City Council**

CEN*

3 8002 02149 919 1	
Askews & Holts	Jan-2014
	£6.99

Printed in U.S.A.

HARLEQUIN®
www.Harlequin.com

CONTENTS

Dear Reader,

We hope that your college years were filled with fond memories—football games with tailgating parties, studying all night and meeting your roommate for the first time. Aside from these remembrances, there might also be that one love that you left behind and wondered, what if...

This *Hollington Homecoming* collection presents four wonderful stories that take you on an exciting adventure back to homecoming weekend. You will be reminded of what it feels like to revisit your old stomping grounds and connect with friends and lovers. Your heart will beat with nostalgia as you read these sensual class-reunion tales and are swept off your feet by the power of passion.

In Pamela Yaye's "Passion Overtime," PR rep and event planner Kyra Dixon has been given the plum job of helping sign hunky pro-football star Terrence Franklin as Hollington's new head coach. But Kyra and Terrence have some unfinished business. Essence bestselling author Adrianne Byrd's "Tender to His Touch" introduces trendy designer Beverly Turner, who wants to let loose and have some fun at her reunion. And her wish just might come true when she meets Lucius Gray.

Enjoy this escape down memory lane with *Hollington Homecoming, Volume Two,* and look for *Hollington Homecoming, Volume One,* available now wherever books are sold.

Happy Reading,

Harlequin Kimani Arabesque

PASSION OVERTIME
Pamela Yaye

Acknowledgments

Jean-Claude Yaye: You are such an amazing person, and from the moment I met you, I knew you were the perfect man for me. One day soon, we'll travel back to Korea and recreate our first date. Only this time, I won't play hard to get! (ha ha)

Aysiah Yaye: Mommy loves you very much. You are the funniest, most interesting kid I know and I feel so blessed to be your mom.

To the best parents ever, Daniel and Gwendolyn Odidison: Writing this book made me reflect about my college years, and what stands out most are all the times we all sat around the kitchen table talking, laughing and just hanging out. I love you both with all my heart and live to make you proud in all that I do.

Bettey Odidison: You are my biggest supporter, my best friend and the perfect sister in every way. I love you and am counting down the days until our next girls-only vacation together.

Kenny Odidison: Bro, you never cease to amaze me. Not only an incredible man, you're a loving, doting father. Kayla is truly blessed to have you as her dad. Love ya!

As always, I have to thank my agent, **Sha-Shana Crichton,** my critique group, my coworkers, and all my friends and family around the world who support my work. I hope you know that I appreciate you all. Thanks for everything!

Chapter 1

"Terrence Franklin just pulled up in a yellow Ferrari sports car!"

Kyra Dixon jumped as if she'd been zapped with a stun gun. Blistering-hot coffee sloshed over her mug and splashed onto her slingback sandals. She felt a tightening in her chest at the mention of her ex-fiancé's name and calmed her nerves with a deep breath. Masking her annoyance, she turned and smiled grudgingly at her boss. "Good morning, Mr. Morrow."

"Can you believe it? He's finally here. I glanced out my office window, and there he was signing autographs and posing for pictures by the fountain." Straightening his tie, he studied his profile in the coffeepot, a wide, goofy expression on his face. When he swung back around, his smile had doubled in length. "I asked Nikki to show Terrence into the conference room," he explained, nodding furiously. "I wanted us to have some time to go over our game plan."

"Our game plan?" she repeated, frowning. "Walter, I think I can handle a washed-up, ex-football player. I've been the public relations director at Hollington College for almost seven years. I know what I'm doing."

"Terrence Franklin is more than just an *ex*-football player. He's a living legend!" Tugging on his olive-colored suspenders, Walter rocked on the balls of his feet with gusto. "This is the biggest moment of your career, Kyra. For me, too!"

His face was flush with excitement, and he was practically slobbering on his starched white shirt. "I think you're worrying for nothing, Walter. Terrence Franklin isn't the superstar athlete he once was. Getting him to sign on as head coach will be a piece of cake."

"Kyra, Kyra, Kyra." Shaking his head in disapproval, he wagged a finger at her, as if he were scolding a wayward child. "We don't have much time, but I'm going to give you a crash course on professional sports. Try to keep up."

Spare me, she thought, adding another sugar cube to her coffee. Raising the mug to her lips, she listened halfheartedly as her boss spoke in a loud but reverent tone about the National Football League. Football was America's favorite pastime. People watched it, talked about it and die-hard fans gambled on its outcomes. And, a player with the right personality could bring millions in revenue to any given city. Gesticulating wildly with his hands, his breathing grew deep and labored, like a pregnant woman on the verge of giving birth.

"Not only is the kid good-looking, he has more charm than a Hollywood movie star!" His big, bold laugh was like a blast of a trumpet. "He's a Heisman Trophy winner, an eight-time all-star and the only running back to be voted most valuable player two consecutive seasons. And he's here, at Hollington College!"

Her legs trembled like a toddler on stilts, but she didn't slide to the floor like she had the morning Walter called to say her ex-fiancé was interested in the head coaching position. Even though Kyra despised Terrence and everything he stood for, she had to admit that his stats were impressive. Since being drafted by the Dallas Cowboys, he'd broken long-standing records, amazed fans with his heroic plays on the field and built a cult following.

In ten seasons, he'd become the most talked about, most admired and most electrifying pro athlete. And every time Kyra turned on the TV, he was hawking the next big thing. Terrence was the golden boy of the National Football League and the media couldn't get enough of him. Terrence had gotten injured during a nationally televised playoff game, but his coach had assured fans that he'd make a speedy recovery. Then, in a move that shocked the entire sports world, he'd announced his retirement and walked away from it all.

"Terrence is a superstar, and—" he leaned heavily on the word "—a Hollington alum. He's given thousands to charity, and even partnered with the Make-a-Wish Foundation a few years back. Exceptional athletic ability and womanizing aside, he's a good man, and an excellent role model for kids and teens alike."

Kyra snorted. Big friggin' deal. Her boss might think the former NFL running back was the salt of the earth, but she knew the real Terrence Franklin. The arrogant, showboating Casanova who didn't have a loyal bone in his body. The one who craved the spotlight and female attention. In his third season, his off-the-field antics had tarnished his squeaky-clean image and after a wild night at a Las Vegas club Super Bowl weekend, the media had dubbed him Flash. Terrence seemed to derive great pleasure from shocking people. But what did she care? He wasn't her problem, but if he took the head coaching position, the cavorting and partying had to stop.

"Kyra, you don't watch football, so you don't get how truly gifted he is."

If he only knew. Since the day Terrence had stepped onto the field as the newest running back for the Hollington Lions, she'd watched every single one of his games. And she'd been there, along with Terrence's family, when he was presented with the coveted Heisman Trophy. But admitting to her boss that she'd once been engaged to Terrence would only complicate things. Walter was a fair, easygoing man, who trusted her, and she didn't want to disappoint him.

The hours were long and the accolades few, but Kyra loved working at her alma mater. And she wasn't going to let her feelings stand in the way of doing her job. Besides, her history with Terrence wasn't the issue. Convincing him to sign on as head coach of a losing team was going to be challenging enough without their past getting in the way. Yes, keeping mum about their relationship was definitely the way to go.

"Terrence Franklin is the fastest man ever. Carl Lewis? Maurice Green? Those guys have nothing on him. And if he ever decides to come out of retirement, the NFL and its fans will be waiting."

"You really think so?"

He nodded fervently. "Terrence is one of the greatest running backs to ever play the game. Right up there with Deion Sanders, Emmitt Smith and…"

She sipped her coffee. A season ticket holder of the Atlanta Falcons for years, Kyra, and her two younger brothers had braved traffic, freaky weather and long lines every Sunday afternoon to cheer on the home team. They were there when Terrence scored his first touchdown in a Dallas Cowboys uniform. Saw him twist and spin out of tackles and shoot into the end zone like a human cannonball. And hollered feverishly when he shattered another decade-old record.

Kyra's mind returned to that chilly afternoon ten years ago at the Georgia Dome when the Cowboys were playing the Falcons. Over the deafening roar of the crowd, she'd actually heard the thunderous beat of her heart. After celebrating with his teammates, Terrence stopped in the middle of the field, and lifted his eyes to the rafters, as if taking everything in. He'd stared up at Section A, and for a panic-stricken moment, she'd feared he would see her. It was a ludicrous thought, of course. He didn't have extraordinary vision, after all, just lightning-quick speed. But in that moment, it was as real as her raging, out-of-control heartbeat.

"I love this school," Walter confessed, his eyes filled with pride, "but I'm tired of watching our guys get butchered out there on the field. Attendance is at an all-time low, players are arguing between plays and even the cheerleaders sound depressed."

Kyra opened her mouth, but he spoke over her.

"It's up to us to get Terrence here. Without him, the team doesn't have a chance of winning their division. And building that new stadium would all be for naught."

She waited patiently for him to run out of steam, but when she glimpsed the time on the clock, she decided to cut in. "We better get going," she suggested, putting down her empty mug. "We don't want to keep Wonder Boy waiting, now do we?"

Down the hall in a bright airy room off the main office, Terrence Franklin sent a text message to his financial adviser. Buying stocks in the auto industry sounded risky. Sure he had the money, but he hadn't become a millionaire by making impetuous decisions. Maybe later, after his meeting with Kyra, he'd give it some more thought.

An image of Kyra, as he remembered her from their college days surfaced. Had it really been ten years since he'd seen her? It seemed like just yesterday they were walking through the halls of Hollington, hanging out in "the quad" with their friends and sharing their first explosive kiss.

He had been just another college student, juggling school, football and an active social life. Then he'd met Kyra. He knew from speaking to her sorority sister, Tamara Hodges, that she was a sheltered good girl, shielded from the temptations of the world by her minister parents. Before meeting the vibrant management student, he was a boozing, partying misfit who didn't take his education or his future seriously. But after their first date, he realized he'd have to clean up his image if he wanted to be with a girl as special as Kyra Dixon.

Intent on having her, he'd quit drinking and stopped clubbing with the guys. A year later, he proposed. He'd been the one to break things off, but Terrence knew if it wasn't for Kyra's unwavering support, he never would have made it to the NFL.

Terrence turned away from his memories. He wasn't going there. Not today. It was bad enough he'd had another dream about her. Since returning to Hollington he'd thought of nothing else but Kyra and the love they'd once shared.

Smiling ruefully, he shifted in his chair. *Well, that's a lie.* She'd crossed his mind over the years, too. Times when he'd least expected it. The day he'd signed with the Cowboys. The afternoon he'd moved into his beach condo. And every time he smelled exotic fruit.

Footsteps pounded in the hallway. Then, the door swung open and a flabby, silver-haired man, who he guessed was Walter Morrow, burst into the room with more exuberance than Richard Simmons. Terrence stood, hand outstretched, game face on. He took a step forward, but his legs buckled like a folding chair.

Momentarily speechless, his gaze swept over the woman with the familiar scent. Walter welcomed him to Hollington, but Terrence didn't respond. His eyes were glued to Kyra and the longer he stared, the harder it was to think. She had a fresh, modern look that was sexy but not overdone, and seeing her again after all these years made his heart race a hundred miles an hour. He was known to say, "You've seen one pretty face, you've seen 'em all!" But today, Terrence was prepared to eat crow. Kyra wasn't the typical beautiful woman. She was infinitely more. More natural, more graceful, more sophisticated. There was a simplicity about her, some-thing warm and compelling and, though it was hard to believe in this day and age, genteel.

"Terrence Franklin, the pleasure is all mine."

He felt a sharp pop in his shoulder and snapped out of his daze. Mr. Morrow was pumping his hand so hard, his knuckles cracked.

"It's good to be back at Hollington." His decision to return to his alma mater had been twofold. He'd make some plans for the future and reconnect with Kyra. He'd never forgotten the sacrifices she'd made for him, and he was going to make things right with her if it killed him. Staring at her now, he said, "This school holds a lot of special memories for me."

"That's right. You rushed for ninety-three yards against the Wildcats in your first game!" Mr. Morrow's face clouded with nostalgia. "I wasn't president of Hollington back then, but I was in the bleachers that night. You were incredible and the energy in the stadium was electric!"

"Thank you, sir."

"Excuse me, but I just have to ask. What's Terrell Owens *really* like? He's a hothead, isn't he? A real live wire, I bet," he speculated. "Come on, you're out of the league now, you can tell me. I promise it won't leave this room."

Football had been his life since he picked up his first pigskin at the age of nine, but Terrence didn't want to discuss his teammates, his endorsement deals or any of the other usual crap fans liked to talk about. Uninterested in the conversation, he stared at Kyra, desperate to make eye contact. *Why wouldn't she look at him?*

As if remembering Kyra was standing behind him, Walter turned and gave her a hearty push forward. "This is the little lady I've been chatting up over the phone. Terrence Franklin, I'd like you to meet—"

"Kyra Dixon," he finished smoothly. "It's been a long time, hasn't it?"

Mr. Morrow's cheeks sagged when his jaw fell open. "You guys know each other?"

"We took a few classes together," she was quick to say, "and we knew a lot of the same people on campus."

Her smile was polite, guarded, filled with manufactured warmth. He'd been haunted by her face for all these years and he knew forced emotion when he saw it. "Welcome back to Hollington, Mr. Franklin. We're glad to have you."

Disappointed by her lukewarm greeting, he dug his hands into his pockets and shook off feelings of frustration. He wasn't doing play drills in the scorching Dallas heat or working out with his trainer, but he needed a moment to catch his breath. This was insane. He'd dated models, dancers and an impressive collection of singers and actresses, but he'd never been more nervous than he was right now.

"I wish I could stay, but I have a board meeting in fifteen minutes," Mr. Morrow explained. "I'd cancel, but everyone's expecting me."

Thank God. I thought he'd never leave. While Terrence waited for the man to disappear, he studied Kyra closely, carefully, examining every aspect of her appearance. Light eyes, plump glossy lips, curves stacked on top of curves. Her hair had a soft sheen to it and was cut in a dramatic, cheek-grazing bob. The reddish-brown hue was a sharp contrast to her coffee-with-cream complexion and played up her soft, pale eyes. Underneath her mustard blazer was a white blouse and a belted skirt that emphasized her soda pop bottle shape.

Terrence licked his lips. He'd just finished a bottle

of vitamin water, but he was suddenly thirstier than a Kenyan marathon runner. High-heeled sandals gave Kyra height, and reminded him of those clunky shoes she used to wear back in the day. The PR manager hated her diminutive height and still did everything in her power to appear taller. Five feet four inches was listed on her driver's license, but she used to swear on a stack of bibles that she was five-six.

"Terrence, we'll talk later this week," Walter promised, pausing at the door. "If you need anything, anything at all, just let Kyra know. She'll take good care of you."

"What was that all about?" he asked, when they were alone. "Why didn't you tell him the truth?" He added, half-teasing, "You're not embarrassed of me, are you, Kyra?"

The corners of her lips tightened. "We're going to be spending a lot of time together in the coming weeks and I'd like if we could put the past behind us."

Her eyes were so pretty, so deep and incredibly bright, he couldn't concentrate on what she was saying. Kyra was all business, but that didn't stop Terrence from wanting her. He wanted to touch her, hold her, feel the delicious heat of that shapely body. But he knew better than to touch her. Not yet, anyway. After, when she'd loosened up and quit being so tense, he'd show the public relations director that he was a changed man.

The sound of his name on her heavily painted cherry-red lips brought him back to the present. "Fine. If that's what you want, I'll go along with it."

On the football field he was flashy, brazen, daring even, but here, in Hollington, standing inches away from his first love, his confidence deserted him. He was just another man, lusting over a ridiculously beautiful woman, and though he was a smart, articulate guy, he didn't have the words to tell Kyra just how stunning she was. "Anything else on your mind?"

"I know you're very busy, so let's get started."

Terrence pumped more shine into his smile. "I have all the time in the world."

"Well, I don't."

His face must have showed his surprise, because she suddenly looked contrite.

Gesturing to one of the chairs around the table, she sat down and crossed her legs. Shoulders squared, hands clasped, she looked like a woman in control of herself and her surroundings. And for now, she was. "I promise to be brief."

Terrence followed her lead. Seated, his eyes roving appreciatively over her chest and hips, he tried not to stare at her moist, luscious mouth.

"Mr. Rawlins quit unexpectedly, leaving us scrambling to find a suitable replacement, and although the interim coach is doing a fine job, President Morrow made it very clear that you're the only one he wants for our team."

"What do you think, Kyra?"

"I think you'll bring excitement back to Hollington and connect with the freshman players." Another artificial smile. "Why don't I tell you more about the specifics of the job, and we'll go from there?"

Kyra tucked a chunk of hair behind her ear. Sunlight splashed through the window and bounced off the diamond ring on her hand. Panic swelling in his chest, he checked to see which finger. Second from the left. *What? Kyra was married?*

Twenty minutes passed. Kyra delivered her pitch and though her enthusiasm was contagious, he didn't hear more than five words. How was he supposed to concentrate when she smelled so damn good? No one could concentrate under these conditions. Not even the Pope, and he was the king, or rather, the father of cool.

"I was hoping you'd stop me when I got carried away," she confessed, dropping her hands in her lap. "What do you think so far?"

"I think you're beautiful."

Terrence couldn't be sure, but he thought he saw surprise flash in her eyes. "It's eleven thirty," he told her. "Why don't we continue this discussion over lunch?"

Kyra got to her feet. "I can't. It's been a zoo around here all day and I'm busy getting everything ready for reunion weekend."

"You can't take an hour out of your day to have a bite with an old friend?"

"I'm afraid not, but we can set up another time next week to discuss the coaching position. Also, other people in the Hollington organization will want to speak to you about this fantastic opportunity." Her voice was light, her words carefully chosen, but he heard the chill in her tone. To signify the end of their conversation, she strode over to the door and opened it. "I'll show you out."

Terrence knew what a brush-off looked like and Kyra had always been an expert at letting a guy down easy. His gut feeling was that the curvy PR director was going to be a tough cookie to crack, but Terrence wasn't worried. He was made to compete, to win, to perform at the highest level, and it didn't matter if he was shooting hoops or playing blackjack. He played to win. "Ladies first," he announced, gesturing for her to precede him. "Why don't you tell me more about the players on the team?"

Falling in step with her, they strode past narrow offices and sunlit conference rooms. To block out the noises around them, he leaned in, purposely brushing against her. Kyra hopped as if she'd been jabbed with a pitchfork. The message was clear: look, but don't touch.

Convinced she was appalled at his behavior, Terrence decided to cool his Nikes. This was her turf, her world, and if he came on too strong, she'd think he was just another pompous athlete trying to score some tail. For now, he'd sit back and let Kyra take the lead. Hell, why not, when she looked so damn sexy doing it?

Chapter 2

Kyra felt Terrence's hand on her lower back, and narrowed her eyes in disgust. Where did he get off touching her? Her first thought was to smack his hand away, but she didn't want to appear uptight. President Morrow wanted Terrence to coach the Hollington Lions and until the ex-footballer accepted the job, she had to play nice.

Refusing to shy away from his gaze, she stared up at him, marveling at how youthful he looked even after all these years. The edges of his fine, dark hair were trimmed, giving the thirty-two-year-old sports star a clean, polished appearance. His short-sleeve shirt and jeans couldn't disguise his long athletic physique. Terrence Franklin reeked of masculinity and although Kyra wasn't attracted to him, she loved the way his muscles filled out his designer shirt.

"Have you been working at Hollington since graduation?"

The friendly expression on his face didn't fool her. The former NFL running back was trouble, and Kyra knew if she ever let her guard down, she'd be sorry. "No, I worked at an advertising agency for a few years before applying here. This is my—"

Their conversation came to a halt when the door to the registrar's office flew open and a group of bright-eyed students rushed out. "Hey, look, it's Terrence Franklin!"

Worried she might get trampled on, Kyra moved off to the side and watched in amusement as Terrence greeted the awe-struck freshmen. A small crowd gathered around him, and though he smiled apologetically at her, it was obvious he enjoyed signing autographs and connecting with his fans.

When the crowd cleared, he apologized for the interruption. "I'm sorry for making you wait. I know how busy you are getting things together for reunion weekend."

"It's no problem. You're one of the most recognizable athletes in the world, and that's why the board of directors wanted you here at Hollington. To bring excitement and enthusiasm to the college."

"Coaching at my alma mater would be a dream come true and I'm really grateful for this opportunity. Hopefully, this will be the start of a long, successful partnership."

Kyra avoided his gaze. Truth was, she found it hard to believe anything that came out of Terrence's mouth. After all, he'd lied when he said he loved her and made her the butt of their friends' jokes when he dumped her.

They continued down the hall towards the reception area. "How's your family doing? Is everyone all right?"

"Uh-huh." His crippling smile and fragrant cologne made her thoughts turn to mush. An aromatic aphrodisiac, his scent aroused her senses and elicited an unexpected physical response. Her voice caught in her throat, and her skin prickled with desire. Over the years, Kyra had dated scores of cool, dreamy types, but no one aroused her like Terrence did.

"I hear your dad's church is one of the fastest-growing in the South."

Mindful of him watching her, she produced a smile. Her father's ministry didn't impress her and although he'd been heralded as a dynamic bishop, Kyra rarely attended services. Work kept her busy and she'd much rather organize her filing cabinet than listen to one of his fire-and-brimstone messages. "Yes, he's got quite the following."

"I'd love to see them again. Maybe one of these Sundays I'll visit their church."

Nodding, she allowed herself a fleeting look in his direction. Terrence had a voice made for radio and a body for the big screen, and suddenly articulating her thoughts was harder than riding a unicycle backwards. All smiles and good looks, he stared at her with such genuine interest that her thoughts scrambled like marbles on concrete. "Mom and Dad are still going strong. In fact, they were recently invited to the Mayor's Luncheon and honored with a humanitarian service award for their dedication to the community."

Terrence extended his congratulations and when she nodded in response, he asked if she was looking forward to the reunion. "Kevin Stayton and I have kept in touch, but I'm anxious to see the rest of the crew."

"Me, too. Tamara and I have years and years of catching up to do."

"What about us?"

"What *about* us?" she repeated.

Stopping abruptly in the middle of the hallway, his eyes burning into her very soul, he put a hand to her shoulder. "Kyra, we haven't seen each other in ten years. Don't you think we should talk?" His smooth, mellow voice deepened. "I went off to play in the NFL, but I never stopped thinking about you. You were always in my thoughts."

Kyra gulped. Her throat was tight and she feared what might come out. Squeaking wasn't cool. No matter what Terrence said or did, she had to keep her head. In college, he'd been a charmer, and there was no doubt in her mind that he'd perfected his skills over the years. Ten minutes earlier, he'd been offering compliments and making such intense eye contact she'd fumbled through her speech. All of her rehearsals in the bathroom mirror had been in vain because the moment Terrence smiled at her, she lost the use of her tongue.

"Can you believe it's been ten years since we graduated? It seems like just yesterday we were going steady and stealing kisses in our American history class."

Heart accelerating, mouth dry, she discreetly dried her palms on the sides of her skirt. After a long, meaningful silence, her mind cleared and her voice returned. "Enjoy the rest of your day, Terrence. I'll be in touch."

"When?"

The question hung in the air for several seconds. Kyra felt like there were pop rockets in her stomach. The office was crawling with students, faculty members and visitors, and the telephone buzzed every five seconds, but none of it seemed real. And why should it? Terrence Franklin, the man she'd planned to marry, the man she'd lost her virginity to, was staring at her with those deep, penetrating eyes.

"I'll give you a call once I free up some time in my schedule." Another lie. Hiring a coach for the Hollington Lions was priority number one. He knew it, she knew it and so did her boss, so who did she think she was kidding?

"How long have you been married?"

Kyra frowned. "What makes you think I'm married?"

He indicated to her left hand. "You're wearing a wedding ring."

What? Only married women like diamonds? Kyra didn't owe Terrence an explanation. They weren't friends, they weren't lovers. Hell, they were barely acquaintances. Besides, what he didn't know wouldn't hurt him. Or rather, hurt her. Her confidence returned, and a smile touched her lips. Yes, this arrangement would work out nicely. She'd pretend to be married and Terrence would never be the wiser. And her parents said it didn't pay to lie. Who knew?

"Could we get together tonight to discuss…"

Kyra started to speak, but trailed off when she felt a hand wind around her waist. She turned to her left, and a smile came. A huge, toothy grin that could eclipse the morning sun. Charles had chosen the best possible time to make an appearance, and Kyra suddenly felt like hugging him. But they'd only been dating for a few weeks and she didn't want to give him the wrong impression, even if it would knock Terrence down a few pegs. "Charles! Oh my God, what are you doing here?"

"Surprising you," he announced. "Don't tell me you're busy making arrangements for homecoming, because I've been looking forward to seeing you all week. I'm taking you out to lunch, and I won't take no for an answer."

"Of course, Charles. You know how much I like spending time with you. I've…"

Terrence coughed loudly, breaking her concentration. Annoyed, she glanced over at him. His jaw was clenched so tight, the muscles in his neck were throbbing. *Thank you, Charles!* she thought, grinning with satisfaction at Terrence's displeasure. She could be wrong, but he looked jealous. Though she'd graduated at the top of her class and bought her first home last year, nothing was more satisfying than seeing her ex green with envy.

"Hey man, what's up? I'm Terrence."

"Charles Roberts." His ocean-blue eyes were hard stones, and his forehead was creased. "Are you also in PR?"

"No, I play…I mean, I played professional ball."

Charles snuck a glance at Kyra for confirmation, and she nodded. "Terrence played for the Dallas Cowboys," she explained, mustering the appropriate amount of excitement. "He was also voted offensive player of the year three times during his career."

"You forgot eight-time pro Bowler," Terrence added with a sly wink. "And tell him about those soup commercials. Big Mama loves those!"

Kyra laughed. She couldn't help it. The commercials were a riot. Only Terrence could make figure skating look cool and she'd read recently that the company had seen a twenty percent increase in sales since the spots started running.

"Kyra, go grab your things," Charles ordered, pulling back the sleeve of his suit jacket and consulting his diamond encrusted watch. "Our reservations are for twelve-thirty and if we're late they might give away our table."

Turning on her heels, she shot into her office, grabbed her purse off her desk and returned to the reception area in ten seconds flat. Couldn't risk Terrence pumping Charles for personal information, now could she? "I'm ready," she sang. "Let's go. I'm starving."

But Charles didn't move. "You've been keeping secrets from me." He wiggled his eyebrows. "I knew you were recruiting a new coach for the Lions, but you never mentioned Terrence Franklin was your old college sweetheart."

Kyra stopped breathing. For a moment, she stood there, frozen, her gaze bouncing between the two men. "We were kids. It meant nothing. It was over ten years ago," she offered, by way of explanation. Her words came out in a clump, and she heard the quiver in her voice. Wonderful, she sounded like Miss Piggy on speed.

"It sure sounds serious," Charles countered. "Is it true you were engaged?"

Kyra cranked her head to the right. Terrence looked as innocent as Jack the Ripper. "Yes, but it was a long time ago. So long in fact, I hardly remember."

"Kyra's being shy. We had some really great times back then," Terrence mused, as if overtaken by nostalgia. "Cruising around in my Jeep, kicking it in the quad, eating at that crummy waffle house on Ninth."

Kyra felt hotter than a furnace. Why was he doing this? Was he trying to get a rise out of her? When Terrence reached out and patted her arm, her veneer cracked. *Two could play that game,* she decided, gritting her teeth. Facing Terrence, she met the challenge in his eyes, and smiled with a sick, saccharine sweetness. "I'm surprised you even remember any of that. I mean, with all your groupies and whatnot."

Returning her gaze to Charles, but watching Terrence out of her peripheral vision, she said, "He left for training camp and I never heard from him again. Well, unless you count that email he sent dumping me."

The light in Terrence's eyes went out, and his mouth went slack.

Kyra nodded to herself. Mission accomplished. From now on, Terrence would think twice before embarrassing her. "Honey, let's go," Kyra purred, tugging on Charles's arm. She'd never used the pet name before, but now was as good a time as any. "I've missed you, baby, and we have so much to talk about."

Charles frowned at her but said nothing. She was smiling so hard, her teeth ached, but when Terrence averted his gaze, satisfaction flowed through her. It appeared he couldn't stand to see her with someone else. How did he think she felt every time she flipped on the TV and saw him at a Hollywood premiere with a gorgeous blonde draped in diamonds and Versace?

"Kyra, I'll wait to hear from you," he said.

She thought she heard a note of sadness in his tone, but Kyra refused to feel guilty for living her life. Terrence was her past and as long as she kept telling herself that, she'd be fine. Remembering her earlier conversation with her boss, she inflected her voice with cheer.

"It was good seeing you again, Terrence. Welcome back to Hollington."

"Thanks for taking time out of your very busy schedule to meet with me."

"Take care."

The elevator pinged and Charles stepped inside.

Then, in a twist of bad luck, everyone inside got off on their floor, leaving the elevator empty. Faced with no alternatives, Kyra got on and strangled a groan when Terrence followed. Staring intently at the control panel, she wondered how long the awkward silence would last. *Is it just me or is this elevator moving slower than normal?* she thought, praying the stupid thing wouldn't stall. Stranger things had happened, and last night there had been a full moon.

"Terrence, how long are you in town for?" Charles asked, glancing up from his BlackBerry handheld device. "You're not hanging around until homecoming weekend, are you?"

"I wouldn't miss it for the world."

"You have a place here in Atlanta?"

"I have a five-bedroom spread in Savannah," he bragged, "but the school put me up in a place a few blocks from here."

While Charles and Terrence discussed the sinking real estate market, Kyra noted each man's physical attributes. Though Terrence was several inches taller, Charles had meatier arms and outweighed him by at least twenty pounds. Olive-toned, with a sprinkling of gray throughout his short, brown hair, Charles Roberts was on the fast track to being CEO of the largest insurance company in the nation.

Kyra's eyes slid down the hard lines of Terrence's

chest. The NFL player might have been every woman's dream, but he was her worst nightmare. For starters, he was broad, lean and had more muscles than a professional body builder. He possessed everything she liked in a man and more. Sexy shaved hair, deep brown eyes, ripped arms. And then there was his voice. There was a very sensual feel to it. It was commanding, but soothing and evoked feelings of calm. Charles spoke in a polished, refined way and though Terrence had graduated with a double major in English and education, his speech was cooler, laid-back, street.

"We should all hang out some time," Terrence suggested, as the elevator came to a grinding halt. "Kevin owns a nightclub in the city called Bollito. Ever heard of it?"

Charles started to speak, but Kyra grabbed his arm and with a burst of superhuman strength, practically dragged him out of the elevator. Going clubbing with Terrence was out of the question. Not today, not tomorrow, not ever. He'd made his choice ten years ago, and Kyra didn't believe in second chances, especially not for someone like him.

"Is everything all right?"

Kyra snapped out of her daydream. Instead of enjoying a quiet lunch at one of her favorite restaurants, she was replaying her conversation with Terrence in her mind. Thanks to its celebrity investors, big shots such as Russell Simmons and Justin Timberlake, Azure Lounge & Bar attracted a steady stream of powerful executives and rising stars. "I'm sorry. I haven't been very good company, have I?"

"No, but I forgive you," Charles said.

Kyra couldn't tell if he was joking, and didn't have the energy to ask. Troubled about her meeting with Terrence, and hungrier than a hiker lost in the woods, she reached for another garlic bun from the oversized glass bowl.

"Why don't you let me order you another appetizer?"

"Because I've already eaten a huge plate of pepper-corn ribs!" She sliced the bun in half, decided against adding butter and took a bite. "I'd like to lose a few pounds before homecoming, and it's already September 5. If I keep eating everything in sight, I'll never fit into the gown I bought."

"You're beautiful no matter what size you are."

Kyra's mind drifted off. Terrence had once whispered those very words to her, and after one drink too many at a raucous house party, they'd returned to his apartment to "talk." She remembered that night in remarkable detail. The potency of his cologne. The feel of his lips on her ear, his hands on her breasts and the rush of pleasure to her core when he plunged deep inside her slick walls.

"You feel the same way, Kyra, don't you?"

Embarrassed that she'd been swept away by her thoughts, she smoothed a hand over her flushed cheeks. Not wanting Charles to know she'd been fantasizing about another man, she nodded in response to his question and choked down so much water, she felt the button on her skirt pop off.

"I want us to be exclusive," Charles confessed, his awestruck tone teetering on desperation. Eyes glittering like diamonds, he took her hand and caressed her palm. "I think we're good together, don't you?"

Her shoulders tensed. It was too soon in their relationship to make grandiose declarations. Charles traveled a lot for his company, and Kyra was lucky if they saw each other once a week. Furthermore, she considered him more of a friend than a potential lover. "I'm really glad we exchanged numbers," she said, unsure of what else to say. "It's nice having someone to hang out with on the—"

"Hold that thought." He swiped his cell off the table, pressed it to his ear and chirped, "Charles Roberts. Talk to me."

Kyra stared at him, hoping her furrowed brows conveyed her disapproval. Talking on his cell phone at the table was her biggest pet peeve and they'd discussed it at length last week. Now he was back at it.

"Here we go," the waiter announced, pulling up beside the table and setting down two enormous plates. After refilling her glass, he left.

"I'm sorry about that," Charles said when he finally ended his call, "but I'm in the middle of a monster business deal."

Not wanting to ruin their lunch, she accepted his apology. "It's all right. I understand. Everyone gets a bit crazy when—"

His utensils fell on his plate with a clank, startling her.

"My food is cold." Charles spit into his napkin. Rising from his chair, his gaze darted maniacally around the room. "Where is that stupid waiter?"

Having worked as a waitress to put herself through school, Kyra had zero tolerance for rudeness and told him so. "Charles," she began, refusing to be embarrassed in front of the other well-dressed patrons, "your food is cold because you were on your cell phone for ten minutes. What did you expect the server to do?"

The waiter returned. "How is everything tasting?"

"I'd like another steak." Charles pushed his plate forward. "This one's cold."

With a curt nod, the young man was off and running back into the kitchen.

"Charles, that was unnecessary—"

"It's my accountant." Phone pressed to his ear, he stood and stalked through the dining room. Kyra watched him walk away. Charles was acting like a petulant child, and she wasn't going to let him get away with humiliating her. He had to learn to treat her—and everyone around him—with more respect. His behavior was something she'd expect from an actor. Or a rapper. Or a buff, wickedly handsome NFL running back.

Sighing, she glanced out the window, unwanted memories rolling through her mind. Ten years ago, she'd met Terrence on the Hollington College campus, and as she thought about that first meeting, a smile filled her lips. Rushing toward the fine arts building, she'd rolled her ankle and narrowly missed wiping out in front of Terrence. Kyra had seen the star running back around campus, but they'd never talked before. So when he ditched his friends and commanded her to hop on his back, she'd been stunned.

Five minutes later, she was climbing aboard the T-train, as he'd teasingly called it. Arms swathed around his neck, legs wrapped at his waist, he'd carried her to the north building and returned at the end of her African dance class with a pair of pink jelly shoes. To show her appreciation, she'd treated the handsome footballer to lunch.

Terrence was the big man on campus and she was a bookworm, but they'd hit it off immediately. Then one night after they'd had too much to drink they'd ended up back in his dorm room. One thing led to another and the next thing Kyra knew, she was down to her panties, pulsing with a tangible mix of desire, passion and lust. Terrence was her first, and though they'd stumbled in the dark, knocking things over and laughing hysterically at their inanity, she'd counted it as one of the happiest moments of her life.

Within weeks, they were inseparable. They ran with the same crowd, had the same friends and made plans to get married after the NFL draft. "Once things settle down and I finish training camp," he'd promised. Things never did settle down and that magical day she'd always dreamed of never happened. Pressured by his manager to maintain his cool, single guy image, Terrence had broken off their engagement via email, never to be heard from again. Until now.

Why, after all these years, was she rehashing the past? Seeing Terrence again had stirred something in her. Something that had died the day she'd read that email message. Over the years, Kyra had dated some great guys. Powerful, accomplished men who knew how to treat a woman right. But Terrence stood out in her mind for several reasons. Though he'd been a struggling college student, with a rusted white hooptie and staggering debt, he'd spoiled her silly. He brought her breakfast in bed, walked her to and from class and made love to her with unspeakable warmth and tenderness. Humility had never been his strong suit, but he was chivalrous and respectful of her feelings.

"Ms., I brought a new steak entrée."

Kyra came to. Oh brother. Not this again. Squinting, as if blinded by the angry glare of headlights, she
searched the waiting area for Charles. Where was he?
Deciding she'd had enough of Charles and his rudeness
for one day, she opened her purse, tipped the waiter
and rose from her seat. "Thanks, Miguel. Everything
was great."

He looked confused. "You're leaving? What should
I tell the gentleman when he comes back?"

"I don't know," she sassed, winking mischievously.
"Be creative!"

Chapter 3

"Good morning, Kyra Dixon speaking."

"Just the voice I wanted to hear."

Her heart turned to wax. Terrence was more persuasive than a door-to-door salesman, but if she was going to survive the next eight weeks with him, she had to keep her guard up. "It's good to hear from you," she lied, with forced enthusiasm. Swallowing a yawn, Kyra flipped open her daily planner and scanned her list of appointments for the day. "I'm glad you called. I was going to contact you this afternoon."

"You were?" The inflection of his voice conveyed surprise. "When I didn't hear from you, I thought maybe you'd forgotten about me."

I wish, she thought, remembering last night's restless bout of sleep. Faded memories of her youth had filled her with nostalgia, and every time she closed her eyes, she saw Terrence, his mouth stretched into that cocky, lopsided grin, his arms outstretched like a compassionate lover. To distance herself from the troubling image, she asked Terrence how his day was going.

"I hope you've been enjoying this gorgeous weather, because it's going to start cooling down soon."

"Do you remember my cousins Neal and Damon?"

"Vaguely." It was a lie, but Kyra wanted to obliterate memories of their past and lying seemed to be the only way.

"I've been kicking it with them. We played pool and had some sushi last night. You used to love eating new foods. Ever tried Japanese?"

"No." Kyra stared down at the phone, the lines on her forehead bunched into a frown. Okay, now she was just being silly. What would it hurt if she admitted that she liked sushi, too? Before she could retract her words, he spoke.

"You lied to me," Terrence said. "You're not married. Why didn't you say anything when I asked?"

"Because I'm not going to discuss my personal life with you."

"Do you know what I love most about being back here?"

Kyra could hear the smile in his voice and pictured his broad grin.

"The people. Everyone's so polite and welcoming." He paused expectantly. "And then there's you."

Right, she thought, rolling her eyes to the ceiling. *He couldn't wait to return to Hollington to see me—the woman he'd dumped and humiliated.* Loosening her grip on the receiver, she propped an elbow up on the desk. All Kyra wanted to do was sign Terrence and get on with her life, but he seemed bent on rekindling their friendship. That was too bad. It wasn't going to happen.

"My evenings are free. Wide open," he told her. "I have nothing to do but watch TV. It would be great to hang out, you know, for old times' sake."

Her heart accelerated. Kyra felt like she was hanging upside down on a cliff. He sounded like the old Terrence. The one she used to love, the one who made her laugh, the one who'd once licked whipped cream and fudge off her breasts.

Deleting the image and his suggestion from her mind, she sat straight up in her chair. Remembering she was the one in control of this conversation, and not Terrence, she asked if he was free tomorrow. "The Lions practice at nine o'clock and I'd like you to come and meet the team."

"Cool. I'll see you then." He added, "Oh, and Ky?"

The phone slipped from her grasp, but didn't fall. Why was he using her pet name? They weren't friends anymore, weren't lovers, so why was he being cute with her all of a sudden? "Yes, Terrence?"

"Don't work too hard."

Someone knocked on the door. "I have to go, but I'll meet you in front of the stadium at nine o'clock sharp."

"I'll be there, ready and waiting."

Kyra put down the phone. "Come in," she called, adjusting her plum-colored suit jacket. It was probably her boss, wanting to see if she'd made any progress with Terrence yet. He'd been on her back all day, offering ideas on how to win the former NFL running back over. "Nikki, is that you under all those flowers?"

The bouquet was enormous. So big, it covered the

top half of Nikki's body. If it wasn't for the intern's teal high heels, Kyra wouldn't know who was carrying it.

"This is a surprise," she said, coming around her desk. Her office was inundated with the scent of pineapple and upon closer inspection Kyra realized it was a bouquet of fruit, not flowers. The white ceramic vase overflowed with stems of cantaloupe, guava and watermelon.

Who knew? she thought, popping a heart-shaped strawberry into her mouth. Charles must be feeling guilty about what happened at lunch, because he'd never sent her flowers before. He'd apologized, promised it wouldn't happen again and admitted he was under extreme pressure at work. Everyone lost their cool sometimes, even sweet quiet guys like Charles Roberts.

Munching on a cube of banana-dipped chocolate, she took the miniature envelope from Nikki's outstretched hands and ripped it open. "Looking forward to creating new memories with you," she read aloud. "I had no idea Charles could be so romantic."

"Mind if I have some?" Nikki asked, setting the bouquet on the desk. "I skipped breakie this morning and the pineapples smell yummy."

Kyra nodded. "In fact, do me a favor and take it to the staff room. I'm liable to have a sugar overdose eating all this fruit."

"I forgot your phone messages on my desk, but Terrence Franklin called earlier. You were in with Mr. Morrow and I didn't want to disturb you." Nikki's face shined.

"What's he like, Kyra? Do you think the tabloid stories about him are true?"

"Every last one," she blurted out. Casting a glance at

her wide-open door, she leaned back against the desk and gave herself five minutes to indulge in some harmless, office gossip. Nikki Wakefield, the department's high-spirited intern, was in her final year of the business management program and saw to it that everything ran smoothly. Once a week, Kyra took the senior out to lunch and it was always a lively, hour-long affair. "He's conceited, macho and—"

"Hella fine!" she shrieked. "Terrence Franklin is living proof that God exists. He's the perfect male specimen, in my book."

"All that glitters isn't gold, Nikki." Kyra put a hand on the intern's shoulder. "He might seem charming, but be very, *very* careful around guys like that."

Nikki's eyes glazed over and Kyra knew she'd lost her. Trim, chesty and blessed with naturally curly hair, the management student had more admirers than a Playboy Playmate of the Year. "The man is gorgeous," Nikki cooed, coiling a glossy curl around her index finger. "You could cover him in green slime and he'd still be fine!"

Tell me something I don't know.

Nikki turned to leave, then spun back around and extended her right hand. "Oh, I almost forgot. Your dad called. He wants you to call him at the church."

Nodding absently, Kyra took the message slip and shoved it into her pocket. Returning her father's call could wait. He was always imploring her to live the Christian way and Kyra wasn't in the mood to hear one of his midday sermons. Not when she had Terrence Franklin hot on her trail.

When Nikki departed, she picked up her pen and got down to work. The business letters weren't going to write themselves, and Kyra knew Walter would come looking for them at the end of the day. But when she wrote the word *fine* instead of *find* for the second time, she got up from her desk and went over to the window.

Students rushed to and from the dormitories, a group of international students kicked around a soccer ball, and couples kissed under the shade of lofty willow trees. Pride filled Kyra's heart. Few people, including her parents, understood why she'd chosen to study at a historically black college. Scholarships had poured in from other prestigious universities, but she'd turned them all down. Here, among students of every shade of brown under the sun, she'd flourished. Her sorority sisters had cheered her accomplishments, challenged her way of thinking and offered a shoulder to cry on when she needed it most.

Raised in a middle-class suburban neighborhood, Kyra had secretly longed to have friends and teachers who looked like her. She'd grown up wanting to be Debbie Allen and when she arrived at Hollington that balmy afternoon in August just days after her eighteenth birthday, she'd felt like a character on *A Different World*. Kyra had loved the community so much she'd applied for the public relations position the second she'd seen it in the newspaper, bought a two-bedroom townhouse in East Point and settled comfortably into her new life.

A girl who couldn't be much more than eighteen pushed a stroller down the street. Kyra rested her head against the glass. Everything she'd ever wanted in life had become a reality, and although she wasn't a wife or mother yet, she knew in time it would happen. Once Terrence signed on to coach the Lions and the excitement of homecoming weekend was behind her, she'd think more about her future.

For the last three months, the reunion had consumed her and now she had to fill the head coaching position. Her quiet life had suddenly become very hectic and something told her, Terrence Franklin, the former bad boy of the NFL, was going to be more trouble than he was worth.

"Beverly, what do you mean you're not going to the reunion?" Kyra asked, her hands propped on her slender hips. "This is a big weekend for the university and I'm counting on you to be there."

"I don't see why," Beverly Turner quipped, straightening a rack of printed skirts. Her trendy, high-end boutique, Hoops, was on North Highland Avenue and a steady stream of twenty-somethings flowed into the store and left carrying enormous white shopping bags with the dainty Hoops logo. The sparkling chandelier, golden cherubs and tasteful furniture gave a chic, intimate feel to the place. "Aside from you and a couple of other people, I haven't kept in touch with anyone from our graduating class."

"Beverly, you were homecoming queen and everyone's expecting you to be there."

"That's too bad, because I'm not going."

"Give me one good reason why you can't go."

"I'll give you three," she chirped, her low Southern twang taking on a hard edge.

Kyra sighed inwardly. Beverly was a deeply thoughtful woman with a gentle disposition, but she was always poised with a comeback.

"For starters, I'm swamped here." Selecting a daz-

zling sheath dress from off the rack, she slipped it off
the gold padded hanger and held it up to one of the mannequins in the front window. "I'm putting together the
final touches for my new spring line, and I have to design a gown for Gabrielle Union to wear to an awards
gala next month."

"You seem stressed, Bev. Why don't you let me take
you out for lunch?"

"So you can pressure me into going to the reunion?"
Beverly shook her head. "No way. I don't have time
for this right now. I'm up to my neck in paperwork and
it's going to take me the rest of the afternoon to fill the
online orders."

"Beverly, you've been dodging my calls for weeks
and the reunion is less than a month away. I need to help
Chloe finalize the rest of the plans for homecoming."

She said nothing, just continued dressing the mannequin and humming to the Smokey Robinson song
playing in the background.

Kyra heaved a heavy sigh. This was not going as
she'd planned. One of her girlfriend's less laudable traits
was definitely her stubbornness, but if she was going to
convince Beverly to attend reunion weekend, she had
to get to the heart of the matter. "So, that's it? You're
not going and there's nothing I can say or do to change
your mind?"

Beverly gave a brisk nod, then changed the subject by
asking how her meeting with Terrence Franklin went.
"I was picking up some fabric at my favorite store on
Monday and it seemed the whole town was abuzz with
the news of his big return."

Kyra thought about the scene she witnessed yesterday at The Tavern. She'd stopped in for lunch, but

when she spotted Terrence and Mr. Morrow eating beside the far window, she'd ordered her chicken salad to go. Shielded by a large, imposing floor plant, she'd watched Terrence in all of his celebrity glory. Fans scurried over to his table for autographs, pictures and hugs. For months, there had been speculation that he would come out of retirement before the trade deadline, and his silence heightened the media's interests and fueled every sports blog in the country. Kyra didn't like that Terrence was playing both sides of the fence, but until he signed on to coach the Lions, she didn't have a say in the matter. "Yeah, his arrival has generated a lot of good press for the school. We've received hundreds of online applications, and we had so much traffic on the Web site yesterday, it crashed!"

"I bet," Beverly agreed. "After all, he is the pride of Hollington."

"I'm lining up as many interviews as I can. I even contacted my old sorority sister, Tamara Hodges, about doing an article on Terrence becoming the Lions coach."

Her eyebrows rose. "You got him to sign on already?"

"Not yet, but I will."

Beverly started to speak, but her words were drowned out by a shrill, piercing laugh. Realizing they needed privacy, Kyra grabbed Beverly's hand and dragged her into the back office. Where the boutique was bright and glitzy, the office was a simple, understated space teeming with fashion magazines, invoices and poster boards. "Now," Kyra began, closing the door and standing in front of it, "spill it. What's the real reason you won't go to the reunion?"

Beverly stood her ground. "You're not going to change my mind, so you might as well save your breath."

"The class of '99 voted *you* Homecoming Queen, Beverly. How's it going to look if you don't show up?"

"Like I'm a popular fashion designer who has orders to fill." Straightening up, she folded her arms across her chest, her gaze drifting to the open window. "Kyra, I'm not trying to be difficult, but I've moved on from beauty pageants and modeling contests. I want to be taken as a serious businesswoman and that's not going to happen if I'm riding on top of a flowered float."

In an effort to keep the peace, Kyra listened to what she had to say without interrupting. Beverly was frowning, and Kyra could tell by the faraway look in her eyes that her mind was somewhere else. "Why does it feel like you're blowing me off?"

"I'd never do that," Beverly insisted, shaking her head. "We're friends, remember?"

"Then can a sister get a discount on that gold Ralph Lauren gown?"

Beverly gave a brief sputter of laughter, her eyes soft with a radiant glow and her oval face bright with cheer. It made Kyra feel good to see her girlfriend smile. All she ever did these days was stay cooped up in her office working. More than anything, Beverly needed to start living again, and three days of partying, drinking and socializing was just what the doctor ordered.

"Hanging out with old friends is just what you need. You've been divorced for almost two years, but you haven't been on a single date. I'm not telling you to go out there and party like Paris Hilton, but live a little, girl! Go to the reunion, and have a good time. And if you see someone who catches your eye…" Kyra trailed off, her glossy, red lips curled into a mischievous smirk. "There are going to be plenty of handsome, eligible brothers at the reunion, Bev. It would be a shame for you to miss out."

A smile broke through. "You must be very good at your job," Beverly teased.

"I try," Kyra sang, laughing. Sensing a subtle shift in her friend's mood, and anxious to get her on board, she continued. "Homecoming weekend is your opportunity to shine. Do you know how much business you'll drum up for the boutique just by being there wearing one of your gorgeous, one-of-a-kind creations?"

"I never even thought of that. It would be great for business, wouldn't it?"

Kyra nodded. A hard-driving perfectionist with an eye for detail, Beverly had created a line of mermaid-style gowns that had been worn on the red carpet by some of Hollywood's leading women. In the last six months, her celebrity clientele had tripled and her name was on every fashionista's lips. "Please, Bev? You're going to have an awesome time during reunion weekend. I just know it."

Beverly shrugged. "Okay, I'll think about it."

"Oh, you're going all right," Kyra vowed, lobbing an arm around Beverly's shoulders, "because I won't take no for an answer!"

Chapter 4

Cyclists in spandex shorts and wraparound sunglasses clogged the bike trail at Centennial Park. Pressing down the heel of her Rollerblade skates, Kyra slowed and waited until she was past the ten-man group before resuming her speed.

Chest heaving, arms swinging like a skier catapulted off a mountain, she shot down the hill on her Rollerblades, feeling as light and as free as a jaybird. Seagulls squawked, dogs barked and the sound of children's laughter rippled on the sultry, red-hot breeze. After a stressful day, in-line skating was just what Kyra needed to clear her head.

Invigorated by the scents and sounds of summer, she skated up the winding path and decided to do a third lap through the park. Kyra didn't know if she'd be able to get out of bed tomorrow, but she wasn't ready to pack up and go home.

Kyra plucked her tank top with one hand and wiped her forehead with the other. Sweat dripped off her face and chunks of hair clung to the back of her neck. Insects buzzed around her, but she was feeling too good to be bothered. Next month, her sorority sisters would be back in town for their ten-year reunion and there was no telling what trouble they'd get into this time.

Punching up the volume on her iPod handheld, she moved her shoulders and hands in tune to the beat. The Destiny's Child song made her reflect on her college days. Lately, she'd been doing a lot of self-examination. Ever since Terrence showed up, she'd been having one flashback after another. Turning away from her thoughts, she chose to admire the bright, fragrant flowers swaying in the breeze.

Joggers ran alongside their dogs and seniors strolled leisurely along the narrow trail. A bare-chested man in shorts and a baseball cap came into view. The corners of Kyra's mouth drooped slightly. He was perfection. A ten. A living, breathing, dream. Six feet four inches of sexy. The word *beautiful* was the most abused word in the English language, but the man jogging towards her was gorgeous. Muscular arms, pert nipples, a chest begging to be touched. Following the hard contours of his waist, her eyes moved slowly up his shoulders to his lips. His cap shielded his forehead, making it impossible for her to see his entire face, but she'd recognize the familiar shape of Terrence Franklin's mouth in the dark.

Her heart swayed like a daisy in the breeze. Should she pretend not to see him, or dive into the bushes? Kyra wiped the perspiration from her face. Sweat wasn't cool, neither was funk. Her tank top was damp and she smelled as if she'd slept in a men's locker room. Since Kyra wasn't sure whether he'd even seen her, she decided to just keep on trucking.

When they were just a few feet away, he stopped and fell into step beside her. "Funny seeing you here," he drawled. "What a pleasant surprise."

Kyra slowed but didn't stop. He sounded sincere, but the expression on his face said *touchdown*. The roguish sparkle in his eye matched his wide grin. Kyra had no proof, but she had a sneaking suspicion Terrence had orchestrated this meeting. But as she considered the likelihood of it, she realized it was next to impossible. Terrence was good, but he wasn't *that* good. There was no way for him to know she'd be on this trail at this time of the day. "Hey, Terrence."

He pointed with his chin to the trail. "Mind if I join you?"

"Actually, I was just leaving," she said, skating backward out of his reach. "I promised my mom I'd come over for dinner."

"Then I'll walk you to your car."

Her legs shook like a straight man in heels, and she suddenly didn't have the energy to stand, but she stayed shoulder to shoulder with him all the way up the hill. His cologne had notes of cedar and stimulated her senses. Then there was his chest…his nipples…the slope of his rock-hard abs.

Kyra fanned her face. It was hotter than a Texas heat wave, but where on Earth was his shirt? Was he an exhibitionist or had some crazed female fan mauled him in the parking lot? "What does SKW stand for?" she asked, spotting the scripted initials on his right bicep.

"Selma Kay Williams."

"Was she an ex-girlfriend?"

"Nope. My great-grandmother." The expression on his face was one of pride. "She was an integral part of my life when I was growing up, and this tattoo is my small way of honoring her memory."

Kyra almost melted onto the hot pavement. It was the sweetest, kindest thing she'd ever heard a man say, and she was touched deeply by his confession.

"How's work?" he asked, feeding her another gorgeous smile. It was definitely one of his best. "Get all that paperwork done that's been keeping you so busy?"

Her eyebrows knitted together. What, was he psychic now, too? "Things are fine."

"I can tell you're very good at your job."

His gaze was powerful, crippling, more potent than a double shot of whiskey. *Good thing I have my sunglasses on,* she thought. *I'd be blinded by all that sexual energy.*

"I hope your boss knows how lucky he is to have you."

Her gaze slid down his physique. Wrong move. Toned arms, muscles as hard as steel, long legs. Terrence Franklin was dark, fine and broad. The kind of man even a woman with amnesia wouldn't forget. There was nothing sexier than a guy who'd just finished working out, and Kyra felt a swoon coming on.

"I spoke to my agent this afternoon," he told her. "Teams have been calling to see if I'm interested in coming out of retirement."

"Are you?" Kyra felt like the ground might slip out from under her. *How could anyone withstand this heat?*

she wondered, running her tongue over her lips. Wanting to put all those Psychology 101 courses to good use, she tore her eyes away from his nipples and asked, "Is returning to the NFL a viable option?"

Silence fell between them.

"When I first busted my knee, I thought I'd be out for a couple months, maybe three, but as time passed, I realized it was a lot worse than the doctors originally thought." He pushed out a ragged breath. "I miss the game, but my surgeon made it clear that continuing my career could result in permanent damage."

"That must have been hard to hear."

Head down, he tugged at his baseball cap, pulling it down past his eyebrows. "I had another five, six seasons left in me, and it was tough walking away from a game I've loved since I was nine."

His voice was hollow, his tone flat. "I never won a championship and that kills me more than anything. More than my knee, more than my friends who turned their backs on me, more than all the women who... never mind that."

"What do you miss most about the game?"

He lifted his eyes to her face, a hint of a smile on his lips. "I'm embarrassed to say this, but I miss everything about playing in the NFL. The thrill, the excitement, the energy. Out on that field, I'm invincible. Fans surround me on every side, screaming just for me. There's nothing like it, Kyra. It's a constant adrenaline rush. It never ends. Long after the game is over, I'm still hyped up and ready for more."

"You had an incredible ten-year run, Terrence. Few players can say they walked away from the sport at the height of their career, healthy, sane and whole. You're one of the lucky ones."

For a moment, he didn't speak. "It's all good, though," he insisted, with a firm nod. "I might be down, but I'm not out. I read for a small part in the new Robert De Niro movie, and my agent assured me I'd get the role."

Her heart fell. A Robert De Niro movie? When was he going to tell her about his acting aspirations. Kyra had dozens of questions, but before she could ask a single one, he said, "Did you like the bouquet?"

Kyra shot him a look. Goodness gracious, how did he know about *that?* Choosing to keep her personal life private, she dodged his question by playing dumb. "I don't know what you're talking about."

"It never came? That's weird. I got an email confirmation hours ago."

"You sent the fruit basket?" Shaking her head, as if unable to believe what she was hearing, she rubbed a hand along her forehead. Charles hadn't sent it? But that didn't make any sense. He should have. After all, he was the one who'd embarrassed her at the Azure Bar & Lounge, not Terrence. "I'm shocked. I don't know what to say."

"You hated it, didn't you? Damn, I should have gone with real roses." Stopping abruptly, he turned to her, his eyes soft and his smile apologetic. "This was my way of starting over. I remembered how much you loved exotic fruit, and thought you'd like it."

"I did," she blurted, wishing she could hit Rewind and snatch the words back. Encouragement was something Terrence didn't need. Her mind was closed to the idea of seeing him outside of work, but she thanked him for the bouquet. "It was very sweet of you, Terrence. The staff loved it." She added, "I saw some faculty members eating from it when I left this afternoon."

"It's the least I could do." Returning the compliment, he inclined his head to the right and gently touched her shoulder. "You're a very special woman, Kyra, and you deserve the very best that life has to offer."

Kyra arched her eyebrows. Terrence lived for drama and excitement, and she was perceptive enough to know the star athlete was only after one thing. Refusing to fall for his slick line, she said, "Terrence, you don't even know me."

"That's why I'm here. I want to change that. We were friends once and—"

She met his gaze head on. "I don't need any more friends."

"Is this about Charles?"

The truth stuck in her throat. "Yes and no."

"Are you guys serious?"

Kyra felt her face flush. She'd given new meaning to stretching the truth, but what choice did she have? Terrence had more questions than Katie Couric during a sit-down interview, and he wasn't easily satisfied. "He's a good, decent man and I'm not willing to jeopardize a great—" she stumbled over the word "—relationship by being friends with you. It's nothing personal, Terrence. It's just not worth it."

"Do you love him?"

How had a conversation about an edible fruit basket led to this? she wondered, retrieving her car keys from her pocket and dangling them between two fingers. There was a time when Terrence had been her best friend. They'd lie in bed for hours, talking, joking and planning for their future. But that was a long time ago. Ten years, to be exact. And she didn't feel comfortable talking to him about her relationship. In part because she didn't know how she was supposed to feel. Nothing about Charles thrilled her. He was just…okay. A hard-working, decent guy who'd be a good husband and provider, so why wasn't she sprinting to the altar?

"My private life is none of your business."

"I'll take that as a no."

They slipped into silence. Unable to control herself, her eyes strayed to his chest and slipped down his stomach. Kyra roped in her emotions before they got the best of her. Lusting led to fantasizing, and in the last three days she'd done enough daydreaming to last her a lifetime. Personal history aside, she was paid to do a job, and flirting with Terrence wasn't one of the requirements. They were working together and it didn't matter how many gifts he sent her, she wasn't going out with him. Not in a romantic sense, anyway. Charles didn't light her fire, but he was safe. He wouldn't hurt her, and that beat tall, dark and sexy any day.

"Are we still on for tomorrow?" Terrence asked.

"Yes. I informed the assistant coach that we'd be coming and Mr. Mayo is very excited to meet you."

"Do you know what I'm excited about?"

Terrence lowered his head and for one fear-packed second, Kyra worried he would kiss her. The closer his mouth came, the faster her heart beat. When his lips were just inches away, she forced a cough. "Oh, look, we're here," she said, backing up. "I'll see you tomorrow."

Feeling a sudden burst of energy, Kyra waved good-bye and skated over to her red car. A minute later, she chucked her Rollerblades into the truck, tugged on her sneakers and hopped into the driver's seat. Lurching out of her stall, she shot through the parking lot and disappeared into rush-hour traffic.

Chapter 5

Terrence watched Kyra shoot across the parking lot, a gleam in his eye and a wry smirk on his lips. Had he ever seen a backside so sweet? In his heart, lust, confusion and remorse battled for supremacy. And like a tourist wandering through the streets of Amsterdam, he couldn't tear his gaze away from her luscious body. Was this just about their intense attraction, or something more? Seriously hot, Kyra Dixon had the carefree disposition of an all-American girl and the sexual energy of a pinup model.

Kyra towed the line between sweet and sexy, but there was a very elegant way about her. A down-home beauty with bewitching eyes and a flirty laugh, she embodied all the qualities he admired in a woman—optimism, passion, honesty.

Terrence had been back in Hollington for seventy-two hours, but he felt as if he'd never left. The energy between them was electric and as he headed back up the trail, he reviewed their brief but noteworthy conversation. A woman in love talked with animation. Her face lit up at the mention of her man's name, and her cheeks flushed with delight. Love literally oozed from every pore. Not only were those telltale signs missing from his conversation with Kyra, her voice had flatlined when he asked if she was in love in Charles.

Terrence was no relationship guru, and he'd never have his own syndicated talk show for the brothers, but he knew complacency when he saw it. Hell, he'd been in that dark, lonely pit before. Since his rookie season, he'd dated one brainless woman after another. Sisters who'd rather spend the day at the beauty shop than volunteer in their communities. They all looked good, and smelled good and filled out their designer dresses better than Kim Kardashian, but they couldn't hold an intelligent conversation. Beauty and brains were the perfect mix, not booty and beauty, as his teammates used to say. Too bad it had taken him ten years to realize the truth.

Kyra exuded a confident-in-her-own-skin vibe and didn't have any of the generic traits he was used to seeing in females on the west coast. He liked his women real, natural, fresh-faced, and the curvy PR director certainly fit the bill.

"I can't believe it, it's Terrence Franklin!"

Turning around, he matched the sultry voice to an oval face with red pouty lips.

"I'm LaTisha." The temptress smiled.

Terrence gave her a quick once-over. It was a punishing eighty degrees, but her makeup was flawless. What kind of woman wore fake eyelashes and diamond earrings to the park? Kyra wasn't even wearing a watch, while this girl looked like she was ready for a semi-nude video shoot. Her fuchsia bra-top overflowed with silicone, and booty hung out of her Daisy Duke shorts. Shoulder-length, honey-blond hair twirled in the wind like strings of nutty putty. Her face was impassive, but her eyes shimmered with mischief.

"You probably don't remember me, but we met at an L.A. night club the year your team clinched the play-offs."

His groupie antennae shot up. Only a woman who memorized team schedules and charted the hangouts of professional athletes would remember a five-second meeting in a packed club. Had she followed him to Atlanta? Before entering the league, he wouldn't have believed it, but groupies were inventive and dedicated to their craft. In Las Vegas, a burlesque dancer once cornered him in the men's room; at a friend's birthday party a pair of twins had bum-rushed him in the hot tub; and at his grandmother's church a few years back, the pastor's teenage daughter had surprised him with a French kiss in her father's office. Terrence hated being suspicious of fans, but when females stepped up to him, caution had to be the order of the day.

"I have a flat," she announced, pointing a finger toward the parking lot, but not singling out a specific car. "Think you can help me out?"

LaTisha appeared to be in her late twenties, but he couldn't be a hundred percent sure. Her outfit said junior section at Macy's, but her body language suggested she was mature, conspicuous, experienced. Glad Kyra wasn't around to witness this blatant display of entrapment, he pulled his keys out of his back pocket. He'd had enough sun for one day and they were starting to attract curious stares from sunseekers passing by. "I wish I could help," he lied, starting for the marked crosswalk, "but I gotta jet."

The woman pursued. "It'll only take a minute and I promise to make it worth your while." He heard a hint of anxiety in her voice. "You'll be thanking me later. I can do things with my tongue that will make your head spin."

Stopping beside his luxury sports car, he yanked open the door and retrieved his cell phone from the center console. Back in the day, he would have fallen for this obvious ruse, but now his eyes were wide open. If he wanted to be with a quality woman, someone with poise and class and substance, he had to start making better choices. "I'll call a tow truck for you. What's the make and model of your car?"

A delicate hand touched his forearm. "I don't believe in beating around the bush, so let me spell this out for you." She leaned in and whispered in his ear, "Change my flat, and I'll thank you in the backseat of your car."

"I have a girlfriend," he lied, wishing that it were true.

A coy, mysterious look came over her face. "I'm not greedy." Her smile displayed every tooth. "I don't mind sharing."

"Still not interested."

"Not interested?" Her bottom lip curled. "Are you blind? Look at me. I've been in *Playboy* magazine *twice* and hooked up with Lil Wayne last month. I'm the hottest…"

Terrence slid into his car.

"Hey, what about my tire?" she yelled, bending down

and knocking on his window. "You're not going to leave me stranded, are you?"

To silence her, he depressed the power-window button and said, "Wave down park security. They'll help you."

"But I want you," she cooed, propping her chest up on the window sill. "Come on, Flash, help me out."

A man in tattered sweats stopped at a rusted blue car. He was wide and chubby and his stomach lapped over his Chicago Bulls basketball team T-shirt. The guy didn't look strong enough to bench five pounds, but Terrence wasn't looking for a workout partner. He needed to get this girl off his back before she caused a scene. "Hey, you!"

The guy looked up, and recognition flashed in his eyes. "You're Terrence Franklin! Holy crap. Dude, I'm like your biggest fan ever!"

"Do me a favor," he began, motioning to LaTisha with his index finger, "change her flat. She'll show you where her car is parked." Terrence didn't wait for an answer. Starting the engine, he whipped the Ferrari into reverse and tore out of the parking lot.

Terrence stopped at the intersection of Twelfth and Piedmont. What a trip. Didn't these women ever quit? If they weren't pushing up on him in the mall, they were leaving lewd messages on his MySpace website page or waving him down at the gas station. In retrospect, LaTisha had been tame compared to the other groupies he'd encountered over the years. At least she hadn't flashed him or hopped into his car and refused to get out.

Picking his cell phone off the passenger seat, he glanced down at the screen, hoping he'd received a text message from his favorite intern. There wasn't one, but he smiled to himself anyways. A believer in fate, not luck, he knew his chance meeting with Nikki Wakefield two weeks ago at the Dallas Airport wasn't just another coincidence.

"You're my boyfriend's favorite running back!" she'd said after he scrawled his signature on her boarding pass. "He's going to be stoked when he sees this."

When Terrence saw the familiar logo plastered across her white backpack, he broke into a smile. "You go to Hollington College?"

"Yeah, I'm a senior."

"Do you know who Kyra Dixon is?" he asked, nervous energy flowing through him. "She works in the public relations department."

Nikki blew a bubble with her gum and popped it. "Of course, I know who she is. Kyra's been my faculty adviser for years."

"What did you say your name was again?" They'd boarded that noon flight to Atlanta and by the time the plane touched down, he knew how Kyra took her coffee, where she liked to shop and what her favorite radio station was.

He'd been at home, reviewing an endorsement contract, when he'd received Nikki's text message. It hadn't been easy getting to Centennial Park during rush hour, but he wanted to see Kyra and he'd decided a long time ago to give their friendship his all. Ten more minutes on the I-95 and he would have missed her, but as fate would have it, they'd run into each other out on the trail.

As he thought back over their talk, he wondered if he was going about this thing with Kyra all wrong. He had tender memories of their relationship, but every time he

referred to the past, she'd quickly change the subject.
Calling off their engagement had been a mistake and
he hated himself for hurting her. Instead of being honest about his fears for the future, he'd withdrawn. He'd
ignored her calls and laid low in the weeks leading up
to graduation, but he didn't know how else to cope with
his growing list of problems. Breaking up with Kyra via
email was a cold, classless thing to do and even now,
a decade later, Terrence was still ashamed about what
he'd done. Regardless of what Kyra said, what he'd done
wasn't cool. The indiscretions of his youth were a sore
spot for him, and he'd always planned to make it up to
her. They had to create new memories together, and
what better way than over dinner tonight?

Following the flow of traffic, he remembered the
touch of sadness behind her smile. Did Kyra truly believe he'd forgotten all about her? He had often thought
about contacting her, but didn't know what he'd say if
she answered his call. It had been years since his last
serious relationship and every time he thought about his
future, Kyra came to mind. It was more than just her
smile or her sexy walk. Deeply compassionate, she had
a sense of community about her and lived to help others. Not like his ex-girlfriend, Lourdes Spendoza. She'd
had no trouble blowing his money, but the minute he got
hurt, she'd packed her designer bags and hit the road.

Should he call her now or wait until he got back
home? What if she had plans with her...Terrence
couldn't even bring himself to say the word. *He* was
the right man for Kyra—the *only* man for Kyra—and
he was going to prove it.

His cell phone chirped, and he knew instantly the
message was from Nikki. The light turned red, and he

stepped on the brake. The scent of fresh bread carried on the breeze and through the driver side window. His stomach grumbled, but he was too busy reading Nikki's message to think about tea and crumpets. Turning down the music, he sat back in his seat and read the message out loud.

On Friday nights Kyra and her friends go to The Tavern to play trivia. Starts at 8 p.m. Don't wear jerseys or boots when you're out with her. Kyra hates the thug look, so dress real casual.

Terrence scratched his head. He didn't know squat about trivia, but his cousins, Neal and Damon, had been honor roll students back in university. If anyone could win at trivia, it was those two. Copping a cool, self-assured grin, he threw his sports car into drive and dialed Neal's home number.

Chapter 6

"Please tell me those guys aren't the Hollington Lions," Terrence said. Head cocked to the right, he gestured toward the football field with his index finger. Sunlight reflected off his sunglasses, and although Kyra couldn't see his eyes, she heard the disappointment in his voice. "You said they were a hard-working bunch with a desire to succeed."

"They are," she insisted. "They're still not in the best shape yet, but they'll be ready in time for the home-coming game."

Coach Mayo appeared. "All right boys, gather around."

No one moved.

Undeterred by their lack of enthusiasm, the interim coach spoke about the importance of team work and perseverance. "This is a new day, boys. A new season. We're going to go out fightin', you hear me? Compete on every snap, on every play, on every down. Now, let's warm up and give a good showing this morning!"

Feet dragged across the field. The players formed a crooked circle around Coach Mayo and stretched to the count of ten. After, he instructed them to run five laps around the football field.

Worried about the impression Terrence was forming of the team, Kyra searched for the right explanation to give about the players. "They're really great kids," she began. "The quarterback, Javarius Nelson, is the first person in his family to go to college, and three of the defensive linemen are here on full scholarships."

"Now I know why they were 6-7 last season." Terrence plunked down on the wooden bench. "What the hell am I getting myself into?"

"They just need some direction, some discipline, a strong, firm hand." Taking the seat beside him, she held the team files on her lap, prepared to refer to them if he had any questions about specific players. "They've had some injuries in the past and as a result, had a rough few years. Their confidence is shot. Terrence, you know what a losing streak can do to a player's mental game. You also know that the right coach can make all the difference." He didn't respond, so she ploughed ahead. "Only you understand what kind of pressure these kids are under. We're all convinced you can help turn this around."

His expression troubled her, but she knew under his guidance, the Hollington Lions could be a championship-contending team again. Gifted with natural talent and an unparalleled love for the game, he had the skill and know-how to make it happen. "Terrence, you were a high school All-American, and you had the highest finish ever in Heisman balloting. Everyone here respects your leadership skills both on and off the field. That says a lot about your ability."

Someone cursed, words were exchanged and pushing ensued between players. The coaching staff rushed over to break up the scuffle.

"This is painful to watch," he confessed, hanging his head and rubbing a hand over his face. "They're turning against each other instead of working together. Not an easy thing for a losing team to get over."

"You can do this. I know you can." Her voice was strong, firm, unwavering. "You rushed for two hundred and fifty yards in your first NFL game and scored three touchdowns against the crushing defense. This—" she pointed at the field "—will be a walk in the park for someone with your tenacity and fortitude. If you could go toe-to-toe with a big bully like Joe Bilkie, then you can do anything."

"You saw that game?" he questioned, shooting a look at her. When she nodded, a sheepish smile tugged at his lips. "Mom said I shouldn't have punched him. She said I should have been the bigger man and walked away. What do you think?"

"I think you should have socked him in the gut!"

Terrence had a good laugh. "I knew you'd say that. It didn't matter what I did out there on the field, you always had my back!"

A pair of beauties in pink shorts jogged by. Dressed simply in a chartreuse blouse and capri pants, Kyra wondered how she stacked up to all of the other women he'd dated over the years. Various images from tabloids and entertainment magazines crowded her mind. He liked them young, stacked and curvy. Kyra watched the cheerleaders making eyes at him, but when she looked at him, he was staring at her. "You attract attention wherever you go."

"Too bad it's never the right type of girl."

"You expect me to believe you're not flattered when a sweet, young thing sashays over to you and slips you her number?" He opened his mouth to protest, but she pushed on. "Terrence, you're not fooling anybody. I've heard the stories. I know what's up."

"Kyra, I hate to be the one to tell you this, but *Spotlight Tinseltown* is *not* a valid news source. Everything you see on TV isn't true."

The air felt light on her face, but her heart raced. It had been ten years since they dated, a full decade since they'd made promises and vows to each other, but she was as skittish as she'd been on their first date.

"Keep this up and I'm going to cancel your subscription to *Celeb Today* magazine," he warned. His unfailing good humor calmed her, but when he casually put an arm around her shoulders in a split-second embrace, she broke out into a sweat. "I'm not as bad as the media makes me out to be. My mom raised me to be a gentleman, and all those afternoons I spent with her talking about respecting black women weren't in vain."

The emotions his smile evoked squeezed her heart. Held on tight and wouldn't let go. Everything about Terrence Franklin aroused her. His voice soothed, his smile compelled and he pulsed with a sexual energy. But he was a player. A dog. A womanizer of the worst kind and she had the emotional scars to prove it.

"I'm glad we made it out here today."

Their eyes met and held. Sparks flew like invisible streaks of lightning. And as if programmed, her face warmed, her legs tingled and butterflies danced in her stomach.

"Being here takes me back. Makes me feel like I never left Hollington."

But you did. And you left me. Shaking off feelings of melancholy, she admired the blue, cloudless sky. Her mind slipped back to the summer of 1998. Terrence had surprised her at this very spot. Right there in the middle of the field. He'd spread out a blanket, then made love to her under a breath-taking full moon.

Kyra pressed her eyes shut. That night—that sweet, enchanted night—was ingrained in her heart forever. It had been a tender moment, and despite all of her attempts, she'd never been able to forget it. Kyra hoped Terrence didn't remember that warm summer evening. Hoped he didn't mention it or reminisce about how willingly she'd given herself to him…

"Man, I'd die to be out there one more time, playing to the crowd, spinning out of tackles, showing the whole world what I can do."

Terrence gazed out onto the field and Kyra stared at him. It was unbearably humid, and as hot as the desert, but he was wearing a black V-neck shirt and tan pants. The former NFL running back had powerful shoulders and a Herculean build, but it was his smile that seduced her every time.

"I used to dread training camp," he said, with an easy laugh. "The days begin well before sunrise and we endure the most grueling practice sessions imaginable, but I'd gladly run a hundred laps if it meant I could play just one more pro game."

"It must be hard knowing you'll never play again."

"Hurts like a bitch."

"Don't worry, your female fans aren't going any-where," she teased, hoping to lighten the mood. "I'm sure they'll give you a hero's welcome at the opening game."

"Is that what you think I miss about playing in the NFL? The women?" Disappointment colored his face. "Most people don't know this, but the Dallas Cowboys organization is very involved in the community. We clean up drug-infested neighborhoods, read to preschool children and paint over gang tags and graffiti. I've done a lot of things in my life, but there's no greater feeling than signing a kid's T-shirt or visiting cancer patients at the children's hospital. Making a difference in some-one's life trumps meeting the winner of some model reality show any day."

"I didn't mean to offend you, I—"

"And while we're on the topic of females, let me just say this. It's not as easy for me to meet women as you think."

"It's an open secret that pro athletes bed women by the hundreds, Terrence. Everyone knows they're dogs." Determined to prove her point, she said, "They jump from one groupie to the next making babies they re-fuse to support."

"No one with a lick of sense would date an ODB."

"A what?"

"A woman who only does ballers. Every league has them." His tone was persuasive, matter-of-fact. "The major leagues have bat girls and soccer has bedposts."

"Are you serious? That's crazy," she said, "and slightly disturbing."

"I have to work plenty hard to meet sisters. Inde-pendent, career-types like you automatically think the worst of me, so I have to work twice as hard to prove that I'm a stand-up guy." He winked. "Because I am, you know. Ask Mom. She'll tell you!"

His good-natured smile almost made her forget he'd once dogged her out. She was sure that her opinion didn't matter anymore to him, didn't hold any weight, but she couldn't resist asking him about the now infamous Spago Smackdown. "Is it true you were dating two actresses on the same network at the same time and got busted leaving Spago with one of them?" she asked, giving in to her curiosity. "Why did they start tearing each other's clothes? And was Jerry Springer really there egging them on?"

Terrence snorted. "That's pure fiction."

Amused, she listened as he defended his reputation. It sounded as if he had years of frustration to get off his chest. Kyra heard the irritation in his voice and the underlying sadness he couldn't conceal. He had several million-dollar homes, luxury cars and all the other trappings of success, but expected her to believe he wasn't happy. Please. Did she have *sucker* written across her head in pink neon marker. That baby-life-is-hard speech might work with other women, but not with her.

"Being a professional athlete isn't easy. You wouldn't believe all the crap I go through just because I've got a little money."

"Confessions of an NFL running back," she quipped, trying to keep a straight face. "How sad. You have women throwing themselves at you, and everything you've ever dreamed of, but it still isn't enough. I don't get it. What more could you want?"

"You mean besides you?"

Her breath caught. A rush of pleasure flowed through

her, immobilizing her and leaving her mute. If the school founders could see her now, they'd be hanging their heads in shame. Four years of university down the drain. Remembering that this was the same man who'd dumped her via email made Kyra's interest wane. Terrence had had his chance, and she wasn't interested in dating him again, no matter how persuasive he was.

"Kyra, I want what every man wants." He leaned over until their arms were touching. "A woman who'll love me for me and not for the things I have."

Her lust level soared. Kyra swallowed the lump in her throat, her thoughts racing like a kid in a toy store. And when he moved closer still, shivers vibrated down her spine.

"And—" He paused for a moment. His gaze was strong, steady, invasive. For a second, one crazy terrifying second, she wanted him to kiss her. To create some space between them and usher in some fresh air, Kyra made three shifts to the right. "I want a woman who's a lady in the street, a sex kitten in the bedroom and a Sara Lee chef in the kitchen!" He chuckled. "I'd like to have a bunch of rug rats and a couple of dogs, too."

Unable to picture the scene he'd just described, she read his facial expression for clues. "You're pulling my leg, right?"

"Nope. I'm going to be the Brad Pitt of the NFL!"

Laughter came.

"What about you? Are you ready to tie the knot?"

Studying her hands, she slid her silver bracelet up and down her wrist. When the silence became unbearable, she said, "I guess so."

"You *guess?*"

Annoyed that he was poking fun at her, she rolled her

eyes. "You're one to talk with your bimbo girlfriends and strip club birthday parties," she shot back.

"All right, you've got me there. I've been a very, very bad boy," he confessed, his words strung together like cans on a string. "I'm not trying to get on your bad side, Kyra. I just figured you'd be married by now."

"I would have been if…"

"If I'd been man enough to step up to the plate?" Facing her, he offered a weak smile. "It's okay, Kyra, you can say it. I was a sorry excuse for a man back then."

Their eyes came together. It felt as if a bowling ball were sitting on her chest. Every breath was a struggle. Insects hummed in her ears, but all she could hear was the gentle timbre of his voice and the deep feeling behind his words.

"Everything was coming at me so fast. Training camp, opening season, the wedding. I'm not making excuses, Ky, I just wanted you to know that it wasn't you. It was me. I was the one trippin'. I was the one who screwed up what we had."

Kyra didn't know if it was the quiver in his voice or the gut-wrenching look on his face, but something compelled her to say, "It was a long time ago, Terrence, and neither one of us were ready for marriage."

"I promised myself that I wouldn't bring up the past, but—"

"Terrence, I'm begging you. Please don't do this."

"Don't do what? Apologize for breaking your heart and—"

"You're giving yourself way too much credit," she snapped, stunned by his nerve. Where did he get off? After signing with the Cowboys, he'd dropped her, and taken up with a stunning, Cameron Diaz look-alike, but that didn't mean Kyra had gone off the deep end. Yeah, she'd set fire to his Letterman jacket and cut up his pictures, but that didn't mean she was bitter. "I was upset, sure, but I moved on. In fact, I took a trip with my girlfriends that fall and had the time of my life."

A challenge rose in his eyes.

Kyra averted her gaze. Okay, so she'd spent the entire trip in bed crying, but listening to every song ever recorded by Aretha Franklin was incredibly therapeutic.

"Just hear me out, okay? I have to do this or we'll never be able to move on. We'll always be stuck in the past."

Refusing to participate in the discussion, she stared absently out onto the field, her mind chock-full of memories. The players were standing on the sidelines, guzzling water and slipping on numbered jerseys. Discussing the demise of their relationship wasn't going to change anything, and Kyra suddenly wasn't in the mood to hear another one of his well thought-out speeches.

"What I did was messed up and I've always felt guilty about the way things ended. I was stupid. A stupid, terrified kid who didn't know if he was coming or going. I listened to the wrong people, and I'm so sorry I hurt you."

Feigning boredom, but secretly touched by his confession, she inspected her manicure, pretending not to notice him eyeing her. Their breakup had nearly ruined her, and Kyra didn't want to relive one of the lowest moments of her life.

"If I knew then what I know now, I never would have left you."

"Terrence, we were kids. We knew nothing about love."

"What are you saying?"

"We were two lonely teens experiencing love for the first time. Or what we thought was love." Her voice cracked with emotion. "Lust is a powerful emotion and we mistook it for the real thing."

"You're wrong." He was transparent, open, as vulnerable as she'd ever seen him. "I know a good woman when I see one, Ky. I loved you more than anything, more than anyone. Don't ever forget that."

A moment of silence passed between them.

"We've come a long way, haven't we?" His smile was back.

"I think so. We've accomplished a lot in our respective careers and we both have a lot to be proud of."

"I'd like if we could start over." Wearing a grin as long and as broad as a four-lane highway, he offered his right hand. "Friends?"

Touching him was dangerous, deadly, riskier than selling Girl Guide cookies in Compton. Kyra was finally headed in the right direction and she didn't need a great-looking athlete playing with her head. Or her heart. Having Terrence here—at Hollington, the place where they'd met and fallen in love—was confusing enough without him playing mind games with her. Kyra sensed his interest in her, and didn't want to make a habit of seeing him on a personal level, but she liked the idea of calling a truce. Just to prove she was really over his betrayal. Steeling her nerves, she reached out and shook his hand. "Friends."

His touch shot chills down to her toes. She saw the question in his eyes, felt the warmth of his remarkably soft skin and knew something special had just passed between them. Passion was synonymous with desire, but Kyra refused to believe that after all this time, the chemistry between them still remained. This wasn't going to happen. She wasn't going to fall for his smooth speech and muck up what she had going with…damn, what was the name of the guy who'd taken her to lunch last week?

"You know why I returned to Hollington, don't you Kyra?" His gaze was so deep, so penetrating, she felt naked before him. Like that night they'd made love on that bearskin rug, in front of the fireplace, to the soothing sound of D'Angelo's whispery vocals. "I came to see you."

"Terrence, we could never be more than…" was as far as she got. Gripped by his megawatt smile, his invigorating scent and his touch, she gulped down the rush of emotion threatening to overtake her. Several deep breaths later, Kyra ordered herself to get a grip. Terrence had the bravado of the James Bond icon and more sex appeal than a Chippendales dancer, but she refused to be duped again by his suave moves.

"There you are," a familiar voice said.

Kyra dropped Terrence's hand as if it were a roasted stone. Smile frozen in place, she swiveled around on the bench and met her boss's gaze. "Mr. Morrow, hi, um, what are you doing here?"

Chapter 7

Secretly pleased by the interruption, Kyra looked on as her boss led Terrence onto the field. Fifty feet away, she could still hear Mr. Morrow's rich, booming laugh. Introductions were made, players were split into teams and, to her surprise, Terrence donned a red pinny and joined the smaller of the two squads.

Digging her cell phone out of her purse, she got up off the bench and walked over to the sidelines. Kyra smiled when she heard her best friend's message. After striking up a conversation at the Georgia Conference for Women three years ago, Aimee Phillips had quickly become someone she could depend on. The Houston native had parlayed her love of down-home cooking into a culinary career, and Kyra was thrilled the personal chef was relocating to Atlanta.

Anxious to speak to Aimee, she pressed Redial and put the phone to her ear. On the third ring, her girlfriend's light, breathy voice floated over the line. "What took you so long to call me back?" Aimee asked once they'd exchanged greetings. "I called you hours ago."

"It's been one of those mornings. Crazy from the moment I rolled out of bed, and growing longer by the second!"

"It couldn't be any worse than the day I'm having."

"What's up? You sound bummed. Is everything okay at the…"

Momentarily sidetracked by Terrence's impressive moves on the football field, she lost the ability to think and talk at the same time. Glued to the spot, her eyes slipping and sliding all over his bulging forearms, she waited for her mind to clear. A minute passed. Then another. Kyra was having a mental lapse again, but ever since Terrence had arrived at her office, daydreaming had become a daily occurrence. And when their eyes met, desire washed over her like water from a brook. Blessed with the face and physique of a model, he had the height, the build and the kind of personality that women of all ages found hopelessly attractive. Biting the inside of her cheek, she turned away from his powerful, muscled body and regained the use of her tongue.

"What are you doing tomorrow?" she asked, remembering her girlfriend was on the line. "Are you visiting your parents this weekend?"

"No, they're out of town."

"Great. So you can join me and Shaunice at The Tavern for trivia night."

"Kyra, you know you're my girl and everything, but that sounds kind of corny."

"Don't knock it until you try it. Last month we won the grand prize."

"What, a year's supply of corn chips?"

"No, thirty-five hundred dollars."

Aimee's voice perked up. "What time did you say it started?"

Giving in to her laughter, she raised her head just in time to see Terrence yank off his pinny. Walter paused to speak to Coach Mayo before falling in step with the former NFL running back. The men strode off the field, wearing identical smiles.

A minute later, Kyra slapped her cell phone shut and slipped it into her purse. "The kids sure looked happy to see you," she said when Terrence pulled up beside her.

"As they should be. Flash is the real deal!" The excess skin around Walter's chin jiggled and his shoulders shook with merriment. "You should have seen the wide-eyed expression on their faces when Terrence asked if he could play. They looked like they were going to pass out!"

Terrence pointed his chin towards the field. "They're a good bunch. If they study the play book and listen to the coaching staff, they might have a chance this year."

"With you at the helm, they'll have more than just a chance. But we can discuss your vision for the team over lunch." Walter clapped him on the shoulder. "There's a great restaurant up the street that has the biggest steak burgers you've ever seen."

"Don't say no more. I can eat any time of the day!"

"All right," Kyra began, putting on her Prada designer sunglasses, "you guys go have lunch and I'll catch up with you both this afternoon."

Mr. Morrow frowned. "Nonsense, you're coming with us. We'll talk football, and then you can show Terrence around our fine city."

"But Terrence went to school here," she pointed out. "He knows the area better than I do. He doesn't need me to show him around."

"Oh, but I do," he insisted, his eyes wide and innocent. He'd perfected the deer-in-headlights look, and unfortunately for Kyra, her boss was eating it up. "I want to check out the aquarium and the Atlanta Sports Museum."

Walter nodded. "Great, it's settled. Kyra will show you around after lunch."

"It sounds wonderful." Kyra forced the words out through clamped lips. "We should hurry, so we don't get caught in the lunch rush."

Terrence gave her an affectionate touch on the arm. "Ladies first."

Hating the pompous smirk on his lips, she hurled a dirty look at him. *Why was he doing this?* Is he trying to get a rise out of me? Summoning a smile for her boss's benefit, she licked the dryness from her lips. Terrence's eyes were filled with laughter, and though she took a step forward, he didn't remove his hand.

Brampton's Bar, a high-end restaurant located downtown, served breakfast until closing and its extensive wine list and eclectic menu brought patrons in from neighboring counties. Prompt seating, efficient servers and a peaceful ambience made the establishment the talk of the town.

"We should order a bottle of wine," Mr. Morrow announced, stopping a passing waiter. "Terrence, I know you haven't accepted the coaching position yet, but I feel like celebrating! This could be the start of another Hollington dynasty!"

Terrence winked at Kyra.

A Southern girl from a family of big, strapping men, Kyra had always been taken by strong, silent types with impeccable manners. He greeted the manager as if they were old friends, chatted up the hostess as she led them out to the patio and entertained Walter with stories about his most harrowing days in the NFL.

A cell phone beeped, and Kyra reached into her purse.

"Sorry, it's mine." Putting down his fork, Terrence cleaned his mouth with his napkin and pushed away from the table. "Normally, I wouldn't answer, but I've been waiting to hear back from my agent all day. Do either of you mind if I take this call?"

Mr. Morrow flicked a hand as if to dismiss his apology. "Go on, Terrence. I'll see you at practice on Monday." He gestured towards Kyra. "You're in good hands. Kyra will take great care of you."

"I don't doubt it." Confident to the point of appearing cocky, he winked at her and rose to his feet. They were sequestered behind soaring hedges of fiscus trees that shielded them from prying eyes, but as Terrence strode off through the patio, Kyra noticed that everyone, from the businesswomen downing wine to the teenager with the fashion sense of T-Pain, turned and stared admiringly at the former NFL running back.

Mr. Morrow ingested a mouthful of chicken. "Think we could convince Terrence to invite some of his celebrity friends to the Winter Wonderland Ball?"

Kyra thought about it for a moment, then said, "I'll see what I can do."

"I don't have to tell you how important it is that we get Terrence here at Hollington," he began, stroking his jaw reflectively. "We have a brand new stadium and have practically given tickets away, but the stands are still empty."

"That'll change once Terrence becomes head coach. Soon, every seat in the stadium will be filled. Mark my words, Walter. You'll see."

"I love your enthusiasm." His head remained bent, but he was watching her intently. "You're in the last year of your contract, right?"

Kyra nodded. She tried to look interested in what her boss was saying, but how could she focus when Terrence was staring right at her? His smile lacked its usual warmth. At ten feet away, he was too far to be heard, but the troubled expression on his face told her the conversation was not going well.

"You've given your heart and soul to this school and you're one of the best PR directors Hollington's ever had." He was smiling, but the expression on his face was solemn. "I'm going to level with you, Kyra. What happens this season is going to have an enormous effect on your future. If Terrence signs on as head coach, I'll see to it that you get a raise and a long-term contract."

As if I don't have enough pressure, she thought, annoyed.

"I have to run. I'm chairing this afternoon's board meeting and I don't want to be late." Ending the conversation, he stood and slipped his beige suit jacket over his shoulders. "Take good care of our star coach. See to it that Terrence has everything he needs. Spoil him. Roll out the red carpet. Be extra nice."

She slaked her thirst by sipping her ice water. "I'll try my best."

"That's what I like to hear." Walter took another

swig from his wineglass, and then was gone. But before Kyra could enjoy a quiet moment with her thoughts, Terrence was back.

"That was fast," she said.

"I didn't want to keep you waiting."

"Everything okay?"

"Yup."

"Liar." Leaning forward in her chair, arms folded casually on the table, she studied him for a full minute. "The clenched jaw says it all, but if that's not enough, you're gripping your glass so tight your veins are popping."

Slowly, his frown fell away and was replaced with a grin. "You still know me better than anyone else."

Kyra swallowed. Her tongue felt like dead weight, and it didn't matter how much she moved it, it wouldn't oblige. Needing a diversion, she forked broccoli into her mouth and chewed. "So, what's up? Why do you have a long face?"

"I'm in talks with a network to host my own show, but negotiations have stalled. They're trying to lowball me, and my agent thinks we should bail."

"Wow," she breathed, her voice laced with awe, "you've got your hands in everything. Movies, television, endorsements."

His hearty laugh drew the attention of the brunette at the next table. Winking, she formed her pouty lips into a coy smile. Terrence looked away. "I try to stay busy. I'd lose my mind if I had nothing to do."

"I'd kill to have some more free time."

"That's what you think, but after a few weeks, you'd be itching to go back to work," he argued. His eyes were sharp and wide and showed how much he was enjoying their banter. "There's no substitute for getting out and being with people."

"Maybe for a social butterfly like you, but I have plenty to do at home. I have so many projects on the go, I had to make a list!"

Squinting, he leaned forward. She saw the amused sparkle in his eyes and wondered if she'd revealed too much. His smile had always been her downfall, and that hadn't changed in the time they'd been apart. Every time he flashed those pearly whites, she went soft. "Tell me what's on your list."

"It's nothing. Just a few things I enjoy doing."

"Come on," he prodded. "Don't be shy. I'd love to know what you do for kicks."

Was it the sweltering heat that made it impossible for her to think, or his intrusive gaze? Convinced she was reading too much into his questions, she told him about the extensive renovations that had been done to her house last month. "I still have to clean out the garage, unpack boxes and find a company to landscape before winter. Then, there's my scrapbooking projects, and all the orders I have for my holiday candles."

"You still make aromatherapy candles?"

Nodding, she bit back a smile. "I'm surprised you remember."

"How could I forget? I had the best-smelling dorm room in Rupert Hall. You always accused me of flirting with the other co-eds, but it had nothing to do with me and everything to do with your products!"

"It didn't help that you liked strutting around without your shirt on."

"I was trying to impress you."

Kyra gulped down some water.

"Scrapbooking, huh? I should get you to help me organize all the pictures, and mementos I've collected during my career."

Not wanting to offend the superstar athlete, she said, "Not a problem, I'd love to help out. Just say when—"

"How does tonight sound?"

"Sorry, I'm busy." Unsettled by his steely gaze, Kyra lowered her eyes and pushed out a breath. She needed to steady her nerves before she embarrassed herself. "Back to your deal with Fox. How are you going to find time to host a Sunday morning sports show, with all the other things you've got on the go?"

"I'll find the time. Sleep's overrated. As long as I get five hours, I'm good to go."

"You should take it easy," she advised. "After ten years and countless hits, fractures and broken bones, you need sufficient rest."

"Kyra, no one retires at thirty-two. I might not be healthy enough to play football, but I have a few good years left in me."

"You never were one to heed advice."

"That's true." They were two, meaningless words, but his voice was thick with feeling. His expression sobered. "My mom told me to marry you, but I wouldn't listen. That was the worst decision I ever made and I've regretted…"

Pressing her back flat against the chair, she uncrossed her legs and wrung her hands fretfully in her lap. Kyra wanted to tell Terrence to stop, wanted to tell him to quit living in the past, but the words stuck in her throat. They were lodged so deep she could hardly breathe. Sucking in some fresh air, she decided to deal with his erroneous statements head on. Laughing, joking and reminiscing about the good old days took Kyra back to one of the happiest times in her life, but she had to draw the line. Right here, right now. She wasn't about to take up with an arrogant skirt-chaser who'd betrayed her once before.

"I'm glad Walter contacted me about the coaching position." He gazed at her, his eyes bright, his big, handsome smile more endearing than a fluffy, white kitten clawing at the back door. "I have a lot to be thankful for. Job offers are starting to roll in, I'm feeling stronger than I have in years and then there's...*you*."

Kyra wanted to laugh, but didn't. Terrence Franklin had some nerve. He'd broken her heart when he'd dumped her, but arrogantly thought she could be placated with smooth lines and wide smiles. Waiting impatiently for him to wrap up his speech, she tried not to stare at his thick, juicy lips. An unscrupulous charmer, he lived for the intrusive glare of the spotlight and seemed to derive extreme pleasure from seeing her sweat. Kyra didn't care if he had a perfect smile, bulging biceps and a tight butt. She wouldn't date him if he were the last man on Earth. But if all that was true, why was she sitting in the stifling heat, shooting the breeze with Terrence when she had tons of paperwork waiting for her back at the office?

"I'm grateful for this opportunity." His hand grazed hers. "If it wasn't for the job offer, I would have missed the chance to see you again."

It took Kyra a moment to organize her thoughts, but when she opened her mouth, a lie rolled off her lips. "Terrence, you're a nice guy, and I'm sure you'll make some woman very happy some day, but with our history we could never be more than friends."

"You're getting a head of yourself, aren't you? We haven't even had our first kiss yet." He changed the subject so fast Kyra was convinced she'd misheard him. "What are your plans for the weekend? Got anything special going on?"

"Nothing much. Visiting my parents, cleaning the house, maybe a little baking. What about you?"

"My cousins are huge trivia buffs and they need a third man for their team, so I'll be at The Tavern tonight kicking some butt."

Her eyes ballooned. "You play trivia?"

"I know. Geeky, huh?"

"No, not at all. You graduated with high marks in all of your English courses, but you always downplayed how well you did," she said. "I just couldn't imagine an NFL superstar like you hanging out with us at The Tavern on Friday night."

"I'm more than just a handsome athlete, you know. I'm smart, too!" His smile increased tenfold. "You should come by the bar and watch me do my thing."

"I'll be there, but not to watch you," she told him, with a dismissive shake of her head. "My team, the Foxy Cleopatras, are the reigning champs."

"Well, prepare to be dethroned!"

"It's not going to happen, Terrence. We've been undefeated for weeks."

"But there's a new sheriff in town," he countered, "and *I* hate to lose."

"I don't know what your cousins told you, but trivia night at The Tavern isn't for the faint of heart. The questions are hard, the competition is tough and the crowd's wild."

"I played in the NFL. I can handle a bunch of suits and nerds."

"Who are you calling a nerd?" To underscore her disgust, she gave a snort of disdain. "What's your team name?"

"The Verbal Ninjas."

"That's original," she drawled.

"It doesn't matter what we're called. You're going down!"

Kyra burst into uncontrollable laughter. "Keep dreaming, pretty boy! You have a better chance of being struck by lightning than beating me!"

"Wanna bet?" He slanted his head to the right, studying her, examining her, wondering how to make this deal work to his advantage. "If I win, you have to cook dinner for me tomorrow night and if I lose I'll take care of your landscaping."

"You?" The skepticism in her voice was palpable.

"I had my own landscaping business when I was a kid. Ten dollars a yard. It wasn't much, but it kept me out of trouble."

In jest she said, "I'd hate for you to ruin your sneakers."

"Then you better bring your A game, because I play to win!" Terrence fished some bills out of his wallet and placed them on the silver billet. Grinning like a Cheshire cat, he stood and came around the table. He pulled up behind her chair and placed a hand on her shoulder. "How about that tour? I thought we could start at…"

Terrence murmured in her ear, and chills zipped down her back. Against her will, but too dumbfounded to protest, Kyra rose on wobbly, sweat-drenched legs.

She commanded her feet to move, and they reluctantly obliged. With a hand fixed to the slope of her back, his touch more dizzying than a French kiss, he escorted her through the sun-drenched patio and out onto Stayler Avenue.

Chapter 8

Known for its fine dining, designer boutiques and ten-thousand square-foot mansions, Highland Hills was home to some of the most prominent businessmen in the state. And on Friday nights, the movers and shakers in the community crammed into The Tavern for old-fashioned steaks, vintage wine and scintillating conversation.

Desperate to escape the pelting rain, Kyra yanked open the wooden door and rushed inside, almost knocking over a teenage girl with dyed blue hair. Housed in a historic bungalow, The Tavern had long been regarded as a Georgia landmark and the framed portraits hanging at the entrance paid tribute to the city's founders. With its extended bar, and muted lighting, the century-old restaurant was the ideal place for after-work drinks or a cozy first date.

Shaking the water from her umbrella, she peered into

the dining room, canvassing the area for her girlfriends. Every Friday, the women met for food, conversation and cocktails. Shaunice Berkley was a devoted mom to her preteen daughter, but she never missed an opportunity to hang out with her girls. Being an emergency room nurse was a stressful job, and Shaunice often joked that if it wasn't for happy hour, she would have been carted off to a psych ward a long time ago.

In the same instance she found Shaunice, she spotted Terrence. As if by design, he passed right in her line of vision. Kyra stood there for a moment, weighing her options.

Should she greet Terrence or make a beeline for her table? If she ignored her girlfriend, she'd hear about it later, but it didn't seem right dodging Terrence. After all, it was her job to entertain him while he was in town.

"Kyra! Over here!" Terrence yelled, drawing the attention of everyone in the lounge. When she didn't move, he strode over. He smiled as if he thought he was cute. And he was. Casual, in a white polo shirt, jeans and a buckskin jacket, he looked even sexier than he had that afternoon out on the football field. Wearing thousands of dollars' worth of bling, in a place that the upper class frequented, he stuck out like a priest at a biker bar. His crooked grin, arresting eyes, and homeboy swag made all the women in the room sit up and take notice, including her.

Remembering all the laughs they'd shared that afternoon, she tore her gaze away from his delicious mouth and waved in greeting. Terrence was an affable, easygoing guy, so why did she get flustered whenever he was around? She enjoyed his wit and his personality, and his bad-boy vibe only emphasized his appeal.

Showing admirable poise, she pushed out a breath and greeted him with a tentative smile. "Hey. How's it going?"

"You made it." To her utter surprise, he bent down and pecked her cheek. "I've been watching the door for the last fifteen minutes."

Kyra tripped over her tongue. His voice had a soporific effect on her and she suddenly felt light-headed. Why did this keep happening to her? Around Terrence she became more self-conscious than a preteen girl buying her first training bra. Recognizing the danger of being so close, she moved her body away from his. "Traffic's usually crazy on Friday nights, but the rain made the drive ten times worse."

"This is your last chance to back out of the bet," he told her. "My cousin Damon is even more competitive than I am and he suggested the loser pay the winner's tab. Think your friends will go for it?"

"Bring it on, bucko! We're going to mop the floor with you!" Laughing, she agreed to meet up with him after the game and crossed the room toward her friend.

"Is that Terrence Franklin?" Shaunice asked, gripping her forearm.

"Yeah, that's him."

"He looked mighty happy to see you."

Kyra told her about the bet. "I'm not worried. We've got this, right?"

"Not if Black Barbie doesn't show up. Where is Aimee, anyway?"

"Shaunice, I told you to quit calling her that," Kyra scolded. "How would you feel if I made fun of you behind *your* back?"

"Aimee's plastic. It fits." She lifted her martini glass to her thin, glossy lips. "I don't know what men see in her. She's as fake as a blow-up doll!"

"You sound jealous."

Her eyes thinned. "Me? Jealous? Never. I might not have dimples or three bags of human hair flowing down my back, but I've got it going on." She punctuated her words with heavy sighs and excessive eye rolling. "In my opinion, she's nothing but a fake…"

Kyra shook her head. That confirmed it. *Jealous.* Shaunice's problem was and always had been that she was intimidated by anyone who was different. She was Kyra's loudest, most aggressive friend by far. No one was exempt from her sharp tongue and critique, but she had always been a good friend to her. "How are things going at work? Still working all that crazy overtime?"

Flying high over the promotion she'd received on Monday, Shaunice chatted about her plans for the bonus. Her friend kept up a continuous stream of chatter, but Kyra's thoughts were on Terrence. Every so often, she'd steal a glance at him and after several seconds, look away. This time, she gave herself permission to stare. Frowning, she scrutinized the women who had surrounded his table. Didn't he have any male fans? she wondered, as another leggy blonde joined the group. Being surrounded by a troop of sinewy model types would make the average man puff out his chest, but Terrence looked bored.

Kyra heard a buzzing sound. Plopping her handbag down on her lap, she rummaged through it for her cell phone. Concealing it under the table, she flipped open the screen and quickly read the text message.

What's your pleasure? A Cosmopolitan, or a Candy Cane Martini?

Hiding a smile, she glanced up at him. His eyes were all over her. Terrence thought the world belonged to him and arrogantly believed they could pick up where they left off. Overconfident and full of pride, he was the type of man who never gave up. The type who'd stop at nothing to win. They'd never be more than friends, but there was no harm in letting him buy her a drink, was there?

"What are you over there smiling about?" Shaunice asked, glancing over Kyra's shoulder. "Hey, I thought we agreed not to answer our cell phones during dinner. It was *your* rule, remember?"

Feeling guilty, she switched her phone to vibrate and made a show of dropping it into her purse. "Happy now?"

"Very," Shaunice said, wearing a cheeky smile, "and don't let it happen again!"

Two waiters arrived, carrying trays of appetizers and cocktails.

"Courtesy of the Verbal Ninjas," the server explained, placing a drink in front of each woman. "Enjoy the lemon piña coladas, ladies."

Kyra softened. So, he did remember. Pushing an errant piece of hair off her forehead, she sent Terrence a smile of thanks. He didn't respond. Instead, he studied her with all seriousness, as if he were putting together a hundred-piece puzzle. And maybe he was, because when it came to their relationship nothing made sense.

The bar filled up and soon every seat was taken. Kyra was on her third cocktail when the disc jockey from WTSU 95 took the microphone and greeted the crowd. Glancing around the room for Aimee, Kyra opened her cell phone and punched in her girlfriend's number. When the call went to voice mail, she left a message.

"Let's get this party started!" the emcee bellowed, pumping his fists. "The first team to fifty points wins!"

Allowing herself another quick glance at Terrence, she pushed away her dainty cocktail glass and sat up ruler-straight.

He mouthed, "Good luck," took a swallow of his beer and faced the host like a diligent student awaiting instructions from his teacher. An act if she'd ever seen one. To the casual observer, Terrence was just another participant, enjoying a night of trivia, but Kyra knew this was much more than just a game. And when he answered the first three questions correctly, Kyra knew she'd been had.

"How many albums has Michael Jackson sold worldwide?"

Shaunice smacked the buzzer. "750 million."

"Five points for the Foxy Cleopatras!" The emcee paused expectantly. "How many countries border the African country of Libya?"

A man with a nasally voice answered. "Four!"

"Wrong. The correct answer is six. Who did the Atlanta Braves beat to win the 1995 World Series?"

"The Cleveland Indians!" Terrence shouted, up out of his seat.

Kyra snorted. Of course, a sports question. Hell, everyone in the state of Georgia could get *that* one right.

"We're down to the last question, and the Verbal Ninjas and Foxy Cleopatras are leading all teams with forty-five points each. Whoever answers the next question right will win a thousand big ones, y'all!"

Kyra tasted her water. If she botched the next question, she'd be cooking Terrence dinner at his house tomorrow night. What was she thinking, agreeing to such outlandish terms? He'd goaded her into the bet and she'd fallen for his trick—hook, line and sinker. It was the oldest con in the book, but she'd been too busy lusting to see what he was doing. How long could they spend together before crossing the line? Kyra would never dream of sleeping with Terrence, but she couldn't keep pretending that she wasn't attracted to him. Not when her heart thundered every time he walked into a room.

Leaning forward, hand poised to strike, she calmed her nerves. Losing to Terrence wasn't an option, so she smacked the buzzer before the host even finished reading the question. "Nineteen fifty-five!" she shouted, high above the din. "Martin Luther King received his doctorate in nineteen fifty-five."

"Correct! The winners, for the third consecutive week, are the Foxy Cleopatras!"

Shaunice cheered, whooping and hollering like the missing member of the Village People. Kyra followed her friend to the front of the restaurant and burst out laughing when Shaunice snatched the prize money out of the emcee's hands.

They were back at their table, sharing a complimentary slice of chocolate raspberry cheesecake when Terrence sidled up to their table with two dark, equally attractive men.

"That was some game," Terrence said, after introductions were made, "but just for the record, I knew the answer to the last question."

"Too bad your hand isn't as fast as mine!"

The group laughed.

"Terrence, what's it like being back in the A after all these years?" Shaunice asked, setting down her cocktail glass. "Did you miss it?"

"Definitely. I grew up in Pittsburgh, but Hollington will always be home. I played ball, received my degree and fell in love for the first time, too."

Kyra coughed.

"We saw your first NFL game," Shaunice told him.

"Really? I'm flattered."

"When you ran out onto the field, Kyra screamed so loud I spilled soda all over my jeans." Shaunice tugged on her earlobe. "I still can't hear properly out of this ear!"

Eyes wide, mouth ajar, he turned to Kyra. "You saw my debut game?"

"Oh, yeah, she's a sports nut," Shaunice explained. "She likes the Falcons, but the Cowboys are her favorite team."

A grin on his lips, Terrence turned towards his cousins. "I think Shaunice deserves a celebratory glass of wine, don't you think so, fellas?"

"For sure," Damon agreed. "Winning is tough work."

Under the table, Kyra clutched Shaunice's hand. Speaking through the side of her mouth, she begged her to stay. "Please don't leave me alone with him."

"You're a big girl," she whispered, "I can't pass up this opportunity! His cousins are single and hot!"

Then, in the likeness of Jezebel, she rose from her seat, linked arms with Neal and Damon and waltzed off as if she were the belle of the ball.

"So," Terrence began, taking a seat in the now vacant chair, "you're a fan."

"A fan of football, not one of those insane Franklin Fanatics."

"Oh, so you've been on my website, too." His smile was ridiculously wide. "Ky, I have to admit that I'm shocked. You gave me the impression that you didn't care."

"I don't."

"You do. Why else would you be keeping tabs on me?"

"Keeping tabs on you?" she repeated. "You're joking, right? I loved football long before we ever met. I have two brothers, remember?"

He didn't answer, but his smile said he wasn't buying it. Resting his elbows on the table, his gaze more devastating than a four-alarm fire, he watched her intently. "What time should I come by tomorrow?"

"For what?"

"A deal's a deal," he drawled. "I'm your handsome landscaper tomorrow."

She started to protest, but he interrupted. "Pick a time or I will."

"Anytime after ten will be fine," she replied, prying the words out of her mouth.

"Great. Then I'll be there at noon."

Kyra laughed.

"I have a hell of a time waking up in the morning."

"I bet. Parties at the Playboy Mansion never end before sunrise, do they?"

"I'd much rather spend an evening with you than watch a bunch of blondes play-fighting in a pool of chocolate pudding."

"Is that what happens at those parties?"

"Why don't we talk about us?" he proposed. "What are you doing later?"

Good question. What was she doing? Feeling dry-mouthed and woozy, Kyra gripped the side of her chair to keep from passing out. No more piña coladas, she decided, shifting nervously in her seat. "I don't know. It's up to Shaunice."

Terrence stared deep into her eyes. Kyra looked away, but she could still feel the heat of his gaze. Wondering where Shaunice was, she searched the over-crowded room. Being alone with Terrence, even in a public place, was risky. He was openly flirting with her, trying to seduce her right then and there in The Tavern.

"Being here with you is just like old times." Voice full of longing and regret, he leaned forward, brushing his fingers against her hands. "Can I ask you something?"

He looked serious, but Kyra felt the strange compulsion to laugh. Noting the hitch in his voice, she lifted her head and pressed her back flat against her chair. Terrence was moving closer and was just inches away. Worried her mouth smelled like onions, she discreetly checked her breath. Kyra didn't want Terrence to kiss her, but if he did, she didn't want him to recoil in disgust.

"Do you think you could ever date a guy like me?"

His voice fell gently on her ears. It was rich and soulful, the sweetest sound she had ever heard. She stared at him, wondering what it would be like to feel him inside her again. Back in university, they'd been inexperienced lovers, but now, at thirty-two, Kyra knew how she liked to be loved. Gaining control of her thoughts, she said, "I did date a guy like you, remember? And it nearly broke me."

When Terrence didn't respond, she continued. "We shouldn't be discussing this," she began, lowering her voice so they couldn't be overheard. The strength of his gaze worried her. Nothing drove Terrence like failure, and she feared what he might do if she rejected him. If she wanted to keep their relationship pleasant, she had to handle him with kid gloves. "If you take the coaching position, we're going to be coworkers, Terrence. I don't want us to start the year off on the wrong foot."

"I've achieved success beyond my wildest dreams and now I want what every man wants. Someone strong and sexy to come home to at the end of the day."

"Have you considered placing an online ad?"

His eyes shone with jollity. "You mean on one of those dating sites?"

"I can help you to set up your profile." Kyra had to calm down to finish her sentence. Giggling, she dug into her purse and produced a pen and notepad. "How does Sleepless in Atlanta sound?"

"I'd let you fix me up," he confessed, slipping an arm over her shoulder and giving her an affectionate squeeze. "I've always thought you had great taste. Still do."

He made a move as if he was going to kiss her, and Kyra froze. Panic flooded her body. Her tongue was heavy and she felt like her lips had been wired shut. She wanted to protest, but couldn't find the words. Heart thumping wildly, she parted her lips, frantically gulping mouthfuls of air.

"Sorry I'm late."

The sound of Aimee's voice yanked Kyra from her

daze. "Oh, hey, girl," she greeted, glancing up at her friend. "What took you so long to get—"

"Terrence?"

He cranked his head to the right. "Aimee?"

"I haven't seen you since that night in Houston." Features contorted into a glare, Aimee pushed a hand through her sleek, golden hair. Slanting her head to the right, she studied him through her extra-long eyelashes. "What are you doing here?"

Confused, Kyra divided her gaze between them. Antarctica isn't this cold, she thought, rubbing her hands over her chilled shoulders. Aimee toyed with her diamond bracelet and Terrence was staring off into space, but their mutual animosity was clear. Kyra sat there silently, passively, waiting patiently for an explanation, but when they lapsed in silence, she decided to get to the bottom of things. Addressing Aimee, she said, "Did you guys hang out in the same crowd?"

Aimee shot Terrence a surreptitious glance, but he was too busy studying his Nikes to notice. Kyra frowned. Things were getting weirder by the second. In all the time she'd known Terrence, she'd never seen him look so uncomfortable.

"We dated for a while," Aimee said.

Terrence coughed. "I wouldn't use the word *dated*. We went out once or twice."

"Once or twice?" Aimee's eyebrows shot up. Glaring at him, the wrinkles in her forehead jammed together in a clump of crooked lines and she stuck a hand on her hip. If it wasn't for her designer clothes, she'd look like a deranged clown. "He's lying," she spat, anger seeping through her tone. "It was a lot more than a couple dates."

Kyra remained seated, without moving a muscle, unable to believe the scene unfolding before her. Terrence had slept with Aimee? Kyra didn't know why she was surprised. Everyone wanted Aimee Phillips. Her hazel-blue eyes were offset by creamy brown skin, and high cheekbones. The product of a black man and a white woman trying to make a go of an interracial marriage in the early seventies, Aimee had lived most of her life being teased by whites, ostracized by blacks and thoroughly confused about where she fit on the color line. But since relocating to Atlanta, Kyra had seen her friend blossom. After decades of fighting for acceptance, she'd finally come into her own.

Kyra didn't think the evening could get any worse, but when Terrence excused himself from the table and Aimee launched into a lengthy play-by-play about their hot and heavy summer romance, Kyra felt sick to her stomach.

Chapter 9

At ten o'clock the next morning, Terrence turned onto Penrose Drive and searched for house number forty-nine. The suburban neighborhood of East Point featured impressive homes, neat lawns and a surfeit of shiny convertibles.

Terrence found Kyra's condo at the end of the block. Decorative flower plants flanked the porch and fine calligraphy script beautified a pair of wooden rocking chairs. Trees arched gracefully along the entrance, and behind the row of mailboxes was a small pond. A red Dodge Viper car was parked in the driveway. Knots of tension twisted in his stomach. That wasn't Kyra's car. So whose was it? Charles's?

His luxury sports car rolled to a stop, but Terrence didn't take his foot off the brake. What was Charles doing here? Had he come for breakfast or had he spent the night? He hadn't considered, not even for a moment, that Kyra might be in love with Charles Roberts. She rarely mentioned the guy, and when she wasn't working late she was with her friends. Terrence didn't want anyone up under him 24/7, but if Kyra was his woman, he'd want to see her all day, every day.

He'd been smiling ever since he'd reunited with Kyra and thoughts of her snuck up on him when he least expected it. Yesterday, he was confident that he was making progress, but now he was back at square one. Still annoyed about his run-in with Aimee last night at The Tavern, he released a long, pained sigh. Aimee's arrival had ruined everything. And he knew that she'd badmouthed him to Kyra after he left the table. That's just the kind of girl Aimee Phillips was. He shook his head at the inanity of the situation. Of all the women in his past, he'd been dogged by a sister who could be the spokesperson for the Gold Diggers of America.

Terrence considered his options. Coming clean about his fling with Aimee would open the door to other conversations about his past. Did Kyra really need to know about that raucous weekend in Rio? Or about the DUI he'd been charged with last year?

His knee was acting up, but he wasn't going to pass up an opportunity to see Kyra. He'd popped a couple of aspirin, had a shot of whiskey and jumped into his car. His decision was an easy one to make. He was going to do what he'd always done in the face of adversity. Forge ahead. After all, Charles Roberts was the least of his problems. Kyra's temporary boyfriend wasn't the biggest obstacle. Their past was.

Terrence released his seat belt. He had his work cut out for him. It was going to be an uphill battle to win

Kyra's trust, but he was nothing if not determined. Shoving his keys into his pocket, he reached across the seat and grabbed the bags of takeout.

Strolling up the walkway, he took the steps two at a time and rang the doorbell. A half-minute later, he heard light footsteps. Terrence wasn't sure how he'd feel if Charles answered, but before he could reflect on it, the door swung open. Terrence didn't know if he should be surprised or relieved. Aimee didn't speak, but her arched eyebrows and upturned mouth spoke of her annoyance. "What do you want?"

Staggered to see her, he greeted the personal chef with all the kindness he could muster. "How's it going, Aimee?"

Her frown deepened.

A dead ringer for the late singer Aaliyah, she wore her hair parted down the middle and a revealing, bone-white dress that offered two cupfuls of cleavage. "You look very nice today. Are you catering an event this—"

"You didn't drive over here to hand out compliments, so get to it."

"I'm here to see Kyra."

"She's busy." Her tongue clicked against her teeth, making a loud, annoying sound. "You really should have called first. Showing up uninvited is in poor taste, Terrence, even for you."

"You don't understand. I—"

"Oh, I understand perfectly," she snapped, making a face that could rival Ugly Wanda. "Don't think for a second that I'm going to let you play my best friend, Terrence. I know your MO and I'm onto you, so don't even try it."

The devil doesn't wear Prada, he thought, *she wears*

Apple Bottoms. Like a menacing-looking security guard at a gated mansion in the Hollywood Hills, Aimee was barring his entrance into Kyra's house and seemed to take great pleasure in insulting him.

"Kyra's expecting me," he told her, annoyed that she was spoiling for a fight at this ungodly hour. "If it wasn't for the accident on Ninth, I would've been here an hour ago."

After five miserable hours of sleep, he'd dragged himself out of bed and made the hour-long trek to East Point to have brunch with Kyra. He wasn't here to listen to Aimee run her mouth. That was one of the reasons he'd stopped calling her. She talked constantly and had something to say about everything. In her mind, silence was the enemy, and if there was a break in the conversation, she felt it was her duty to fill it with mindless jibber-jabber. "Are you going to go and get her for me?"

Aimee shook her head, her ponytail swishing back and forth. "She's getting dressed and I'm on my way out, so call her later," she suggested, gathering her purse. "Now, get out of my way. I'm running late."

"No problem. You go about your business and I'll wait for Kyra in the kitchen."

"Oh no, you don't." Arms folded, she sneered at him with open contempt. "There's another man in Kyra's life and I don't think he'd like you sniffing around."

"It's not like that. Kyra and I went to Hollington together. We're old friends."

Surprise colored her cheeks. Her green-eyed glare spoke of her malevolence, but she loosened her grip on the door handle. "You're not interested in Kyra romantically?" she asked, her tone accusatory. "Last night at The Tavern, you sure *looked* interested. You had your arms around her and you were drooling like my brown lab!"

Appearing nonchalant, he hung his thumb off the front pocket of his jeans. "We're old friends," he told her, producing a smile. His mother had taught him nothing good could come from lying, but if he wanted to get past Aimee, he had to tell her what she wanted to hear. "Kyra's seeing someone and I'm not looking to catch a beat down. I'm just landscaping her yard. Nothing more than one friend helping another."

Aimee's frown fell away and was replaced with a smile so bright it could power the entire state of Georgia. Eyes centered square on his face, she twined one leg behind the other and wet her lips with more flair than Marilyn Monroe. It was like letting the air out of a balloon. Her face softened, the tension in her shoulders receded and she looked like she'd been worked over by a masseuse.

Terrence thought he heard movement behind her and peered inside. The shutters were open, and the sun was making mosaic shapes on the mahogany floors. Cool blue walls blended easily with the opulent, crystal chandelier, the oak staircase and luxurious draperies. He felt connected to Kyra, and Aimee—or any other temptress who tried—wasn't going to come between them.

After a nasty spill off his motorcycle a few years back, he'd heeded his coach's advice and cleaned up his act. No more late nights at the club, no more bar fights, and no more girls like Aimee Phillips. He wanted more than just another pretty face and a bangin' body. He wanted the total package. Someone thrilling and fun who wasn't concerned with where he ranked on lists of richest athletes.

"Oh, I see. Well in that case, we should definitely hook up while you're in town. I'm moving down here soon, and I could really use a friend." Aimee asked if he needed a date for Snoop Dogg's album release party and thrust her breasts in his face for good measure. "Are you game?"

Terrence shook his head. Aimee hadn't changed one bit. The personal chef was still looking for someone to take care of her. And not just anyone, either. It had to be someone famous and ridiculously wealthy who could use their celebrity status to open doors for her. Though she'd once ditched him and hooked up with a hot-shot baseball player with a fleet of luxury jets, Terrence harbored no hard feelings toward her. Why would he when he had Kyra? Aimee had perfected the naughty-but-nice look and had the longest legs outside of Nevada, but Kyra was the type of woman he'd been looking for. Authentic, straightforward and more beautiful than words, Terrence knew that he could always count on Kyra to tell him the truth. Aimee had the loyalty of a stray cat, and though she was an attractive woman, she couldn't be trusted.

"Aimee, you're still here?"

Terrence stepped around Aimee and pushed open the door. Without makeup, Kyra barely looked legal, and the fuchsia bandana covering her hair enhanced her youthful appeal. Her extra-long tank top and shorts were loose-fitting, but her beauty was unmistakable. It shone from within, from her core, from the depths of her soul. Aimee was decked out in white, but Kyra was the one who looked innocent. And when she greeted him with a cheery wave, his heart thumped louder than a hundred conga drums.

He held up the bags. "I brought brunch."

"Something smells delicious." Aimee pointed a jeweled finger at the bag. "Do you have poached sausages in there?"

Terrence nodded. "I have breakfast enchiladas, too. They're Kyra's favorite."

Groaning, Aimee rubbed a hand over her stomach. "I wish I could stay, but I have a meeting downtown with a potential client."

"Then you better get going. Traffic's thick heading south." Terrence didn't mean to be rude, but when Aimee stomped off, he knew she'd taken offense. An eye roll, a flick of her hair, and she was gone. Not wanting to appear eager, he waited until he heard the door slam, before setting his sights back on Kyra. "Great house," he said, glancing around. A marriage of classical and urban architecture, the two-storey home featured an arched opening, cherrywood furniture and generous shelf space. "The decor's very cool. Eclectic but modern. I like it."

"Your place is probably ten times this size."

"It's not the size of a house that makes it a home," he told her. "It's the people who live there and the love and respect they share."

"Uh-oh. Someone's been watching too many Jimmy Stewart movies."

"Who?" Terrence scratched his head. "Is that the guy in all those old movies you used to force me to watch?"

Her laughter filled the room. It was a soft, almost musical sound and her eyes were sparkling. Terrence felt his heart inflate. Finally, something was going right. Kyra was laughing, and that was always a good thing.

"I forgot, you never liked the classics. *Baby Boy*

is more your style, isn't it?" Kyra wore a coy, closed-mouth grin and if it wasn't for the distance between them, he would have kissed her. He'd never been one to push up on a woman, but he was only human. How could anyone withstand that delicious smile? Desire consumed him and the more he fought it, the more he wanted her. It was that age-old cat and mouse game; he was enjoying the chase.

"So, what were you and Aimee talking about?"

"Nothing." To put her mind at ease, he decided to tell the truth. "Kyra, I don't know what she told you, but we were never a couple. We went out a few times, but nothing happened between us."

Kyra shrugged. "It's no big deal. I was just curious."

"I'm going to set up brunch out on the patio," he said, anxious to distance himself from his past. "Why don't you meet me outside with a pitcher of your famous watermelon lemonade?"

"But—"

"Ky, don't argue. Just let me do something nice for you." In four long strides, he was in her personal space. She smelled like orchids and her lips looked sweet. Terrence was a quick study and though he'd only been back in Hollington for a week, he had a good picture of who Kyra Dixon was. The PR director was a woman of incredible poise and strength, but beneath all of her admirable qualities was someone who was hurting. Terrence had to show her how special she was. With that thought in mind, he slipped a hand across her shoulders and led her through the French doors.

Chuckling, Terrence put down his glass and sat back in his wicker chair. "Come on, Kyra. Everyone knows women lie more than men. Weaves, acrylic nails, five-inch heels to make you taller." He lifted the tablecloth and paused when he saw her red painted toes poking out of her sandals. "It's all part of the female conspiracy, and every time a guy buys a woman and her girlfriends a round of cocktails, he feels like a sucker."

Kyra giggled. "We get all dolled up to go out because that's what *you* men like. You guys drool over curvy centerfolds and we sisters are just trying to stay in the game." She pointed a finger at him. "And just so you know, no one wakes up looking like a sex kitten. Eva Menendez has bed head and bad breath just like the rest of us!"

Their laughter floated on the afternoon breeze.

"Sounds like someone has a touch of celebrity envy," he teased, wiggling his eyebrows. "God, I hope you don't have a secret aspiration to be an actress or something because I'm sick of meeting women whose life goal is to be on the big screen."

"I couldn't handle all the scrutiny that comes with being famous. Hell, I'd get a tummy tuck, too, if I was dissed on one of those gossip Web sites."

"I'd die before I'd let you do that. You're perfect just the way you are."

"And all natural!" she added, laughing.

"That you are, baby. That you are."

Kyra took a bite of her four-cheese omlette. Chasing it down with water, she noticed the defiant slope of his jaw and the odd look on his face. She wanted to know what he was thinking, but didn't have the courage to ask. Steering the conversation to a safer topic, she asked about his plans for the weekend. "Are you going to Snoop Dogg's party? It's all Aimee could talk about during our workout."

"That depends. What are *you* doing tonight?"

He looked deep into her eyes and when he smiled, her heart murmured. Kyra made a point of dropping Charles's name into the conversation, but every time their fingers accidentally touched, she had an overpowering desire to kiss him. To just lean over and plant one on him. Her face flushed at the thought. She'd obviously lost grip with reality, and if she knew what was good for her, she'd stay on her side of the table. "Charles is taking me to the theater."

"Mind if I come?"

"Right, like you'd skip the biggest party of the year to see an all-woman play."

"I would," he affirmed with a quick nod of his head. "I'm sick of the single scene. If the right woman came along, I'd propose in an instant."

Her mouth creaked open.

"Don't look so surprised, Kyra. I haven't been an Eagle Scout, but I'm not as bad as the media makes me out to be. Pro athletes need love, too!"

"With your wild bachelor lifestyle, I find it hard to believe you're ready for a monogamous relationship."

"Having a wife and family is all that really matters."

Kyra wasn't convinced. "Why the sudden change of heart?"

"There's nothing sudden about it. I've been partying like a rock star since I entered the NFL, and now it's time to grow up. At least, that's what Big Mama says!"

His deep, rumbling laugh brought a smile to her lips. He sobered, and spoke openly about the challenges of being wealthy in a country obsessed with looks and celebrity. Kyra listened, enraptured by the sound of his voice. In that moment, Terrence reminded her of the sweet, caring guy she'd fallen for all those years ago. And if she was being honest with herself, he'd never, ever left her heart. In spite of their acrimonious breakup, he still represented everything she wanted in a man. Sincere, down-to-earth, chivalrous. In her book, Terrence was still one hell of a guy and the more he talked about family and community, the more she fantasized about kissing him.

"I want someone to come home to. Someone who has my back." Pain filled his dark brown eyes. "You can't put a monetary value on love, Kyra. It's a special thing, and hard to find. I want a wife, kids and a happy family. *That's* my definition of success."

"You really mean that?"

His gaze pinned her to the chair. "With all my heart."

Chapter 10

Kyra didn't know when or how it happened, but their fingers had twined. Pulling away, she leaped to her feet. "It's too late for this conversation. You came to help me landscape, right? Well, we should get started," she insisted, glancing nervously around the backyard. "Did you notice the evergreen out front?"

He stared at her for a long, nerve-racking moment. "You want the limbs thinned and the lower branches cut off, right?"

"Yes. And I have a long list of things to do, but it's probably going to take you a while to cut and dispose of the branches."

Terrence stood. "Two hours max. I'll be finished by three o'clock, so make sure you have something else lined up."

"All right, Mr. Belvedere. Odd jobs coming up!" she

joked, trying to put the intensity of their conversation behind her. "Can I loan you out to my friends and family?"

"I wouldn't advise it. Two sisters once got into a screaming match because I asked one out and not the other." He sounded solemn, but his eyes were filled with humor. "Women don't like to share. Not shoes, not clothes and certainly not NFL running backs." Terrence winked, then turned and strode towards the shed.

Kyra tried not to stare, but lust consumed her. Terrence was in tip-top shape and his infectious grin and cool, homeboy strut gave him star power. Do big or go home was his personal philosophy and Kyra wondered if that was the strategy he employed when snagging women.

The afternoon passed quickly. Every hour, Kyra went to check on Terrence. As promised, he finished at three o'clock and after safely storing the electric chainsaw he zipped off in his truck to dispose of the branches.

Soaking up the sun and the warm, fresh air, Kyra dropped to her knees and made quick work of unearthing the weeds in the garden. After a long, hot summer and weeks of renovations, she was glad these mundane tasks were getting done. Charles had offered to help, but his schedule left him with no free time.

Humming to herself, she balanced the vegetable basket on her hips and returned inside. Kyra washed and bagged the tomatoes and stuck them in the fridge. Spotting the jug of iced tea, she decided bringing her landscaper a cold drink was a good idea.

Kyra didn't see Terrence when she stepped out onto the porch, but she could hear the chug of her old lawn mower. Her elderly neighbor, Mrs. De La Cruz, was sweeping her walkway and smiled in greeting. The aroma of freshly cut tulips filled the air. It was a sweet, delicious scent that reminded her of her college days.

Despite the punishing heat, the residents of East Point were out in full force. Children ran through sprinklers, splashing each other and shrieking with delight. Groups of women, decked out in shorts, sandals and smiles, stood clustered on the sidewalk fanning themselves. Terrence rounded the corner, and Kyra felt a rush of extreme pleasure. When he shot her a playful grin, she realized what all the fuss was about. For young, stay-at-home moms, watching a half-naked man mow the lawn was more exciting than watching a high-speed chase.

Kyra's hands shook, and for a moment she thought the glass might slip from her grasp. Longing flowed through her, when Terrence shot her a smile. "I thought you might be thirsty," she said, descending the steps on rubbery legs.

Grinning broadly, Terrence shut off the lawn mower and strolled across the lawn. He took the drink and finished it in two, long gulps. "Ummm. Think I could get another one of those? I'm dying out here."

"Think you could put back on your shirt?" she blurted, glancing around. "This is a working-class neighborhood with lots of, ah, small children."

He screwed his features into a frown, but Kyra knew he was enjoying all of the attention. Unlike other celebrities, the intrusive glare of the spotlight didn't seem to bother him. "I know I've let myself go since I retired, but I don't look that bad, do I?"

Let himself go? Her gaze spilled over his shoulders and down his abs. Allowing her eyes to do what her hands couldn't, she openly admired his super-ripped physique. Terrence put the *F* in fine and had a body that deserved to be displayed. He was the perfect male specimen. Light eyes, sensuously wide mouth offset by even, white teeth. And that chest! The definition of his arms and the powerful cut of his abs made Matthew McConaughey look flabby. His nipples were round, dark, and looked like a pair of chocolate chips. "Don't take anything else off," she warned, peering over his left shoulder. Now, her neighbors were using their camera phones to snap pictures. "I don't want these women rolling around in my flower bed, fighting over you!"

Terrence chuckled. "Don't worry so much, Ky. It's all good."

"In case you haven't noticed, I'm not one of those wild, out-of-control types that you seem to gravitate towards. I'm a quiet, small-town girl who'd rather play trivia than party at some overpriced club."

"That's why you're not happy," he said, his handsome head cocked to one side. "You're stuck in a mind-numbing rut of work, work, work. You need some excitement, but don't worry. I'm here now. I'll make everything better."

He flexed his muscles, and Kyra sucked in a breath. "You don't know what you're talking about. I'm very happy."

"No, you're not."

His insistence only strengthened her resolve. "Yes, I am," she countered, drawing out her words to ensure they sunk in. Kyra wasn't going to get into a discussion about her personal life with Terrence. Why did he care whether or not she was happy? Proud of herself for standing up to him, she met his stare head-on. Terrence wasn't the only one who could read people. She could, too, and his smooth-as-silk persona wasn't fooling anybody. Worried about his future, and his fading star, he boasted of his wealth and accomplishments to prove that he still mattered.

"Who was he?"

A frown wrinkled her forehead. "What are you talking about?"

"You don't trust men, specifically black men, and I want to know why. Who hurt you so bad that you've built this cold, hard shell of protection around your heart? Was this really all my doing?"

Kyra blinked hard. The hurt and betrayal she'd tried to conceal for years threatened to overtake her, but she didn't falter. Terrence must have sensed her impending collapse, because he gently touched her arm. She was wary of him and worried that she was opening herself up to the man who had betrayed her trust. Kyra quickly composed herself. Better not to let him see her vulnerability. "I've been hurt, but who hasn't? Everyone's outlook on life is clouded by their past experiences, including you."

Embarrassed, and anxious to move beyond the awkward moment, she stepped out of reach. Most of the onlookers had returned to their air-conditioned homes, but across the street, a pair of silver-haired women sat on lawn chairs whispering.

"There's more to this than you're letting on," he insisted.

"No, there isn't." Intent on knocking Terrence off his high horse, she opened her mouth, poised to fire a stinging retort at her one-time love, but the words died on her lips. Kyra wasn't upset because he'd badgered her, but because his observation was dead-on. It was true. She *didn't* trust men. The man she'd loved most had betrayed her trust, so why would she give Terrence or anyone else the opportunity to hurt her?

"You're not the only one who's been dogged, Kyra. You wouldn't believe some of the characters I've met over the years." She didn't speak, and he continued. "I love spoiling my family and buying my mom things she never dreamed of, but fame and fortune isn't all it's cracked up to be. Remember that Notorious B.I.G. song, *Mo Money Mo Problems?* Well, that's my life in a nutshell."

"There's something I'm curious about." He tipped his head back, studying her, those dark, mysterious eyes producing a searing heat. "This guy Charles. Are you really into him? I mean, he doesn't seem like—"

Following his train of thought, she interrupted, saying, "He's a great guy."

"A great guy?"

"You can believe what you want, but he's a perfect gentleman and he treats me like a queen." Another cliché, but Terrence was staring at her and it was all she could think of in the face of such extreme pressure.

"The eyes never lie, Kyra."

Unsure of what to say, she waited for the words to come.

Then, in a move that stunned her, he touched her cheek. A satisfied look on his face, he spoke so quietly, she couldn't hear his soft utterance without inching forward. "I'm going to restore your confidence in men. And in me."

Kyra didn't respond. Now she understood why the former NFL running back was still single. Being handsome couldn't expunge personality flaws, and Terrence had an ego larger than the Statue of Liberty. "What are you going to do? Wine me, dine me and buy me expensive things I don't need?"

"I have my ways." Four short but devastating words.

Chapter 11

"What do you mean Charles's still in Denver?" Kyra demanded, clutching the cordless phone. "We're going to the theater tonight."

"Mr. Roberts requested I contact you, and extend his apologies," explained the woman, who'd identified herself as his personal assistant, Mrs. Sutton-Brown.

Swallowing a curse, she leaned against the granite counter, seething inwardly. Kyra couldn't believe this. What kind of man had his employees do his bidding for him? She'd had enough of Charles's insensitive behavior, but dumping him wouldn't solve her immediate problem. She had a stunning Roberto Cavalli designer dress hanging outside of her closet and nowhere to go.

"Would you like to leave a message for Mr. Roberts?"

"No, thank you." Kyra disconnected the call. Her

conversation with Mrs. Sutton-Brown festered on her mind. And the endless ticking of the grandfather clock only reminded her that she had nothing to do and nowhere to go. Women arrived at the African American Theater of Arts dripping in diamonds and draped on the arms of fine, dark men, but since she didn't know anyone who fit that bill, she'd asked Charles to be her date. Now, she couldn't think of a single person to invite. Her mother was home, but Kyra knew she couldn't invite her to the raunchy, sexually explicit show.

"I'm gonna jet."

Kyra surfaced from her thoughts. Hands pressed against the wall, his face glistening with sweat, Terrence stood with his head poked inside the French doors.

Managing a smile, she picked up the phone and put it back into the cradle. "Have fun at Snoop's party."

"Is everything all right?"

"Yeah, why?"

"Because you just dropped the phone into the garbage!"

Kyra stared down at the silver canister. Realizing her mistake, she retrieved the cordless, wiped it off with a paper towel and tossed it on the counter. "God, I'm so annoyed I could scream."

He stepped inside. "Chill out, Kyra. It was an honest mistake."

"No, that's not what's bothering me." Terrence asked what was wrong and before she knew it, she was telling him about her conversation with Mrs. Sutton-Brown. "Can you believe he had his assistant call to say he wasn't going to make it?"

"Maybe he's tied up in meetings."

Kyra wasn't buying it. "Charles doesn't go anywhere

without his BlackBerry. He couldn't have taken thirty seconds out of his day to call or send a quick text?"

"Sometimes we have no control over what happens."

"So it's okay to leave someone in the lurch just because something more important came up?"

His face soured. "Kyra, I can't speak for him."

"Then speak for yourself." Voice dripping with disdain, she said, "Is that the kind of thing you ball players do? Get someone else to do your dirty work for you?"

"That's not how I operate," he told her, "And I'd move heaven and earth before I *ever* stood you up."

Dirt specked his T-shirt, but didn't detract from his smoldering hot looks. Attracted to his strength, and his killer wit, she considered asking him to be her date. Kyra liked how Terrence made everyone around him from the waiter to the valet feel special. And if she arrived at the theater on Terrence's arm they'd make the front page of every newspaper in the city. More good press for Hollington College. "Have you ever been to the African American Theater of Arts?"

"The theater is one of my great loves." After a long beat, he broke out laughing. "I'm kidding, but I take Mom to see classical music every Mother's Day. It's not my thing, but if it makes Mom happy, then I'm happy!"

Kyra laughed when he called himself a mama's boy. "A man that takes care of his mother is a good man in my book."

"I'll have to remember that." Terrence paused. "Is there anything I can do to help? I know I look like a sack of potatoes right now, but I clean up pretty well."

"Forget I said anything. You have plans tonight and—"

"You've been to one rap party, you've been to them

all," he joked. "It's no biggie. I'll catch up with Snoop at the next video awards show."

"Then, in that case, I'll meet you outside of the theater at seven."

"No, I'll pick you up."

Wary of his motives, but glad she was going to put her designer gown to good use, she agreed. As Terrence turned toward the sliding glass door he asked about the play. "What are we going to see?" he asked good-naturedly. "One of those big, overblown musicals or a witty play?"

Biting back a smirk, Kyra smiled innocently and shook her head. "No, *The Vagina Monologues.*"

Terrence checked his watch. If they didn't leave for the theater in the next ten minutes, they were going to be late. Not that he minded, though. Seeing a raunchy, feminist show was going to blacken his reputation and when his old teammates found out, he'd be the laughing stock of the league.

Terrence was listening to his voice-mail messages, when Kyra appeared at the top of the staircase, smiling apologetically. "I'm sorry I made you wait," she said, in a rush of words, "but I couldn't find the tickets."

They don't make sisters like that anymore. Struck dumb, he managed a weak nod. His collar was choking him, and his legs didn't feel strong enough to support his weight. The elegant cut of her gown drew his attention to her compact waist, and the sapphire-blue shade was an attention-grabber. Though her look wasn't overtly sexy, he had a growing erection.

"Ready to go?" she asked, staring up at him.

Without thinking, he grazed his fingers across

her cheek. His mouth dried and he couldn't right his thoughts. Terrence lowered his head, but before their lips touched, he pecked her cheek. As surely as walking on hot coals would blister his feet, he knew if he kissed Kyra, he'd never be able to stop. "Kyra, you're stunning. What attracted me to you from the very beginning were your eyes, but tonight, it's the entire package."

Red, rosebud lips flared into a cheeky smile. "You were right, Terrence. You *do* clean up well." Laughing, she reached out and smoothed a hand over the lapel of his blazer. His heart grew soft. He'd been touched by an angel and Terrence knew he'd never be the same again. To keep from twisting a curly lock of dark hair around his fingers, he stuck his hands in his pockets and waited for his feelings of longing to pass. "Great suit," she said. "I love the color. Is it Armani?"

"No, Calvin Klein." Bursting with pride, he told her about his conversation with his agent. "They want me in their new ad campaign."

"Well, you certainly have the body for it," she said easily. "I'm sure you'll make the company a boatload of money."

Grinning ruefully, Terrence stepped forward and placed his hands gently on her waist. "So, you think I'm hot, huh?"

"No, *you* think you're hot!"

They laughed. Terrence tried to control his breathing, but it was a losing battle. "Come, my fair lady," he said, in his best theatrical voice. "Your chariot awaits."

On the drive to the African American Theater of Arts, Terrence amused Kyra with tales from his childhood and his quiet, suburban life now in Pittsburgh. They were mobbed by fans when they stepped out of the limo, and as onlookers cheered their arrival and cameras flashed, Terrence reached for her arm, pulling her close.

Hand in hand, eyes locked, they entered the modern, brightly lit auditorium. On the outside, Kyra appeared calm, but on the inside, she was battling her own demons. And when Terrence bent down and whispered in her ear, she was more confused than ever. Kyra wasn't the type of woman to play mind games or send mixed messages, but when Terrence said she looked beautiful, she felt her body fill with a delicious heat. Feeling blissfully happy, she kissed him softly on the cheek. He smiled and the knots in her stomach disappeared. Her feelings for Terrence were growing, deepening, and although the realization scared her, Kyra refused to let anything spoil their night.

At midnight, after a decadent six-course meal, Kyra and Terrence left the trendiest restaurant in downtown Atlanta and slipped into their waiting limo. Reveling in the beauty of the night, Kyra sank back in the cushy leather seats and stared outside the tinted window. Trees and pedestrians whipped by as the limo sped down the block.

"Slow down, Mr. Chapman," Terrence ordered, his voice firm, but his tone light. "I have a princess back here, and I promised her a smooth ride."

Kyra's eyes grew heavy but cocktails, rum-laced brownies and dirty dancing could do that to a girl. The excitement of being with a fine-looking brother turned her on, and every time Terrence touched her, she shivered. No one had ever planned such an elaborate date for her, and she'd felt like Cinderella since the moment he picked her up.

Allowing herself a glance of his profile, she sighed wistfully. Exquisite in a honey-colored suit, he was a walking advertisement for a men's fitness magazine and easily the best-looking man she had ever dated.

On cloud nine, she closed her eyes, smiling to herself. Never would she have imagined an evening as magical as this. They'd met the all-star cast, and even attended the celebrity after-party. Kyra felt as if none of this were real and worried she was going to wake up tomorrow and discover that it had all been a dream.

Kyra must have drifted off to sleep, because she heard distant voices and had the distinct feeling that someone was carrying her. It was a challenge, but she pried her eyes open. She was curled up on the seat, nestled in Terrence's arms, and smooth jazz was playing. Definitely Najee. "How long have I been out?" she asked, smiling up at him.

"You make it sound like you were drugged."

"Was I?" she teased, raising an eyebrow. "I'm so tired I can barely move."

"That's why I'm taking you home."

"You said we could swing by Snoop's party."

He shook his head. "They'll be other parties. Besides, you've had a long day, too much to drink and you were moaning in your sleep."

"I was?" Kyra sat up. "What was I saying?"

"Oh, the usual." His lopsided grin widened. "*'Terrence, you're such a caring, thoughtful man. I love you, boo.'*"

Kyra giggled. "You're such a liar. You *wish* I'd say something like that."

"You're right, Ky. I do."

His confession was explosive, and for a moment,

Kyra couldn't think of a single thing to say. The strength of his gaze made her wet and kindled the fire between her legs. He lifted her hands to his mouth and kissed them. Stifling a moan, she turned away from his deep, penetrating eyes. Terrence wasn't the right man for her, so why was she hungry for his kiss? She could assert herself without being rude, and she would, right after he finished stroking her back.

"Would you be mad if I kissed you?"

No. Yes. No... Before she could respond, he lifted her chin, and slowly brushed his lips against hers. Desire was in the air, more stifling than smoke fumes, but when he parted her lips with his tongue, she pulled away. "This isn't right."

Still grinning, he stared blankly ahead and spoke to the driver.

When the limo pulled up in front of her house, the driver dashed around to the passenger side. A gentle wind whipped Kyra's hair around her face when the door opened. The scent of rain was heavy in the air and the dark, gray sky suggested an impending thunderstorm.

Terrence helped her up and didn't release his hold until they were inside the foyer. "Thanks for accompanying me to the play, Terrence. I had an amazing time."

"I'm glad *somebody* did."

"Get off it. You enjoyed the show as much as I did."

"It was torture!" He chuckled loudly. "I'd rather have my chest waxed."

Kyra wasn't buying it. "For someone who hated the show, you sure did a lot of cheesing for the cameras," she pointed out, and they laughed.

After a night of wine, music and stolen kisses, she

spoke freely, sharing all the feelings and emotions flowing through her. "Honestly, this is one of the best dates I've ever been on in a long time. I've never felt so spoiled or pampered."

"Oh," he drawled, raising an eyebrow, "so this *was* a date?"

"Your birthday's coming up, isn't it?" Intent on changing the subject, she searched her mind of the correct date. "If I'm not mistaken, it's only a few weeks after the reunion, right?"

Terrence placed a hand over his chest. "I'm touched that you remember. And you're right. I'll be thirty-three years young on October 20."

"How will you celebrate? A night at the strip club with your friends, perhaps?"

"Naw, I did that last year." Her eyes flew open and he released a deep, belly laugh. "I'm only kidding. I have no plans—" he paused expectantly "—unless my favorite PR director wants to make me dinner."

"All right, it's a deal. I'll make you an authentic Southern meal."

"I'm looking forward to it." He squeezed her shoulders, his facial expression one of genuine concern. "I better get out of here. Have a good night, Kyra."

"Wait!" Wearing an innocent face, she pushed a hand through her short, tight curls. Her thoughts were a web, a maze, more confusing than a thousand-piece puzzle, but deep down, Kyra knew she didn't want Terrence to leave. "Do you want a beer or maybe a cup of coffee before you go?"

"If I stay, all bets are off," he told her, his fingertips caressing her warm skin. "I want you, Kyra, but not for just one night. When we make love, I want to possess all of you. Your heart, your mind and your body."

Make love? The thought consumed her mind. And the combined effects of his cologne, his touch and that disarming smile of his rendered Kyra speechless. She couldn't put her feelings into words, but her body was red-hot. On fire for a man she'd once loved with an all-consuming passion.

"It's been ten years since we dated, but nothing's changed, Kyra. I still want you. I never stopped." Terrence lowered his head toward her, and she did the unthinkable. Reaching hungrily for him, she parted her lips and pressed herself hard against his chest. Losing herself in the kiss, she closed her eyes, enjoying the feel of his full, moist lips and the tender intimacy of the moment.

Chapter 12

Cork, an upscale wine bar in downtown Atlanta had been reserved for the private cocktail reception for Hollington's most elite alumni. Anxious to join the classy, upscale event, Terrence handed the keys to his Ferrari luxury sports car to the tuxedo-clad valet and strode confidently through the sleek glass doors.

The party was in full swing. It felt good to be back at the place that had launched his football career and when he entered the large, open space filled with tall, round tables and stools, he was given a hero's welcome. Surrounded by a crowd of well-wishers and energetic Dallas Cowboys fans, he slipped off his tinted shades and slowly combed the room for his favorite PR director.

Soft music played in the background, enhancing the peaceful ambiance. A server offered Terrence a glass of Shiraz, but he politely declined. Sipping wine and nibbling on hors d'oeuvres wasn't his style, but Kyra would be in attendance and Terrence liked the idea of spending the night talking to her outside the college.

"There's the man with the lightning-quick speed!"

Terrence cast a glance to his left. His friend, Kevin Stayton, was grinning like a leprechaun. "You all right, man? You look a little banged-up."

"I took a hit in practice today," he explained, remembering how the defensive linemen had slammed him to the ground. By the time he'd returned to the rental house that afternoon, his knee was killing him. If not for the aspirin and several shots of whiskey he'd downed an hour ago, he'd still be writhing around on the couch in pain. "I underestimated how good the Hollington Lions defense is and they hammered me every time I caught a pass!"

Kevin tasted his wine. "I'm glad things are working out for you, T. I know you miss playing ball, but life isn't over just because you're not in the NFL."

"You're right, it's not. We've all had our share of disappointments and everyone in here has a story to tell. All we can do is get up, dust ourselves off and keep trucking."

"Did you tell the players that before or after they knocked your ass down?"

Both men chuckled. They stood around, talking about Kevin's newest business ventures, tomorrow's football game and the parade on Sunday afternoon.

"Have you seen Kyra?" Terrence asked, trying to appear nonchalant.

"Yeah, she's around here somewhere. And looking mighty fine, too."

"Back off, Kev. Go get your own girl!"

Laughing, Kevin rested his empty glass on one of the raised tables and smoothed a hand over his tie. "Speaking of which, it's time for me to introduce the woman of the hour. See you around, T."

Terrence nodded and watched the successful entrepreneur approach President Morrow, who was standing near the small, raised stage. Kevin raised the microphone to his mouth and greeted the stylish, thirty-something crowd.

"Good evening everyone," he said. "I want to welcome all of you to Hollington's annual homecoming weekend, and the tenth anniversary of class of '99!"

The group broke into feverish cheers and applause.

"I'm Kevin Stayton and I want to take this time to acknowledge the woman who is responsible for planning and organizing this event. Chloe Jackson has been working tirelessly to make this weekend a success and…"

Terrence caught sight of Kyra and his jaw went loose. Always chic and well put together, she wowed in a crimson vest, fitted white blouse and matching pants. Dangling silver earrings and a wide bracelet accessorized her attractive designer outfit.

Watching her, he battled feelings of desire. A part of him wished that they could go back. Start over. Pretend that they didn't have a past. Truth was, he'd loved her deeply and wanted to marry her. But Kyra had never been able to fully open up to him, and despite his commitment to their relationship, she'd always doubted his love. He'd felt under the gun, scrutinized, as if she were just waiting for him to mess up. Her blunt, tough-girl exterior eventually drove a wedge between them, and when he was nominated for the Heisman trophy, they began arguing more and seeing each other less.

Terrence stood there, in complete awe of her beauty. Kyra emanated confidence, sophistication and sensuality in equal parts and when she laughed, the sparkle in her eyes brightened the entire room.

Content to simply observe her, Terrence stood with his elbows resting against the bar, studying the petite woman he couldn't seem to get out of his mind. She was having a very animated discussion with some other faculty members and as the minutes ticked by, he considered interrupting her. He grew restless as the reception began to wind down and worried that Kyra would leave before he got a chance to speak to her.

Determined to connect with her, Terrence strode over to where she was standing. With all the other noises in the room and the music playing, he could hardly hear what Kyra was saying. Coming up behind her, he rested a hand on her lower back. Kyra spun around. Her shoulders squared when he tried to pull her close, and her tight, guarded smile conveyed her disapproval.

Terrence frowned. Was he missing something? A week ago, they'd shared a passionate, head-spinning kiss in the foyer of her house and now she was giving him the evil eye. Before he could ask Kyra what was wrong, Professor Griffey shoved a glass of red wine into his hand and greeted him affably.

"It's good to see you again, Terrence. We were just discussing where to go when this little soiree wraps up. I bet you know the best places to kick back and unwind."

"There are a few cool spots in walking distance from here," he said. "Why don't we all head over to the Azure Bar & Lounge? It's a mature crowd and the drinks are—"

"Terrence, can I have a word with you?" Before he could answer, Kyra spun on her heels and marched off. He caught up to her in the private tasting room at the back of the bar. "Tomorrow's the big game."

"I know," he said, confused by her cold, brisk attitude. "What is this all about? Why are you getting upset?"

"Because we're all depending on you." She cleared her throat, but the hostility in her tone remained. "If you show up at the game hung over, you'll be sending the wrong message to the players. In case you haven't noticed, they all look up to you."

"I haven't had anything but soda to drink all night. And just because I'm going to the club tonight doesn't mean I'm going to shrug off my responsibilities."

"Great, I'm glad we cleared that up." Back in control, she turned and started toward the open door. "Have a good night."

"You can't drive me away this time, Kyra."

She stopped. Hands clenched at her sides, she pivoted back around. Her eyes narrowed dangerously and were filled with contempt. "Drive you away?" Her words came out in an angry shout. "Is that how you assuaged your guilt? By convincing yourself that I was the one to blame for our breakup?"

Terrence dragged a hand down his face. This was it. The moment he'd been waiting for. Ready to set the record straight, he pushed out a breath, saying, "Kyra, I loved you deeply, but you never gave me your whole heart. Just a piece. I thought getting engaged would bring us closer together, but it only made things worse."

Honesty was cathartic and as Terrence spoke, he felt like a weight was being lifted off his shoulders. "Getting engaged only intensified your doubts. You were convinced that I was going to find someone else and leave you, but that was never the case."

"But it *was* the case. You dumped me the second you landed in Dallas and never looked back." Her eyes misted with tears, but her voice was strong. "And as for me pulling away from you, you're right, I did. It all became too much. The girls, the parties, the recognition. Everyone wanted a piece of the great Terrence Franklin and I knew it was just a matter of time before I got replaced."

The desire to comfort her was unbearable. Moved by her words, he placed his hands on the side of her shoulders, hoping to offer comfort. "Kyra, look at me."

She kept her head down. Lifting her chin with his finger, Terrence searched his heart for the right words. "You are, and always will be, the only woman I want."

Kyra remained silent. Voices drifted in from the bar, intruding on their conversation.

"The past is behind us." With the tension at its breaking point, he went one step further. "I've never met anyone who makes me feel like you do, Kyra. You're the one I let get away, and I still love you. I know you don't trust me, but I'm willing to do whatever it takes to have you back in my life."

Pulling away, she held up her hand to prevent him from going any further. "I can't deal with this right now." The animosity in her tone gave him pause. "There's a lot going on and I…I need to get back to the party."

Deep inside, Terrence knew she was lying. That was

fear talking. Watching her leave, he decided he'd waited long enough to make his move. He'd been the one to break things off, so it was up to him to get them back on track. Their physical attraction was explosive, and they shared the same hopes and dreams for the future. As he stood there, thinking about Kyra, he remembered something his high school coach once said. *If you're not going to give a hundred percent, why play at all?* The words registered, inspired, imbued him with self-confidence. Terrence hadn't become one of the greatest running backs in the NFL by playing it safe, and he refused to lose Kyra again.

The seconds on the clock ticked down. Staring intently at the scoreboard, face pinched in concentration, Terrence rubbed a hand across his sweaty forehead. The clouds parted, making room for the sun and as his gaze panned the sold-out crowd he spotted Mr. Morrow. That had to mean Kyra was nearby. And she was. Seeing her striking two noisemakers, decked out in a cute red Hollington Lions shirt and fitted jeans, brought back memories of all those times he'd looked into the stands and saw Kyra cheering him on.

A broad grin fell across his lips as he studied her. The chemistry between them had never died; it was as clear as the morning sky and Terrence wanted her more than ever before. A slim Mexican guy took the seat beside Kyra, and his smile faded. Watching her talk to the handsome stranger was enough to make Terrence lose his lunch. If Coach Mayo hadn't gripped his arm and pointed him toward the field, he would have stormed over and told Ricco Suave to take a hike.

Terrence turned just in time to see the football fall

to the ground. One of the Hollington players scooped up the ball, broke tackle and sprinted down the field at breakneck speed. Vigorously pumping his fist, Terrence shot up off the bench. Cupping his hands over his mouth, he ran along the sidelines, yelling, "Go all the way, Earl. All the way, big guy!"

The freshman sailed into the end zone, and the fans went wild. When the referee blew his whistle, signaling a touchdown, Terrence jumped into the air, applauding the home team. *Ten, nine, eight,* he recited. The play clock ran down to zero and the entire Hollington team flooded the field. The Lions had beaten the defending state champions, and the energy in the stadium was exhilarating.

From her third-row seat, Kyra watched the action on the field, impressed by the athleticism and tenacity of the Hollington Lions. Caught up in the excitement, she clapped exuberantly as the marching band wowed the crowd with their spirited moves.

Fans whistled as the school mascot ran through the stands waving the Hollington flag. A cool breeze swept over Kyra. Pulling on her jacket, she watched Terrence celebrate with the team and laughed when the players hoisted him up on their shoulders.

On a high, she waved, hoping to catch his attention. Terrence gave a thumbs-up sign, and Kyra sucked in a breath. Terrence was naturally cool. Without even trying. He just was. And the sports hero looked good in everything—jeans, suits, T-shirts—all looked fabulous. Ultracasual in Nike sportswear and sneakers, the former NFL running back emanated a suave, sexy vibe that attracted women by the dozens.

Recalling what happened last night at Cork made knots form in the pit of her stomach. Offended by his comments, she'd stormed out of the private tasting room, desperate to put some space between them. Convinced Terrence would show up later at the Azure Lounge & Bar, Kyra had decided against joining her colleagues at the popular nightspot, and headed home. Running away from Terrence wasn't one of her finest moments, but she couldn't risk being alone with him again. Not when there was so much at stake.

Part of her wanted to believe him, but another part— a bigger part—feared that he would hurt her again. And what would she do then? Kyra tried not to think about Terrence and the love they'd once shared, but she was reminded of him at every turn. Even at night her mind wouldn't rest. She thought of him and nothing else. But how could she still desire a man who had once so callously dumped her?

His words rang in her ears. *Kyra, you never gave me your whole heart. Just a small piece...* Was it true? Had she unknowingly driven him away? Soul-searching didn't provide any answers, but it gave her the strength to face the truth. Deep down, Kyra had never felt that she was good enough for Terrence. She'd always worried that he'd find someone else. Someone younger, thinner, more beautiful. Being replaced terrified her; in the end, her darkest fears had been realized.

Last night he'd looked at her with such affection, and sounded so sincere, she'd almost forgotten their bitter past. Could Terrence have been acting? The less she seemed to care about him, the more interested he was in her, but that didn't mean he was lying, did it? Tired of analyzing everything Terrence said and did, Kyra struck the thought from her mind. The schism between them wasn't going to be solved overnight, but she was ready to move on. She'd always had a sweet spot for Terrence, and time had only intensified her feelings. Their familiarity with each other was unparalleled, and Kyra liked that she could be herself around him.

Intent on speaking to him, Kyra collected her things and hustled down the steps. Anxious to put the past behind them, she walked into the tunnel leading to the locker room. Young, attractive girls were lined up along the wall, fluffing their hair, adjusting their miniskirts and applying lipstick. Hands molded to hips, shoulders thrust back, the group resembled a hoochie mama chorus line.

Feeling dowdy in her jeans and red Hollington sweatshirt, Kyra waited patiently as Terrence made his way through the tunnel, praying inwardly that he'd pick her. He did.

"Kyra, we won!" Grinning, Terrence held his hands up high above his head in triumph. "I'm so proud of the guys. They fought hard for that win, and if they keep it up, there'll be no stopping them this season!"

"All they needed was to get their confidence back," she affirmed. "I know you haven't made a decision yet about the coaching job, but I hope you'll take the time to seriously consider coming back to Hollington. The team needs you."

People rushed past them, waving, screaming and shouting greetings at Terrence. They stood there, staring intently at each other, oblivious to the world around them. Breaking the silence, his face weathered in concern, he spoke softly to her. "I'm sorry if I upset you last night at Cork. I just wanted to apologize for how things ended between us, and clear up any misconceptions."

He stroked her cheek with the back of his hand, and her thoughts took a detour. It was a classic Terrence Franklin move, but Kyra didn't pull away. She *wanted* him to touch her. To kiss her. To love her just one more time. And the gentle yearning of his voice made her instinctively inch forward.

"Why don't we go to Ralph's Kitchen for a celebratory burger?" he asked, reaching for her hand. "You used to love eating there."

A smile came. "You're right, I did, but Ralph's closed years ago."

"Then," he leaned heavily on the word, winking at her as if he were letting her in on a secret, "we'll have to find somewhere else to create new memories."

Chapter 13

Chloe Jackson was the first person Kyra saw when she sailed through the elegant, gold-encrusted doors of Bollito Nightclub on Saturday night. The much-in-demand event planner was standing outside of the coat-room, chatting with a woman in a black cocktail dress and long, straight hair.

As she shouldered her way through the crowded lobby, she caught a glimpse of Chloe's companion. It was her long-time friend and sorority sister, Tamara Hodges. Forgetting that she was at Atlanta's trendiest nightclub, she shot across the dark, gleaming floors, calling their names. "Tamara! Chloe! Wait up!"

Tamara glanced over her shoulder and shrieked so loud, the security guard standing nearby dropped his walkie-talkie. "Hey girl!" Kyra threw her arms around them both. "I almost didn't recognize you, Tamara. You look amazing!"

"Thanks, and I love your dress. *Très* sexy."

"The VIP area's been set up just for the reunion party, so let's go hang out in there," Kyra suggested. "We can talk without being interrupted."

"I can't stay long. I have to check in with—"

"Chloe, we'll have a drink and then you can go about your business." Kyra linked arms with her. "Now come on, I want to hear all about you and Kevin!"

Gold velvet drapes separated the private balconies from the rest of the club. Plush leather sofas, glass tables and flickering candles accented the muted brown walls and hushed lighting. While they waited for their drinks to arrive, the three women chatted about last night's reception at Cork and that afternoon's nail-biting football game.

"Do you think you could introduce me to Justice Kane?" Kyra asked, facing Tamara. "I read your interview in *Luster* and he seems like a really cool guy. President Morrow is big on fundraising and wants the Winter Wonderland Ball to be a smash."

Tamara tasted her soda. "I'll see what I can do, but I can't promise you anything." Head tilted back, she studied Kyra for a long moment. "How has it been with Terrence being back in town?"

Dodging Tamara's question, she turned to Chloe and said, "Is Kevin around? I'd like to congratulate him on the success of the club." Admiring the lavish decor, she ran a hand along the back of the plush couch. "This place is real classy. We need more establishments like this. The over-thirty crowd likes to party, too, you know!"

"I heard that," Tamara agreed, sensing her friend's desire to change the subject. "I like being around people my own age. No offense to any of these young whip-persnappers who snuck in here tonight, but they need to take all that bumpin' and grindin' somewhere else. This is a sophisticated club. No hoochies allowed!"

The women erupted in laughter.

"You guys, I really have to go," Chloe said, standing.

"You haven't even been here for five minutes!" Pointing at Chloe's full cocktail glass, Kyra frowned disapprovingly at her. "Chloe, reunion weekend is for you, too, you know. You've been running yourself ragged all weekend. Take a load off, girl!"

"I will, later. There's still a lot that needs to be done," she explained. Smiling, Chloe waved and strode purposefully out of the VIP lounge.

The familiar, bass-heavy beat of "Push It" filled the club. "The DJ's playing my song!" Kyra shrieked, rocking from side to side. "This song takes me *way* back!"

"I know, he went deep into the vault for this one," Tamara joked, retrieving her cell phone and checking for missed calls.

Curious to see which other Hollington alumni were in attendance, Kyra stepped out onto the private balcony and looked out over the dance floor. Hands clapping, bodies swaying, dancers rocked to the infectious hip-hop beat.

Her gaze panned the crowd, and landed on everyone's favorite running back. Behind the shelter of the private balcony, she scoped the gorgeous ex-athlete out. In a three-button suit, vest and matching fedora tilted dangerously to the side, he was easily the best-looking man in the club. Terrence had amassed enormous wealth over the years, which made him an easy target for gold diggers, but tonight he wasn't surrounded by a flock of beauties. He was talking to President Morrow and members of the student council, and though his restless gaze spoke of his boredom, he wore a gracious smile.

Kyra would never admit it to anyone, but she loved having Terrence around. He had a wonderful sense of humor and was always up for a good time. Misplaced trust had been her downfall before, but she couldn't shake the feeling that he'd changed. He was the same fun, charismatic guy he'd been in university, but he was infinitely more considerate, more patient and more caring.

Their eyes met through the jam-packed club. Caught staring, her face flushed with an oven-like heat. The man was every woman's fantasy. A living, breathing, wet dream. The crowd went mad when R&B singer Justice Kane took the stage, but Kyra's gaze was glued to Terrence. He lifted his glass in a silent toast, then downed it in a smooth, fluid swig. He said something to President Morrow, then disappeared in the thick crowd.

"Looking for me?"

Kyra jumped as if she'd been caught with her hand in the cookie jar. Or in this case, with her eyes all over Terrence Franklin. Arranging her lips into a smile, she turned toward Charles, and greeted him. "Hi. You made it."

"Yeah, but I can't stay long. I promised my parents we'd stop by the country club for drinks. They're really anxious to meet you."

Meet his parents? Kyra wasn't going to let him dictate when and where she went, and told him so. "Charles, it's reunion weekend. I haven't seen most of these people in ten years. And to be honest, I'm not ready to meet your parents. We've only known each other for a few—"

He cut her off. "Let's not worry about it now. We have plenty of time to socialize with your friends before we have to leave."

Didn't he hear what I just said? Seething inwardly but determined not to let Charles ruin her night, she waved at her sorority sisters dancing down below. Beside her, Charles complained about the overpriced drinks.

Wishing she was somewhere else, Kyra searched for a quick getaway. No emergency door, no fire extinguisher, no trap door. Where were her girlfriends when she needed them? Unfortunately for her, Beverly was the only person around, and she was sitting in a secluded corner with a striking dark-skinned man. Kyra hadn't seen Tamara since she'd left in search of the washrooms ten minutes earlier, and Chloe was busy seeing to the items on her growing checklist.

"Let's get out of here. All this rap music is giving me a headache."

"It's not rap. It's R&B," she told him.

For weeks, Kyra had considered breaking things off with Charles, and as she listened to him reproach the waiter for taking too long with the bill, she scolded herself for not dumping him sooner. "I'm going to go check on my friend, Tamara. She's been gone a really long time and I'm starting to get worried."

"We better get going. I told my parents we'd be at the country club by ten."

His breath could start a campfire. To create more space, she inched over to the left. Kyra fingered the stem of her cocktail glass to keep from wringing his neck. Charles must be more drunk than she thought, because he was getting more annoying by the minute.

Charles guzzled the rest of his drink. Up on his feet, he swayed slightly, before righting himself. "Go say goodbye to your friends, and I'll bring the car around."

Stunned, her mouth ajar, she stared at him disbelievingly. The insurance sales rep was obviously off his rocker if he thought she was leaving with him. Charles might think he was invincible, but after chugging four drinks, he could hardly stand straight. "I'm not going anywhere with you. You're so drunk you can barely stand."

"Shut your mouth," he snarled. "Someone might hear you."

Kyra started to speak, but broke off when the music stopped. Standing, she peered out over the dance floor. When she saw Kevin Stayton holding the microphone with his free hand outstretched to Chloe, Kyra rushed over to the balcony. Her friend dazzled in a stunning pomegranate-red dress, but she looked as if she was about to faint.

"I am delighted, thrilled, relieved and proud to introduce Chloe Jackson to everyone as my future wife."

Sighing deeply, Kyra wondered if she'd ever find a love so magical and real. Kevin's voice was strong, his words convincing and his eyes filled with pure admiration. With all the passion and emotion of a man in love, he boldly declared his feelings for Chloe Jackson. It was a romantic, heartfelt moment, and though Kyra was thrilled for her friend, she couldn't ignore the ache in her heart. She'd never thought of herself as inferior to anyone, but didn't she deserve a relationship as loving as the one Chloe had?

"I'm going to go get the car. Meet me out front in five minutes."

Mustering what little patience she had left, she faced him, saying, "Charles, this isn't working. I think we'd be better off as friends."

Lips curled into a sneer, he stared right through her, as if he hadn't heard a word she'd said. "We're not going to discuss this here. It's a party, right? Why would you ruin it by getting all emotional on me?"

He tried to kiss her, but she turned her head. Chuckling, he glanced around the room, smiling at no one in particular. "You're so drunk you probably won't even remember this conversation in the morning."

Realizing he couldn't be reasoned with, Kyra decided to save her breath. "I'll call a cab to take you to the country club. You're in no condition to drive."

Charles grabbed Kyra's arm so hard, she winced.

"No, we're leaving together," he spat through clenched teeth.

Startled by his aberrant behavior, she smiled tightly, ignoring the knife-like pain in her arm. Kyra never imagined someone as proper as Charles Roberts would be capable of hurting her. His seeming gentility had obviously been an act, put on to impress her and make her believe he was an upstanding guy. "I'm only going to say this once," Kyra said, controlling the tremor in her voice. "Let go of my arm, Charles, or you'll be sorry."

Terrence was offering a toast to the class of '99 when he spotted Kyra up on the second-floor balcony. He'd never been the type to fawn over a woman, but the PR director made his head spin. Tonight, she was a goddess in gold and he couldn't help picturing her naked, in nothing but those black, ankle-tie pumps. Not only did she rev his engines, she challenged his way of thinking and made him hungry to settle down—with her.

Needing a distraction, he turned to the bartender and ordered another drink. Kyra's overall animosity toward all men—the good ones and the jerks—made it almost impossible for him to get closer to her, but he wasn't giving up.

When Terrence spotted Charles, he shook his head. Letting Charles have Kyra wasn't an option. She was his dream girl. The type of woman he could see himself marrying. And if the businessman thought he was going to ride off into the sunset with the stunning PR director, he was sadly mistaken because Terrence didn't play to win, he played for keeps.

Watching and waiting, he plotted his next move. The party was a hot bed of good-looking women, but Terrence only had eyes for Kyra. He was drinking champagne, planning the perfect date for her, when he saw Charles grab her arm. The lights were low, but he saw the startled expression that flashed across Kyra's face. Slamming down his glass, he pushed his way through the crowd and bolted into the waiting elevator.

Heart racing, adrenaline flowing, he shot across the hall, and didn't stop running until he was inside the VIP room. Expecting to find Kyra in tears, or worse, fighting off Charles, he glanced around, searching the room anxiously for her.

Terrence felt a tap on his shoulder and spun around. Kyra. His joy at seeing her was indescribable and in the space of a few seconds, his emotions vacillated from anger to relief. "Kyra, I'm so glad you're okay! I was worried about you."

"Why?"

He'd obviously misread the situation, but couldn't shake the feeling that something was wrong. "I saw Charles grab your arm and thought..."

Spreading her hands at her sides in a dramatic gesture of helplessness, she lifted her head and batted her eyelashes at him, playing the role of the damsel in distress to the hilt. "What, you thought he was up here pushing me around? I told Charles if he didn't let go of me, things would get *real* ugly, *real* quick, and he took off running. I might be petite, but I'm no wallflower," she explained in a strong, confident voice. "I don't need you charging in here to save me, Terrence. I can take care of myself."

Nodding, he impeded a smile. Nothing made Kyra angrier than being disrespected, and he should have known that the feisty PR director wouldn't need his help.

"I'm surprised you're not out there dancing with your sorority sisters," he said, gesturing with his head to the dance floor. "You used to love a good party and I remember having to drag you out of the club on more than one occasion."

Kyra laughed. "I'm going to get out there, don't you worry!"

"Good. I'll buy you a cocktail and then you can show me what you've got."

They shared light, playful banter while they waited for their drinks to arrive. His easygoing personality made him a hit with the ladies, but when their former classmates asked him to dance, he said no. Wanting privacy, Terrence led Kyra over to the sofa loveseat positioned against the far wall.

A scintillating conversation about relationships ensued. Kyra could have easily spent the rest of the night talking to Terrence. He was interested in what she had to say, made her laugh and complimented her outfit on more than one occasion. His words were genuine, heartfelt. Not rehearsed worn-out lines. Terrence made her feel incredibly special. It was more than just what he said. It was the concentrated expression on his face, the strength of his gaze, the way he lovingly caressed her hands. And when a sensual Motown ballad filled the air, Kyra stood and went willingly into his open arms.

Chapter 14

Kyra was laughing so hard, she couldn't put the key into the lock.

"It looks like somebody's had one too many drinks!" Terrence teased, gripping her elbow to steady her shaky movements. Chuckling, he pushed open the door, stepped aside and waited for her to enter before clicking the lock.

Kyra dropped her keys on the oak table. "Thanks for giving me a ride, Terrence. I'd still be waiting for a taxi if I hadn't run into you and Kevin outside of Bollito's."

"You said you were going to congratulate Chloe, but when you didn't come back, I figured you were brushing me off." Terrence stared at her, his gaze strong and penetrating. "What happened to that sweet, innocent girl I used to know? She never would have run off on me."

Realizing he was teasing, she laughed. "This whole

weekend has been amazing, and I'm actually a little bummed that it's coming to an end. I hope another ten years don't go by before we all get together again."

"Whether or not I accept the head coaching position, I plan on seeing a lot more of you, Kyra. Even if it means flying in every weekend to play trivia with you at The Tavern." Stepping forward, he closed his arms around her, gathering her tightly to his chest. "Do you know what my biggest regret in life is?"

Kyra sucked in a breath. Tomorrow, she might regret letting Terrence hold her, but tonight she relished the familiar touch of his hands. They hadn't been this close in years, but being with Terrence felt right.

"I should have married you when I had the chance. It's not that I didn't love you, Ky. I was scared. Scared that we wouldn't make it." Cupping her cheeks affectionately, he bathed her lips with his mouth. He kissed her with finesse, with ease, lightly licking the slope of her lips and tracing his hands along, over and down her bare shoulders.

The deeply satisfying kiss whetted her appetite for more. His chest was a wall of muscle, and her nipples hardened against his muscular physique. Melting into the embrace, she curved her arms around him, praying he wouldn't stop. Falling in love with Terrence was a recipe for disaster, but a few hours of passion were not only welcome, but needed.

His soulful whispering was her undoing. At heart, she was the same young, whimsical girl who'd once lived for his kiss and his love. His voice was as sensual as a feather drawn across her back and sent shivers down to her toes.

Lost in wild delight, her body throbbing with desire, she rubbed his chest. Kyra started to unbutton his dress shirt, but Terrence covered her hands with his own. "Mind if I use your bathroom?" A wicked grin fell across his mouth. "I had this sexy PR director grinding on me at Bollito and she wouldn't let me out of her sight!"

"You're such a liar!"

Terrence chuckled when Kyra rolled her eyes. "Do you have any aspirin?"

"Sure, there's some in the cabinet. I'll get you a glass of water."

"Make it a beer instead."

"Alcohol and aspirin don't mix," she told him, her tone matter-of-fact. "Go on, and I'll meet you in the living room." Kyra turned towards the kitchen, but Terrence grabbed her hand, pulling her to him for another kiss. Longing rushed through her, and his light kisses ignited her passion. "Hurry back," she quipped, breaking away.

After downing a couple of aspirin, Terrence washed his hands and opened the bathroom door. Sticking his head out into the hall, he cocked his ears and listened intently. He could hear Kyra moving around the kitchen and decided this was the perfect time to give himself a private tour of her condo. He'd been to the house twice since landscaping her yard, but she wouldn't let him see inside the master bedroom. Curiosity had been gnawing at him ever since, and if he was quick, he could be in and out without her ever knowing.

He glanced over his shoulder, gripped the handle and pushed open the door. He was instantly struck by the dizzying scent of vanilla. The bedroom, with its satin sheets, jumbo floor cushions and elevated sleigh bed, exuded charm and positive energy. Tall windows and rich saturated reds and browns reinforced the cozy feel of her home.

The velvet love seat sure looked inviting. Lowering himself onto the couch, he picked up the remote laying on the glass table and hit the power button. Terrence was flipping channels when he heard Kyra calling his name.

"Did you get lost on your way back to the living room?"

Terrence laughed. "No, I'm just taking a load off. I wanted to catch the tail end of *Lost* and liked the idea of kicking it in here." Winking, he draped his long arms around the couch. "Everything's just so darn cute!"

Her eyes gleamed and glowed, and he knew she was trying hard not to laugh. "There's a TV out there," she said, pointing down the hall.

"I know, but I'm starving and it smells like tropical fruit in here!"

They laughed.

"All right. Let me get my rusty butt off your adorable little couch." He started to stand, but Kyra put a hand on his shoulder. "Stay. *Mi casa es su casa.*"

"I was hoping you'd say that. Nice outfit," he said, loving the sexy way her bottom filled out the cotton shorts. "All you need is a pair of pom-poms and you could join the cheerleading squad! Bet that would increase ticket sales!"

Her giggles filled the room. Kyra went into the kitchen, and returned minutes later carrying a plate of turkey sandwiches. "I love this show," she gushed, flopping down beside him on the couch. "Matthew Fox is so damn sexy it's nauseating! If it wasn't for him, I never would've started watching."

Caught up in the action-packed drama, they fell quiet. "That did the trick." Terrence put down the plate. "Guess I can't convince you to make me another one, huh?"

"Terrence, you had three!" she criticized, poking him in the shoulder. "Don't push it, buddy. You're lucky I even let you eat in here. As soon as you leave, I'm going to bust out my handheld vacuum!"

"All right, I can take a hint. I'm out of here."

He stood, but she gripped his arm. "Don't go."

"All right. I guess I could hang out a while longer."

"No, I want you to spend the night."

His grin fell like porcelain on wood.

"I want you, Terrence," she whispered, reaching for his hands and placing them around her. Suddenly, thoughts of making love to him ruled Kyra's loose mind. Her heart was beating loud and fast. Fast enough to require immediate medical attention, but instead of taking a moment to catch her breath, she went one step further. "We've been fighting this thing between us long enough. I'm attracted to you, and I know you feel the same way."

He lifted, then lowered his eyebrows. "I can't stay here. It wouldn't be right."

As Kyra gazed up at him, her body was filled with an unquenchable desire, and for the first time in her life she decided to act on her impulse. Hooking up. That's what the freshman class called it. One night of explosive sex without strings. She'd never had a one-night stand, but bumping and grinding at Bollito was a powerful aphrodisiac. Mind made up, she reached hungrily for him. They were going to make love tonight, and there was nothing Terrence could say to stop her. "You're not going to make me beg, are you?"

Blank-faced, he stared down at her, his mouth wide enough to land a commercial airplane. "You've had too much to drink, Kyra. This is not you, and I don't want to do something you're going to regret in the morning."

"I know exactly what I'm doing." And to show him just how serious she was, she drew his hands from around her back and placed them on her breasts. Longing to feel more of him, she pushed her hips against him, massaging him with her pelvis. She felt his erection, and her lips drew back into a smirk of triumph. "Do you have protection?"

Terrence couldn't believe this was happening. He was a spontaneous, go-with-the-flow type of guy, but when Kyra nibbled on his earlobe, he tensed. This wasn't him. When he saw something he wanted, he went after it. The word *no* wasn't part of his vocabulary, but for the first time ever Terrence wasn't interested in satisfying his carnal pleasures. It didn't matter that Kyra was grinding on him like a Sean Paul dancer.

He searched for a way to let her down easy. Kyra was guarded with her heart and although he'd been fantasizing about making love to her for weeks, he wasn't going to take advantage of her. But when she licked the rim of his ear, his heart leaped into his throat and the fevered voices in his brain got louder. *Man, what's the matter with you? You're Terrence Franklin. An NFL superstar and world-class lover. Hit that! You have a reputation at stake.* "Naw, Kyra, I can't. We—"

Kyra silenced him with a kiss. A kiss so powerful and intense Terrence thought he might black out. His conscience told him to leave, to scoop up his jacket and bolt, but his feet were glued to the floor. Everything about Kyra was hypnotic. Her eyes, her smile, the way she licked her lips. Her touch was light, her lips sweet and when she unzipped his pants and gripped his shaft, a violent shudder racked his body.

In a last-ditch effort to be the upstanding man his mother had raised him to be, he broke off the kiss. Taking a deep breath, he stared up at the ceiling, praying the man upstairs would triple his dose of self-control.

"Let's get into bed," she urged, her low, sensual voice saturating his thoughts.

"No, I'm, ah, gonna jet." Terrence couldn't get the words out fast enough. "I'll just go ahead and let myself out."

He backed into the side table, and let out a curse.

"Terrence, you're not going anywhere," she vowed, her moist lips shaped into a delicious pout. "Why don't you take off your clothes and join me in bed?"

Smiling brazenly, she yanked off her T-shirt and kicked aside her shorts. Blowing out a breath, his heart thumping out of his chest, he rubbed a hand over his head. Terrence didn't want to look at her nipples, but he couldn't help himself. Kyra was stacked. Her breasts flowed out of a satin bra, and the little red ribbons on the panties drew his gaze south. She was throwing so much heat his way, he needed a handheld fan.

Hands fashioned to her hips, oozing a righteous, spell-blinding air, she reeked with a sexual confidence that should be bottled and sold. Nothing was sexier than a sister who was proud of her body, and Terrence couldn't help wondering how and when she'd become such a vivacious woman. Kyra Dixon and Victoria's

Secret lingerie was a match made in heaven and when she took off her bra, he resisted the urge to check his pulse. The sight of her dark, erect nipples made his mouth water. His mouth was so dry he couldn't talk, and he felt his penis strain against his boxers.

Adrenaline kicked in and lust pulsed through his veins. God had given Kyra wonderful curves and he was dying to caress each and every one. With great effort, he focused his eyes on her face and not on those full, luscious breasts. He started to speak, but she pressed her fingertips to his mouth. "Why are you fighting something we both so desperately want?" Pressing light kisses from the side of his neck up to his ear, she offered words of reassurance. "Nothing's going to happen that you're not comfortable with, Terrence. Now just relax and do what comes naturally."

Terrence frowned. What the hell? That was *his* line! He felt like the carpet had been pulled out from underneath him, and he didn't know how much more rubbing, kissing and fondling he could take.

"Desires are nourished by delays," she explained, yanking his shirt down his shoulders. "The longer you wait for something, the more you want it, and we've waited long enough." Then she planted a kiss on him. It was filled with so much heat, he staggered back like a drunkard.

Terrence lost the battle with his conscience. He was in seventh heaven, riding a pleasure wave, pumped up with endorphins, and higher than a bald eagle soaring in the sky. Breast-obsessed, he cupped them in his hands, and kissed them with reverent affection. Like a potter molding clay, he caressed and stroked her until her entire body was soft to the touch. Kyra had goddess good looks and a body made to worship, but that was not what he found irresistible about her. It was her personality, her spirit, the way she treated everyone around her.

Aroused by the sight of her naked body, he shrugged off his pants and joined her on the bed. Tonight, she'd transformed her wholesome, girl-next-door charm into red-hot allure. Kyra was and always had been the object of his desire, and though he felt the timing was wrong, he had to have her.

Sprawled flat on his back, he waited anxiously for her to rejoin him in bed. She did, and after slipping on the condom, he brought her back into his waiting arms. Powerless against her touch, but determined to do the right thing, he gently cupped her shoulders, forcing her to meet his gaze. His eyes probed her heart, and when she smiled reassuringly at him, Terrence knew there was no need for words.

Terrence buried his face in Kyra's hair. She smelled like exotic fruit, and he gulped mouthfuls. Lowering his mouth, he used his tongue to outline the rim of her areola. Her breasts were perfect, round and full, her nipples two erect buds. Panting, she parted her legs, welcoming him inside. He curved a finger inside her, swirling, thrusting, slipping in and out of her sex. Lifting her hips up off the bed, he used his thumb to arouse her, soaking up her moans of pleasure. Snug, tight inside her, he stirred his penis slowly around her slick walls. Holding her to him in a sensuous embrace, his mouth reached hungrily for her lips. He dropped kisses on her cheeks, neck, shoulder and chest. Every part of their bodies was connected. Like a choir, they moved as one, rousing each other with soft words, fervent kisses and sweet melodies.

A scream tumbled off her lips. Terrence was loving her so deeply, so fully, that she couldn't think straight. Weakened, Kyra fought through the passion-filled haze. Without a single word, Terrence conveyed his love and desire. His breath tickled her ear, causing bolts of pleasure to spark in her core. And when he hiked her legs in the air and clutched her hips like a life raft, Kyra had the most powerful, most blinding orgasm ever. Terrence climaxed seconds later. They snuggled close and spent the rest of the night talking, laughing and reminiscing over the years they spent at Hollington.

Sex complicated things. It could destroy a perfectly good relationship, so when Kyra woke up the next morning and felt Terrence's arms around her in a tight, forceps-like grip, she knew there was only one thing she could do: run like hell! But instead of crawling out from under the duvet blanket, she allowed herself another minute of cuddling. Terrence was stuck to her like hinges on a door, and she could feel the heat radiating off his naked body. Enjoying the feel of his hard chest against her back, she closed her eyes and drank in the scent of their lovemaking and the gentle sounds of the early morning.

Memories of last night flooded her mind. It had been damn hard getting Terrence into bed, and to close the deal, she'd had to employ everything she'd learned in her Fit to Strip by Carmen Electra class. Something about Terrence brought out the sexy beast in her, and he'd done things with his hands and mouth that made her orgasms out of this world.

They'd barely made it off the sofa love seat when she'd pounced on him like a mountain lion spotting a snow-white rabbit. Kissing him, undressing him and massaging his muscles had whet her appetite for slow, luxurious lovemaking and when he slipped inside of her and lifted her up off the bed, she'd boldly met him thrust for thrust. Now, instead of getting dressed and executing the perfect early-morning getaway, she was lying on her back like a slab of granite, watching him sleep.

Terrence murmured beside her, and her heart sighed with contentment. He was the most passionate, most generous lover she'd ever had. Kyra gently caressed his cheek and noticed he had tiny, flesh-colored bruises along the side of his neck.

Frowning, she leaned forward, studying the marks. "Oh, my God!" Kyra clasped a hand over her mouth. *Those aren't bruises. They're hickeys!* A giggle caught in her throat when she remembered how they'd teased and played in bed last night. *If Terrence has hickeys on his neck, that means I have some on my...* Curiosity tickled her thoughts, but she didn't have the energy to move. She'd unleashed her inner sex goddess and now had a cramp in her back leg, but she wouldn't be surprised to see love bites on her inner thigh.

Soft, mellow streams of light flowed through the blinds. Without looking at the alarm clock, Kyra knew it was nine-thirty. Brunch would start in a few hours and she'd promised her mom she'd attend the morning service, so why was she still in bed, rubbing up against Terrence? *Because you're not cut out for love 'em and leave 'em sex.*

Deciding her thoughts couldn't be further from the truth, she reached out and traced a finger along his lips. Allowing herself a moment of quiet reflection, she realized that she *was* reluctant to leave his side. Terrence had pleased her thoroughly, expertly, and she wanted to stay in his arms for as long as possible. Throwing herself at Terrence wasn't something Kyra was proud of, but she'd done it, and she didn't regret anything that happened between them. Contrary to what her single friends thought, making love to a hot, muscled brother trumped an electronic vibrator any day.

Her mouth broke into a rich, decadent smile. *Terrence sure knows how to please a woman,* she thought, toying playfully with his ear. *Most men need a map and a GPS to find the G-spot, but Terrence has more moves than an acrobat!* Their kisses were packed with tons of heat, but it had taken time for them to find their sexual rhythm. He preferred a softer, lighter, touch, while she liked the fast, fervent urgency of it all.

His ripped, muscular body was a visual delight, and though they'd only made love once, Kyra understood what made him tick. A caring, sensual lover, he gave new meaning to the word *submission.* He'd focused on pleasing her, not fulfilling his sexual desires. Terrence delivered plenty of foreplay, and teased and aroused her until she climaxed. His moves on the football field were nothing compared to his expertise in the bedroom, and just looking at him made her wet.

Kyra sighed softly. Everything about him was perfect. His chiseled jaw, the set of his shoulders, his sweet-as-caramel French kisses. They'd graduated from friends to lovers in the span of twenty-four hours, but what now? Making love to Terrence had been an impulsive act, and though they'd used protection, Kyra knew nothing would be able to protect her heart. It was too late to second-guess herself, and moreover, if she'd acted on impulse, then why was she anxious to do it again?

Cursing him and his playboy good looks, she made it up in her mind not to see him again. Terrence was dripping with confidence, stunningly handsome and the most charming man she'd ever met. And every time their eyes collided, she felt something stir within her. Something sensual and erotic and more explosive than the atomic bomb. But that didn't mean she had to become his plaything. She would call the shots this time around, not him.

Kyra couldn't stop herself from touching his chest. Too slow to evade the snares of lust, she kissed him slowly, and tenderly, loving the feel of his mouth. She held his face in her palms, then swept her lips over his ear, before returning to his lips and settling into another long, sensual kiss. "Terrence, are you awake?"

"Mmm…" he answered drowsily. "I am now."

"Did you sleep okay?"

"Like a newborn." His eyes were half-open, but he was wearing his trademark broad grin. "How are you?"

Her thoughts went blank. The draw of his smile, coupled with his chocolate-brown eyes and full lips, instantly put her in the mood—again. For the first time ever, she'd permitted herself to let go of her emotions, but Kyra didn't want to make a habit of falling into bed with Terrence. No matter how yummy it was. "I'm a little hung over," she confessed, with a bashful smile, "but I'll be all right after I have my morning coffee."

He smiled. She smiled. Then, their lips came together for a slow, soulful kiss packed with more heat than a blowtorch. Ripples of pleasure zipped down her back, tickling the baby-fine hairs on her neck and the space between her legs. Kyra felt as if she'd lost control of her mind and her body had taken over. She drew closer to him, raised her chin and brushed her fingertips along his jaw. Making love to Terrence had been a total-body experience, one that she was hungry to relive again, but wouldn't because…because…. Damn it, where was her moral compass when she needed it?

"Are you going to let me take you out to the Hollington brunch?" he asked. "The Grand Hyatt hotel restaurant is my favorite spot, but we can go wherever you'd like."

Kyra shook her head. "I can't. I have…a few errands to run before I go to the brunch." She was lying and though his eyes revealed nothing, she knew he didn't believe her. But eating together at the most popular restaurant in the city was a bad idea. Needing a moment to sort her thoughts, she turned and faced the window. She felt his chin on her shoulder and giggled. "Cut it out, Terrence. That tickles."

"You didn't mind it last night."

"I was drunk."

"Right." He nipped at her ear. "Since you won't let me take you out, I guess we'll have to have breakfast here."

"I don't have anything in my fridge, but—"

"Who said anything about eating?"

Eyes wide, she shot a look over her shoulder. Something stirred within her. Something sensual and naughty and hot. His fingers drew circles on her stomach, arousing her desires and kindling her need. Terrence reached down and touched her wetness. She purred. Sensitive to his touch, she felt tingles radiate from her ears to her toes and back up again. Arching her head back, her mouth ajar, she reached for him, rubbing a hand over his head. They caressed and stroked and massaged until they were clinging to each other.

Kyra heard a packet rip open, and once he was sheathed, turned and ensnared his lips in a kiss. His tongue probed her mouth, urging her, inviting her, taking her to heights and depths she never knew existed. Spoiling his ears, neck and cheeks with kisses, she warmed him with her mouth, and embraced the secret fantasies floating around her head. Focusing on every sensation, she opened her eyes. He looked relaxed. As if he'd just enjoyed a soak in the hot tub.

"Kyra, this is more than just a night," he told her, raising her chin. "It's a lot more. And I don't care what it takes. I'm going to make you mine if it's the last thing I do."

Knowing that her voice would betray her, she clamped down on her bottom lip, and listened in awe as words of praise and admiration streamed from his lips. "You're irresistible, Ky. A masterpiece. The most beautiful work of art…"

Moans of pleasure drowned out his words. He was inside her now, moving in a slow, controlled pace. Last night, their lovemaking had been frenzied, wild, carnal, and though it was what she'd needed at the time, she enjoyed the way he stirred his erection inside her, slow, easy and steady. They'd reached another level of their lovemaking, and when she stared into his eyes, her heart flitted like a butterfly in the wind. Words escaped her. Pressing her back flat against him, she parted her legs and wrapped his hands around her in a heartwarming embrace.

Alternating between in-and-out thrusts and deep,

penetrating circles, he held her close to his chest and swept her damp hair off her neck. He rocked inside her, and when she groaned in his ear, he lost his grip on his self-control.

Chapter 15

The blissful afterglow of good lovemaking stayed with Kyra for the rest of the morning, and when she pulled into the park and spotted Terrence standing outside one of the large white tents, a fresh wave of desire filled her body. He was talking to Kevin and Chloe, and seeing the couple all hugged up, gave Kyra hope that one day she'd have a loving, committed relationship of her own.

Flattening her hands over her pink, scoop-neck blouse, she inhaled the delicious scents carrying on the breeze. Laughter rang out, music played and the festive atmosphere reminded Kyra of the Dixon family reunion in North Carolina last year. Children raced around, teenagers danced and couples were spread out on blankets eating picnic-style. The event was geared toward families of all alumni regardless of graduating year. Chloe had arranged to have face painters, dozens of oversized tents, and a child-friendly menu.

Kyra wanted to talk to Chloe, but since she wasn't ready to face her one-night stand, she hustled across the field and ducked into the closest tent. She was filling her plate with grits when she caught whiff of a familiar scent.

"I hope you saved some corn bread for me."

Casting an amused look over her shoulder, Kyra lifted the piece of bread to her mouth and took a hearty bite. "Sorry, this is the last one."

Terrence took his hand from around his back and there, in his outstretched palm, was a single, yellow daisy. Still holding her gaze, he began to pluck the thin petals from the stem. "She loves me—she loves me not. She loves me—she loves me not." On he sang until there was only one petal left. "She loves me not?" Terrence clutched a hand over his chest. "How will I ever go on?"

Kyra burst out laughing. Terrence had always been a joker, but now he was crazier than ever. He was bubbling with good humor, and Kyra couldn't help wondering if it had anything to do with their steamy grind between the sheets that morning.

"I've been looking all over for you," he said, hooking an arm around her waist. "I thought we agreed to meet at noon."

Her gaze roved around the park. Good, no one was watching. "I couldn't decide what to wear. I must have tried on a dozen outfits before selecting this top."

"Good choice, but you should know by now that you don't have to impress me."

"I'm not." When he made a sad face, she laughed. "I want Justice Kane to perform at the Winter Wonderland Ball and Chloe said he might be here."

"Cool, then we'll go talk to him *together*."

On shaky legs, she followed Terrence through the tent. They found a long, vacant table and within seconds of sitting down, it filled up. "Were your parents mad that you missed church this morning?"

Narrowing her eyes, she shot him a sideways glance. "No, why?"

"Because back in the day, your pops used to blow a gasket if you didn't go. Remember when he showed up during pledge week and held an impromptu service in the quad with the guys of Alpha Delta Kappa?"

Kyra groaned. "Don't remind me. I still cringe every time I think about it."

"He had good intentions."

"No, he wanted to control me. My dad never wanted me to come to Hollington. He felt I wouldn't get the right education at a secular school."

"He actually said that?" Terrence had a hard time suppressing his curiosity. "Why? What did he have against Hollington?"

Kyra shrugged. "My dad always dreamed that his children would follow in his footsteps, and since I was the oldest, I had to set the right example for my brothers. I had two choices—either go to Bible college on their dime, or make it on my own."

"Your mom supported him?"

"That's what a good wife does, isn't it?"

"Why didn't you ever say anything?"

The tender sound of his voice awakened strong feelings in her and when he took her hand, an image of them making love rose in her thoughts. "Terrence, there was nothing to say. Lots of kids work to put themselves through school."

"If I had known, I would have—"

"What? Picked up more shifts at Popeye's Chicken fast food restaurant?"

He chuckled. "Hey, it was a good, honest job and the extra money helped me pay for your promise ring."

"I always wondered how you came up with a thousand dollars," she said. "I thought maybe you were doing runs for the local bookie or something!"

His smile fizzed. "How did you know what I paid for the ring?"

"After we broke up, I…I, ah, pawned it."

"What did you do with the money?"

"I used it to pay for a belated graduation trip to Cancun."

Terrence opened his mouth, but closed it when he felt an arm on his shoulder.

"Terrence, my good man!" Dean Rudolph, a tall, robust man was a lovable character with a buoyant personality. He greeted Kyra and took the seat to Terrence's left. "I hear you'll be taking over our football team soon. You'll have our boys looking like champions in no time. The way they played yesterday surely was the result of them wanting to impress you. But you haven't accepted the coaching position yet—sorry if I'm getting ahead of myself."

Terrence was anxious to finish his conversation with Kyra, but he didn't want to affront the older man, and soon his excitement for the game took over. Throwing out strategies, winning plays and his NFL experiences made him feel alive. Being offered the head coaching position at his alma mater was an honor, but he also liked the idea of making an impact at the high school level. Then, there was his acting career. He'd auditioned for a small role in the new Robert De Niro film and nailed the part on the first take. Fear of the future had gnawed at him for months, but now that he had job offers and appointments to fill his day, things were finally starting to look up.

He was so entrenched in his conversation with Dean Rudolph, he didn't realize Kyra was gone until he reached for her hand. Worried that she was off somewhere with R&B heartthrob Justice Kane, he told Dean Rudolph he'd see him at the parade and left.

Terrence did a quick search of the grounds and sighed in relief when he found Kyra talking to a fair-skinned woman by one of the buffet tables. Not wanting to appear eager, he stood off to the side, watching her. Behind the facade of suburban contentment, was a passionate, erotic woman who'd rocked his world not once, but twice. He'd never felt anything this potent, or this real. They had great conversations, complemented each other perfectly and laughed often.

Terrence burned with desire. And when she turned and smiled at him, it was like a shot to the heart. He was filled with an overpowering sense of longing. A longing so deep and so strong, he couldn't fight it for a second more. Needing her back in his arms, he crossed the field toward her.

"I'm going to have to buy you an ankle bracelet," he joked, coming up behind her, "because every time I turn around, you're gone!"

Kyra laughed. "Terrence, you remember Beverly Clark, don't you?"

He did, and said, "Of course. You were Homecoming Queen."

"Congratulations on all of your success, Terrence."

"Are you enjoying the brunch?" he asked, deciding he liked this friendly, attractive sister. "It's like one big ole party out here, huh?"

"You can say that again. Chloe said that brunch would be open to the community, but I wasn't expecting such an enormous turnout."

"This is nothing," he told her, "wait until the parade. The streets are going to be chock full with—"

Terrence felt an elbow jab into his side, and when he looked at Kyra, she was frowning. He almost laughed out loud. She was even sexier when she was annoyed.

"Beverly's a little nervous about being on the float," she explained, rubbing a hand along her friend's back. "But she has nothing to worry about, right, Terrence?"

"Just the thought of being on display in front of all these people is making me feel sick," she confessed, fingering the lace neckline of her cream-colored blouse. "I'm a fashion designer, Kyra, not a beauty contestant."

"You'll be fine." Kyra's voice was bright and full of cheer. "Would it help if we stayed with you until it's time to head over to the stadium?"

So much for our romantic afternoon, Terrence thought, feeling disappointed. If he'd had his way, they'd be back in Kyra's bed, making love for the third time. Terrence grew bored quickly, but when Kyra spoke, he listened. He loved that she was so confident, so strong, so funny. He'd never been this drawn to a woman, and though he wanted to spend the rest of his days and nights with her, he knew he had to temper his enthusiasm.

"It's a fun, family-filled event. You have nothing to worry about."

"Kyra's right," he agreed. "You're among friends, Beverly. So, go out there and make the class of '99 proud!"

She gave a low, shaky laugh. "Right, that's easy for you to say. You're not the one on top of that stupid float."

"You're gorgeous, Bev," Kyra told her. "With that pearly-white smile, and shapely figure, you're a force to be reckoned with!"

"I second that."

A lean, well-muscled man with cropped hair and hazel eyes smiled down at Beverly. Her frown fell away and was replaced with a smile so bright, Terrence slipped back on his sunglasses to protect his eyes.

"Hi, Lucius."

Terrence whipped his head to the right. Where did that thick, sultry voice come from? If he didn't know better, he'd think that Beverly Clark had a split personality. Gone was the long face, pursed lips and shaky voice. Now, she was staring up at the stranger with interest and open admiration.

"Well, knock me over with a feather, if it isn't the great Terrence Franklin!" Lucius chuckled. "I've been wanting to talk to you since Friday, but every time I turn around, you've got fans hot on your heels."

"Hey man, what's up?"

"You don't remember me, do you?"

Terrence shook his head, and the stranger shrugged his shoulders. "I figured as much, but I'd hoped that you'd remember the offensive lineman who took all those hits for you in that state championship game."

"Lucius Gray?"

"Attorney-at-law," he added, with a laugh.

"Man, you were one hell of a player. How come you didn't go all the way? With your competitive edge and strength, you could've had your pick of NFL teams."

Lucius pointed a finger at his chin. "I like this face far too much to let it get stomped on every Sunday afternoon!"

Everyone laughed.

"Beverly, can I steal you away for a second?" the charismatic attorney asked.

Wanting to be alone with Kyra, Terrence slipped a hand around her waist, and squeezed affectionately. "We'll see you guys later," he said, nodding at Lucius.

"All right, man, have a good one."

They strolled back across the field in silence. The lines of friendship and passion were blurred, but that didn't stop him from tightening his hold around her. Her perfume stirred his loins and when her arm grazed his chest, he strangled a groan. Oblivious to his inner turmoil, she put a hand to his forearm. "I have to go track down Chloe and Tamara." Her smile was cheaper than plastic. "I'll see you later, okay?"

His head spun faster than a carousel. Was she trying to ditch him? Truth was, he wanted Kyra again and couldn't stop seeing images of her naked body in his mind. As far as he was concerned, making love had solidified their relationship and he wasn't going to let Kyra run off again. Remembering their conversation last night at Bollito, he asked, "What time does your dad's appreciation dinner start?"

Kyra's shoulders sagged. With all that had happened in the last forty-eight hours, the reception for her dad at Victory Outreach Church had completely slipped her mind. Worse still, she hadn't bought him a gift yet. "Six o'clock."

"Great, that gives us time to swing over to the mall and pick something up."

"Most of these people are here to see you, Terrence, and I'm not going to take you away from all your fans."

"You're not," he told her, the matter decided. "We'll go find a gift for your dad, and catch up with the parade on Main Street."

"I'd rather go alone."

"But I need your help." He paused, trying to concoct a believable story. "My grandmother's birthday is coming up and I don't know what to get her. I was hoping you could give me a hand."

"You never mentioned this before," she pointed out, tilting her head to the right, studying him intently. "When is your grandmother's birthday?"

"Tomorrow," he lied. Clasping her hand, he ushered her past the tent, praying she wouldn't see Justice Kane at the buffet table. Terrence wasn't letting Kyra out of his sight for the rest of the day. They'd shared something special last night, and he refused to let her downplay it. His heart was open to her, full of love and more passion than he'd ever known. He owned cars, houses, and had more money than he could spend in a lifetime, but no one to share it with. Kyra was that woman—the right woman—and now that he'd been given a second chance, he was going to make the most of it. "Maybe we can grab some souvenirs from that specialty store on Ninth."

"Souvenirs?" Frowning, she shook her head, seemingly confused. "You're not somewhere warm and exotic like Costa Rica. You're only a few states away."

Terrence chuckled. "I know, but what Big Mama wants, Big Mama gets!"

Chapter 16

By the time Terrence and Kyra reached Union Square, the temperature was pushing seventy-three degrees. The trees along Main Street curtailed the intensity of the sun, but every time he glanced at Kyra, he felt like he'd been blown over by gale-force winds.

It was ideal weather for firing up the grill or taking a dip in the pool, and Terrence wondered what, if anything would sway Kyra to have dinner with him tonight. He had steaks in the fridge, a bar filled with wine coolers and a fully stocked pantry. An intimate party for two, he thought, chancing another look at her.

Terrence knew what he wanted, and she was standing right in front of him. Kyra was the template of the perfect woman. And although they hadn't seen each other in ten years, nothing had changed. Despite their past mistakes, and years of life experiences between them, they still had *it*. Mutual respect? Check. Compatibility? Check. Sexual chemistry? Shoot, Brad and Angelina had nothing on them.

Matching her quick strides, he avoided a collision with a squealing toddler. Masses of people, with grinning faces and home-made signs, clogged the sidewalk. A four-block radius of shops, galleries, and fully restored old buildings, Union Square was a community pulsing with life and vitality. Teenagers squirted water guns, children squealed and diners sat on patios chugging imported beer.

Out of the corner of his eye, he noticed a trio of brunettes chatting outside of Starbucks. Ten years ago, his unexpected surge of popularity had gone to his head, and it had ruined what he had with Kyra. He wanted more than just a sexual relationship and didn't want her to think bad of him, so when the women waved at him, he ignored them.

Terrence liked to think he was a man in control, but one whiff of Kyra's fragrance and he was lost. He found his first love as irresistible as she'd ever been and he wasn't just captivated by her looks. With Kyra, he could just be himself.

"I don't know how you feel about this, Terrence, but I want to go all out for the playoffs." Her eyes glowed with the excitement. "We'll kick off the post-season with a Friday afternoon pep rally, and then a party to celebrate Sunday's victory!"

"If I accept the coaching position and we make it to the playoffs, our first game would be against Duke University," he pointed out.

"I know."

Terrence raised his eyebrows, his face clouded with

disbelief. "And you think we're going to mop the floor with them?"

"They're toast," she told him, making a cutting motion across her neck, "and so are all the other teams in our division. You're going to take the Lions all the way, and Hollington's going to reclaim its place at the top!"

Terrence chuckled. Her enthusiasm, like her smile and bottomless optimism, was contagious. "If I could sail into the end zone on a bum knee, then I guess I could lead the Hollington Lions to the championship."

"We're all behind you, T. You've *got* this."

"T, huh?" His smile grew until it covered his entire face. "So, we're back to using our old pet names. That didn't take long, did it?"

"I'm sorry. It just slipped out."

"I'm teasing, Ky. You can call me T, or anything else you like." Without thinking, he stopped her with a hand on the arm. Main Street wasn't the place to have such an intimate conversation, but he didn't want the opportunity to discuss their relationship to pass him by. She didn't look angry, but he'd heard something in her voice. It could be nothing or it could be everything, but either way, he was going to find out. "Last night meant something to me, Ky. It wasn't just sex. It was special."

"Can I be honest?"

"I wouldn't have it any other way." Her phony smile wasn't lost on him, and he knew instinctively that she had regrets about them making love.

"Last night was just that, Terrence—one night."

"And this morning?"

"A lapse in judgment."

Terrence felt as if he'd been whacked in the head with

a two-by-four. Is that all it was? One night of meaning-less sex?

"Let's keep things casual. We're friends and—"

"I don't sleep with my friends."

"Neither do I, but it takes a lot more than chemistry and passion to sustain a relationship. We had our night. Let's just keep it at that."

He paused. Kyra was his dream girl, and now that they'd shared a night together, he was more determined than ever to win her heart. Truth be told, he wanted to spend every waking minute with her. *Damn.* He was trippin' big-time. Kyra was exactly his type, and mak-ing love last night had sealed their fate. He'd possessed her body, not once but twice, and was itching to make love to her again. "Kyra, I've never met anyone like you. You don't play games or beat around the bush, and I respect that about you."

"I'm flattered, Terrence, really I am, but let's face it. You and I have about as much in common as those two strangers crossing the street." She gestured toward the intersection, but he didn't turn to look. "I live a quiet, drama-free life and you're Mr. Saturday Night. Guys like you need—"

"Guys like me?" he repeated, cutting in. Being ste-reotyped as a deviant, sex-crazed athlete infuriated him, but he wasn't going to lose his cool. "What are you say-ing? That I'm incapable of being faithful?"

"I learned pretty early on that men can't be faithful no matter how hard they try." Realizing how harsh it sounded, she softened her voice. "Don't get me wrong, there are still a few good men out there, but for every Prince Charming, there are a hundred dogs."

"Are you scared that I'm going to hurt you again?"

Terrence put a hand on her arm. "Is that why you're pushing me away, because you think I'm trying to play you?"

She said no, and turned her head away from him, but not before he saw the grieved expression on her face. Being tackled by a defensive lineman didn't hurt as much. Sweet one minute, acerbic the next, her confession suddenly brought into question the integrity of their relationship. Struggling to right his thoughts, he nodded when Kyra suggested they go into Macy's and followed her through the sliding glass doors.

Since entering the NFL, his life had been marked with excitement and drama, but in Hollington, he was just Terrence and that suited him just fine. And as he watched Kyra move through the racks, admiring shirts, and suits and dresses, he realized he had to reevaluate his plan. He was trying to do too much too soon. Outside on the street, he'd felt condemned and judged by her, but what did he expect? She'd anchored him and kept him sane when his life was spinning out of control, and how had he repaid her? By dumping her when he made it big. The only way to prove to Kyra that he'd changed was to show her. Terrence was nothing if not tenacious, and he knew it was just a matter of time before they'd be dating again.

In the men's department, Kyra selected a pair of cuff links for her dad and, after Terrence's prodding, decided to have them personalized. "I still haven't found something for my grandmother," Terrence said, watching her. "Do you have any ideas?"

"Does she like jewelry?"

"Which woman doesn't?" Chuckling heartily, he followed her over to the jewelry counter. "Maybe I should get her a brooch. She's been collecting them since I was a kid and now her collection could rival Elizabeth Taylor's!"

Kyra pointed a manicured nail at the glass case. "What about that one? It's a heart-shaped brooch set on pink diamonds."

"Is there something I can help you with?" a dull, sleepy voice asked.

Terrence lifted his head, and the woman behind the jewelry counter broke into a wide smile. "Can we look at that case?"

"Certainly, Mr. Franklin."

Resting the tray upon the glass, the salesclerk asked if he'd be interested in seeing the platinum collection. Before he could decide, a second, more expensive tray materialized. "I'll get two. My mom will kill me with her bare hands if I don't bring something for her, too!" He picked up Kyra's hand and kissed her palm. "Do you see anything you like?"

"Thanks, but no thanks."

"But you didn't even look," he argued, signaling the clerk back over. He took great pleasure in spoiling his friends and family, and he wanted to do something special for her. This could be his chance to redeem himself in her eyes. To prove to her that he was genuinely contrite over the mistakes of his youth.

When the clerk reopened the case, Terrence asked to see her most expensive pair of earrings. "Go on, choose something."

"Is this how you guys get girls?" Kyra asked, her face aghast. "You shower women with gifts and diamonds until they agree to go out with you?"

Terrence didn't answer. Tongue-tied, he stood there watching her, stumped. If she was going to stereotype him as just another fallacious ex-athlete, they were never going to work. "I don't know what other men do, but I believe in treating my woman well. If that sets me back a few bills, so be it. Besides," he added, "I love spoiling women, especially sexy, independent, don't-need-a-man types like you."

She screwed her pretty face into a glare. "But we barely know each other. You'd spend five thousand dollars just like that?"

"Barely know each other? Kyra, you know me better than anyone else."

"Terrence, we haven't seen each other in years. We're virtually strangers now."

"But, I've seen your birthmark and sucked your..." Purposely trailing off, a grin playing on his lips, he watched her eyes widen and her cheeks flush. And when she swung her gaze in the opposite direction, Terrence knew he had Kyra right where he wanted. "We better get going. I don't want us to be late for your dad's appreciation dinner." He winked at her. "I can't wait to see your family again."

"But what about the parade?"

"We'll catch the reunion float on the walk back to campus, and then we'll jet."

"I don't know about this," she began, pushing a hand through her hair. "My dad's really uptight and if I show up with you...I just don't think it will go over well."

On impulse, he bent down and kissed her. She tasted like fruit, inciting a physical and sexual hunger in his body. "What was that you were saying?"

At six-thirty that evening, Kyra sailed through the front doors of Victory Outreach Church on Terrence's arm. A tantalizing scent hung in the air, inciting grumbles from her stomach and animated chatter flowed into the sun-lit vestibule.

"Sister Kyra!"

Recognizing the deep, low-pitched voice, she turned and smiled at the bearded man with the kind eyes. "Hi, Deacon Fisher. How are you?"

He squeezed her shoulder, the expression on his face one of joy. "It's so good to see you. We've missed you around here."

Unsure of what to say, Kyra gestured to Terrence. "Deacon Fisher, this is a good friend of mine—"

He flapped his hands as if he was swatting a bee. "No introduction necessary. I know who this talented young man is. Terrence Franklin. Played nine seasons with the Dallas Cowboys until he got cut."

Kyra saw the muscles in Terrence's neck tighten, but his smile stayed intact. "It's a pleasure to meet you, Deacon Fisher."

"Why don't you two follow me inside?" he proposed with a flick of his head. "We're just finishing up dinner, but I'd be happy to go around back and fix you a—"

"No thanks. We're not hungry."

"We're not?" Terrence whispered, falling in step beside her. "I smell—" he sniffed the air "—honey glazed chicken. You sure we can't have a little plate before we leave?"

Kyra laughed. "Fine, Terrence. One plate, but that's it. We're only staying long enough to drop off the gift. Got it?"

As they continued down the hall, Kyra admired the clean, modern building. Glossy posters and business cards were tacked neatly to the bulletin board, the painted walls were a soothing ivory shade, and the coat racks were packed with jackets and silk shawls.

To chase away the butterflies fluttering around in her stomach, she took a deep breath. Showing up late to her dad's appreciation dinner with a superstar athlete at her side was sure to cause a stir and when they stepped into the banquet hall, eyes bulged and jaws fell open. It was so quiet Kyra could hear an infant wailing in the church nursery. Then, after several tense seconds, everyone resumed eating.

From across the room, Kyra saw the quick rise and fall of her father's eyebrows, but her mom, dressed tastefully in a plum-colored suit, was waving wildly. Up on her feet, she came around the table, her long, thin arms outstretched. "Sweet pea, I'm so glad you made it. How was reunion weekend?"

"It was great, Ma."

Mrs. Dixon turned her attention to her daughter's tall, handsome date. "It's nice seeing you again, son. How is your lovely mother doing?"

"Great, Mrs. Dixon. She sends her love," he said, returning her smile. "I can't believe it. It's been years since I saw you, but I'm the only one who got older!"

Mrs. Dixon's laugh perfumed the air. "Well, thank you, son. Having a smart, responsible daughter helps keep those dreaded wrinkles away and it helps that Kyra has such a keen eye for fashion!"

Still seated, her father extended a hand. "Welcome to Victory Outreach. I speak on behalf of the other ministers when I say we're very pleased to have you."

Kyra stared at her father. His smile was plastic, his voice was flat and his eyes were panning the room. She saw his gesture for what it was. An act. One he'd perfected over the course of his ministry. One that was so smooth and so polished he could beat a polygraph. He was doing his duty as head pastor and nothing more. "If you don't have a church to attend, you're more than welcome to worship here with us."

Wanting to cut their conversation short, Kyra handed her father the small gift bag. "This is for you, Dad."

"Kyra, honey, you didn't have to get me anything." He stood and put an arm around her. "I'm sure I'll love whatever it is."

For the next hour, Kyra chatted with her brothers and discussed the highlights of reunion weekend with Terrence. At seven-thirty, she was good to go, but just as she turned to say goodbye to her parents, the assistant pastor saddled up to the podium and asked for the congregation's attention.

"We've heard from esteemed members of the community about what a blessing Reverend Dixon is to this church, but now I'd like to open the floor to you—the congregation." The assistant pastor stepped away from the podium and a tall, willowy woman with braids took his place. "Five years ago, I was an abused housewife," she said, in a voice softer than a whisper. "If it wasn't for the kindness and generosity of Reverend Dixon, I probably wouldn't be here today."

Within seconds, the line behind the podium had doubled in length and people hurried to make their way to the stage. Kyra's gaze slid to her father. His eyes were crinkled behind his eyeglasses and he was shaking his head solemnly. "I can't believe this, Rose...this is all so overwhelming."

Mrs. Dixon kissed her husband's cheek. "You've

touched a lot of lives, honey, and the members want to show their gratitude."

Kyra felt a tickle in her throat. She'd never been close to her father, but when she heard the humility in his voice, she wondered if their relationship could ever be repaired. Battling feelings of fear, anger and sadness, she lowered her eyes to her lap. To preserve her sanity, Kyra had pushed what happened that fateful afternoon in June to the back of her mind, but she'd known that she'd never been able to trust her dad—or any other man again.

Chapter 17

Kyra breezed past the staff room so her boss wouldn't catch her ducking out early. It was only three o'clock, but she was tired. Tired of working late, tired of arguing with Mr. Morrow about effective fundraising strategies and tired of doing everyone else's job.

The last two weeks had been filled with long, drawn-out team meetings, but tonight, she was going to put her feet up and enjoy a quiet evening for one. *That is, unless Terrence calls and invites me out for dinner,* Kyra thought, smiling to herself.

Since the reunion, her opinion of Terrence had changed. He used humor to mask his feelings, but once she'd scratched the surface, she discovered that he cared and respected everyone. Players complained that he was too strict, but since Terrence had started working out with the team, no one had missed practice or skipped class.

When Terrence was around, laughter abounded. He was a perfect gentleman and so damn charming, she'd started to believe he cared about her. They text-messaged each other throughout the day, had lunch in town and talked for hours on the phone.

Kyra was inside the elevator, waiting impatiently for passengers to file on, when she realized she didn't have her wallet. Remembering she'd put it in her top drawer after ordering some books online, she began the arduous task of debarking the jam-packed elevator. Squeezing out from behind a pendulous man who made Rueben Studdard look thin, she mumbled her thanks and dashed back down the hall.

Kyra opened her office door and almost tripped over her feet. Nikki was crouched behind her desk, riffling through her bottom drawers. The intern was so busy with her search, she didn't even notice her standing there. "Nikki, what are you doing?"

Hands pressed to her chest, she stepped back from the desk. "What are you doing here? I thought you left."

"And I thought we were friends."

Nikki lowered her head.

She'd shamed the girl into silence, but that didn't make Kyra feel better. Knowing Nikki as well as she did, she knew there was something else going on. "Is this about your tuition?" she asked, remembering the intern's outstanding bill. "If you needed money, why didn't you just come to me? I paid my way through college, and I still remember what a stressful time in my life that was."

Kyra didn't tell Nikki that she'd considered dropping out her junior year. Her friends had tried to talk her out of it, but after coming up short on her rent for the third consecutive month, she'd decided to withdraw from her spring semester courses to square her debts. Then, just days before her scheduled meeting with the academic advisor, a large sum of money had been deposited into her bank account. To this day, Kyra still didn't know who'd done it. None of her girlfriends had that kind of money, and although Terrence had wanted to help, he was strapped for cash, too. Her parents had poured every penny they had into their church, and she knew the bank wouldn't give her mom and dad a loan if Bill Gates was the co-signer.

Yes, she knew exactly what Nikki was going through. Most people didn't think ten thousand dollars was a lot of money, but it had changed her life. Without the stress of working a second job, she was able to focus on her studies and made the dean's list for the first time that semester, a tremendous accomplishment in a university that had some of the brightest students in the country.

"Nikki, there's no excuse for what you did, and if President Morrow finds out about this, you'll be suspended, or worse, expelled."

"This is bad." Face marred in anguish, she dropped her hands at her sides, and released a plaintive sigh. "Terrence is going to be so disappointed when he finds out—"

"Terrence? What does he have to do with this?"

Nikki came around the desk, shut the door and motioned for Kyra to sit down. Plunking down on one of the padded chairs, she swung her feet restlessly back and forth. "I'm going to tell you something, Kyra, but I don't want you to get angry."

Thinking the worst, she gripped Nikki's arm. "You promised me you wouldn't go back to dancing, Nikki.

I don't care how much that sleazy club manager offered you, you can't put a price on your—"

"Relax, Kyra," she said, interrupting. "I'm not shaking my ass for money."

"Good." Her frown returned. "All right, so tell me what the big secret is and what it has to do with you snooping in my desk."

"I met Terrence at the Dallas Airport on my way back to school in August," she began. "I didn't say anything because…"

Remembering the fiasco at The Tavern with Aimee and Terrence, she blurted, "Oh, my God! You slept with him, too?"

Nikki laughed. "No, he's fine as all be all, but I love Rocco. We're getting married as soon as he's done his time."

Making a mental note to introduce Nikki to the Lions' adorable backup quarterback at next Sunday's game, she asked the intern to continue. "Okay, so you met Terrence at the airport. What does that have to do with this?"

"We got to talking and discovered that we both knew you." Her smile deepened, and her voice was suddenly dreamy. "He told me you guys were engaged back in the day, and said he wanted to spend time with you while he was here."

Kyra impeded a smile.

"So," she continued, "when he asked me to email him a list of your favorite restaurants, bars, shopping centers and other places you like to go, I said sure. Who am I to stand in the way of true love?"

"That's how he knew I'd be at Centennial Park that afternoon…" she trailed off, as realization dawned. For the past month, they'd bumped into each other at the most unusual places. The gas station, the grocery store and even last Friday at a fast food restaurant. "This community is so small I just assumed it was a coincidence."

Nikki shook her head. "Nope. Mr. Man is sweating you hard, girl!"

"He sent me a text message a few minutes ago, asking if I knew what your plans were tonight. I was looking for your planner when you walked in," she explained. "Hey, did you know you left your wallet in the top drawer?"

Battling feelings of anger and hope, she nodded absently in response.

"You should be really careful of where you put your stuff, Kyra. You never know who might be lurking around."

"You're right about that," she murmured.

"I'm sorry for sneaking around behind your back," she confessed, lowering her eyes to her lap. "Blame Terrence! He's so nice and charming, it's hard to say no."

I hear you, Kyra thought, remembering how he'd snuck a kiss yesterday at dinner when her brothers were shooting pool. As strong and assertive as she was, she was no match against the suave superstar athlete.

"And not only did he get me and my girlfriends into that Snoop Dogg party, he gave me two hundred dollars for my trouble."

"I'm going home. I can't deal with this right now." Kyra stood, wrenched open her top drawer and retrieved her wallet. As she turned to leave, a thought came to mind. "Do me a favor, Nikki. Call Terrence back and tell him I'll be attending the charity fundraiser at the Hilton hotel tonight."

"Should I arrange a town car to pick you up or will you be driving yourself?"

Smirking, her eyes tinged with mischief, she said, "Oh, I'm not going."

"Ooh, you're cold! Remind me never to get on *your* bad side."

Kyra laughed. She'd gotten back at people before, but this was going to be one for the record books. "Take notes, Nikki. It's called payback, Kyra Dixon style!"

"Sweet pea, pick up, it's Mom!"

The sound of her mother's voice jolted Kyra awake. She heard the plaintive sound of birds and watched the sunset ablaze in crimson and orange. Her breathing slowed, but her legs continued tingling with desire. Kyra didn't know women could have wet dreams, but she had the telltale signs of someone on the verge of an orgasm.

A groan of frustration rose in her throat. Not only was she not making love to Terrence on rose-scented sheets, she wasn't in the comfort of her bed, either. She'd dozed off on her patio chair and now had hideous drool stains on her fitted cashmere top.

Smiling to herself, she listened to her mom chatter merrily on the answering machine. The phone base was inside the living room, but her mother's sweet, Southern drawl carried for miles.

"Hey, Mom," she greeted, after locating the cordless on the end of her lounger and pressing the receiver to her ear. "What are you doing up so late?"

"I couldn't sleep, sweet pea, and I was hoping we could talk."

Kyra didn't have psychic ability, but even Dionne Warwick could see where this was headed. "This is about Terrence, isn't it?"

"We have some concerns and—"

"You mean *Dad* has some concerns," she corrected. Arms crossed, eyebrows furrowed, she stared up at the deep, blue sky. "Mom, why do you always do this?"

"Do what, sweet pea?"

"Call and relay Dad's complaints." Kyra brew out a breath. Her parents' relationship fooled most people. On the outside, it appeared that her mom wore the pants, but nothing happened without her father's say-so. He called the shots and her mother dutifully obeyed. "If Dad has something to say to me, he can call me himself. Is he so busy transforming lives that he can't pick up the phone to talk to his daughter?"

"Mind your tone, Kyra. You might be grown, but I'm still your mother."

Feeling guilty, she took a moment to right her thoughts. The grasses whispered, the wind whipped leaves. "Mom, I'm sorry for raising my voice at you. I'm just sick of Dad acting all high and mighty."

"Kyra, don't talk about your father like that. He only wants the best for you." Then her mother continued, "Your father is a great judge of character and he doesn't feel Terrence Franklin is the right man for you."

"He's in no position to judge," she snapped, with renewed annoyance.

"What's that supposed to mean? Not only is your father a good man, he's a loving husband and an upstanding member of the community. You were at the appreciation dinner. You heard all of the glowing things that people had to say."

Unmoved and growing annoyed, Kyra listened with half an ear as her mother praised her father's long list of accomplishments.

"Is...is Terrence there with you now?" She spoke in a whisper, and her voice was lit with curiosity. "You're not shacking up, are you?"

"No, Mom, he's not here. Terrence and I aren't a couple, but if we were Dad would have absolutely no say in our relationship. I don't tell him how to run the church, and he can't tell me how to run my life."

"I'm going to go get your father. The two of you really need to talk."

"Mom, don't!"

Silence descended on the line. Then, after a painfully long moment, her mother spoke. "Okay. I'll let you go, then. I'll see you kids at church on Sunday."

"Terrence won't be there. He has other plans."

"Oh?"

Kyra shook her head. It was amazing how one word could convey so much. In her mother's eyes, missing church was right up there with assault with a deadly weapon, and before Kyra could explain, her mother chirped, "That'll be the second Sunday he's missed."

"Really?" Kyra said, trying hard not to laugh. "I haven't been keeping track."

"You should. How a man feels about God says a lot about him, sweet pea. If he doesn't love Jesus, he isn't going to love you!"

Laughing, she turned the receiver away from her mouth, so her mom wouldn't hear her. *The gospel ac-*

cording to Rose Dixon, she thought, pushing herself up from the patio chair. "Mom, I have to go. Try not to worry, okay, Ma? I can handle Terrence."

After promising to call her mom tomorrow, Kyra hung up. She was inside the kitchen, fixing herself a sandwich when the telephone rang again. Worried it was her dad phoning back, she checked the caller ID box. When she saw the number on the screen, a smirk overwhelmed her lips. "How was the charity fundraiser?" she asked, picturing Terrence surrounded by geriatric patients clutching bingo markers. "I heard it was a huge success."

"Oh, I had a great ole time. I was the only person there under fifty and had my cheeks pinched so many times they're swollen!"

Kyra laughed so hard she dropped the bottle of mayonnaise. It rolled across the floor, before stopping at the heel of Aimee's silver metallic shoe. Her girlfriend scooped up the bottle and smiling her thanks, Kyra gave a small wave. She'd been so busy talking to Terrence she didn't hear the front door open, and could only imagine what Aimee was thinking after witnessing her wild outburst.

"That'll teach you to spy on me!" she said, resuming her conversation with Terrence. "You're lucky I didn't write your name and phone number inside the woman's bathroom."

"You wouldn't dare," he argued. "You want me all to yourself."

"Ha!" she exclaimed. "You wish!"

"You're right. I do."

His words made her smile.

"Do you know what tomorrow is?"

"You mean besides Saturday?" she asked, affecting surprise in her tone.

"Come on, Ky. Don't tease me."

"Oh, that's right, tomorrow's your birthday."

"I'm touched that you remember."

"How could I forget? You've been talking about it all week!" Kyra laughed. "What time should I expect you for dinner?"

"There's been a change of plans." He sounded all business, take-charge, as sexy as sin. "You've had a tough week and you deserve to have a little fun. We're going out, so be ready at seven."

"Don't have to twist my arm," she joked. Not wanting to be rude to her friend, she quickly wrapped up her conversation. "I'll see you tomorrow, then."

"I'm looking forward to it."

Feeling giddy, she returned the phone to the cradle and cleaned the crumbs off the kitchen counter. "Hey girl, how was your date?"

"Boring as hell." Aimee poured herself a bowl of cereal. "I am *so* done with dating celebrities. All he wanted to talk about was himself. I don't know how he can be part of a hit group with *that* much ego."

Perched on a stool in an indigo-colored dress, eating a bowl of cereal, Aimee looked chic, but out of place in the simple, modest room. "You're going out tomorrow?"

Now seated on the stool across from Aimee, Kyra sliced her sandwich in half and took a bite. "Yeah, it's Terrence's birthday. I was going to make him dinner, but he suggested we go out instead."

"He probably heard what a horrible cook you are and decided not to risk a trip to the emergency room!"

Kyra chucked an oven mitt at her. "Shut up. I'm a great cook!"

"Thanks for letting me crash here while my place gets fixed up," Aimee said, turning serious. "I could've stayed with my parents, but it would've tacked an extra twenty minutes to my commute."

"It's no problem. Stay for as long as you need." Standing, she picked up her plate and Aimee's empty cereal bowl. "Having you here reminds me of my old college days."

"And Terrence, too, right?"

Tension built. It was thick, suffocating, more intolerable than L.A. smog.

"You never told me why things ended?" Kyra said, trying to project an air of casual nonchalance. "What happened?"

"Are you sure you want to know?"

Not trusting herself to speak, she gave a brisk nod.

"He cheated on me," she spat. "Terrence is a smooth-talkin' player just like every other guy in the league."

Kyra forced air into her lungs. Her mind was spinning and she felt a burning sensation in her chest. "Are you sure, Aimee? I know he attracts a lot of female attention, but he seems so—"

"Normal?" she offered. "Open your eyes, Kyra. It's all part of his act. Terrence comes across as being sincere, but he'll nail anything that moves."

Aimee's words turned over in Kyra's mind. Something didn't sit right with her. If Terrence was an iniquitous womanizer, why had he rejected her the night she came on to him? Instead of yielding to her advances he'd tried to talk her *out* of making love.

"Now don't get me wrong, he isn't all bad. Terrence

might be a mangy, cheating dog, but he can throw down in the bedroom!"

"I don't want to hear this."

"But you do!" Lips curled in a smirk, Aimee opened her mouth and touched a finger to her tongue. "That brother is hot, hot, hot!"

Chapter 18

The Peninsula Hotel was on a block swarming with boutiques, cafés and art galleries. Just off the main floor, inside the Italian-inspired lounge, international businessmen and local celebrities reclined in velvet chairs, downing flutes of rose champagne.

A group of tourists rushed off the main-floor elevator, and Terrence reached for Kyra's hand, pulling her possessively to his side. Gratified to be seen on his arm, Kyra held on tight. It felt good being with such a popular, engaging man, and the fact that he was tall, ripped and ridiculously handsome was a definite plus.

Terrence bypassed the front desk. Having been to the hotel once before, Kyra knew they were going in the wrong direction. "Terrence, the restaurant is back that way."

He only smiled. They walked the length of the corridor, turned right and stopped in front of a single elevator. "Thanks for making time in your schedule for me tonight," he said, once they were alone inside the elevator. "It means a lot to me, Ky."

"I couldn't leave you high and dry on your birthday."

Terrence didn't laugh. "Is that what this is? A pity date?"

"Of course not, we're friends and—"

"Stop saying that, Ky." His voice was soft, but firm. "We're not friends. You're my girl. I thought I made myself very clear the other night."

Their eyes locked and a delicious warmth flowed through her. Kyra broke the spell by looking away. In the silence, her thoughts drifted back to Wednesday night. Terrence had showed up at her door carrying an armful of movies, Chinese takeout and a bottle of her favorite wine. They'd had dinner by candlelight and wine by the fire. There, he'd bared his heart to her. He wanted a relationship, but if she couldn't make a commitment to him, he'd rather they just be friends. And to prove his point, he'd grabbed his coat, said good-night, and left her sitting there—hot, horny, and flustered.

"Ky, what's going on? You've been distant all night." He observed her carefully, thoughtfully, his face lined with concern. "Are you upset with me because I haven't made a decision about the head coaching position yet?"

Kyra stared. He was expecting an answer, but she didn't say anything for a long moment. Gradually, one by one, Aimee's words came back to her. *He cheated on me...he'll nail anything that moves...Terrence Franklin can't be faithful for five minutes.* Breaking things off with him was the right thing to do, and although she'd thought about nothing else for the last twenty-four hours, it wasn't going to be easy. "Aimee's been a really good friend to me and I don't want to hurt her."

He looked puzzled. "What does she have to do with us?"

"She told me what happened between you."

"We were never a couple, Kyra. It didn't mean anything."

"Maybe not to you," she snapped, annoyed by his flippant attitude. "You hurt her, Terrence. She didn't come out and say it, but I could tell."

Grumbling under his breath, his voice a raspy bark, he raked a hand over his head.

"Kyra, Aimee's a lying, scheming gold-digger."

"You're the one who screwed around, not her."

"Tell me this. How could I cheat on her if we never had sex? And as for me cheating on her, that's a load of crap. After I ran up on her with one of my teammates at an awards show, I quit calling her."

Hearing the slight inflection of his voice, she closely studied his face. His eyes were narrowed and his shoulders were rigid. He tried to look cool, unfazed, but he failed. Unsure of what to say, but wanting to comfort him, she reached out and took his hand. "I believe you, Terrence. You don't have to explain yourself to me."

"I'm not going to let anyone come between us, Ky. Not after all we've been through." Terrence met her gaze head-on. He waited a moment for his words to sink in, then brought her into his arms. "You're the only woman I want and I'd never do anything to hurt you. You have to believe that."

Moved by his honesty, she apologized for starting their night off on the wrong foot. "Happy birthday, Terrence. I hope everything you wish for comes true."

"It already has." He pulled her close. Consumed with lust, he ran his hands down the slope of her hips, and parted her lips with his tongue. Terrence felt as if he were going to boil over and when Kyra took his hands and placed them underneath her dress, he wanted her even more. "That's the best birthday gift I've ever had," he confessed, chuckling.

Terrence pressed the single button on the panel and the private express elevator began its ascent. Luminous skyscrapers, twinkling lights and a bevy of round, brilliant stars created a stunning, panoramic scene. The 360-degree view of the Atlanta skyline took Kyra's breath away, but when the door slid open, she shrieked with excitement.

An enclosed area with tables, fire pits and limestone flooring, the restaurant lounge had a South Beach feel and a sultry, romantic ambience. Jazz played, and peach-colored candles filled the air with their tranquil scent.

"It's gorgeous up here," she finally said. "I didn't even know this place existed."

"It's Atlanta's best-kept secret, and for the rest of the night, it's all ours."

Kyra closed her sagging mouth. "Wow. That must have been expensive."

"Don't worry your pretty little head about that," he told her, kissing the tip of her nose. "It's my birthday, and I wanted to do it big!"

They settled into one of the cream-and-white cabanas and within seconds of sitting down, an older gentleman arrived with the first course. Not wanting to be bothered with the rigamarole of ordering entrées, Terrence had met with the senior chef yesterday and selected each course with Kyra in mind.

Seated side by side on the pillowed couch, sampling a seafood appetizer, they discussed their plans for Thanksgiving weekend. Waiters arrived with the main course promptly at eight o'clock and when Kyra saw the flaming tray of filet mignon, she clapped wildly. They shared a pitcher of mint julep and by the time they finished eating the dessert, she had a slight buzz. The epitome of chic, in a bubblegum-pink dress, and stilettos, Kyra looked vibrant, healthy and ready for a good time.

"Time for presents!" She reached into her purse, retrieved a small package and held it out to him. "Read the card first," she instructed.

He did, and erupted in laughter when he read her short, personalized note. "So you think I'm over the hill, huh?"

"Just a little." The twinkle in her eye spoke of her mischief. "That's why I think you'll be a phenomenal coach. You have the experience and wisdom needed to guide…"

Terrence cupped her chin. "Not another word. We've discussed the head coaching position ad nauseam. The only thing I want to talk about now is us." Her scent filled him with a fervid desire, but he cooled his heels. He didn't want to be lumped in with all the do-wrong brothers she'd dated in the past, so he wisely pulled away.

He raised the package, shook it, and laughed when she poked him in the shoulder and quipped, "Get on with it, man!"

Underneath the blue wrapping paper was an embroidered leather book. Terrence flipped it open and read the inscription on the first page. *Pleasure is the flower that passes; remembrance the lasting perfume,* it said. "I can't believe this," he said, staring down at the picture of him in his Little League uniform. "Did you break into my place?"

Her smile turned naughty. "I'll never tell!"

There were more pictures, more memories, more color snapshots of his ten-year football career. It was the most thoughtful gift anyone had ever given him, and he told her so. "Kyra, I love it. It's going on the mantel as soon as I get home. Thanks, baby."

"You're welcome."

"Now it's your turn."

"My turn? For what?"

The elevator chimed. The waiter returned carrying a dainty, silver tray and set it down on the table. Terrence picked up the gold box. "This is for you."

"Why? It's not my birthday."

Accustomed to dating women with expensive tastes, he was taken aback by her reaction. "Kyra, I want you to have this. It's a symbol of how I feel about you. About us."

After much prodding, she reluctantly took the box and tugged on the pink ribbon. The locket was the size of a jawbreaker, speckled with diamonds and the words Love, Trust And Loyalty were written in calligraphic letters. "Terrence, I…I can't accept this."

"Of course you can. You're my girl, and I want you to have it." Deaf to her protests, he unclasped the chain and fastened it around her neck. The pendant shimmered in the moonlight, matching the brilliance of her wide smile. "I didn't think it was possible, but you're even more beautiful."

Staring down, she turned the pendant over in her hands. "It's almost identical to the one you got me for my twenty-first birthday. The one…"

You threw at me the morning I left for training camp.

"Terrence, it's gorgeous."

Passion shot through his body like a bolt of lightning. The wind pulled at her dress, giving him a better view of her thighs. His eyes ran down her hips, then his hands followed suit. Kyra moved into his arms, and they shared a deep, soulful kiss. One that stole his breath, his thoughts and his self-control. A great tenderness came over him when she nuzzled against him, and wrapped her hands around his waist. "Have you given any thought to what we talked about the other night?"

Only every second of every day.

"Kyra, I want a future with you."

"Don't you think this is a little premature? We've only been on a few dates."

"But I've loved you from the moment I first saw you." He took her hand, his fingertips playing over her soft flesh. Her placid expression worried him, but he had to speak his mind. "You're perfect for me in every way. I want you, Ky, God knows I do, but not like this. Not if you can't commit to me."

"You're serious about this, aren't you?"

"More serious than I've ever been about anything."

His words touched her deeply. She smiled, but her hands were shaking and her eyes filled with water. He swam out of focus, and for a moment, she didn't know what to say. Kyra was conflicted over what to do and for good reason. Aimee, her parents, and—

"It doesn't matter what anyone else has to say," he told her, speaking to her thoughts. "I don't care if I have to spend all week in church. I'll do whatever it takes to win over your parents."

"Don't let my dad hear you say that! He'll work you to the bone!"

Their laughter alleviated the tension.

"I've changed, Kyra, and I swear that I'll never hurt you again. You have my word on that, baby." Kissing from her cheek to her neck, he whispered, "I love you, Kyra, and I want you to be my girlfriend. Can we go steady again?"

Her smile returned. "I thought you'd never ask."

Chapter 19

Terrence's rental house was three blocks away from Hollington College. Freshly painted, the attractive, three-bedroom duplex featured dark maple wood, a spacious main floor and a fully fenced yard with an expansive deck.

"Want a quick tour?" His grin widened. "There's a hot tub upstairs. Interested?"

Kyra laughed. It had been her job to get the house ready for his arrival, and she probably knew more about the rental property than he did. "Maybe later. You promised me a back rub and I came to collect!"

"I *only* work in the bedroom," he joked, pecking her cheek. "Let me grab some music." Opening the entertainment unit, he perused the rack of CDs inside. "Sade, Dru Hill, oh yeah, we gotta have some Prince."

"The light on your answering machine is blinking."

Kyra pointed at the black, square box. "You have two new messages."

Standing, a pile of discs in hand, he strolled over to the end table. "My agent is the only one who has this number. Do you mind?"

"Go ahead," she said, picking up the remote and aiming it at the flat screen. "I'll just watch a little TV while I wait."

"Not so fast." Terrence folded his arms around her. "I want you to share in my good news. Today's the day I officially launch my acting career."

"It is?" Hearing the disappointment in her voice, she forced a smile. What was she going to do now? She'd promised Mr. Morrow those signed contracts by the end of the month, and now Terrence was talking about his acting career.

"You're about to witness history. Watch out Matt Damon! Here comes *Flash!*"

Chuckling, he hit Play on the machine. A man with a deep throaty voice spoke in rapid-fire speech. "Yo, Terrence, what's up? It's me, Glen. Just got the call from the casting director of the Robert De Niro flick. It's a no-go. They decided to go with someone else. And *Celebrity Apprentice* isn't interested, either. Keep your head up, man. I'll check back with you in a couple weeks." Click.

Kyra didn't know what to say. "Terrence, I am so sorry."

"For what?" He shrugged his shoulders. "Other opportunities will come. I just gotta be positive and keep doing my thing."

"You definitely have the right attitude about it." Although he smiled, she could tell he was disappointed. Overcome with sympathy, she reached out and touched a hand to his cheek. "That's why we want you to coach the Lions. Terrence, you have a great outlook on life and I'm absolutely convinced that you're the right man for the job."

"What about you, Kyra? Am I the right man for you?"

The build-up was insane. What was he waiting for? *Why doesn't he just kiss me, already?* The room was so quiet Kyra could hear wind chimes tinkling outside. Her gaze swung from the window to his face. Deep brown eyes stared back at her. Tonight, she didn't have the strength to turn away from him. Not here. Not now. Not when he'd dropped a small fortune on dinner and surprised her with such a beautiful gift.

"I love you," he whispered, working his hands over her shoulders, his mouth closing in on her lips. "More than words can ever explain."

Gripped by his impenetrable stare, she blinked hard to clear the tears from her eyes. He spoke with such heart and sincerity, she couldn't speak. Wanting to please, she pinned him against the wall. Inflamed with desire, she moved her warm body down his sculpted torso. Her nipples grazed his chest, and a moan ripped from his mouth.

Kyra lowered herself to her knees. Her hands fluttered over his chest, and down his stomach. Holding his gaze, she pulled down his boxers and tenderly stroked his shaft. Cupping his butt, she moved him in and out of her mouth, loving the feel of his erection against her lips.

Eyes closed, head back, Terrence dug his hands into her luscious hair. Kyra licked from his navel to his penis, and he groaned deep in his throat. His self-control, which he'd been fighting to hold on to since she'd walked into the conference room six weeks ago, ebbed away like the shadows of the passing night.

"Terrence, you taste so good…"

Blood rushed to his groin. Numb and dazed, he dropped his head and closed his mouth. Despite her very buttoned-up persona, she liked to use the dirtiest language in bed and when Kyra called him Big Daddy he chuckled long and hard. Her short, fast, in-and-out movements aroused him, and just when he thought he'd implode, she slowed and started the explosive pattern all over again.

Standing, she closed her hands around him and lovingly caressed the back of his head. Terrence found a condom and rubbed his erection against her thighs. Kissing passionately, they tumbled onto the couch like a pair of human bowling pins. "Terrence, stop! I still have my shoes on!"

"I love your stilettos. They're staying on!"

Kyra shrieked with laughter.

Head angled to the right, Terrence ground against her with a savage intensity. Hooking a leg around his waist, she carefully ran the tip of her stiletto along his thigh. Frantically unhooking her bra, he shrugged the straps down her shoulders, then slowly and reverently cupped her breasts in his hands. He bit her neck playfully and she moaned her pleasure. Seeing her physical reaction thrilled him, so he did it again. "That hurts *so* good!" she quipped, wearing an extra lusty smile. "Do that again, baby…"

Grabbing her breasts, he alternated between licking, sucking and fondling each chocolate-brown nipple. His touch was exhilarating and drove her to the brink.

He massaged her clit through her panties, then yanked them aside and dipped a finger inside her sex. Moving her hips slowly back and forth, she rocked against him, creating a beautiful, erotic rhythm.

Stunned by the strength of his passion, he cupped her face and lavished kisses on her warm cheeks. "I could never get enough of this…could never get enough of you," he rasped, the voice he heard in his ears not his own. "I love you, Ky, and I need you in my life. I'm sorry that it took me this long to come back to you."

Terrence shed the rest of his clothes. Running his tongue along her bare skin, he gathered her up in his arms and kissed away her falling tears. Sensitive to her needs, he told her she was gorgeous, stunning, the smartest, most appealing sister he knew. And it was true. Kyra was all the woman he needed. His primary concern would always be to make her happy, so he reined in his desires and teased her clit with his tongue.

Kyra ran her nails over his back, and he cursed under his breath. Terrence couldn't hold back any longer. He eased inside her in one fluid motion, swirling around her core. Riding her senselessly, he stroked her like a man possessed. His thrusts got deeper, wilder, more frenzied. Terrence rotated his hips, thrusting back and forth, plunging yet deeper inside her. The last thing Terrence remembered before being hammered by a hard, crippling orgasm was the sound of her salacious moans in his ears.

Terrence lifted the tumbler to his mouth and choked down his whiskey. Despite making love to Kyra twice, sleep eluded him, and after she'd drifted off in his arms, he'd come into the living room and poured himself a drink.

Returning the glass to the coaster, he settled back into his seat, staring blankly at the forty-inch TV screen. In his mind's eye, he saw her riding him, teasing him, driving him to the brink with her tongue. Laughter was a sexy aphrodisiac, and he liked how Kyra played and joked in the bedroom. Kyra Dixon was his dream. The type of woman he wanted to marry. *Had* to marry.

Kyra touched his life in ways that no one else ever had, and he felt lucky to have her back in his life again. So much so, he hadn't given a second thought to losing out on the Robert De Niro movie. Opportunities for ex-NFL running backs were few and far between, but with Kyra by his side, he could handle anything.

Terrence put his feet up on the ottoman and felt a sharp pain in his back. Grimacing, he popped open the bottle of aspirin, tossed a couple into his mouth and drained his glass.

"I thought I heard the TV."

Swallowing hard, a fist-size knot in his throat, he slowly lifted his eyes to Kyra's face. Standing in the darkened hallway, looking dangerously sexy in his white undershirt, she pushed a hand through her hair, a shy smile playing on her lips. "Terrence, are you okay?"

Lowering the empty tumbler, he picked up the remote and muted the TV. He wanted to go to her, but the pain in his shoulder had spread down his back and he didn't think he could walk without limping. "Sorry about the noise. I didn't mean to wake you."

She nodded absently, her forehead creased with wrinkles. "When I woke up and didn't see you, I got worried. I just wanted to make sure you were all right."

Terrence patted the space beside him. "Sit and keep me company for a while."

"It's three in the morning," she said, padding into the room and settling beside him on the couch. "I can't believe you're sitting in the dark watching old *Martin* reruns."

"I couldn't sleep."

"You always were a night owl. Back when we were dating, I'd wake up in the middle of the night and find you studying your play book or watching game film."

Worried she might misconstrue his absence from their bed, he said, "For years I thought I was just a light sleeper, but after my rookie season, the team doctor confirmed that I had severe insomnia."

Leaning in, her breasts pressed against his arm, she stroked the back of his neck. "How could you play football on only a few hours of sleep every night?"

"I learned to live with it. There's no bellyaching in the NFL. Either you go out and get the job done, or risk losing your spot."

"Has it gotten better now that you've retired?"

"A little. Over the years, I tried everything from hypnosis to meditation, but nothing really worked. Now, if I get five hours of sleep, I'm happy."

"How about your knee? Is it acting up again?"

"It's nothing a little Jack can't cure," he joked, reaching for the bottle and topping up his glass. "In a couple days, I'll be as good as new."

Kyra picked up the bottle of aspirin and her eyes went wide. "Terrence, it's empty. How many of these have you had today?"

"I have three every few hours."

Her mouth fell open. "And you wash them down with whiskey?"

"Don't look so worried, Ky. I've been doing this for years. It's either that or live in constant pain." He added, "Lots of athletes self-medicate."

"That doesn't mean it's right." Hand propped up on the couch, her expression grim, she examined him closely. "Drugs and alcohol don't mix, Terrence, not even over-the-counter ones like Advil and Motrin."

"When my back is acting up, it's the only thing that helps." Terrence frowned. His explanation sounded weak, asinine, like something a drug addict might say. "I don't have a problem, Ky. That's not what this is. It's just a…a bad habit."

The light from the television illuminated the fear in Kyra's pale brown eyes. Feeling guilty, he folded his arms around her, and kissed the top of her forehead. "Baby, I didn't mean to worry you. I'm fine. I swear."

"Motrin and booze might seem harmless, but what you're doing can have dangerous consequences."

Terrence had a bitter taste in his mouth. Something in her tone made him feel small, foolish, as if he was living a lie. Did she really believe he had a problem? Her words buzzed in his mind like bees in a cornfield. His body had taken a beating over the course of his ten-year career, but he'd never abused drugs and alcohol. He had to make Kyra see the truth, had to prove to her that he wasn't just another reckless athlete.

After several long, painful minutes, Kyra broke the silence. "Two years ago, my Aunt Bridgett and Uncle Lewis were in a tragic car accident. Sadly, after three days in a coma, she passed away."

Terrence took her hand. "I'm sorry, baby."

"My uncle was in the hospital for weeks," she continued, her voice filled with sadness. "Not only did he have to deal with the grief of losing his wife of seventeen years, he was plagued with chronic back pain. Doctors prescribed painkillers, but his symptoms only got worse."

"Is he better now?"

"Luckily, he was referred to a herbalist who specializes in promoting health through nutrition, herbs and exercise. He's still not a hundred percent, but he's coming along."

Eager to know more, he said, "Tell me more about your uncle's treatments." Terrence listened intently, his eyes glued to her pretty oval face. What continually amazed him about Kyra was her genuine concern for others. Maybe it was her ties to Pi Beta Gamma, or maybe it was because she'd been raised in the church, but he'd never met a more loving, generous woman.

He held her closer, tighter, worried that she was angry at him, or worse, disappointed. In light of what he'd seen his teammates do over the years, downing aspirin with booze was tame. Until tonight, he'd never considered the risks of what he was doing, but deep down he knew Kyra was right. He didn't want anything to build a wedge between them, and more than anything, he wanted her respect.

"Do you think this herbalist woman can help me?"

"It's worth a try, isn't it?"

As his eyes glided down her body, his hands reached out and teased. "Set something up for next week and we can go see her together."

"I'll call first thing tomorrow."

He looked at her, and shook his head. "I didn't have a choice, did I?"

"Nope." Kyra giggled. "You should know by now that I always get my way."

"Spoken like a true diva."

"I'm not a diva," she protested, poking out her bottom lip. "Just politely persistent! Terrence, you were going to see Marie Vasteles whether you liked it or not. I would have kidnapped you if I had to!"

A laugh burst out of his mouth. He didn't doubt it. When Kyra got an idea in her head, there was just no stopping her. Just another thing about her that he loved. She was his heart, his dream, the woman he'd been looking for his whole life. With her, he could block out everything around him and just enjoy the moment. For all his talk and bravado, he enjoyed being in a committed relationship and loved when she snuggled in his arms.

They talked, and laughed until the sun crept over the horizon. When she rested her head on his shoulder, Terrence was struck by the strength of his feelings. He loved her—not because the sex was amazing or because she took care of him, but because she told him the truth. And when she fell asleep in his arms, he swept her up and carried her into the bedroom where they made love for the third time.

Chapter 20

"I'm so sorry I'm late." Tamara threw her arms around Kyra, embracing her in a fierce Pi Beta Gamma hug. "I had my first meeting with the florist and she insisted on showing me every single arrangement in her shop! I love roses as much as the next girl, but I'm not about to spend twenty grand on a bunch of flowers."

"You only get married once, right? Might as well do it big!"

The women laughed.

Appearing with menus, the hostess led them to a table beside the window. Situated in downtown Atlanta, three blocks from the Centennial Tower, Fusion Café was a sleek, uptown bar with a tasty eight-page menu that spanned the globe. To start, they ordered a chicken appetizer, garden salads and a pitcher of soda.

"I still can't believe you're engaged!" Kyra confessed, setting her menu aside. "Four months ago you were interviewing A-list stars, and now you're planning a wedding, moving to L.A. and—"

"Pregnant!"

Kyra gasped. "Oh, my goodness, Tamara! That's wonderful. I'm so happy for you." Reaching for her girlfriend's hand, she gave it a warm squeeze and congratulated her again. "Micah must be over the moon. He's wanted you forever, and now he has you *and* a little one on the way."

Nodding, her face glowing with happiness, Tamara laughed softly. Five-seven, with fair skin and hazel green eyes, she was a gorgeous, fun-spirited girl who enjoyed life. She'd always been the bright, happy type, but today, she seemed lit from within. "Micah's been fawning all over me ever since he learned about the baby. I'm not used to all this attention," she confessed, wearing a shy smile. "It's sweet, but kind of overwhelming, too."

"Don't complain," Kyra scolded, pointing at her girlfriend with her fork. "I'd switch places with you in a heartbeat."

"I have it pretty good, don't I?"

"Damn right, you do! The last time I saw you, you were really upset about your breakup and now you're rocking a gigantic ring and smiling from ear to ear."

"Oh, my God, I never told you how he proposed!" Turning serious, Tamara put down her fork and wiped her mouth with her napkin. Ensuring she'd be heard above the chatter, she slid her chair closer. "We're both avid hikers, so when Micah suggested we spend the weekend at a quaint mountain lodge, I was all for it."

"Wow, you really have changed," Kyra observed, her

eyes combing over her girlfriend's face. "Back in the day when Pi Beta Gamma used to organize The Boys & Girls Club summer camps, you'd whine about having to sleep in a tent!"

Both women laughed. A waiter arrived with their orders and when he left, Tamara continued. "We decided to take a stroll along the grounds and ended up on this beautiful hill overlooking a small lily pond. I was going on and on about the hybrid rose exhibit going on in town, but when I suggested we check it out, Micah didn't answer. I turned around and there he was. Down on bended knee, holding my ring."

Staring at her left hand, she smoothed a finger over the pear-shaped diamond. "Micah said he couldn't live another day without me, and I burst into tears. I was crying into his handkerchief when a helicopter appeared out of nowhere, trailing a banner that read, 'Tamara Hodges, will you marry me?'"

Tamara's eyes filled with tears. "Sorry, I'm a little hormonal." Smiling through her tears, she said, "Enough about me. I want to hear what's going on with you and Terrence. Chloe said you guys have been hot and heavy ever since reunion weekend."

A smiled overwhelmed Kyra's lips. Of all the men she'd dated, Terrence was the most romantic. He was creative and spontaneous and was always looking for ways to show his love. They were comfortable with each other, and every time they made love, Kyra felt closer to him than ever before.

"So it's true?" Tamara wiggled her eyebrows. "I don't even have to ask if he's *the one.* It's written all over your face. That cute, little-girl smile says it all. You're in love!"

"We're in a good place," she said, fingering the locket absently. The diamond chain was far too expensive to be wearing it around the office, but Kyra couldn't bring herself to take it off. Since Terrence had surprised her with it, it had remained firmly fastened to her neck. Touching it now, she marveled at how quickly her life had changed. Four months ago, she was convinced that she'd have to launch a worldwide search to find her dream man and now she had Terrence.

It was an open secret that they were dating, but Kyra had been stunned when Mr. Morrow cornered her in the student union center and asked if they were serious. His Phil Donahue smile had showcased every tooth and his eyes had been light-bulb bright.

"Terrence and I might be a couple, but he's not making my job any easier. He still hasn't accepted the head coaching position, and Mr. Morrow's really been applying the pressure. Girl, things are so bad, I dive into my office every time I see him coming down the hall!"

Comfortable with Tamara, and confident she wouldn't be judged, she shared her deepest fears. Kyra could picture her future and saw Terrence standing right there beside her, but her thoughts were ruled with doubts. "I love Terrence, but I can't help thinking about our past. Do you think I'm in way over my head? I mean, you've heard the stories about Terrence. Do you think he's incapable of settling down?"

"Girl, please, behind every woman is a man who used to have bad-boy tendencies," Tamara said, chewing a mouthful of salad. "From what I saw on reunion weekend, you have nothing to worry about. Terrence obviously loves you, Kyra."

Feeling better, and not wanting to monopolize the

conversation, she asked Tamara about her new life in L.A. Glowing with health and happiness, Tamara spoke about the wedding and the plans for the baby's nursery. It was miserable-looking outside, but her sorority sister's enthusiasm was catching. In no rush to return home, Tamara suggested they go see the new Jennifer Aniston movie. Kyra agreed, and when her girlfriend left to use the bathroom, she dialed Terrence's number.

"Hey babe, how are you?"

The sound of her boyfriend's voice made her heart race. A smile formed on her lips, but inside she was feeling a storm of emotions. Everyone was coupling up and riding off into the sunset. First Chloe, then Tamara. Next, Beverly would be calling to say she'd eloped. Since reunion weekend, Beverly had been secretly dating someone but refused to say who the mystery man was.

On the phone, Terrence spoke about his appointment with Marie Vasteles. He'd been to see the herbalist twice since and though he was still having trouble sleeping, he admitted to feeling stronger and more alert. "We're meeting at The Tavern at six, right?"

"Do you mind if we stay in tonight?" she asked, fiddling with her napkin. "Shaunice is working late and I'm just not in the mood to play tonight. Tamara and I are going to see a movie, but I should be home by nine."

"How's Mom and baby doing?"

Frowning, Kyra gripped her cell phone, pressing it closer to her ear. "You knew Tamara was pregnant? Why didn't you say anything?"

"Micah called and told me the good news a couple days ago. They didn't waste any time, did they," he joked.

"I know. Tamara's practically bursting with joy, and every word out of her mouth is either about Micah or the baby. It's sweet."

"We better hurry up and jump the broom before we get left behind!"

"Terrence, don't joke about things like that. Marriage is important to me and—"

"Who said I was joking? Just because we haven't talked about marriage, doesn't mean I haven't been thinking about it, too." He added, "But we can discuss our future when I come over tonight, all right?"

Kyra melted. One of the things she'd always loved about Terrence was his ability to read her. Everything was so easy with him, so right. It didn't matter what they were doing or where they went, they always had a good time together. Being with him was an adventure, and Kyra had never felt more alive. And when they got off the phone a few minutes later, a seductive plan was forming in her mind. A bottle of wine, a blindfold and her boyfriend would be flat on his back singing her praises.

"Baby, where are you?" Terrence called, kicking off his shoes. A soft light streamed into the foyer, and as he walked down the hall the scent of strawberries grew stronger.

Inside the living room, potted candles emitted a peaceful glow and Kyra was standing beside the entertainment unit holding two flute glasses. Wearing a multicolored tunic sweater, leggings and skinny heels, his girlfriend looked incredibly youthful and fun.

"Hi, honey." She walked over, and handed him a glass. "I'm glad you made it."

Terrence returned her smile. "You look tempting."

"Thanks. That's the look I was going for."

Her large brown eyes were fringed with incredibly long lashes, and despite slaving over a hot stove for the last two hours, she smelled like fruit.

"Looks like you went to a lot of trouble." His gaze toured the room. A bed of extra large pillows were in the middle of the floor, gold plates sat on a small raised mahogany table and dried flowers stood in round decorative vases. "Umm, is that your delicious garlic cheese loaf I smell?"

"Uh-huh." Kyra reached up and kissed him, but when she tried to pull away, Terrence held on tighter. The tantalizing text message she'd sent him earlier had riled him up, and he needed more than just a peck on the lips. Deficient in self-control, he ran his hands down the slopes of her hips and inhaled her sweet, floral perfume. "I think we should skip the main course and start with dessert."

"You would!" she quipped.

Terrence reluctantly released her arm. He watched her leave, mesmerized by the erotic rhythm of her walk. Sliding a hand into his coat, he checked to make sure the ring box was still in his inner pocket. He'd been carrying around the diamond for the last three days, but tonight it felt as if it were burning a hole into his chest. He relished the thought of Kyra being his wife and although they hadn't discussed tying the knot, he was confident she'd say yes. Or at least her mother had assured him she would.

"Dinner is served!" she said in her best French accent. Kyra sailed into the living room carrying a ceramic dish, and when she sat down beside him and fed him a stuffed mushroom, Terrence knew he'd never look at food quite the same way again.

They ate, laughed and shared long, deep kisses between sips of red wine. He'd always loved her eternal optimism, but as she told him about her afternoon run-in with President Morrow, he couldn't help feeling guilty.

Terrence hated to see her stressed out and soothed her fears with a kiss. If not for his uncertainty about his future, he would have already popped the question. Inside, he could feel himself changing, growing, become a more caring, considerate man. And it was all because of Kyra's love. He felt her hands on his chest and shuddered. Her touch, though soft and warm, made him hot all over. In three weeks, he'd be going back to Pittsburgh for Thanksgiving, and the thought of being without Kyra terrified him. He'd invited her to come home with him, but she hadn't given him an answer yet. *Will I be returning home alone, or with a gorgeous, new fiancée?*

"I know you're probably sick of me asking you this, but have you come to a decision about the head coaching position? Mr. Morrow wants an answer by next Friday and I promised him I'd let him know what was happening one way or another."

Seated with her legs outstretched and her hands clasped, she looked worried and vulnerable. "This has been a tough decision, Kyra, one I haven't taken lightly. I—"

Terrence broke off when he heard Aimee's voice in the distance. Let down that their intimate party for two was about to be interrupted, he motioned with his head toward the foyer. "I thought you said she was going back to Houston this weekend?"

Kyra shrugged. "Her plans must have changed."

"We'll talk about the coaching position later," he whispered, lifting her chin for a quick kiss, "*after* we have dessert!"

A minute later, Aimee sashayed into the living room and greeted them with a wave. "Hola!" Eyebrows arched, she sank into the armchair and swung her legs over the side. "What are you guys up to?"

"Nothing much. Just a quiet evening at home." Kyra finished her wine and returned the empty glass to the tray. "Is everything all right?"

"Uh-huh, things are fine." Aimee plucked a chicken spring roll off the plate, studied it, and then pushed it into her open mouth. "Not bad. It's a bit salty, though. I would have boiled the meat first before grilling it. It's still tough inside."

"That's just the way I like it." Terrence pulled Kyra to his chest and gave her a wet, sloppy kiss. Aimee was a vain, know-it-all and for the life of him he couldn't figure out why Kyra was her friend. Uninterested in what Aimee had to say, he smiled at his lady love, marveling at her natural, feminine beauty. "Thanks for dinner, baby. It was delicious and—"

The TV drowned out the rest of his sentence. "Do you guys mind if I watch TV in here? That dinky little set in the spare bedroom is a piece of junk."

Terrence started to speak, but Kyra said, "No problem. We'll all watch together."

Smothering a sigh, he stood and picked up the dirty dishes. This was the second time Aimee had popped up in the middle of their date, and as he stalked out of the living room, he thought he saw a small triumphant smile on her lips.

Chapter 21

Kyra sat up in bed. Blinking sleepily, she stared down at the empty space beside her. Last night, she'd remained in the living room with Aimee, while Terrence watched TV in the bedroom and by the time she finally came to bed, he was asleep. It wasn't the ending to their date that she'd imagined, but it wasn't too late to make it up to him. Wondering where he was now, she slipped out from between the covers and grabbed her robe.

Worried that Terrence was sitting in the living room downing aspirin with whiskey, she hurried from the bedroom. Despite the hour, Kyra was sharp and alert and as she descended the staircase, she heard a low, humming sound coming from the kitchen. The microwave. Shaking her head, she allowed herself a wry smile. Of course. Terrence was heating up the leftovers.

Voices echoed off the hardwood floor. Her feet skidded to a stop when she heard Aimee's girlish laugh.

"Kyra's my girl and everything, but she's not the right woman for you, Terrence. You need someone worldly, and sophisticated."

"Is that right?"

To keep from falling, Kyra reached out and gripped the banister. Fear filled her heart, and it felt as if her mouth were packed with sand. Terrence joked and even teased other women, but he always knew where to draw the line. So why was he in the living room flirting with Aimee?

"Why did you lie to Kyra about us? We never hooked up and you know it."

"It's not too late. You could come back to my room." Her high-pitched tone grew husky. "Kyra will never know. It'll be our little secret."

Heart pounding, eyes stinging, Kyra choked down the emotion clogging her throat. Waves of sickness and dizziness washed over her. Why would Aimee do this to her? She'd taken her in when no one else would. Her betrayal was like a stiletto in the back, but what hurt more than anything was her cold, superior attitude.

In a fury that verged on madness, Kyra flew into the living room just in time to see Aimee fling her arms around Terrence. He pushed her away, but she didn't release her hold. Her breasts fell out of her tank top and her shorts were cut so high, Kyra could see her red G-string. Aimee was so busy grinding against Terrence, she didn't notice Kyra standing in the doorway. "Get out of my house. *Now.*"

Aimee flinched. "H-hey girl. What are you doing up? I thought you were—"

"Ky, I know this looks bad, but it's not what you think," Terrence interrupted, reaching for her. She pushed his hands away, but he grabbed her arm. "Nothing happened between us. I don't want her, baby. I only want you."

"I told you he was a dog!" Bottom lip quivering, face flushed with heat, Aimee produced a stream of fat sloppy tears. "I came downstairs to get some water and this…this creep propositioned me!"

"What?" Glaring, teeth clenched, Terrence gave his head a hard shake. "I came on to you? Are you kidding me? I wouldn't sleep with you for all the money in the world."

"You're just mad because I turned you down." Disgust peppered her words as she spoke. "Why would I want an old, washed-up athlete when the *new* quarterback of the Falcons is blowing up my phone? You're a has-been, Terrence, and nobody wants you."

Putting an end to Aimee's rant, Kyra pointed at the front door. "You have five minutes to get out, or I'll *put* you out."

"B-but it's four o'clock in the morning," she stammered. "Where am I supposed to go at this time of night?"

"I don't care, I just want you out." Kyra couldn't resist adding, "Why don't you call the Falcons' quarterback?"

"You're going to let a guy come between us?"

"I heard you, Aimee. I heard every filthy, backstabbing word that came out of your mouth." Her voice cracked, but she didn't give in to her emotions. "I don't want to have anything to do with you anymore, so leave."

"I didn't mean it," she protested. "I just wanted to

see if he'd go for it. Please don't do this, Kyra. You're the only friend I have."

"And now I know why. You might want to rethink throwing yourself at men who don't belong to you." Deeply saddened, she bit the inside of her cheek to keep from crying. Despite what Aimee had done, Kyra was going to miss having her around. "Go and get your stuff, or I'll start tossing it into the trash."

Her pupils dilated. "You wouldn't."

Patience exhausted, Kyra spun on her heels, determined to make good on her threat.

"Okay, okay, I'm leaving." She made a great performance of straightening her clothes, then stomped out of the room and up the stairs.

"Kyra, it's not what it looked like."

"It looked like you were about to screw my best friend."

"You think I'd actually be stupid enough to sleep with Aimee while you slept upstairs?" His voice was low. "Is that how little you think of me?"

"I don't know what to think anymore."

"I couldn't sleep so I came down here to get something to eat," he began, meeting her gaze. He looked tired, as if their argument had sucked the life out of him. Unsparing in his criticism of Aimee, he told Kyra about the stunt she'd pulled last week out in the garage. "I'm sorry, Ky. I thought Aimee was just messing around. I should have said something, but I didn't want to cause problems between you guys."

Silence descended. Minutes later, Kyra heard Aimee in the foyer. The front door slammed, and the tears she'd been holding in threatened to break free. Terrence stroked her shoulders. His touch stilled and quieted her, but she didn't go willingly into his arms.

"Do you want me to leave?" He swept an errant strand of hair off of her cheek. "I understand if you want to be alone. You've had a rough night, and the last thing I want to do is cause you any more pain."

Kyra wanted him to stay, but the words stuck in her throat. What she needed was time. Time to sort out her thoughts and feelings. His hands skimmed her shoulders, warming her weary body. Kyra had zero desire to make love, but when they returned upstairs, that's just what they did.

Flopping down on a padded swivel chair, Kyra scooted forward and slid her hands under the nail dryer. It was Wednesday afternoon, and although it was storming outside, Unique Nails was filled to capacity.

Rain dribbled down the window, and lightning flashed in the sky. Strong winds blew, breaking twigs off trees and swirling litter in the huge parking lot.

Hearing Shaunice's voice behind her, Kyra glanced over her shoulder. Her best friend was perusing a shelf lined with nail polish, pausing every few seconds to read labels and admire bottles. "It doesn't take ten minutes to pick out a color," Kyra commented, noting the time on the wall clock. "At this rate, we'll never get out of here."

"Okay, I think I'm going to get Passion Pink." Cotton wedged between her toes, she waddled on the balls of her feet to the station where a slim manicurist was waiting. Seeing the stack of women's magazines on the desk reminded Kyra of the last time she'd been at the salon. She and Aimee had sat in the waiting room, sipping their lattes, laughing hysterically at the fallacious stories about their favorite celebrities.

Sighing heavily, Kyra crossed her legs and leaned back in her chair. Every time she thought about what Aimee did, she was consumed with anger. The personal chef had proven to be a backstabber, skilled at deception. But Aimee's tactic had backfired, bringing her and Terrence closer than ever. In the last two weeks, Aimee had left dozens of teary messages on the answering machine, but Kyra hadn't returned any of her calls.

Her boyfriend's face rose in her mind, and her heart surged with love. Terrence had become a permanent fixture at Hollington since the reunion and when they weren't meeting for brunch or strolling around the campus, they were at home, planning their first vacation together and making love.

In honor of their two-month anniversary, Terrence had surprised her with a romantic dinner at home. They'd had a great meal, with good wine, conversation and deep, rousing kisses. The sensual feel of his voice quickly put her in the mood, and when he scooped her up and strode down the hall, Kyra felt breathless with anticipation. For her pleasure, he'd dressed the king-sized bed in burgundy satin sheets and filled the room with more candles than a Vatican church. Ne-Yo was playing on the stereo, sharing his sexy, soothing voice. Kissing, they stroked and fondled each other as they quickly shed their clothes. Then, the next thing she knew, they were on the floor, naked, making love in the middle of the rug like they had ten years ago.

"I hope we're going for drinks after this," Shaunice said, plunking down beside her. "You don't have plans with Terrence tonight, do you?"

"No, his cousins are taking him to a basketball game. Where do you want to eat?"

"It doesn't matter, as long as we don't have to wait in a long line."

Kyra pulled her hands out of the dryer and checked her flaming-red nails. Pleased, she reached into her purse for her wallet.

"Aimee called me last night."

Head bent, she continued rummaging around in her bag. Maybe if she pretended not to hear Shaunice, her friend would get bored and move on to something else.

"She said Terrence came on to her," Shaunice reported, one eyebrow raised. "I'm not trying to take sides, but are you sure about what you saw? Maybe it just looked like Aimee was touching him…"

Kyra checked her reaction. It wasn't Shaunice's fault that Aimee was a liar. Squeezing her lips together to keep from cursing, she sat upright, facing her girlfriend. Aimee's version of events had more holes in it than fishnet stockings, but hearing Shaunice defend her made Kyra angry enough to scream. "Why are you taking up for Aimee? I thought you didn't like her."

"You're right, I don't, but you do, and I'd hate for your friendship to end over a misunderstanding. Men come and go, but girlfriends are forever."

"A misunderstanding?" Her high-pitched voice rose above the raucous chatter in the nail salon. "I know what I saw. She badmouthed me in my own house and threw herself at my boyfriend!"

"Things aren't always what they seem, Kyra. How do you—"

"What's that supposed to mean? You think I imagined the whole thing?"

They fell into silence. After several minutes, Shaunice spoke.

"We've been friends for years, but you never once mentioned being engaged to Terrence Franklin. How come? I had no clue he was your old college sweetheart until Aimee told me."

"It was a long time ago, and I didn't say anything because I was embarrassed about how things ended. I moved on and never looked back."

"I know, but you still should have said something. I hate being kept in the dark," she protested. "And if I had known Terrence was your one true love, I wouldn't have told him about all the brothers in your little black book!"

The women chortled.

"I thought all that drama with Aimee would have put a strain on your relationship, but I can tell by the way you sashayed up in here that the fire's burning hotter than ever!"

"Shaunice, things are so much better this time around. There's no drama in our relationship, just love." Kyra knew she was gushing, knew she sounded sappier than a card commercial, but whenever she thought about Terrence, her heart went soft. "We have fun together, and I couldn't have asked for a more loving man."

"It's great to see you so happy, Ky. After all you guys have been through, you deserve a happy ending." Shaunice leaned over and hugged her. Straightening, her eyes bright with humor, she asked, "So, do you get a bonus for signing Terrence?"

Kyra cleared her throat. "I don't think so, but I'll let you know for sure once I turn in the contracts."

"I still can't believe you pulled it off. Getting Terrence to sign on with the Lions was a tall order, and to be honest, I didn't think you could do it."

"You should know by now not to underestimate me. I always get the job done!" Laughing, she rose from her chair. "I'm going to the ladies' room. I'll meet you out front."

Kyra smiled, but she felt like a fraud. Why had she lied to Shaunice about signing Terrence? The deadline Mr. Morrow had given her was tomorrow, and Terrence still hadn't given her an answer.

After using the bathroom, Kyra washed her hands. Staring at her reflection in the mirror, she wondered what more she could do to persuade Terrence to sign on to coach the Lions. He'd had more than enough time to make a decision, so what was he waiting for? Kyra's thoughts couldn't be controlled, and soon her mind was overrun with questions. Had Terrence decided not to take the job? Was he trying to find a way to break the news to her?

Remembering Shaunice was waiting, she exited the washroom and strode back through the salon. Still thinking about Terrence, she searched for her umbrella in her purse. Terrence was taking her out on Saturday night, and before the night was over, Kyra was going to find out what decisions he'd made for the future. Relationship aside, she had a job to do and, like Shaunice had so aptly pointed out, she had to deliver.

Chapter 22

On Friday morning, Kyra strolled through the student center. Oblivious to the sounds around her, she slipped off her tweed coat and draped it over her right arm. Her thoughts were on Terrence, and as images of their late-night tryst in the back row of the IMAX theater surfaced, a smile filled her lips.

Exhausted, she patted back a yawn. As she passed the faculty dining room, she noticed the sideway glances her colleagues were shooting her way. Worried she'd had a wardrobe malfunction, Kyra glanced down at her suit. Toilet paper wasn't stuck to her shoes, her skirt wasn't jammed into her panty hose and she didn't have coffee stains on her blouse, so what was everyone looking at?

When Kyra stepped off the elevator onto the second floor, Nikki leaped to her feet, hustled around her desk and put an arm around her. Features touched with concern, she wore a tight sympathetic smile. "Are you okay?"

"Of course I am. Why wouldn't I be?"

"I don't know, I just thought you'd be upset about the article in the *Daily.*"

"What are you talking about, Nikki? What article?"

"Why don't you go get settled in your office and I'll bring you a cup of coffee?"

By the time Kyra hung up her coat, Nikki was inside the room, handing her a white coffee mug. Clutching the newspaper to her chest, she lowered herself onto one of the padded chairs. "Before I show you the paper, let me just say that you and Terrence are a great couple. He loves you, Kyra, and I know that—"

Kyra stuck out her hand. "Give me the paper, Nikki, then get back out front before Mr. Morrow catches you socializing," she teased.

"He's out of town, remember? Won't be back from Seattle until Friday."

"I almost forgot he was attending the Leadership for the Future Conference. It's going to be quiet around here for once, huh?"

Quiet, the expression on her face one of concern, Nikki reluctantly handed over the newspaper. "If you need anything, or just want to talk, I'm here."

Puzzled, she watched Nikki's hurried departure. What had gotten into everyone? Unless…had Terrence made a decision about the head coaching position and given the *Atlanta Daily World* the scoop? Kyra glanced down at the newspaper and cupped a hand over her mouth. Eyes wide, heart racing erratically, she choked down a mouthful of tears. The longer she stared at the bold, black headline, the harder it was to breathe. Ex-Football Star Named In Paternity Suit! Underneath the caption was a full-length photo of Terrence and a voluptuous Latin woman kissing outside of an L.A. nightclub.

Her legs caved and she slumped into her chair like dead weight. Grabbing ahold of her emotions, she smoothed a hand over her cheeks and sat upright in her chair. Shaking off feelings of despair, she studied the eight-by-eleven picture intently.

It felt as if someone was grabbing her throat. Gripping the newspaper, she perused the cover story, pouring over every scandalous word in the front-page article. According to an unidentified source, Terrence had hooked up with the former Dallas Cowboys cheerleader last year and after the baby's birth promptly skipped town. *So that's the real reason he came to Hollington? To escape his baby mama?*

Her mind was spinning, turning, analyzing every facet of their relationship, searching for clues pointing to this. But there weren't any. Terrence made her feel understood and, most importantly, worthy of his love. It was a powerful feeling, one she'd never experienced, one that overwhelmed her at times to the point of tears.

Water filled her eyes, blurring her vision, and clogging her throat. Facing the computer screen, her hands shaking uncontrollably, she punched in her password and logged on to the Internet. When Terrence's picture popped up, Kyra thought she was going to hurl. How had this gotten out so fast? There were more pictures, more videos and dozens of stories dating back to his rookie season. Kyra understood the boys-will-be-boys mentality, but there was no excuse for consorting with strippers and then posting the outrageous video online.

And when she saw the date the pictures of his trip to Rio had been posted, her heart rate spiked. Three weeks before he'd returned to Hollington.

As she watched various news bites, she found herself ingesting every shocking word. Pressing her eyes shut to ward off tears, she ignored the relentless peal of her cell phone and concentrated on her breathing. She'd known from the beginning that Terrence was too good to be true, so why hadn't she listened to her intuition? Could she have been wrong about Aimee, too? Maybe Terrence *had* propositioned her in the kitchen.

Kyra needed a moment to think. Propping her elbows up on the desk, she massaged her temples. Replaying last Sunday in her mind, she ignored the crippling pain spreading from her head to her heart. Anger flared in Kyra's stomach. No, she knew what she saw. Terrence might be keeping secrets, but he hadn't made a play for her ex-friend.

The telephone buzzed. Knowing she couldn't hide out in her office for the rest of the day, she opened her eyes and cleaned the tears from her face. Kyra exhaled, turned away from the computer screen and readied herself for the media onslaught. "Good morning. Ms. Dixon speaking."

"Have you seen this morning's newspaper?"

"Yes, Mr. Morrow, I have."

"This couldn't have happened at a worse time. The Lions are playing on Sunday in the biggest game of the year." He sounded agitated, and she could hear the sports channel theme music in the background. "Kyra, what are we going to do to fix this mess?"

"Nothing. Terrence's personal life is none of our business and—"

"Like hell it isn't!" he exploded. "I've been fielding calls from outraged parents, board members and alumni who feel this story is casting a negative light on our fine school. If it were up to me, I'd toss him out on his ear."

"Sir, with all due respect, I think that would be a mistake. I still believe Terrence Franklin is the right man for the job. You've been saying as much for the last eight weeks," she pointed out. "The story will die down in a couple days and life will return to normal." But even as Kyra said it, she knew it wasn't true.

"How do we know he doesn't have a whole fleet of baby mamas out there? It's not like we did a background check on him. The guy could have a drug problem or outstanding gambling debts for all we know. I don't put anything past these athletes. They have absolutely no morals and think they're..."

Kyra tuned out. She didn't want to hear this. Not now, not ever. Not when she was torn up inside, and battling a headache strong enough to knock her flat on her back. Mr. Morrow didn't understand. Terrence had changed drastically since leaving the NFL. He didn't party anymore and always kept his promises. The energy between them was electric, and their lovemaking was a sensual, passionate experience.

But what Kyra loved most was that he was committed to their relationship. He put her first and didn't allow anyone—not his boys, not his manager or other women—to come between them.

"As of today, Terrence is no longer welcome on campus, and I don't want him to practice with the Lions, either."

"Mr. Morrow, I can't enforce that."

"You can and you will." His voice grew louder. "This

isn't up for discussion, Ms. Dixon. You might be the PR director, but I'm the one who makes the final decisions around here. Keep that man off of my campus. Have I made myself clear?"

Trembling uncontrollably, Kyra lowered her head, dropping her face into her clammy hands. *I can't believe this is happening. What am I supposed to do to fix this?* Mr. Morrow's words reverberated in her ears. How could she distance herself from the man she loved? The man she wanted to marry and start a family with? It was a heart-wrenching decision to make, one that she didn't want to make, but one that she couldn't afford to put off. It had to be done. If she wanted to keep her job, and her heart intact, she had to distance herself from Terrence permanently.

Terrence lurked in the darkness, waiting for Kyra to get out of her car. Hiding in the bushes outside of her house was a harebrained idea, but she'd left him no other choice. Kyra had ignored his emails, text messages and all of the voice mails he'd left for her throughout the day. At his breaking point, he'd called the public relations department and demanded to speak to her, but after ten minutes on hold the line had disconnected. Kyra was going to hear him out, tonight, even if he had to kidnap her.

Stars glittered in the night sky and the moon shed a soft glow over the quiet street. Terrence heard a car door slam, and peered through the branches. Kyra's fragrance perfumed the air, rousing his memories of happier times, of brighter days, of all the moments they'd spent talking, laughing and loving each other.

Yesterday, while he was shaving, she'd sauntered

into the bathroom, kissed him passionately and dropped her purple, satin robe. They'd made love well into the night, and after, she'd given him a slow rubdown that put him to sleep.

His head was pounding and it felt as if a tennis ball were jammed in his throat, but Terrence would sooner choke to death than have Kyra think he'd betrayed her.

High heels pounded the pavement. Not wanting to startle her, he came from around the side of the house. He called to her, but she looked right through him. Dumbstruck, he watched as she strode past him as if he were an invisible man and marched up the steps.

"Kyra, I've been calling you all day, but you didn't answer your phone."

To block her path, he slid in front of the door. Kyra stared up at him and what Terrence saw in her eyes made his blood run cold. She shot him a hostile glare. One so cold and malevolent he had to look away. "Are you all right?"

She tightened her grip on her purse and for a moment, Terrence feared she was going to wallop him with the black designer handbag. "Get out of my way."

"You're not going to give me a chance to explain?"

Lips pursed tight, she rolled her eyes skyward. "No, Terrence, you don't deserve one. You're a liar and I have absolutely nothing to say to you."

"We need to talk, Kyra. Let's go inside and work this thing out."

She shivered in the cool night air and her cheeks were flushed from the cold, but she ignored his suggestion. "Going into the living room isn't going to make this any easier."

"I know," he agreed, "but I'd rather not discuss this out here."

"I don't care what you want."

"This is silly. You're freezing and—"

"You've been lying to me for the last two months and you have the nerve to make demands?" The harshness of her tone startled him. "All you've ever cared about is yourself. Today was one of the worst days of my life and all you can think about is what you want. I've been fielding calls from the media, and my friends and family since nine o'clock this morning. Do you have any idea how humiliated I felt when President Morrow called me about the paternity story?"

"Kyra, I didn't lie to you. I don't care what's in the newspapers. I've been up-front with you from day one, so don't make me out to be the villain in this." Angry at himself for raising his voice, he took a moment to re-group. "The media isn't reporting the whole story. Just the parts they think are entertaining."

"Who is she?"

In the untoward silence, he took a good hard look at her. Kyra dazzled in a fitted red suit and her soft, natural-looking makeup was flawless, but he could see the tracks of her tears. Her eyes were lined with sadness, and she was twisting the leather off her purse strap, obviously battling a case of the nerves.

"Terrence, tell me who she is." Her voice cracked, but she quickly recovered. "Is she a groupie? Someone you screwed at the back of an L.A. nightclub?"

"No, I met Lourdes at a health food store." Terrence smoothed a hand over the back of his neck. "Within weeks, she quit her job and moved in with me. Things were fine until I got hurt. She couldn't deal and left. End of story."

"She left because you couldn't play football anymore?"

"Lourdes got accustomed to living the good life and didn't want to stay home taking care of me. Three months after I announced my retirement, she hooked up with a pro basketball rookie and moved to Miami. Now, she's popped up out of the blue claiming that I'm her son's father."

"Well, are you?"

Terrence shrugged. "I won't know for sure until I take a paternity test. My attorney's trying to set something up later this week."

Kyra looked away. Out into the sky, as if facing him was suddenly too much to bear. "President Morrow doesn't want you for the coaching job anymore."

"I don't care about that, Kyra. I care about you." Not telling Kyra about Lourdes had been a mistake, but he wasn't losing her over it. He was ready to trade his independence for a committed relationship, and Kyra Dixon was the only woman he wanted. "I know I screwed up, Ky, but I never meant to hurt you."

"How long have you known about the baby?"

"I found out when the story hit the papers," he told her. "I was completely blindsided by this. Contrary to what was reported, Lourdes hasn't attempted to contact me and that confrontation outside of my house never happened. That's pure fiction."

Longing to hold her, he moved forward until they were just inches apart.

"You never told me about your trip to Rio. Or your

DUI last year. You were arrested and your blood alcohol level was above the legal limit."

Terrence slid his tongue over his teeth. "None of that stuff matters anymore, babe. It happened in the past and I've moved on."

"That's all you can say? 'It happened in the past and I've moved on,'" Kyra snorted. "Well, it matters to me, and that weak-ass excuse isn't going to fly."

Terrence didn't react. What mattered now was how they were going to fix this, not what had happened a year ago, but when he suggested they go back to his place or better yet, check into a hotel, Kyra wrinkled her nose. "Let's get away from it all and—"

"And what? Pretend you don't have a baby mama doing interviews with every news media in the country? Oh, and let's not forget about all of the stories and videos that have flooded the Internet in the last eight hours. There's the DUI charge and…"

Refusing to argue, he listened with uncharacteristic calm. "This is not getting us anywhere, Kyra. We're talking in circles and you're getting angrier."

"You're right. This is a waste of time."

"I didn't mean it like that," he protested, angry that she was twisting his words. "I was bummed about my knee, and the loss of my football career and had too many beers one night. I paid my fine, did my hours of community service and vowed that it would never happen again. And it won't."

"You know what, forget that I asked. It's your life, your business."

"Don't say that. It's not true. I want to marry you, and build a life with you." He reached inside his coat and opened the box. "I've been carrying this engagement ring around for weeks. I wanted to propose, but it was never the right time."

Kyra turned her head away.

"Don't throw away what we have," he pleaded. Reaching out, he drew his hand along her cheek in a sweet caress. "I know you're mad, and I understand if you're not ready to get married now, but I can't live without you, Ky. It was wrong of me to hide my past from you, and I promise from now on to be up-front about everything."

When she didn't answer, his confidence died, along with his hopes and dreams for the future. Terrence didn't want to press the issue, didn't want to come across as being desperate, but he had to know where they stood. "Do you forgive me?"

Her voice was so low, so pained, he could barely hear her. "I can't."

"Why not?"

"Because I can hardly stand to look at you, that's why." Tears fell, but she slapped them away. Laughing bitterly, she shook her head. "I should have known that something like this would happen," she confessed, repugnance in her tone. "This isn't the first time you've broken my heart or publicly humiliated me. You'd think by now I'd get it. You're just not the kind of man I can trust."

Stunned, her searing words reverberating in his mind, he listened to her say their relationship was over. "Kyra, I'm not going to let you go," he vowed, forcing her to look at him. "We've been through too much to give up now."

"You don't have a choice," she snapped. "I don't want you."

Terrence kept a cool head. She didn't mean it. Her words hurt, pierced, but he wasn't going to fall for her deception. Fear clogged his throat, and the thick, cloying taste was enough to make him sick, but he soldiered on. Nothing was going to ruin his future with Kyra. Not when he finally had her back, finally had her love. "There's no one in this world I want more than you. I love you and I know you love me."

"Of course you love me. You have no one else." She wore a joyless smile. "Now that all the groupies are gone and your endorsements have fallen through, you're anxious to settle down, aren't you, Terrence?"

"It's not like that. That's not what this is about."

"Yes, it is. Your star is fading fast, and you figured you'd come down to Hollington and hook up with good ole Kyra," she surmised. "But I'd rather be single for the rest of my life than end up loving another lying, cheating man."

"Kyra, I never cheated on you. Why don't you believe me?"

"Because you're a liar, that's why. And I can't trust anything you say."

Terrence shoved the ring box into his pocket. Coming here had been a mistake. He didn't need Kyra— the one person he thought he could trust—turning her back on him when he needed her most. All of the other women in his past had bailed, so why did he think she'd be any different? *Because Kyra doesn't care if you have millions in the bank,* a voice protested. *She'd love you if you were living in a FEMA trailer.*

"Please leave." Stepping past him, she jabbed her key into the lock. Without looking back, she issued a stern warning. "Stay away from the college or you'll be escorted off the grounds by campus security. The last thing the school needs is any more bad press. I'm sure you understand. I mean, this isn't your first public scandal, is it?"

Terrence started to speak, but the door slammed in his face, stealing his words.

Chapter 23

Sweat trickled down Kyra's back. She was burning up in her wool sweater and jeans, but she hadn't planned on walking to her parents' house. Scowling, she glanced back down the street at her car. Kyra was going to go up both sides of Allan Walker when she went back to his garage tomorrow. It hadn't even been a week since he'd changed the ignition module thingamajig and now her car had overheated again. Left with no other options, she'd put on the hazard lights, locked the doors and set out.

The traffic light turned green, but the driver of the shiny yellow convertible stopped to let her cross. Terrence. His name fell into her thoughts like a gentle sprinkling of rain. *It had only been a week since they broke up, so why did it feel as if she hadn't seen him in six months?*

The fallout from the paternity scandal had built an irrevocable wedge between them that could never be mended. There was a hole in her heart, and every time someone said his name, knots formed in her stomach.

Sadness penetrated her soul. And as her childhood home came into view, Kyra was reminded of the last time she'd raced down this road, clutching her mother's hand, fighting back sobs. To ward off the memories, she closed her eyes, allowing the sun's gentle rays to shower her with warmth and tranquility.

Kyra rang the doorbell and the door swung open. Her mother's round face broke into a bright smile. "Hi, sweet pea," Mrs. Dixon greeted, hugging her. "What brings you by? I thought you had plans with your girlfriends tonight."

"My car broke down on 18th Street. I called you twice, but there was no answer."

"Sorry, I had the blender on," she said. "Come in. I just started dinner."

Inside the kitchen, cooking utensils covered the granite countertop and the scent of sautéed mushrooms filled the air. Kyra washed her hands, put on an apron and started slicing the onions. Sunlight trickled in through the blinds and a light breeze flowed in through the screen door.

"How is everything at work?" Mrs. Dixon asked, sliding the turkey casserole into the oven. "When you didn't come by for dinner, I figured you probably had to work late."

Kyra nodded. "It's been a crazy week, but everything's coming together nicely for the Winter Wonderland Ball."

"And Terrence?"

Surprised by the question, she furrowed her eyebrows, frowning openly at her mom. "What about him?"

"Have you two kids talked since he returned to Dallas?"

Kyra shook her head.

"Do you want to talk about it, sweet pea?" Mrs. Dixon cleaned her hands on a dish towel. "It's no good keeping things bottled up inside. Resentment's bad for the heart."

"There's really nothing to talk about, Ma. Things just didn't work out."

"But," she protested, "Terrence was ready to marry you!"

"Who told you that?"

"He did, when he came by last Sunday and asked us for your hand in marriage."

The knife fell from Kyra's hand. So, Terrence *had* been telling the truth. Recovering quickly, she said, "It doesn't matter anyways. I never would have married him. Marriage is a commitment I'm not sure I'll ever be able to make."

Mrs. Dixon gasped. "How can you just up and decide marriage isn't right for you? Your father and I have been happily married for more than thirty years and—"

"I know all about Dad's affair," she said, interrupting. "Why did you stay, Mom?"

Mrs. Dixon's head jerked back. Her mouth fell open, but as if suddenly voiceless, nothing came out. Feeling her way to the table, she sank down onto one of the chairs and lowered her head in her hands. Rose never would've imagined that her daughter would remember that fateful afternoon in June. But she did. And not only did Kyra remember, she wanted to talk about it.

To heal, she'd placed that unforgettable day in the furthest corner of her mind. It was as if it had never happened. But it had. And like a recurring dream, it was rearing its ugly head.

Desperate for answers, Kyra joined her at the table and took her mom back to the day that had changed her life forever. "I remember us running from the house. I was too young to understand what was going on, but I heard you and Aunt Bridgett talking in the bedroom that night and put two and two together."

"To understand what happened, Kyra, we have to go back to the very beginning."

She'd expected her mom to play dumb and was relieved that she didn't. Kyra's eyes swept over her mother's face, and her lips softened into a smile. If she looked half as good as her mom did at fifty-eight, she'd have no complaints.

"I knew I was going to be Mrs. Lawrence Dixon the moment I met your father," Mrs. Dixon said whimsically. "*God,* how I loved that man. We'd go for long, romantic walks along the pier and make love for hours."

Kyra coughed. She hadn't expected her mother to go *there.* And as much as she appreciated her mother's candor, she didn't want to hear everything. "Spare me the details, Mom. I don't want to hear about your sex life."

"Why is it so hard to believe that your father and I were once madly in love?"

Feeling guilty, she tried to soothe her mother's obviously bruised feelings. "It's just hard to picture you and Daddy... you know."

"Well, believe it. We were in love just as much as you and Terrence, probably even more." Smiling softly, she reached out and cupped Kyra's chin. "I couldn't have asked for a better life, and then we had the prettiest little daughter."

After an extended pause, Mrs. Dixon cleared her throat and continued.

"Things were great, until Deacon Hewitt left the church and took more than half the members with him. I had to get a job at Kroger's grocery store and I think it devastated your father's pride that he couldn't support us. The bills started piling up, and finally out of desperation, he took a part-time position at an auto body shop. But just when we were getting back on our feet, we were pregnant again with your brothers."

"Is that why Daddy cheated? Because he felt like he was less of a man?"

Head bent, she raked her fingers through her short, dark hair. "Cicely was the secretary over at Motor Mechanics. She made time for your dad and gave him gifts. He was flattered. Any man would be."

A question Kyra had never considered before rose in her thoughts. "Did this Cicely woman know Daddy had us?"

Anger flashed in her mother's eyes. "Some women just don't care, sweet pea."

"What happened when you and Aunt Bridgett returned to the house?"

"Luckily for your father, we busted in there before anything more happened than what I saw. I almost ripped him apart with my bare hands—and Miss Home Wrecker, too. What hurt the most was that he'd brought that…that woman into our home."

"Is that why we moved into this house?"

Mrs. Dixon nodded. "I told your father to find us another place or kiss us goodbye. I wasn't going to step one foot into that house again. For weeks I thought of filing for divorce, but I just couldn't do it. I didn't want to—"

"Take us away from Daddy, right?" Kyra interjected, her voice an anguished whisper. "You stayed so that we could have a better life and that's always bothered me, Mom. You deserve to be happy, too."

"I *am* happy, sweet pea. I've lived a truly wonderful life." Rose patted her daughter's hand. "And my decision to remain married to your father was never anything that noble. I stayed with Lawrence because I couldn't imagine living without him. He's the only man for me, and I truly believe we're soul mates."

The news was stunning. Her mom hadn't stayed to keep the family together; she'd been a woman desperately and hopelessly in love. *Just like me.* A mental snapshot of Terrence rose in Kyra's mind, but she pushed the image away. "How long did the affair last? Did Dad love her? Was she—"

"If you dig around in the past, you're bound to find skeletons," warned Mrs. Dixon. "Let it go, sweet pea. It's over. And this might be hard for you to hear, but I'm a better wife and mother because of what happened that day. I don't take your dad or anyone else I love for granted anymore."

"But—"

"Lawrence and I grew up in an era where marriage meant something, not like today where people get divorced over nothing," she explained. "Your father swore it wouldn't happen again and I've never once regretted my decision to take him back."

"Do you still love Dad?"

"Of course, I do, sweet pea! Why would you ask me something like that?"

Kyra shrugged. "Well, earlier you made it sound like things had changed."

"The passion may not be as intense as it used to be, but the love has always remained. What we have is rare and I'm grateful I didn't allow your father's lapse in judgment to ruin the good thing we had." Deep worry lines wrinkled her smooth, brown skin. "Sweet pea, your father loves you and he'd do anything for you, including refinancing the house so you wouldn't have to quit school."

Her eyes widened. "Dad was the one who put that money into my account?"

"We were hurt that you didn't come to us, but once your Aunt Bridgett told us you were dropping out of school, we knew we had to do something." Rose smoothed a hand over her daughter's cheeks. "It doesn't matter how old you get, Kyra, you'll always be your father's little girl. And there's no one he loves more than you."

After a prolonged silence, Kyra said, "Mom, can we keep this between us? I don't want Dad to know about this."

"It'll be our little secret." Her mother patted her hand and stood. "I'm going to go finish dinner. But if you were wondering, your father is in his study."

Emotionally drained, Kyra slumped back onto her chair, her mind spinning out of control. She'd resented her father for a mistake he'd made twenty years ago, but if not for his sacrifice, she never would've graduated from Hollington.

Her stomach lurched when she stood up. Exiting the

kitchen, she pushed out a deep, soothing breath. Apologizing to her dad was going to be the hardest thing she'd ever had to do, but it was time. Time to put the past behind her once and for all.

Kyra paused outside of her dad's study and took a moment to collect herself. She didn't want to have to face her father, but she owed him an apology—for living in the past, for resenting him and, most importantly, for withholding her love.

While she was gathering her nerve, the door swung open and her dad stepped out into the hall. "Hi, honey, when did you get here?"

Overcome with emotion, Kyra felt her eyes water and her mouth go dry.

"What's the matter? Is this about Terrence?"

"No, Dad, it's about you and me…" she stumbled over the words. Kyra squeezed her eyes shut, fighting valiantly against the tears threatening to overtake her. But the pain she'd been holding inside for the past twenty years finally broke free and she sobbed in her father's arms. "I've been horrible to you, Dad, and you don't deserve it. I'm so sorry."

"Ah, honey, you could never be horrible to me," he insisted, hugging her. "We love each other too much, right, honey?"

Kyra didn't think she'd ever stop crying and when her dad kissed her on the forehead and called her his little girl, she cried even harder.

Chapter 24

"We'll rescind the offer in writing through Mr. Franklin's attorney. All in favor?"

The climate in the room changed when Kyra stepped inside. The stunned expressions on the faces of the six men and women seated around the glass table made a laugh bubble in her throat, but there was nothing funny about this clandestine meeting. If not for the conversation she'd overheard in the faculty dining room, Kyra wouldn't have known the board of directors was in the building. "As PR director of this school for the last seven years, I think I have earned the right to speak on this matter."

Mr. Morrow furrowed his brows and the lines around his mouth tightened. "That's not necessary, Ms. Dixon. This no longer concerns you."

"Terrence Franklin is just another rich, irresponsible athlete with no morals," insisted Chairman Wagner. "It's imperative that we distance ourselves from this man and his troubles *immediately*."

Treasurer Browne addressed Kyra. "You took up with Mr. Franklin months ago, so I'm not surprised you're judgment is skewed. Why don't you go back to your office and iron out the details for the Winter Wonderland Ball, so we can conclude this meeting?"

Angered, she readied herself for a fight. If she was going to save Terrence's job, she had to take drastic action. Producing a smile as fake as the man's knockoff designer luxury watch, she very calmly said, "If you rescind the coaching offer to Terrence Franklin, there'll be no Winter Wonderland Ball. At least not with Justice Kane as the celebrity guest."

Eyes bugged, heads swiveled and lips parted mutely.

"I'll resign from my position and take my celebrity contacts with me." Kyra was bluffing, but she saw the look of fear that spread across her boss's face. Justice Kane had already agreed to perform and although Kyra was angry at Mr. Morrow for calling this secret meeting, she'd never do anything to embarrass her alma mater.

"Calm down," admonished Treasurer Browne. "There's no need to make threats."

The wind tapped against the windows, momentarily drawing her gaze away from the older man's face. "My opinion has little to do with my relationship with Mr. Franklin. If another Hollington alum was in this predicament, I'd fight for them to keep their job, too. I'm doing this because it's the right thing to do."

Her boss gave a twitch of his moustache and smoothed out the curved ends. Like a game of pinball, his eyes jumped back and forth between the board of directors. "You've certainly given us something to think about, Miss Dixon, but I'm sorry. We simply cannot allow Mr. Franklin to coach the team. What kind of message would we be sending the players if we did?"

"Did you ever pledge a fraternity, Mr. Morrow?" Kyra asked.

He scratched his cheek. "No, I was too busy with my studies."

"Well, I'm Pi Beta Gamma and the sorority is built on three basic principles. Labor, love and loyalty. We don't turn our backs on our sisters or our fellow man. It doesn't matter how far they fall, we're there to pick them up."

"What do you expect us to do? Ignore his long, felonious past?" Mrs. Littleton huffed. "I've been reading the papers and watching the news, and Terrence Franklin is not the kind of man who should be coaching our kids."

Dean Rudolph disagreed. "Who better to show our boys what not to do than a former NFL great? Six months ago, when we met to discuss hiring Terrence Franklin, you all could barely contain your excitement." Dean Rudolph fixed his stare on Treasurer Browne. "You said Terrence was a living legend who you'd be honored to have coach the Hollington Lions."

Kyra almost threw her arms around Dean Rudolph. She was still outnumbered, but it felt good knowing there was at least one person in the conference room on her side. "I'm going to leave you to your vote, but if you rescind your offer to Terrence, expect my resignation tomorrow." Kyra turned to leave, but her boss called out to her.

"Wait. I have something that I'm sure will change your mind." President Morrow flipped open his leather-bound case, and took out three sheets of paper. Pointing at them, he said, "This is your new five-year contract, Kyra. You can expect an eight-percent raise, an extra week of paid vacation, and your own personal secretary." Smiling smugly, he leaned back in his chair. "Now, tell me. Do you still feel the same way?"

Kyra's deepest desire was to be the managing director of the department, and this new contract would bring her one step closer to her dream. "Yes, sir. I do."

Adamant that she would not support their decision, she asked the board of directors to be sympathetic toward the ex-NFL running back and thanked them for their time. Heart beating out of control, she crossed the room on unsteady legs. Stepping out into the hall, she slumped against the wall and released the breath she'd been holding.

"You drive a hard bargain, Miss Dixon."

Kyra whipped around, and her eyes widened in surprise. "Terrence? Oh, my God, what are you doing here?"

"We have some unfinished business to discuss," he answered, stepping forward. Casually dressed in a chocolate-brown sweater and jeans, he looked relaxed and undeniably handsome. "Let's get out of here."

They strolled down the hall in silence, but Kyra was intimately aware of his presence, as she'd been that morning of their first meeting. When they reached her office, she quickly grabbed her things and flipped off the lights. Within seconds, they were walking out of the administrative building.

The fields that skimmed the dormitories were neatly

trimmed, and the grounds were clean. Students hung out in the center square, and faculty members strode toward the parking lot. Kyra could feel the sharp bite of winter in the evening breeze and pulled her scarf tight around her.

"This is where it all started, remember?"

"Every time I passed the quad or ate in the cafeteria, I thought about you," she confessed. "I couldn't help wondering what could have been."

He raised his eyebrows. "And all this time I thought you just wanted me for my body!"

His joke broke the tension and lightened the mood.

"Kyra, I really appreciate you fighting for my job, but that's not why I'm here. I made a decision about my future long before news of the paternity scandal broke."

"You did? What did you decide?"

"I'll tell you all in good time, but first, we need to talk about what happened the night I came to see you."

Staring up at him, her hands quivering slightly, she slowly blew the air out of her lungs. "Terrence, I owe you an apology," she began. "You told me the truth and I didn't believe you. But I want you to know it wasn't you. It was me. I was battling demons from my past and projected my fears and insecurities onto you."

He looked disappointed. "That's it? That's all you got? No hug, no kiss, no weepy declarations about me being your one true love?"

Kyra smiled despite herself. "Can you be serious for a minute?"

The corner of his lips twitched, and she knew he wanted to laugh.

"I should've believed what you told me about Lourdes. I couldn't see the truth, even though it was staring me in the face. You were right, Terrence. Everything the media reported was a bunch of lies."

"Not all of them," he said, with a soft chuckle. "I am still one of the best running backs to ever play football!"

"Humility never was one of your strong points," she quipped, giggling.

A thoughtful expression came over his face. For a long moment, neither one of them spoke. "I talked with your dad. He told me how some of the mistakes he made deeply affected you. I wish you would have shared your feelings with me, but at the same time, I understand why you didn't."

"I'm so angry at myself for the way I've treated my dad. I've scrutinized everything he's ever said and did, because I was convinced that he was still cheating on my mom, but he wasn't." Head lowered, she rubbed her hands over her face. Kyra struggled to break free of her thoughts, but her doubts persisted. Without warning, the truth tumbled out of her mouth. "I've always been afraid that the man I loved would end up doing what my dad did to my mom."

"I'd never, ever cheat on you. You know that, right?" She nodded, but he cupped her chin to focus her gaze. His voice was passionate, his eyes ablaze. "Have I ever given you reason to believe that I wouldn't be a hundred percent committed to you?"

"No, but sometimes I feel a little insecure."

"Ky, no one in this world can ever take your place and nothing's going to go wrong as long as we have each other." Terrence reached into his pocket and unfolded a single sheet of paper. "I wasn't going to say anything until I got the official report, but I'm not the father of Lourdes' baby."

"Terrence, I don't need to see that. I believe you," she said softly. "And it didn't matter how things turned out. I was going to call you and apologize. What we have is special, and definitely worth fighting for."

They wore the same goofy smile.

"Your dad said you're taking the family on a cruise Thanksgiving weekend." Taking her hand, he twined his fingers with hers, gently caressing her flesh. "I came back to see you, but you're leaving for three days."

"I've wasted a lot of time being angry at my dad and I want to make it up to him," she explained, relishing the feel of his soothing touch. "We're going to sail the seas, eat some good food and do the limbo in Jamaica, mon!"

"Do you have room on this trip for one more?"

Masking a smile, she shook her head. "Nope, sorry, all the seats are fully booked. There's nothing I can do."

"Not even for your new fiancé?"

Kyra squealed. Eyes wide with glee, she jumped into his open arms. Feelings of unspeakable delight filled her as Terrence clasped her hand, tugged off her leather glove and slipped an enormous white solitaire diamond onto her finger. "Oh, my God, Terrence, it's beautiful!" she shouted excitedly. "Yes! Yes! Of course, I'll marry you!"

"Can you let me propose before you say yes?" Terrence chuckled when Kyra giggled and swatted him playfully in the arm. "What? I memorized my speech and I'd hate for it to go to waste. I don't want to brag, Ky, but it's one of my best."

"Just shut up and kiss me!" she quipped, throwing her arms around him. Kyra pressed her lips against his and used her mouth to express just how much she loved him. She felt his hands on her neck, gently stroking her skin, then around her waist. His fragrant scent settled over her, reminding her of all the times they'd talked and laughed as they strolled around the Hollington campus. "I know the perfect place for us to get married," she whispered, gazing at the student union building.

"It'll be perfect as long as we're together." Terrence palmed her cheeks and she nuzzled her face against his hand. "Ky, there isn't a thought I have that doesn't include you. Wear this ring as a sign of my love, my loyalty and my commitment. You're the only woman I desire, and I can't wait for us to build a life together. It's what I've dreamed of all these years."

Kyra felt like whooping for joy. She was so happy she wanted to dance in the middle of the street. "I insulted my boss and all but lost my job, but none of it matters, Terrence, because I have you."

He wore a rueful grin. "You always were a little firecracker," he teased, gathering her to his chest. "What am I going to do with you?"

"Just love me unconditionally. That's all I ask. Baby, I love you more than anything in this world and I promise to make you the happiest man alive."

"Great," he rasped, nibbling on her earlobe. "You can start tonight, Mrs. Franklin. How do you feel about spending the rest of the weekend at a nice hotel?" Winking, he added slyly, "We can practice for the honeymoon!"

Kyra reached up and kissed the man of her dreams with all the passion flowing through her. As they kissed, her heart inflated with joy and tears spilled down her cheeks.

"What do you say we get out of here and go share the good news with your parents?"

They stood, wrapped tightly in each other's arms, wearing matching smiles. Their friendship had withstood the test of time and as they strolled past "the quad" Kyra knew their love would last forever.

* * * * *

TENDER TO HIS TOUCH
Adrianne Byrd

This book is dedicated to: Sandra Kitt,
Jacquelin Thomas and Pamela Yaye.
It was a pleasure working with you talented ladies

Prologue

Beverly Clark's eyes were wide open when her alarm clock blared at five-thirty. She flung out an arm and shut off its loud and annoying buzz. However, she didn't climb out of bed. Instead she remained nestled in her white cotton sheets, staring up at her popcorn ceiling.

She hated that damn ceiling.

It reminded her of cottage cheese or, worse, something she used to study under a microscope in her old science lab class eons ago. One of these days she was going to take Spackle or a chisel to the damn thing and scrape that junk off. Beverly huffed, rolled over onto her side and stared at the clock. Its loud ticking sounded as if it had been hooked up to an amplifier. In no time her heart and the muscles along her temples thumped in precise harmony.

Maybe she should just stay in bed today.

Why not? What difference would it make? It wasn't as if anybody cared—or that she had anything to do.

The numbers on the clock blurred and in the next second warm tears slid from her eyes, rolled down her nose, then dripped quietly onto her pillowcase. She pulled in a deep breath, but her lungs felt as if they were trying to resist being revived. Her shoulders trembled and before long her entire body followed suit. It was five forty-five in the morning and she was crying.

A whole fifteen minutes ahead of schedule.

Reluctantly Beverly peeled the sheets back and pulled herself up. Those two simple acts nearly zapped all her energy. From across the room, she caught sight of herself in the full-length mirror and was repulsed by what she saw.

"Oh, God." She raised a hand to her sunken face while her fingers traced the deep lines below her bloodshot eyes. Her full lips looked bee-stung and cracked, and her hair...well, let's just say that it would probably be easier to cut it than comb it. Her hands fell from her face and slapped against her lap. "Look at what's become of me."

Being the daughter of two prominent doctors, Beverly had grown up in an affluent and privileged life. Friends and family had told her throughout the years that she'd been lucky to have inherited her mother's honey-brown complexion and liquid-gold eyes. In her youth, the combination had made her popular with the opposite sex and garnered more than a few sniping remarks from girls who'd assumed she was stuck-up. Those opinions usually changed, though, once people got to know her.

Beauty and charm helped land her the Miss Georgia Teen crown at sixteen and the Miss Georgia crown at eighteen. Plus she was also homecoming queen in both high school and in college. She was smart, too— at least she liked to think she was. She had managed to graduate in the top of her class and at one time had given serious thought to following her parents' example and enrolling in medical school. But after an art teacher pointed out she had a natural flair for fashion, Beverly started spending hours upon hours daydreaming that one day her fashions would be worn on red carpets around the world.

But love intervened and she ended up marrying her old high-school sweetheart, David Clark, right after college despite the protests of her parents. It didn't matter at the time. Surely her parents could grow to love her husband.

David had been a year older and, once upon a time, more mature. They had been so careful planning out their lives. He'd continued his schooling and become a dentist. It turned out to be a great decision. His career had afforded them a great life in the suburbs, but three years ago it all came crashing to an end.

More tears leaked from Beverly's eyes.

From a distance, a car turned into the driveway. She turned her head toward the open window and listened to the smooth rumble of a Mercedes engine as it coasted toward the house. Beverly wiped her face and reached for her satin robe draped over the foot of her bed.

Beneath the window, the engine shut off, the car door opened and then slammed shut. The familiar footfalls of expensive Ferragamo loafers slapped against the pavement and then up the front porch. Beverly stood when she heard keys rattle in the front-door lock.

Inside the house, the heavy footsteps continued through the foyer and then up the staircase. Beverly tried to mentally prepare herself for her daily battle, but on this day she found that she simply couldn't. She just didn't have anything left.

The knob turned and the bedroom door crept open. David poked his head inside, his attention on the empty bed.

"Glad to see that you found your way home," Beverly said, her wintry voice chilling the room. "And here I thought buying that GPS unit was a complete waste of money."

Unable to hide his disappointment, David released a long, frustrated sigh. "I thought you'd still be asleep."

"I haven't slept in years."

He rolled his eyes and pulled his wrinkled tie from around his neck. "Maybe that's your problem." David headed toward the adjoining bathroom.

"My problem?" she said, her eyes narrowing on his retreating back. Beverly followed. "Maybe *my problem* is that my *husband* is out screwing his office manager at all hours of the night while I'm stuck in this suburban prison cooking dinners for one."

"There you go again. No one's screwing around," he said. "And I'm not stopping you from getting out of the house. That's your choice. In fact, I wish you would get out. Maybe the neighbors would stop looking at me as if I've chained you up in the basement or something." He turned on the shower.

"No one's screwing around," she thundered incredulously.

"Do I look stupid to you?" she hissed. "It is six o'clock in the morning. Nearly twelve hours since the office closed *yesterday.* Are you going to tell me that you had some dental emergency that kept you at the office and strategically away from a phone all this time?"

His eyes rolled again as he unbuttoned and then slid out of his pants. "I went out for a few drinks with the guys. I crashed over at Curtis's place."

David finally stopped and looked at her. Guilt was etched in every inch of his handsome face. The same face that she'd once vowed to love for the rest of her life. She now longed to rake her nails down its gorgeous perfection. Why did it seem as if the nightmare of the last three years had not scared him the way it had her? Why was it so easy for him to just move on? If they were truly soul mates why weren't they living in the same hell?

"What?" David asked defensively.

"If you're going to be a playa, then learn to get your lies straight."

"I told you—"

"Curtis called here last night looking for you. He wanted to know whether you two were still going fishing today."

Thick clouds of steam billowed from the shower, then swirled around the fractured husband and wife. The battle of their heated gazes raged on for a few heartbreaking seconds and then finally, resignation flickered across David's face. He'd been busted and his brain failed to come up with a plausible lie.

"Just admit it," she urged in a thin whisper. She half convinced herself that she would feel better if he'd just confess that he'd been having an affair. Confess that the perfume clinging to his clothes right now wasn't just her imagination.

"Beverly—"

"Say it," she choked out.

"Bev—"

"Goddamn it, *say it!*" She snatched a curling iron from the vanity counter and hurled it at him. The bastard ducked and the curling iron slammed against the glass shower stall. It hit a weak spot and the whole thing shattered as if she had unloaded an AK-47 at it.

David leaped away from the shower as shards of glass launched toward him. "All right! All right! I'm having an affair. Are you happy now?" he roared.

Beverly sucked in a breath and stepped back as if he'd punched her. Her mind reeled. She couldn't decide if she wanted to hit him, scratch him or kick him in the balls.

As he realized what he had said, regret blanketed David's face. He reached for her. "Beverly, I—"

"Don't touch me." She pulled away. "I want you out. Out of this house and out of my life!"

"Look, Beverly. I didn't mean to—"

"It's over." She took another huge step back, shaking her head. "I want a divorce," she said evenly.

He wouldn't give up. "We've been through a lot," he reminded her. "We can get through this."

"No, we can't," she contradicted. "We can't…because I don't love you anymore."

Chapter 1

Two years later

A jacketless and tieless Lucius Gray was nearing his tenth hour poring over documents and case files. He kept telling himself that he'd quit for the day—or rather, night—every ten minutes, but his determination to know this wrongful death case backward and forward prevented him from leaving. He wanted all his ducks in a row so he could squeeze Dr. E. J. Stewart and his insurance company into settling the case for a mid-eight-figure settlement.

It wasn't one of his biggest litigation cases, but this particular case hit him hard. The similarities between Mr. Keith Johnson's death and Lucius's father's were just too striking. Dr. Stewart, a cardiologist, kept finding nothing wrong with Mr. Johnson a year after he had a stint implanted and recommended he see an oncologist for his illness. Of course the oncologist found nothing wrong with him and kept referring him back to his cardiologist. All the while, Mr. Johnson's condition grew worse and worse. When he finally passed away, the autopsy showed that he had a lot of blockages in his arteries and his poor heart just gave out. There were so many of them that it was just unexplainable how Dr. Stewart had missed the obvious.

What did it say about the state of the health-care system when doctors were just too busy to do their jobs?

The phone chirped.

Lucius glanced up, annoyed to have had his concentration broken. He punched the speakerphone button. "Yeah?"

"Mr. Gray, I have your wife on line one."

He frowned. "You mean my *ex*-wife, don't you, Maggie?"

"I'm just repeating what *she* said."

Lucius drew a deep breath and pitched back into his chair. Until that moment, he hadn't noticed how hungry he was or how tight his neck muscles had become.

"Mr. Gray?"

"Put her through," he said and expelled a tired breath. In the next second the phone rang and he picked up. "What can I do for you, Erica?"

"You haven't been able to do anything for me in a looooonnng time," she answered in her usual sarcastic tone.

He rolled his eyes. "I really don't have time to fight with you right now. So—"

"I know. I know," Erica huffed. "You're working on a really important case. The story of our marriage."

"So you kept reminding me through the divorce." Lucius's office door crept open and he looked up in time to see Maggie poke her head inside. He didn't miss the tired lines beneath her eyes or how her morning curls had wilted on her head. "Erica, hold on for a moment." He hit the phone's mute button without waiting for his ex-wife's permission.

"I'm getting ready to head out," Maggie said. "Is there anything else you need?"

Lucius glanced at his watch. It was well past seven o'clock. "No. I'm good. Have a good night. I'll see you in the morning."

Maggie nodded and then disappeared back behind the door.

Lucius drew a deep breath and hit the mute button again. "I'm back."

"I can't bring Ruby this weekend. It'll have to be next weekend."

Lucius's grip tightened on the phone. In the five years since his divorce, he and Erica kept playing the same game with their now eight-year-old daughter—the emotional blackmail game. And now that Erica had a new man, Andrew, in her life, she seemed steadfastly determined to have this jerk take Lucius's place. "You said that *last* weekend, Erica."

"It was true last weekend, too," Erica snorted. "And don't act like you're so disappointed."

"I made plans," he said, though it wasn't exactly true. He'd planned to wing it. Maybe take Ruby to Chuck E. Cheese or a movie or something.

"Please." He could practically see Erica rolling her eyes. "Buying her a bunch of junk food and dragging her to your office isn't exactly a trip to Disney World."

Great. She played a guilt card. "It was just that one time."

"Uh-huh," she said dubiously. "Like I said, I can't bring her this weekend. Andrew wants to take Ruby up to Boston."

"Boston?" Lucius barked, irritated. "What the hell is in Boston?"

"Andrew is from Boston…and we're going up to meet his family."

Silence.

"Lucius?"

"So…what? This *relationship* is getting serious?" He was surprised by his annoyance.

"Maybe," she hedged, her tone finally softening.

Lucius closed his eyes and then rubbed the tension from his forehead. It wasn't that he still harbored romantic feelings toward his ex-wife. It was more that the threat of him being replaced in Ruby's life with another man was becoming a reality at a pace that made him more than uncomfortable. "C'mon, Erica. How long have you known this guy? Two months—three?"

"A year," she corrected him.

Had a year passed that quickly?

"Of course, if you ever pulled your head out from your…work, you'd see that life was passing you by."

Lucius heaved another frustrated sigh. "Can we not fight tonight? I have a headache."

"Fine."

The line fell silent, but the tension remained. Finally he said, "I don't know if I like this."

Erica chuckled. "Don't tell me that I've finally done something to catch your attention."

"Is that what this is all about—getting my attention?"

Her laugh deepened. "Please. I've stopped trying to do that a long time ago. You made it perfectly clear that your work is all that matters to you."

"That's not true."

"It feels true." Another awkward silence drifted over the line. "I'll bring Ruby next weekend," she said and then disconnected the line.

Lucius held the phone until the automated voice came on and instructed him on how to make a call. "That went well," he mumbled under his breath. He settled back in his chair, replaying the call in his head and wishing he had handled the situation better. But what had been obvious for many years now was, point-blank, he and Erica just rubbed each other the wrong way.

His gaze fell on a framed photograph of his precocious daughter, Ruby. He struggled to remember exactly how old she was in the picture—maybe four or five. It was an adorable picture of her with her thick black hair parted into two fat ponytails. On the day of the picture, she was so proud to show off the loss of her two front teeth. Her big quarter-size hazel eyes danced with excitement at the possibility of seeing the Tooth Fairy.

Lucius reached over his desk and picked up the photograph. Instantly, his irritation and annoyance at Erica melted away and a broad smile broke across his face. Ruby was a perfect amalgam of him and Erica. She had his warm brown complexion and hazel eyes and Erica's button nose and full lips. "Daddy's little girl," he whispered, feeling his chest swell with pride.

Ruby Elizabeth Gray was the absolute joy of his life—despite what her mother thought. Sure, he had been thrown out of his element from time to time by tea parties with imaginary guests or playing baby dolls with dolls that actually did number one *and* number two. However, most of that came from the fact Lucius grew up in a family dominated by men.

It had been a real shock to him when the doctor told him and Erica that they were going to have a girl. He didn't know what to do with a girl. Up until that ultrasound, he had envisioned mock football and basketball games with *Junior*. Instead he got a little girl that stole his heart like no other. And he was a better man for it.

Lucius slowly rocked his neck from side to side, but his tense muscles refused to relax and his empty stomach rumbled in protest. Sighing with regret, he knew that it was finally time to call it a night. Propelling out of his chair, he quickly stuffed the case files into his briefcase, slid on his office jacket and crammed his tie into his pocket.

As he exited the building of Kendall, Hendrix and Gray, LLC, he contemplated which fast-food drive-through he was in the mood for. Once behind the wheel of his black Cadillac SRX Crossover, he elected instead to finish off some leftovers he had back at the crib. He'd always been careful to take care of his body through regular exercise and a healthy diet, and there was no need to wreck all that for a greasy burger.

It was well past eight o'clock by the time he finally pulled into his large two-car garage. As usual when he headed toward the garage door that led into the kitchen, he tossed a longing look toward his old wood workshop. His *man* space, as Erica used to call it. How long had it been now since he'd lost himself in the hobby of building things—six years...seven?

He had always enjoyed working and making things with his hands. It had a way of relaxing him. However, with the influx of bank and credit fraud, his law firm had enjoyed a healthy spike in litigation and court cases. There just hadn't been any time to whittle the hours away in his workshop.

Soon, he promised himself. He'd make the time one day soon.

Lucius entered the house, flipped on the light switch, placed his briefcase on the counter and made a beeline toward the refrigerator. Thirty minutes later he was settled at the dinner table and casually sifting through the day's mail. He stopped when he came across the envelope from Hollington College.

His smile was instant. "Hollington." He chuckled, opening the envelope. "My old stomping grounds." Suddenly memories of football and frat parties filled his head, as well as the small string of college shawties he'd juggled while struggling to maintain his high GPA.

"'October homecoming weekend,'" he read. His eyes quickly scanned over the invitation card. "Tenth anniversary? Has it been that long already?" He shook his head. Where had all the time gone? Thinking about it, a lot had happened in ten years: marriage, law school, law practice, a baby, working like hell, making partner, working like hell, divorce, working like hell.

There was a theme in there somewhere.

"All work and no play make Lucius a dull man," he whispered. He glanced up and truly took stock of the empty dining-room chairs surrounding the table. Outside, the evening crickets played their songs while his expensively furnished house felt awfully cold... and lonely.

His gaze shifted back to the invitation. Maybe this

was exactly what he needed. A little time out with some old friends…and old girlfriends.

"Beverly, what do you mean you're not going to the reunion?" Kyra asked, her hands propped on her slender hips. "This is a big weekend for the university and I'm counting on you to be there."

"I don't see why," Beverly said, straightening a rack of embellished skirts. Her trendy, high-end boutique, Hoops, was on North Highland Avenue and a steady stream of twentysomethings flowed into the store and left carrying enormous white shopping bags with the dainty Hoops logo. The sparkly chandelier, golden cherubs and tasteful furniture lent a chic, intimate feel to the place. "Aside from you and a couple of other people, I haven't kept in touch with anyone from our graduating class."

"Beverly, you were homecoming queen and everyone's expecting you to be there."

"That's too bad, because I'm not going."

"Give me one good reason why you can't go."

"I'll give you three. For starters, I'm swamped here." Selecting a dazzling sheath from off the rack, she slipped it off the gold, padded hanger and held it up to one of the mannequins in the front window. "I'm putting together the final touches for my new spring line, and I have to design a gown for Gabrielle Union to wear to an awards gala next month."

"You seem stressed, Bev. Why don't you let me take you out for lunch?"

"So you can pressure me into going to the reunion?" Beverly shook her head. "No way. I don't have time for this right now. I'm up to my neck in paperwork and it's going to take me the rest of the afternoon to fill the online orders."

"Beverly, you've been dodging my calls for weeks and the reunion is less than a month away. I need to help finalize the rest of the plans for homecoming."

She said nothing, just continued dressing the mannequin and humming to the Smokey Robinson song playing in the background.

Kyra heaved a heavy sigh. "So, that's it? You're not going and there's nothing I can say or do to change your mind?"

Beverly gave a brisk nod, and then changed the subject. "I was at my favorite fabric store last week and it seemed the whole town was abuzz with the news of Terrence's big return."

"Yeah, his arrival has generated a lot of good press for the school. We've received hundreds of online applications, and we had so much traffic on the Web site yesterday, it crashed!"

"I bet," Beverly agreed. "After all, he is the pride of Hollington."

"I'm lining up as many interviews as I can. I even contacted my old sorority sister, Tamara Hodges, about doing an article on Terrence becoming the Lions' coach."

Her eyebrows rose. "You got him to sign on already?"

"Not yet, but I will."

Beverly started to speak, but her words were drowned out by a shrill, piercing laugh. Realizing they needed privacy, Kyra grabbed Beverly's hand and dragged her into the back office. While the boutique was bright and glitzy, the office was a simple, understated space teeming with fashion magazines, invoices and poster boards. "Now," Kyra began, closing the door and standing in front of it, "spill it. What's the real reason you won't go to the reunion?"

Beverly stood her ground. "You're not going to change my mind, so you might as well save your breath."

"The class of ninety-nine voted *you* homecoming queen, Beverly. How's it going to look if you don't show up?"

"Like I'm a popular fashion designer who has orders to fill." Straightening up, she folded her arms across her chest, her gaze drifting to the open window. "Kyra, I'm not trying to be difficult, but I've moved on from beauty pageants and modeling contests. I want to be taken as a serious businesswoman and that's not going to happen if I'm riding on top of a flowered float."

In an effort to keep the peace, Kyra listened to what she had to say without interrupting. Beverly was frowning, and she could tell by the faraway look in her eyes that her mind was somewhere else. "Why does it feel like you're blowing me off?"

"I'd never do that," Beverly insisted, shaking her head. "We're friends, remember?"

"Then can a sister get a discount on that gold Ferragamo gown?"

Beverly gave a brief sputter of laughter.

"Hanging out with old friends is just what you need. You've been divorced for almost two years, but you haven't been on a single date. I'm not telling you to go out there and party like Paris Hilton, but live a little, girl! Go to the reunion, and have a good time. And if you see someone who catches your eye…" Kyra trailed off, her glossy red lips curling into a mischievous smirk.

"There are going to be plenty of handsome, eligible brothers at the reunion, Bev. It would be a shame for you to miss out."

A smile broke through. "You must be very good at your job," she teased.

"I try," Kyra sang, laughing. Sensing a subtle shift in her friend's mood, and anxious to get her on board, she continued, "Homecoming weekend is your opportunity to shine. Do you know how much business you'll drum up for the boutique just by being there wearing one of your gorgeous, one-of-a-kind creations?"

"I never even thought of that. It would be great for business, wouldn't it?"

Kyra nodded. "How about I contact Tamara and ask her to do a piece in *Luster* about Hoops? It's free publicity and last year the magazine surpassed *Glamour* magazine in sales."

"I'll think about it."

"Oh, you're going, all right," Kyra vowed, lobbing an arm around Beverly's shoulders, "because I won't take no for an answer!"

That was exactly what Beverly was afraid of.

Chapter 2

"Girrrrl, you are going to get laid for sure in that dress." Clarence, Beverly's best friend and self-appointed relationship advisor, snapped his fingers and twirled her around so she could face the full-length mirror.

A cocky grin sloped across Beverly's face. She did look good. The red cocktail dress hugged her curvy body like an extra layer of skin and she debated whether she even needed the thin silver belt. What was even more surprising was how much she loved her new hairstyle.

Clarence swished his hips and smacked his clear, shimmering lips. "Do I know how to hook my girl up or what?"

Beverly happily agreed. The shorter, darker do made her golden eyes pop and easily erased the past ten years from her face. She might actually pull this off.

"Now remember, whatever booty you get, fifteen percent of it is mine."

Beverly howled and then bumped her hip against his. "What the hell am I going to do with you?"

"Love me, sweetheart. That's what they all do with me." He leaned forward and blew air kisses. Dressed in an immaculate pair of shiny denim jeans and a cloud-white shirt beneath a black merino sweater, Clarence was as sharp as any male model strutting down a Prada runway. On his youthful, effeminate face he wore the lightest touch of face powder and lip gloss.

"Well, I better go," Clarence said as he turned away from the mirror and marched out of the bathroom. "It's Friday night and you're not the only bitch trying to get laid."

Beverly laughed as she followed. "Thanks again, Clarence. I don't know what I would have done if you didn't come over."

"Uh-huh." Clarence glanced around the large hotel suite, specifically the huge king-size bed.

"Look, I'm just staying here at the hotel during homecoming weekend because it's a lot closer to Hollington College than my house. If I happened to have a few drinks, it's easier to catch a cab here than risk driving all the way back out to the suburbs."

Clarence wasn't buying it. "Whatever, chickie." He swished his hips as he retrieved his jacket. "You just make sure this big ol' bed doesn't go to waste this weekend. I've been telling you you needed to get your groove back for a while. I'm glad Kyra finally brought you around."

Beverly actually blushed. "I never said I was going to this homecoming to get laid."

"Uh-huh." Clarence popped his lips.

"I came to just have a good time and catch up with old friends." The lie even sounded weak to her.

Clarence rolled his eyes. "Girl, I know a freakum dress when I see it." He headed to the door. "Have a good time and I expect details when I come by Hoops next week."

Beverly chuckled and then added, "Thanks again for coming to my hair emergency. I was ready to pack up and go back home."

"Relax." Clarence reached over and squeezed her hand. "You're the homecoming queen. They're going to love you. And *if* that jerk of an ex-husband of yours does show up, give him a good swift kick in the balls for me."

Lucius was getting excited at the thought of returning to his old stomping grounds. Rumors had been circulating that both Terrence Franklin and Micah Ross would be swinging through the joint. He hoped to get a little face time with his old buddies and shoot the breeze. He had only one last business errand to run over at the downtown Hilton before he headed off to the college. Once he dropped off a few documents with one of his clients, he promised himself to turn off his BlackBerry and just enjoy his weekend.

Hell, he deserved it.

However, Atlanta's Friday bumper-to-bumper traffic delayed his plans for a carefree weekend. While surrounding cars engaged in an endless game of cutting each other off, honking and tossing a few middle fingers in the air, Lucius slipped in his old *The Miseducation of Lauryn Hill* CD. Ten years ago, his senior year in college, this disc stayed on repeat. His boys loved it and, more importantly, so did the ladies.

When his favorite jam, "Ex-Factor," came on, a broad smile carved across his lips as he bobbed his head. This was just what he needed to get in the '99 mood. An hour later, he finally arrived at the Hilton and met businessman Mitch Paulson in the hotel bar.

"Ah, right on time," Paulson said as he stood to shake Lucius's hand. "Can I get you a drink?" He waved and caught a waitress's attention.

Lucius glanced at his watch. "Actually, I—"

"Ah, c'mon." Paulson gestured for him to take a seat. "It's the least I can do after having you deliver those papers on such short notice."

Lucius hesitated, glanced at his watch. No way would he make it over to Cork for the school's private cocktail party on time. Then again, maybe it was better to show up fashionably late.

"Don't be rude, Lucius. Have a seat," Paulson insisted and then added a boisterous laugh. "You know businessmen don't like drinking alone."

Lucius relented with a chuckle. "Maybe just one drink."

Their waitress popped up the moment Lucius took his seat. "Whiskey on the rocks," he ordered.

"Make that two," Paulson corrected, giving the pixie blonde a flirtatious wink.

However, the waitress's blue gaze was busy assessing Lucius. She was cute, but Lucius would most likely always crave the touch and love of a curvy sistah. That was just how he rolled.

When the waitress saw that she wasn't getting any play, she drifted away from the table.

"Ah, well," Paulson huffed and reached inside his jacket and retrieved a cigar case. "I guess I'm losing my touch."

Or you shouldn't try to pick up someone young enough to be your granddaughter.

"Just as well, I suppose. It's not easy keeping up with these young girls," he said, laughing at his own joke. "I damn near threw my back out last year with an eighteen-year-old hell-bent on turning me into a pretzel."

Lucius laughed along, though he picked up on a few notes of sadness.

"Who knows? I probably should've stayed married," Paulson continued. "But…well, back when I was your age I was married to my job more than I was to Sheila."

This always happened when Lucius shared drinks with his male clients. Alcohol loosened tongues and Lucius found himself cast in the role of a pseudopsychiatrist.

"You married, Lucius?" Paulson asked just as their waitress returned with their drinks.

"Divorced."

"Hmmph." Paulson shook his head. "Big mistake."

"I don't know. It seemed to have worked out for the best."

"Sure you say that *now*. Let a few more years roll by." He took a sip of his drink. "Seeing anybody?"

Lucius shifted in his chair as he took a few sips of his whiskey. "Let's just say that I'm keeping my options open."

"How many hours are you putting in at the firm?"

"What is this, an interrogation?"

"Let me guess," Paulson went on, sizing him up. "You look like a workaholic. I'd say about 85 to 90?"

Their gazes locked.

"I'm right, aren't I?" Paulson flashed him a lopsided grin. "Tell me. Have you noticed how cold a house gets at night yet?"

Lucius didn't answer.

"Hmmph." Paulson shook his head. "Believe me. It gets a lot colder. Thing is, I don't ever remember it being that way when I was married. A house is meant to be a home." He leveled his gaze back on Lucius. "And man was never meant to be alone—that's the one passage I remember from the Bible."

Lucius quickly took another sip of his drink.

"A career is great, but a good woman is even better." Paulson scanned the room. "Are you a breast or leg man?"

"I, uh—"

"Aww. Maybe you like a woman with a little junk in the trunk?" He winked.

Lucius would never get used to old white men trying to talk hip. "Yeah. I guess you can say that I like it all."

Paulson's drink stopped midway to his lips. "Then it looks like you're in luck. Check out who just walked through the door."

Curious, Lucius turned around and nearly dropped his glass when his gaze zeroed in on a tall, gorgeous woman in red with deep brick-house curves and a smile that lit up the whole room. Spellbound, he watched her as she strolled over to the bar. Her big breasts sat high and were like—*pow!* Her firm, but still bouncing backside was like—*ka-pow!*

To maintain some semblance of cool, Lucius sipped a little more of his whiskey, but his eyes never left the seductive sway Paulson so elegantly called *junk in the trunk.*

"Better close your mouth and go make a move," Paulson chuckled. "I'd say you have about five seconds before someone else beats you to the punch."

Lucius tossed down the rest of his drink in one gulp and sprang out of his chair without a backward glance. Halfway over to the bar, he realized that he didn't have the slightest idea what to say. His pickup lines were a little rusty.

Across the room, he saw another brother stand up; his eyes locked on the same mysterious woman. Lucius picked up his pace and settled onto the empty stool beside the lady in red, whose soft floral perfume worked like an invisible hook. Before he could speak, she glanced over her shoulder and smiled.

"Hello," she greeted in a velvety smooth voice that dripped with sin.

Lucius responded with the first thing that popped into his head. "Marry me?"

Chapter 3

Beverly laughed. The question had been so unexpected that she couldn't do anything but. The handsome stranger next to her joined in. His intriguing hazel eyes were so bewitching her heart skipped a beat. She estimated him to be six-two, lean but well muscled. His medium-brown skin had a healthy glow, and he had short-cropped hair that was well-groomed. She fought the sudden impulse to run her fingers through it to see if it was as soft as it looked. Bottom line, he was a good-looking man with a smile that took her breath away.

"Okay. I admit that was a pretty cheesy pickup line," the handsome devil admitted.

"But very effective," she said, throwing him a bone. "Maybe I should be asking how many wives you have stashed away."

He held up his bare left hand. "I'm as free as a bird."

She arched a brow at him. Did he think a missing ring meant anything these days?

"I'm divorced."

"What a coincidence," she said.

"Now what idiot let *you* go?" he countered, shaking his head and hitting her with his sexy dimples.

"I know, right?"

They laughed.

"Mind if I buy you a drink?" he asked.

"Well, I don't—"

"C'mon. Just one."

The bartender popped up out of nowhere.

"What'll you have?" her handsome admirer asked.

"Whoooo, boy. It's, um, been a while." She hesitated, not knowing what to order. She was more of a wine connoisseur and didn't know any of the latest cool alcoholic concoctions so she stuck with an old staple. "I'll just have a Long Island iced tea."

"And I'll have another whiskey on the rocks," the stranger said and then turned his attention back to Beverly. "By the way, I'm Lucius Gray." He extended his hand.

"Beverly Clark—well, Turner, actually." She laughed at the slip. "I can't believe I still make that mistake."

When his large hand closed around hers, a delicious warmth raced up her arm, her nipples hardened and she tingled in places she'd long forgotten about. That was definitely a good sign.

"If you don't mind, I have a second cheesy line I'd like to ask you," Lucius said.

"All right." She smiled. "Shoot."

"What's a beautiful woman like you doing in a bar like this?"

"Well, I just wanted to grab a quick drink to help me relax before I head out for the evening."

His gaze roamed over her. "So you're staying at the hotel?"

The bartender returned. "One Long Island iced tea and one whiskey on the rocks. Enjoy."

Lucius waited patiently for an answer while Beverly took a sip of her drink.

"Mmmm. Now that hit the spot."

He chuckled, deciding to keep an obvious sexual retort to himself.

Beverly glanced over at him and read him easily. "Get your mind out of the gutter."

Lucius held up his hand. "I don't know what you're talking about."

"Yeah, right." She sipped more of her drink. "And to your previous question, I'm just staying at the hotel for the weekend. And yourself?"

"No, I actually, uh—" he glanced around "—had a meeting with a client, but it looks like that's already ended."

"I'm not keeping you from your work, am I?"

"No. No. It's all right." He flashed another smile. "We had already wrapped things up. When you strolled in and caught every brotha's attention in that knock-out dress."

"What—this old thing?"

Lucius laughed.

She bobbed her head and then returned to nursing her drink. "So what do you do, Mr. Gray?"

"I'm an attorney...and please, call me Lucius."

"Okay, Lucius," she said, purposely lowering her voice. "It sort of sounds like luscious."

Lucius's eyes darkened with unmistakable desire. "You can call me that if you like," he said, leaning in close. "But *only* when we're alone."

At the feel of his warm breath against her cheek, Beverly experienced a few more tingles. *Good Lord, one drink and she was ready to jump the man's bones.*

"Anyway," Lucius said, "I work for one of the largest African-American law firms in Atlanta. We primarily deal with big litigation cases. You know, health care, pharmaceuticals and insurance fraud."

"Ahh, an attorney," she said noncommittally.

"What? Don't tell me that you have something against lawyers?"

She shrugged. "No. It's just that…well…"

"What?"

"It's just that you might be the first attorney I actually like."

Lucius choked on his drink. When he recovered, he barked with laughter.

Beverly chuckled at his side. "No offense," she added. "But the last time I had to deal with attorneys I was going through a pretty messy divorce."

"No offense taken, I assure you. And to be completely honest with you, I wasn't too crazy about my divorce attorney, either. If you don't mind my asking, how long ago did you get your freedom papers?"

She shrugged. "Two years."

"Ah. So your wounds are still fresh."

Was he suggesting that she still had baggage? "What about you?"

Lucius took another sip of his drink. "Five years. I've officially been divorced longer than I was married. But I did get a beautiful daughter out of the deal."

Beverly's easy smile dimmed as she reached for her glass.

Lucius soaked in her profile. "Are you sure that we haven't met somewhere before?"

This time, she nearly choked on her drink. "Cheesy line number three," she said, dabbing her mouth with a cocktail napkin.

His laughter deepened as he shook his head. "Nah. Nah. I mean it. You look very familiar to me. Do you live here in Atlanta or did you fly in on business?"

"No. I live here in Atlanta," she said. Her face continued to warm beneath the intensity of his gaze. It didn't help that the alcohol from her drink felt as if it suddenly had a direct pipeline to her blood system. "Mmm." She closed her eyes and enjoyed the small buzz.

Lucius's body reacted to her sexy moan. "Damn. I should've had what you're having."

Beverly giggled—something she hadn't done in a long time.

"So what is it that *you* do, Ms. Turner?"

"I'm a fashion designer—local. I own a boutique out in Virginia Highland. Have you ever been out there?"

He thought hard and long about it. "Can't say that I have." His eyes narrowed. "But I swear you seem familiar. Maybe with lighter hair?"

Beverly blinked. "Actually, I recently darkened it."

He continued to scrutinize. "Was it longer, too?"

"Yes!" Now she tried to study him. Had they met before?

"I'm going to figure it out," he assured her. His eyes continued to roam hungrily.

He wanted to taste a sample of her lips, not doubting for a moment that they would be sweet, intoxicating and

downright addictive. He had a nearly uncontrollable desire to bury himself in the soft curves of her body. Good
Lord, he was already thinking about her this way after
just talking to her for a few minutes. How long had it
been since he'd been with a woman? He frowned, trying
to come up with an answer. Ten months. Eleven months.
A year? Surely, it couldn't have been that long—had it?

He reached for his drink again while trying to rein
in his horny body. Hell, if he stood up right now he
would have to figure out a way to walk with three legs.

Beverly glanced at her watch.

Lucius did the same. He was *really* going to be late
to the private cocktail party. But if he played his cards
right, maybe the night would end on a higher note than
trying to see how many of his old college buddies still
had a head full of hair.

"Can I get you anything else?" the bartender popped
up to ask.

Beverly warred with whether she should stick around
and enjoy Mr. Lucius's company or get her butt over to
Cork for the Hollington private cocktail party. It wasn't
any easy decision. It felt good to have a man look at
her the way he did. It made her feel beautiful, desired,
and downright horny. When was the last time that happened? In her mind, she was already experimenting
with different acrobatic positions and she could feel
herself overheating.

Whoooaaa, Beverly. Slow it down.

"Are you blushing?" he asked.

"Huh? What? No!" She blinked and shook her head
clear of those naughty thoughts. "I'll just have some
water," she said.

"Yes, ma'am. Coming right up."

Lucius's evenly groomed brows rose in mild curiosity.

"A woman must know her limitations," Beverly said, meeting his gaze. "I don't want to do anything I might regret in the morning."

He clearly caught her meaning and licked his lips. "I don't know about regret, but maybe you should do something you'll *enjoy.*"

Their eyes locked and the temperature in the bar skyrocketed. *Where was that damn water?*

"Here you go," the bartender said, helping Beverly break the spell she'd fallen under.

"Thank you." She tossed down half its contents in one long gulp.

"Damn. Thirsty?" Lucius asked.

"Just a little." She chuckled.

They glanced at their watches again.

"Am I keeping you from something?"

She hesitated and then gave him an apologetic smile. "I am supposed to be somewhere."

"Oh?"

"It's a cocktail party over at Cork. I—"

Lucius snapped his fingers. "*That's* where I know you from."

Beverly frowned.

"Class of '99. Hollington College. You're *that* Beverly Turner." He balled his hand in front of his mouth and laughed. "You were homecoming queen."

Stunned, Beverly blinked at him. "You graduated at Hollington?"

"Sure did. Four of the best years of my life. Now it's coming back to me." He laughed. "You used to hang with Kyra Dixon, right?"

"Yeah." She continued to struggle to place his face.

"I used to be on the football team with Terrence Franklin. Offensive lineman."

Beverly experienced a flicker of a memory—tall boy, tight ass, hazel eyes. "I think I do remember you," she said, smiling. "What a coincidence."

"I'd say." His smoldering gaze roamed over every inch of her. "Boy, you're just as beautiful today as you were back then."

Beverly's blush deepened. "I love it when a man lies to me."

"We never officially met back then," Lucius confessed. "But I remember peeping you out on more than one occasion." He set down his drink. "Tell you what. Since I'm heading to Cork myself, what do you say I give you a lift?"

It wasn't exactly smart to jump in a car with a man she hardly knew.

He leaned forward and gave her a wink. "I promise, I'm harmless—despite my being a lawyer." He stood from his stool, tossed a few bills onto the bar and then offered her his arm. "C'mon. Live a little."

Beverly could almost hear Clarence cussing her out if she turned down this fine brotha. It would be nice to actually walk into Cork on a handsome man's arm. Plus, who knows how the rest of the night might end up?

Girrrrl, you are going to get laid for sure.

She certainly hoped so. "All right. Let's go."

Chapter 4

Beverly felt wicked as she allowed Lucius to escort her to his car. It had been years since she'd allowed a man to pick her up in a bar. In fact, she would have to think back to all those wild college spring breaks when she'd been so daring. She kept waiting for her conscience to kick in, for reason to stop her from jumping into this man's car; however, that little voice never came. Instead, desire and lust seized her body, making her willing to see just how this whole night would play out.

"After you," Lucius said, opening the passenger door.

Her gaze locked onto his and caused another spark of electricity to flow between them. "Thank you." Slowly, she dipped into the seat.

Lucius closed the door and rushed around to the driver's side. "I can't believe that I'm actually escorting the homecoming queen," he chuckled, gliding into his own seat.

"Oh, please. Don't go on about that." She rolled her eyes. "That was a very long time ago."

He strapped on his seat belt. "But you're riding in the parade Sunday, right?"

"Unfortunately." Beverly sighed and wondered once again how Kyra had talked her into wearing that god-forsaken crown and waving to the crowd. In her opinion, there was nothing worse than an aging beauty queen trying to recapture her youth. Back in the day, she thought nothing of pursuing all those titles—heck, there was good scholarship money attached to those pageants. Now that she was older, she just found the whole thing…silly.

She chuckled. Those were the same words her father used to use. He never once liked the idea of her trotting before a phalanx of judges, normally in a skimpy bathing suit, to be judged. It was sort of funny that it had taken her so long to finally agree with him.

Lucius started the car and Lauryn Hill's "Ex-Factor" poured out of the speakers.

"Oh, I love this song," Beverly gasped. "I used to blast it all the time back in the day." She rocked in her seat and cooed the lyrics to the song.

Lucius laughed and bobbed his head. "Not bad," he praised. "Baby girl got skills."

"I can hold a note or two." Beverly turned down the volume. "Good enough for car concerts only."

"You're selling yourself too short." He hit her with another deep-dimpled grin that had her feeling as if she was sitting next to a childhood crush. There was no explanation for why she reacted the way she did to him. She had known plenty of good-looking men in her life. A lot of them were confident achievers, too, but

Lucius…he had this whole other vibe going. It was this whole sexy-cool thing that had her hanging on his every word—even when he said something cheesy.

A few minutes later, they arrived at Cork—a posh wine bar in downtown Atlanta. The place was so packed that they had to drive around a couple of times before he discovered one parking place in the back of the building. On the outside, the place looked small and quaint, but once inside it was a large open space with dark wood floors. Wine barrels lined one wall while another entire wall was a large mahogany bar behind which were rows and rows of wine bottles.

Tall tables and stools were located off to the sides, leaving the center open for mingling. Soft piano music filtered from hidden speakers and the lighting was somewhat subdued, giving the place a warm, sexy vibe that Beverly was really feeling.

"This is nice," she commented, glancing around. Everyone looked beautiful in their fancy cocktail dresses and casual suits.

"Beverly? Is that you?"

Beverly turned to see a gaggle of women quickly surround her.

"I don't believe it! Look at you. You look beautiful," the leader of the pack exclaimed, taking Beverly by the shoulders and literarily forcing her to do a pirouette.

Beverly beamed a smile at the woman, but after scanning her memory bank, she was unable to place the woman's face with a name. *This is starting to become a trend,* she noted. "Why, thank you," she said when the woman finally released her. "It's so good to see you. How are you doing?" Maybe if she kept the woman talking, she'd be able to figure out who she was.

"Doing good. Just landed a morning spot on CNN and—" she flashed her diamond ring "—married to Damon Woods. Eight years and still going strong." She laughed and batted her long faux lashes. But it was how her voice squeaked and skipped that finally made Beverly clue in to whom she was speaking with. *Darcy Knight*—which meant that the three women flanking her were Kitty Kirkland, Natalie Coles and Keri Evans.

Instantly, a few inches were shaved off Beverly's smile. She and Darcy had an unspoken rivalry back in college *and* high school. It was nothing that was perpetuated on Beverly's end, but Darcy lost both homecoming queen titles to Beverly, as well as placing second in the Ms. Georgia Teen and Ms. Georgia pageants. When they weren't competing, Darcy chased after David like a bitch in heat and she was constantly biting Beverly's look from hairstyles to clothes.

Unfortunately, it didn't look as if the past ten years had been particularly easy on her. At a cursory glance, Darcy's yaki weave didn't exactly match her unrelaxed crown, plus she had on way too much makeup and she'd easily gained fifty pounds. And her happy clique suffered the same fate.

"Is this one of your creations? I heard you were a fashion designer now," Darcy asked, acid dripping from her voice.

"Why, yes. It is. Do you like it?"

"It's...*cute,*" Darcy drawled. "You know I thought about going into the fashion biz, too, but I much prefer to work in something a little more *serious.*"

Beverly blinked, but before she had the chance to respond to that backhand slap, Darcy changed the subject. "So how's David?" Darcy asked, casting a curious look over at Lucius. "Word is you two tied the knot right after college."

"We did," she confirmed. "And now we're divorced."

Darcy and her gang's faces collapsed in mock sympathy. "Oh, I'm sooo sorry to hear that," Darcy said. "Of course, I always thought that you two were an odd fit."

Her girls bobbed their heads in agreement.

Beverly tensed, but then to her surprise, Lucius wrapped a supporting arm around her waist. She looked up into his smoldering hazel eyes while he smiled down at her.

"David's loss is *my* gain," he told the women without breaking eye contact with Beverly.

She smiled. *Talk about a knight in shining armor.*

Kitty, Natalie and Keri sighed while Beverly swore her body was slowly melting in Lucius's arms. This was the closest they had been tonight; it was almost like being wrapped in a cocoon where she detected the faint scent of his aftershave mixed with his sinfully sexy cologne.

"Aren't you Lucius Gray?" Darcy asked, stepping closer.

"Guilty," he said, finally turning to look at Darcy. "And you are?"

"Darcy Woods—well, it used to be Knight." Her smile was suddenly bright enough to rival the sun. "We met once at a, um…frat party." She twirled a few strands of her hair around her fingers.

Beverly tensed as jealousy pricked her skin. Had Lucius and Darcy had a fling back in the day? One look and she could tell he was wondering the same thing.

"Well, I did attend my fair share of those," he admitted.

"Mmm-hmm." Darcy smiled like a sly cat with a se-cret. "At this particular party you had quite a bit to drink and I seem to remember you losing a bet to Terrence Franklin and you and Thomas Barrett had to shave your heads and streak through the center of campus."

"Hey," Beverly said, turning. "I remember that!" Her eyes widened, mainly because that night one of the boys shocked the crowd by being *extremely* well-endowed.

Lucius's face darkened to a deep cranberry. "Ah. *That* night. Not exactly one of my most sober decisions."

"Well," Darcy said, swinging her gaze back to Beverly with contempt clearly written on every inch of her face, "looks like your lucky streak continues."

Lucky? Beverly almost laughed in the woman's face. There were plenty of ways to describe her, especially since she'd left college, and lucky wasn't one of them. "I'd thank you not to presume you know anything about my life."

"Hmmph. Well," Darcy said as if she was suddenly bored, "it was good seeing you again. I'm sure that we'll have time to play catch-up later." She blew Bev-erly a quick air kiss and then ushered her three-ring circus away.

Beverly shook her head, stunned by how the more things changed, the more they stayed the same.

"That was…interesting," Lucius said, glancing back down at her. "How come I get the feeling that you two weren't *really* friends?"

"Picked up on that, did you?"

He chuckled. "How about I get us a drink? You look as if you could use one."

She could, actually. "Thanks."

"Be right back." He winked.

The moment his arm fell from her waist, Beverly's body ached for its return. Again, a strange response to a man she hardly knew.

"There you are!" Kyra threaded her way through a throng of people and then popped up in front of Beverly and wrapped her in a brief hug. "You came."

"As promised," Beverly said, smiling.

"Good." Krya looped her arm through Beverly's. "Please tell me you're having a good time."

"So far so good." She bobbed her head. "Except when I ran into Darcy Knight."

"Oh!" Krya rolled her eyes. "I was hoping her invitation got lost in the mail."

"It's all right. We kept the claws in…kind of."

Kyra's smile exploded. "See. I knew that you could handle yourself. By the way, I love the new haircut and color."

Beverly beamed. "Thanks, I had Clarence hook me up. I swear the man has magic hands when it comes to my hair."

"Well, I think you look beautiful. In fact, you look like you're positively glowing."

Beverly's gaze skittered across the room to the bar, where Lucius scanned a wine menu. "Can I ask you a question?"

"Sure."

"Do you remember a Lucius Gray?" The minute she asked the question she noted a visible change in her friend's face.

"I, uh, yeah…used to play on the football team, I believe. Why?"

Beverly took another cursory glance toward the bar, but noticed Lucius was gone.

"And here we go," Lucius said, suddenly appearing at her side and handing her a glass of red wine. "I hope you like pinot noir," he added, chuckling and circling his arm back around her waist.

Kyra's eyes widened. "You…two…know…each…other?"

Lucius turned and hit Kyra with one of his sexy deep-dimple grins. "Well, I don't believe it. Kyra. Kyra Dixon." He eased from Beverly's side to sweep a startled Kyra into a brief hug. "Don't you look lovely as ever?" He glanced around. "Is Terrence here, too? I can't wait to see him and play catch-up."

Kyra stiffened. "I don't know how you could miss him. He's over there with his big adoring fan club."

Lucius's brows lifted at her tone.

Kyra smiled weakly. "Um, can you two excuse me? I need to go check on something."

Before Beverly or Lucius could respond, she jetted away from their small circle and disappeared into the crowd.

"Was it something I said?" Lucius asked.

Beverly shook her head. "No. It's…a long story."

He clearly picked up the hint and let the subject drop. Minutes later, Beverly and Lucius maneuvered through the crowd like a seasoned couple saying their hellos and reconnecting with old friends. Whenever anyone questioned how long she and Lucius had been dating, no one believed that they had only known each other a few hours. In some respects, even Beverly couldn't believe it. There was definitely a connection between them. The only question was: what were they going to do about it?

"Good evening, everyone. Welcome to Hollington's

annual homecoming weekend, and the tenth anniversary of class of ninety-nine," greeted a voice over the microphone. "I'm Kevin Stayton…"

That was as far as he got before the room erupted into shouts and applause. Even Kevin seemed caught off guard by the response. He quickly put up his hand to quiet the group down and regain control.

"Thanks for that, but the reason why I commandeered the mike from President Morrow is to make sure that everyone is made aware of who is responsible for the important and complex job of organizing this weekend. As it turned out, the best person possible was selected. And she's one of ours, class of '99, y'all!"

There was enthusiastic applause until Kevin again signaled for quiet.

"Typical of her, and some of you will remember this from our undergraduate years, she doesn't like drawing attention to herself. She works quietly behind the scenes but she gets the job done, as all of you will experience during the course of this weekend. Ladies and gentlemen, Chloe Jackson!"

Chloe didn't move, and then someone took her hand and pulled her forward to be recognized. It was Kyra, using her small hands to encourage the audience to keep up the applause.

Chloe half raised her hand in a shy salute and quickly stepped back behind the president.

Lucius leaned close and whispered, "I wonder what that was all about."

Beverly just shrugged. She remembered Kevin Stayton, but for the life of her she couldn't remember ever meeting a Chloe Jackson, but she looked great up there and there was no denying that she'd done a fabulous job with tonight's party.

For the most part, Beverly enjoyed the evening. After several glasses of wine, she grew more lethargic and hid more and more yawns behind her hand. Still, she wasn't quite ready to leave just yet.

"Someone is getting sleepy," Lucius whispered as they rocked to Brandy's old jam "Have You Ever?"

"No, no," she lied and then immediately had to stifle another yawn. "Okay. Maybe just a little." She blushed.

"Then what do you say that we head out of here and go do something that will wake you up?" he asked.

Did that mean what she thought it meant? Beverly's legs quivered and those delicious tingles returned. Seeing that she came to the reception with him, it only made sense that they leave together—unless she wanted to play hard to get and call a cab. Looking into Lucius's twinkling hazel gaze, Beverly realized an undeniable truth: she had no desire to play hard to get.

"Yeah," she answered in a lusty voice. "Let's get out of here."

Chapter 5

When Lucius asked Beverly if she was ready to leave, he had meant to extend their evening by going to a nice jazz club or something. But he knew by the look that she'd given him that she had other things on her mind. And he was way too much of a gentleman to disappoint her. As they tried to maneuver through the crowd, Kevin Stayton cut off their escape path.

"Well, I don't believe it! Lucius Gray!" Kevin declared, thrusting out a hand while simultaneously pounding Lucius on the back. "Nice to see you, you old dog."

"Kevin, how are you?" Lucius greeted, though truth be told he'd rather put off their reunion for another time.

"I'm doing good." He glanced around. "You know your old football buddy Terrence is here, too, but you might have some trouble getting to him through his mad fan club."

"So I heard," Lucius said. "Well, if you could excuse—"

"Hey, I've been meaning to talk to you about something. You're a lawyer, right?"

Lucius cast an apologetic look over his shoulder at Beverly.

"Don't worry. I need to step into the ladies' room for a few minutes anyway," Beverly said with a teasing smile. "I won't be too long."

Lucius turned his attention back to Kevin. And though his old friend was delaying his power play, he kept his cool and concentrated on what was being said.

"Yeah, man. The CHRIS Kids Foundation is this great family program that keeps struggling families from collapsing, losing their children and becoming dependent on public welfare, mental health and juvenile justice systems. I was thinking maybe your firm could help them on this. Now, we couldn't pay you much…"

Beverly smiled and waved her way toward the ladies' room, but once inside, her smile dropped and she drew in a deep, exhausted breath. "Bev, do you have any idea what you're doing?" she whispered to herself as she headed over to the long vanity counter to check her appearance. To her great pleasure, her hair was still fierce. Maybe she needed a quick touch-up on her lipstick. She opened her clutch purse and whipped out a pink tube when a weird hacking sound caught her attention.

She frowned. A toilet flushed and a second later, the door opened and an attractive woman in a black sequined cocktail dress stepped out with an awkward smile.

"Are you okay?" Beverly asked, looking at the woman's reflection in the mirror.

The woman looked up and Beverly instantly recognized Tamara Hodges.

"Hey, Beverly. I'm fine," she responded. "At least I will be in a few minutes."

Beverly abandoned her lipstick touch-up and turned to face the pale woman. "Tamara, it's so good to see you again," she stated with a sincere smile. "It's been a while, huh?"

Tamara nodded. "Time goes so fast. You were my first interview for the *Atlanta Daily* after we graduated."

Beverly remembered, nodding. "You did a great job on the article, by the way—I don't know if I ever told you."

Tamara smiled. "You sent me a nice note thanking me. In fact, I believe I still have it."

That was sweet, Beverly thought. Then again, Tamara was always such a sweet girl even though Beverly had always detected a quiet sadness about her.

Suddenly, she stopped smiling. Next she put a hand to her stomach and rushed back into a nearby stall.

Beverly frowned again. "Are you sure you're okay?" she asked a second time when Tamara walked out.

Nodding, Tamara responded, "My stomach is a little upset."

Beverly had other suspicions. "I hope I'm not being too nosy, but are you expecting a baby?"

Tamara nodded sheepishly.

"Congratulations," Beverly proclaimed with bittersweet tears stinging the backs of her eyes. "I—I'm happy for you."

Lucius glanced toward the ladies' room just as Beverly exited. Her smile had disappeared and she looked as though she was downright troubled. "Is something wrong?" he asked when she returned to his side.

"Uh, no. I just ran into an old friend." She glanced over her shoulder, and then smiled back at him. "Are you ready to go?"

Lucius glanced at Kevin and, at last, the brotha seemed to pick up on the hint.

"I'll holler at you sometime next week," Kevin said, winking.

"Thanks, man." Lucius looped an arm around Beverly's waist and this time he managed to successfully escort her from the party. As they strolled out to his car, Beverly leaned her head against his shoulder. Something had changed and Lucius wondered if he'd have to take a rain check for their promised evening.

He whipped out the car keys from his pants pocket, and quickly opened the passenger door. "Here you go, mademoiselle."

"Thank you," she murmured and took her seat.

Once in, Lucius shut her door and then bounded over to the driver's side. Another glance to his right and he knew he had to do something to recapture the moment. "You know those hors d'oeuvres were nice, but I could really go for something to eat. Are you game?"

Beverly pulled out of her reverie and, for a moment, looked like she was going to reject the offer, but then she apparently thought better of it. "Actually, I am a bit famished."

"Great." He started up the car. "Have you ever been to Sambuca?"

A sparkle returned to her eye. "I love that place." She glanced at her watch. "It's dinnertime on a Friday night—do you think we can get in without a reservation?"

Lucius winked. "Leave it to me. I know a guy."

Sambuca, located in the heart of Buckhead, was one of Lucius's favorite places to dine and dance the night away. On top of offering an eclectic American menu, the casual sophisticated atmosphere was hailed across A-town for the diversity of its live bands. On any given night, its patrons were treated to an evening of jazz, R&B or dance hits.

It was a jazz night, and the low, seductive lighting immediately aided the seductive mood Lucius was aiming for. However, the crowded ring of waiting patrons didn't bode well.

"Yo, Lucius," Spencer, the club's host, greeted, the moment he saw Lucius approach the host/hostess stand. "Long time no see. How have you been?"

"Working, you know how it is."

Spencer tossed up his hands. "I hear you, man. Everybody is hustlin'." He glanced over at Beverly and then gave Lucius a knowing wink. "Good to see you, um, testing the waters again."

Lucius caught his not-so-subtle meaning and struggled to keep his grin from turning sly. "How long is the wait?"

Spencer glanced down at the crammed waiting list. "No reservation?"

"Last-minute decision."

Spencer sucked in a long stream of air through his teeth and stroked this thinly trimmed goatee. "I don't know. The walk-ins list is hitting about an hour wait time."

Lucius reached into his pocket and handed over a couple of folded bills. "How about now?"

"Maybe thirty minutes?"

Lucius added a couple more bills. "And now?"

"Fifteen minutes?"

"You're killing me." He handed over two more Grant bills, bringing the grand total to three hundred dollars. "My final offer."

"Well, looky here. It appears I *do* have a table in section four available."

"Section one," Lucius corrected, wanting a table closer to the stage.

"That's what I said," Spencer said, grabbing two menus. "Follow me."

Lucius returned his arm around Beverly's waist as he escorted her behind Spencer.

The jazz band jammed John Coltrane's "A Love Supreme" as they moved past the stage and then settled into their u-shaped leather booth. He and Beverly sat pretty close at the bottom of the *u*.

"Here you go," Spencer said, handing over their menus. "Your waiter should be with you in a moment."

"Thanks, man," Lucius said.

"Heeey—" Spencer shrugged good-naturedly "—what are friends for?"

Lucius laughed, thinking about how much his *friend* just bilked him for.

Spencer winked, signaling that everybody had a hustle these days. "Enjoy your evening."

He glanced over at Beverly and loved seeing the huge smile plastered on her face.

She leaned over and spoke into his ear, "I love Coltrane."

Lucius perked at that statement. "Now what do you know about Coltrane?"

"Please. My father was a jazz aficionado. Coltrane was like a god in our house." She laughed, thinking about the number of Saturday mornings she woke to the melodious tune of 'Trane's seemingly magical saxophone.

Lucius nodded appreciatively. "A woman who knows her jazz. You're starting to sound too good to be true."

Beverly couldn't help but blush at the praise and then fell into easy conversation about their favorite jazz artists, which morphed into who were their favorite R&B artists and so on and so on. Throughout the meal, Beverly kept marveling over how easy it was to talk to Lucius. There was something about his smooth baritone that she found comforting. She was convinced that she would be content just listening to him read the phonebook.

When another old favorite began to play, this time "What a Diff'rence a Day Makes," Lucius adeptly read her face and offered her his hand. "May I have this dance?"

Beverly tilted her head. "Yes, you may."

They stood together and waltzed over to the small dance floor before the band. As they'd done for most of the evening and now the night, the two glided into each other's arms, their bodies fitting together perfectly.

Beverly sighed as she leaned her cheek against Lucius and rocked steadily with him. When Lucius started to hum along with the music, she closed her eyes and allowed herself to get lost in the moment. Gone was the baggage of her failed marriage and the stress of running her own business. For the first time in years, she allowed herself to just...*be*.

The music ended. For Beverly it was a little too soon. She and Lucius pulled apart and joined the crowd in applauding the band. When it was time to leave there was reluctance on Beverly's part. She could easily dance in Lucius's arms well into the morning, but it was nearing midnight, and the dinner club was winding down.

Strolling out to Lucius's parked car, she had to confess, "This has been a long, wonderful evening."

He opened the passenger door and smiled at her. "I was just thinking the same thing—except for the long part. I kinda thought the night flew by."

Their eyes locked and Beverly's body submitted to an overpowering magnetic pull. At the sight of Lucius's head descending, the muscles in her belly quivered and her heart pounded so loud she feared that the whole world could hear it. When their lips finally made contact, Beverly's eyes fluttered closed and, once again, she was lost.

However, this time was different. In her mind, not only could she hear music, but there was also this wonderful floating sensation that made her feel lush and giddy. She pressed closer, greedy for more.

Lucius eagerly gave her what she wanted—what they both wanted. He had spent the evening wondering what she would taste like and he wasn't disappointed. Her lips were amazingly soft and decadently sweet. A man, if he wasn't too careful, could get caught up.

They remained locked together, the kiss growing hungrier by the second. Lucius pressed her body against the car door. Beverly moaned. Maybe their promised evening was still on. To test the waters, Lucius ran a hand up the front of her dress and cupped one of her large breasts, which easily filled his hand. She didn't pull away. In fact, her mouth opened wider, her tongue delved deeper and mated with his mouth in a way that was so erotic his hard-on was ready to break through the seam of his pants.

However, the sounds of heels hitting concrete and distant laughter penetrated their small intimate sphere and brought them back to Earth. Beverly broke the kiss and panted hard against his ear, "Take me back to the hotel."

Lucius nodded and then helped her into her seat, but when he rushed around to his own door his throbbing cock made it hard for him to think straight, let alone fold into his seat and attempt to drive. But the moment he was behind the wheel, he gave Beverly one look and then sprang across the seat for one more taste of her sweet lips. She received him with as much hunger and passion as she did a few moments ago.

So soft.

So sweet.

So…

Honk!

Lucius and Beverly sprang apart, their hands shooting up as if the entire Atlanta Police Department had suddenly materialized. Instead they discovered, when their heartbeats slowed down a bit, that all that had happened was Lucius's knee—or at least he thought it was his knee—had hit the horn and that there was no one surrounding them.

Beverly laughed, breaking the tension.

Lucius quickly joined in, cooled down and then started the car. He wasn't the most patient of drivers on the road. The urgency to get back to the hotel gave him a lead foot and rendered him color-blind on a few traffic lights. Hell, it *had* been eleven months.

When the Hilton came into view, his heart lightened as if he was once again the college offensive lineman and his team was just a few feet from scoring the game-winning touchdown. That is until blue lights flashed in his rearview mirror.

No. No. No.

Beverly giggled from the passenger seat.

Reluctantly, Lucius pulled over and then was surprised and relieved when the police car whizzed by, clearly intent on a different destination.

"Maybe you should just drive the speed limit," Beverly suggested with a teasing lilt.

"Right." Lucius pulled back onto the road and somehow managed to control his lead foot and his painfully straight hard-on while maintaining his cool. Well, at least he hoped it came off that way. The flip side was that he was coming off like a dog and at any moment he was going to break out and start humping her leg.

Beverly leaned over to turn the CD player back on. Lauryn Hill's mellow rendition of "Killing Me Softly" set the mood. Now that her libido had the chance to slow down, she glanced over at the man sitting beside her. She still had the same assessment she had earlier. *Damn, he's fine.*

But was she really so bold as to sleep with him on the first night? *Hell, yeah!* the small voice in the back of her head shouted. She could actually visualize a little miniature version of herself, complete with a cheerleading outfit, flipping around and shouting, "Give me a *S*, give me an *E*, give me a *X*. What does that spell? *Sex!*"

Lucius pulled into the parking lot of the Hilton hotel and then shot her a smoldering look that had her twitching in her seat. It was decision time, she realized as he stopped in a parking spot and killed the engine. Beverly closed her eyes and wondered if she could really go through with what her body was demanding. As much as she wanted to recapture her long-lost college spirit, she feared that she didn't know how. The trials and tribulations that she'd endured in the past ten years were like shackles to maturity. Taking risks didn't thrill her as it once did, but rather frightened her. It was sad to say, but the last man she'd been with was her ex-husband, David. What if Lucius found her performance in the bedroom…lacking?

It was possible. David had, after all, escaped her bed for the warmth of another's. Slowly but surely Beverly's earlier confidence started to erode and no amount of pom-pom waving from her invisible self could help her.

Lucius opened his car door and then rushed around the luxury SUV to help her out. "Mind if I walk you to your room?"

No woman in this world could look into Lucius's seductive hazel eyes and deny him anything—her included. "I'd like that very much."

Chapter 6

There was something about the way he touched her.

That was the only way Beverly could explain why she was feeling what she was feeling as they stumbled their way into her hotel suite. She dropped her clutch purse on the floor and kicked her shoes off while Lucius peeled out of his shirt, revealing a beautiful, firm milk-chocolate chest with a nice six-pack.

Yum.

Lucius stalked toward her like a panther approaching his prey; his hungry gaze devoured her every curve.

Beverly's body went haywire while her endorphins had her as high as a kite. She gasped when his arm shot out like a python strike, grabbing her and crushing her body up against his. They melded their lips together in the most intoxicating kiss she'd ever experienced. Spellbound, she slid her arms up his hard chest and then curved them around the back of his head, locking him in place so that she could drink her fill of him.

And drink she did, so much so that the removal of her dress was nothing more than a blur. What did crystallize in her mind was when Lucius gracefully and skillfully removed her black lace bra and tossed it across the room. When his large and strong hands cupped and squeezed her full breasts, a mini-orgasm caused her to break their kiss and gasp her pleasure.

Lucius didn't miss a beat and descended his head lower and sucked one of her hard, raisin-sized nipples into his mouth. A bit of flesh scraped across his teeth and a delicious pain set off another mini-orgasm that caused Beverly's knees to buckle.

They fell to the bed. Lucius adeptly rolled her beneath him so that he could continue to squeeze, suck and occasionally bite at her breasts to his heart's content.

Beverly sighed, gasped and squirmed while mentally dancing near the edge of insanity. Just when she was sure that she was about to take that giant leap, his merciless mouth moved to the valley between her breasts and then traveled lower. Her eyes opened slightly and through the mess of her thick lashes, she watched him descend down the middle of her body.

The erotic part was that he was watching her as well. Despite his smoldering hot gaze, Beverly was more transfixed by the sight of his long, glistening pink tongue. When it reached the center of her body and dipped into her belly button, her lace panties grew moist in anticipation of his tongue's next pit stop.

Lucius peeled her panties from her hips and slid them down to reveal the small nest of curls between her legs. He emitted a soft gasp as if he'd just opened a present to find he'd been gifted with something he'd been longing for forever. First, he pressed a kiss against her springing curls and smiled.

Beverly held her breath for so long that her lungs burned and her chest ached, but Lucius was obviously having too much fun, teasing and torturing her. He pressed kisses against first her right thigh, and then her left, which made her open her legs wider and thrust her hips upward.

Instead of responding to what she so clearly and eagerly offered, Lucius continued to press G-rated kisses everywhere but where she wanted. Even when her soft hands combed his head and tried to direct him, he steadfastly refused to succumb to what they both wanted.

Needed.

However, he was determined to wait for the magic word and given her stark impatience, he suspected he was just seconds from hearing it.

"Lucius," she panted. "Please."

Bingo! He smiled. "Anything you want, baby." He slid his tongue through her soft lips and tasted the honey within. "Mmmmmm," he moaned and then dipped in for another taste, this time longer and taking his time twirling his tongue around the base of her pretty pink pearl.

Tears surfaced and leaked from Beverly's eyes as she continued to squirm around, the air now emptying her lungs as she aahed and oohed through his slow feasting. At the feel of her first full orgasm building, she found herself inching her way up the bed as if she wasn't sure she was ready for such an intense impact.

Lucius dogged her every move, following her up the bed until she hit her head against the headboard.

Now she had nowhere to go as the pressure kept building and intensifying. Her mouth slacked open. It was going to be too big—too much, she decided and then tried to push Lucius away. However, that was like trying to move the Rock of Gibraltar. He wasn't having it.

Preparing for the inevitable, Beverly spread out her hands and grabbed large fistfuls of the bed's sheets and held on. "Oh, God," she moaned repeatedly. Her body's temperature climbed until finally she exploded. Her soul splintered into a million little pieces.

For a few precious seconds afterward, Beverly had no idea where she was or how she got there. Her only guess was that she existed somewhere between heaven and Earth. By the time she opened her eyes again, Lucius had yanked off his designer boxers and his hard dick was swinging in the air, like he was gearing up for batting practice.

He possessed a beautiful work of art: thick, long and hands down the biggest she'd personally seen. Her clit throbbed and her breasts ached for what was to come.

Still drifting on a hazy cloud of lust, she reached for him and was pleased with how he felt both hard and soft at the same time. Wanting to return the great pleasure that he'd just given her, Beverly took the head of his cock into her mouth and sucked gently before tracing the smoothness with her tongue.

"Oooh, baby. That feels nice," Lucius cooed, running his fingers through her hair.

Beverly loved the praise and grew bold enough to grab his hard ass with both of her hands, and then drew as much as she could of him into her mouth.

"Damn," he sighed, his knees buckling.

With her mouth full, she looked up at him, wanting

to see what ecstasy looked like on his face. What she saw only turned her on more.

She sucked harder. Faster. Deeper.

Lucius pumped his hips—not enough to choke her, but just enough to deepen his pleasure. Mentally, he was trying every trick in the book to prevent himself from coming too soon.

It wasn't easy.

Beverly's wonderful mouth and amazing tongue suckled and caressed him in a way that had his toes curling and his heart hammering against his chest. He couldn't stand it anymore and jumped back, his dick springing free from her mouth so he could retrieve the gold-wrapped condom from his wallet.

When he came back to the bed, Lucius handed Beverly the packet. "Won't you help me out with this?"

Her long fingers took the condom from his hand and she smiled wickedly as she tore open the packet and then slowly unrolled the condom over his thick pole.

"Ah, you're trying to pay a brotha back, huh?"

"I don't know what you're talking about," she lied prettily.

He climbed onto the bed, easing her onto her back. "You don't, huh?"

Automatically, her long silky legs slid up and hooked around his waist. "Not a clue."

"Now why don't I believe you?" he asked, taking his thick cock in hand and then using it to smack her open clit. "Maybe I should punish you for lying to me?" He smacked her clit again.

Beverly squirmed. What did she do? Now he was going to torture her again before giving her what she wanted. How long could she hold out?

"You know I could just keep you open like this until you confess."

She moaned and squirmed.

Lucius ran his dick from the top of her clit down to the crack of her ass and then back up again. "It's too bad because I really wanted to get a piece of this. But since you don't know what I'm talking about…" He shook his head. "I guess I should just go ahead and get dressed and go back home."

"No. Don't. I was just playing," she groaned and then realized that it hadn't taken her long to break and beg.

"You were just playing?" He placed his dick right at the entrance of her sex and watched her try to ease him in. "Are you playing with me now?"

"No," she sighed. "Please." She was going crazy and no longer cared whether he knew it.

Lucius leaned over, kissed her lips. "Please what?"

She kissed him back. "I need you."

With those words, Lucius eased into her with a slow, gentle thrust of his hips. At the same time, Beverly sank her nails into his back and they both ended up hissing with a mixture of pleasure and pain.

Beverly couldn't believe how much of him she was able to take in. At one point, she thought that she was losing her virginity for the second time, but the truth was that Lucius Gray was a very well-endowed brotha indeed. And just when she thought she couldn't take any more, Lucius completed their joining with one determined, savage thrust.

Beverly cried out, but Lucius's loving murmur and then subsequent kisses dried her tears. Then he began to move and a whole new world opened up behind her closed eyelids. Years of stress peeled off of her, leaving her feeling as light as a feather.

Lucius's cock filled every inch of her and more, but she was determined to ride until she passed out, if necessary. What was amazing was how she had at first felt like Lucius was too much, but then she quickly found that she couldn't get enough. In no time their bodies were coated with sweat.

"Damn, baby. Damn," he repeated continuously in her ear. "You feel soooo good."

The bed was jumping, the headboard was banging and Lucius's and Beverly's bodies were slapping together as if they were all part of some erotic percussion section of a big sex band.

A new heat simmered and then roared to life, signaling to Beverly that she was just seconds away from another mind-bending orgasm. She tried to brace herself, which caused her to tighten her vaginal muscles and, thus, drive Lucius insane.

"I'm coming," they said in unison.

Lucius slanted his mouth over hers. A second later they were victims of an orgasm so violent that all they could do was shudder and collapse against each other. Spent. Exhilarated. Satisfied.

As Beverly slowly came back to her senses, she rained tiny kisses along his shoulder and then up the column of his sweaty neck. That was all it took for Lucius to reboot and harden again.

"Looks like you want to play some more," he whispered.

"How could you tell?"

He chuckled. "You're an amazing woman."

"You're not so bad yourself."

Lucius's brows hiked up.

"I mean…you're an amazing *man*."

He laughed. "That's much better." He pulled back and mopped at her still-hard nipples, eliciting a soft moan from her. "And you're in luck," he said, pausing. "I want to play some more, too."

Her smile blossomed. "Good. Then let's have some fun."

Chapter 7

Beverly woke up Saturday morning with a smile on her face and feeling like a brand-new woman. She started to stretch and uncurl from her C-shaped position only to bump into her new lover's still sleeping form. Stopping in midstretch, she glanced over her shoulder and was instantly awestruck by the beauty of such handsome masculinity.

A calm settled over her as she soaked in his peaceful profile. Her gaze roamed from his healthy hairline to his groomed brows, long lashes and even his light morning beard. Slowly, she pulled away from her comfortable spoon position so she could turn and run her fingers along the light prickly hairs of his jawline. Her smile widened as she realized that she loved the feel of it. Slowly her fingers wandered to trace a line around his lips.

Beverly gasped when he kissed her fingertips.

Lucius's eyes fluttered open, his own smile sliding into place. "Morning."

"Morning," she sighed, amazed at how her body was already tingling again.

He reached out and pulled her close. "How long have you been up?"

She quivered at the feel of his morning erection pressed against the high part of her thigh. "Not long."

"No?" He nuzzled her neck.

Beverly giggled, now being tortured by his scruffy beard against her face. "Stop. Stop. That tickles."

Of course, that just ensured he would continue until she squealed for mercy. Instead of giving in this time, Beverly reached for a pillow and smacked him soundly on the head.

Lucius looked up, confused, but then was hit again. When he went careening to the side, he reached for his own pillow and then declared war.

Beverly tried to scramble out of bed, but received a few pillow whacks that had her diving under the bedding for cover.

"Oh, no, you don't," Lucius said, grabbing her by the ankles and trying to pull her back out. "You started this."

Beverly grabbed hold of the bottom edge of the bed and held on for dear life.

"Ah. You think you're slick." Lucius laughed, yanking the comforter and top sheets from the bed and leaving her completely exposed.

She released the bed, grabbed a pillow and flipped around almost in the same motion. Her swing caught Lucius off guard, but it wasn't powerful enough to knock him from hovering over her. She, however, took a direct blow to the face. Despite erupting into a new series of giggles, she renewed her efforts to try to get off the bed.

Lucius, once again, dogged her every move, including when she fell over the side and crawled toward the safety of the bathroom.

They were halfway across the floor—Beverly, naked and on her hands and knees, and Lucius, naked and dragging her firm backside back toward him—when the suite's door suddenly opened and a startled gasp drew their attention.

"Oh, I'm so sorry. I'll come back later," a young Latina maid said, covering a trembling hand over her mouth and quickly backtracking and slamming the door shut.

Beverly blinked a few times, trying to process what had just happened. Finally, she glanced back over her shoulder to see a very amused Lucius smirking back at her. That was all it took for them to collapse with laughter.

After a long and playful shower, Lucius called room service and ordered up lunch…since they had missed breakfast by a couple of hours. His next call was to the concierge, where he gave his clothes sizes and requested new clothes to be purchased and charged to his credit card.

When they sat down to eat, both cloaked in thick, white hotel robes, they were equally interested in playing footsies as they were with actually eating their meals. Beverly still couldn't believe how she was behaving. It was if she'd taken some magic pill and she was eighteen again.

As if.

But it was nice to pretend. She also ignored the needling question as to what she expected from all of this. Was she officially in a relationship now or was this some weekend fling to help her find her groove again? She bit into her chicken sandwich and eyeballed her lover from across the small table. How nice would it be to wake up every morning to see his handsome face, smiling, laughing and devouring her with a simple glance?

Stop that! she mentally admonished herself. Hadn't she been down that disastrous road before? Hadn't she convinced herself that she was in love before? Hadn't she tried to achieve having the perfect family before?

Soon, her smile melted from her face as a precious memory bubbled to the surface.

Lucius noticed the change immediately. "Is something wrong?"

Beverly jumped as if suddenly remembering he was still in the room with her. "No. Everything is great." She smiled awkwardly.

Lucius's antennae shot up. He'd been around enough women to know not to buy that line. He reached across the table and caressed her hand. "C'mon. Surely by now I've proven that I'm a pretty good listener."

Beverly drew a deep breath and looked as if she was weighing her answer.

The familiar sound of his BlackBerry ringing caught his ear. He groaned and rolled his eyes. Couldn't he have this one Saturday away from the office? It rang again. "Hold that thought," he told her and then bounded out of the chair and searched through the piles of clothes littered across the room for his phone.

Beverly took the moment to regroup and clear her head. *Get a grip, girl.*

"There you are," Lucius said after finally finding the phone, but not in time to answer it. But when he read who the missed call was from, he took a seat on the edge of the bed and returned the call. "Give me just a second," he told Beverly while he listened to the phone ring over the line.

Beverly returned her attention to her lunch until she heard Lucius say another woman's name.

"Erica," he said. "You just called?"

"Where the hell are you?" Erica snapped. "*Your* daughter wanted to see you today so we swung by your place and you're not there!"

"What do you mean you swung by? You were supposed to be going out of town *again,* don't you remember?"

"Well, we changed our minds and Ruby said that she wanted to see you."

Lucius huffed and glanced at the clock. "Fine. I'll be home in a half hour."

"Naw. Don't do us any favors. You're probably out partying with some bimbo while your daughter is in tears."

Lucius gripped the phone and clenched his teeth. "You're out of line. I said I'll be home in thirty minutes so I'll be there in thirty minutes."

"Then you'll be there by yourself because I'm not driving back across town."

Breathe. "Then I'll come to your house and pick her up."

"Well, we won't be there, either. To make her feel better, Andrew and I decided to take her down to Pine

Mountain to see the safari. You know how much she loves animals."

"Then *I'll* take her."

"Next time," Erica said and then disconnected the call.

A seething and incredulous Lucius was left staring at the phone, a long stream of expletives flowing through his mind, but not out of his mouth—though the urge nearly overpowered him.

"Is something wrong?" Beverly asked.

"No. Everything is great." Realizing what he'd just said, he looked up. They smiled. "Why don't we make a deal?" he said, returning to the table. "We leave whatever troubles we have at home." He took her hand again. "Let's just shut everything out and enjoy this weekend."

Beverly's smile returned. "Now *that* sounds like a wonderful idea."

The Hollington Lions homecoming game was against their decades-old rival the Greenville Rangers. It all had the makings of being a really tight and intense game and Beverly was surprised that she was actually looking forward to it. She and Lucius made the last few minutes of the large tailgate party. Like her, Lucius had no problems reverting back to his college days when he kept running across old football buddies that were determined to show off by tossing a football around.

Lucius went a little overboard. Every time he turned or made a play, he checked and made sure she was watching. It was sort of cute, really.

The party wasn't all fun. Darcy and her posse continued to cross Beverly's path and each time they had their noses turned up and their asses on their shoulders. It just confirmed to Beverly that some people never grew up.

The football game turned out to be a real thrill. Lucius and Beverly joined the crowd in shouting and jeering.

Hollington's marching band jammed, playing an array of hits from the '90s, everything from R. Kelly to TLC, and the crowd loved it. Afterward, the college's president took the stage and welcomed the crowd. Chloe Jackson followed behind him.

"Is everybody having fun yet?" she shouted.

The stadium crowd cheered.

"We're just getting started, and there's so much more to come. Just a reminder that there are several places where you can leave your order forms for official homecoming and class photographs. And there will be someone at the brunch on Sunday to collect them as you're getting ready to leave the campus. Be safe, respect school property and don't forget we need your contributions to the alumni association. Hollington is educating our kids better for tomorrow."

There was another outburst of response from the crowd.

Kevin Stayton stepped forward to talk into the mike. "One more thing before we get out of the way and let the performance begin. I think you all need to know who was the moving force behind this weekend. She doesn't think she deserves any recognition, but how about a Hollington shout-out for *Chloe Jackson!*"

Chloe was pushed forward and her image was immediately enlarged and displayed on the screens erected at both ends of the field. She didn't take the mike again, but merely pivoted to wave at the crowd, who applauded her, as the night before. She smiled and quickly stepped back.

Lucius leaned over. "I'm telling you, there's something up between them two."

Beverly shrugged. "They do sort of make a cute couple."

The rest of the game was a complete blowout. The Hollington Lions won the game 27-11 and Beverly and Lucius exited the stadium, laughing and shouting along with the crowd, *"We're number one! We're number one!"*

They were still in a jubilant mood when Lucius carried Beverly piggyback style back into her hotel suite. She squealed when he tossed her onto the bed and then launched himself on top of her.

"Bev, my dear. Has anyone ever told you that you make one hell of a cheerleader?"

Beverly wrapped her legs around his waist and tugged up his shirt. "Rah, rah, rah."

Lucius held up his arms and allowed for his shirt to be removed. He returned the favor by tugging up her black turtleneck, then planting his face in the valley between her breasts and shaking his head like a rabid dog.

Beverly giggled at his childish antics and didn't protest when his hands then made quick work of unbuttoning and unzipping her designer jeans. She went from being amused to being turned on in a matter of seconds. This time, however, she wanted to take the lead and she playfully rolled Lucius over and helped him remove his own jeans.

"Whoo. Somebody is anxious," he joked, folding

his arms behind his head and watching her as she removed his boxers and retrieved a condom from the bag the concierge had delivered earlier.

"You were taking too long," she said, smiling and sliding the condom over his rigid cock. Next, she climbed up and lifted her left leg high over his shoulder, stretching herself wide so she could take all of him when she slid down.

The air left Lucius's body in a long hiss. "Oooh. Damn, baby."

Beverly only smiled and rocked back and forth on his dick like a seesaw.

Lucius grunted and groaned while trying his best not to come too soon, but it was hard. Beverly was driving him wild. Just when he thought that he was losing the battle, Beverly jumped off, flipped around and scooted her booty toward his face while she peeled the condom off and stuffed his hard shaft into her watering mouth.

Loving the instant sixty-nine, Lucius grabbed hold of Beverly's melon-sized ass cheeks, squeezed them and then smacked them a couple of times before parting her open and sliding his tongue so deep he could feel her vaginal muscles tremble. His mouth went to work, smacking and slurping until Beverly's mouth sprang off his dick because she was about to come.

"Ooooh, Gawd," she panted.

Lucius continued even as her cries grew louder.

"Ooooh, Gaaaawwwddd." Beverly's body quaked violently as she came, but Lucius was nowhere near done with her.

"Stand up," he ordered, giving her ass a good smack.

She stood up while he grabbed a new condom.

"Bend over and grab your ankles."

Beverly obeyed without hesitation, but nearly passed out from the pleasure of his long, thick dick sliding into her from behind.

"Damn, baby. You're so wet," he praised and then immediately started pumping his hips. Soon he reached around and grabbed her full breasts, squeezing and pinching her nipples, but then his smooth strokes became like a violent jackhammer.

"Oooh, baby. That's it! That's it!" she screamed as he worked her G-spot. It was amazing how he filled every inch of her. She loved the combination of pleasure and pain she felt each time he pounded into her. "I'm—I'm coming," she panted.

"Then come on, baby. That's what I'm here for."

Her muscles started contracting, causing Lucius to hiss and curse about how good her body felt. It got so good to him that he had to hike one leg up on the edge of the bed so he could sink even deeper into her warm, slick walls.

Beverly was the first to scream out. Behind her closed eyelids a blanket of shooting stars appeared and swirled around her.

Lucius cried out, his thick sausage-like dick springing out from the force of his explosion.

They fell to the bed, sweaty and panting for air. As if it was the most natural thing in the world, they curled up together and promptly fell asleep. When they woke again, they had about an hour to get ready for the reunion dance at Bollitos.

Jumping out of bed, they scrambled around, showering and dressing at a record pace. In the end, Lucius whistled when he saw Beverly twirl around in a short black dress that looked as if it was poured over her thick curves. But it was her legs and thick booty that drew his attention and nearly forced his dick to give a high salute.

"Ready to go?" she asked.

Frankly, he was more interested in getting her out of that dress.

"Later," she said, as if reading his mind. "I promise."

"In that case," he said, offering her his arm, "let's go."

Chapter 8

Beverly and Lucius arrived at Bollitos at eight-thirty and the place was packed. When Beverly learned that the building was owned by Kevin Stayton, she was more than a little impressed with the five-story warehouse building. It looked quite urban and stark from the outside, but inside was another story altogether. Large, multilevel balconies looked down on a huge five-story dance floor. There was different music playing on each floor.

When they walked through the large double doors, Beverly handed over her jacket at the coat room and then excused herself to go to the large restroom down the hall.

"I heard she was going to be waving on some float tomorrow." Darcy's snarky voice drifted to Beverly when she cracked open the door.

Kitty barked with laughter. "Like she's still relevant or something."

Natalie chimed in. "Who cares that she was homecoming queen a decade ago? She's no better than anybody else here."

Darcy's high-pitched laugh grated across Beverly's nerves. "Tell me about it. If her ass was all that, she would've been able to keep her husband." Her voice lowered. "I heard David left because she went crazy after losing—"

Beverly pushed open the door and stormed inside. Darcy and her gossiping group swung apart and then smiled up at her.

"Bev," Darcy cooed. "We were just wondering if you were coming tonight."

Beverly glared at the woman, letting her know that she'd heard every word.

"Well—" Darcy smiled tightly "—I guess we better get back out to the party."

Beverly remained mute, staring them down and ready if any of them said something out of pocket again. When they sauntered past her they were careful not to bump into her. Likely, they sensed she was just seconds from yanking out their ratty-ass weaves from their heads.

Once they were gone, Beverly closed her eyes and sucked in a deep breath. It did little to calm her down. In fact, she could feel a wave of tears rushing forward. She couldn't decide what was worse, that Darcy was spreading lies about her divorce or that she knew the truth about her loss and her subsequent breakdown. Having her years of chronic depression, medication and therapy being discussed and dissected by those cackling bitches had her blood boiling.

"Damn it, Kyra. Why did I let you talk me into doing this?" She moved over to the vanity mirror and stared at her reflection. Suddenly, she didn't like anything she saw: her hair, her makeup or her dress. After all, who was she trying to fool—her classmates or herself?

She drew a few more deep breaths, but her solitude was disrupted when more women began to drift into the ladies' room.

"Hey, aren't you Beverly Turner?" a woman asked.

Beverly blinked back her tears and forced on a plastic smile. "Yes."

The woman's smile beamed. "Hey, I'm Shawna Miller. You probably don't remember me. I used to be in your English and calculus class senior year."

"Oh, hi."

"I have to tell you," Shawna went on, "I admired you so much back in college. You were so beautiful—and you still are. Plus, you had that gorgeous boyfriend, David Clark, and you were sooo popular with everyone. It just looked like you had the perfect life. I heard you were going to be in the parade tomorrow?"

Beverly's smile tightened. She needed to get out of there. "Excuse me," she said and then hightailed it out of the bathroom.

Lucius saw the look on Beverly's face when she came out of the bathroom and was instantly concerned. "Sweetie, are you all right?"

She glanced up at him, her eyes glossy.

"That's it. No more bathroom breaks for you. Every time you leave my side you come back looking as if someone kicked your puppy or something."

His joke was rewarded with a small smile. "There. That's better," he praised.

"I need to find Kyra," she said. "There's no way I'm riding in that parade tomorrow."

Lucius frowned. "Why? Is something wrong?"

"I don't want to talk about it. I just need to find Kyra…or Chloe Jackson," she amended, as if remembering the name. "I could tell her."

Lucius looked around. "Well, I haven't seen either one of them. Maybe they're over near the stage. I heard someone mention a few minutes ago that Micah Ross was here and about to introduce one of his artists."

"Then let's go over there," she shouted, taking him by the hand and pulling him along. She seemed like a woman on a mission again. He wondered what had happened in the ladies' room that spooked her from wanting to participate in the parade.

They maneuvered skillfully around black leather sofas and acrylic tables that flanked the dance floor. But when the lights dimmed, it became clear that they weren't going to be able to see let alone search for anyone. "Hey, let's look for them after the concert," he suggested when he noted her distraught face. "C'mon. It's gonna be all right," he assured her and then led her toward one of the private balconies while everyone else was focused on crowding onto the dance floor.

Beverly allowed him to direct her away. Once they found an empty private balcony, they took their seats on a plush velvet love seat and stared directly down on the main stage. A minute later, college alumni Micah Ross took to the stage to roaring applause.

Lucius leaned over to Beverly. "I still don't remember this dude from school, do you?"

She shook her head. "But he certainly made out well in the music industry. That's no small feat."

After the crowd calmed down, Micah introduced Justice Kane to the stage. Everyone went wild again. The music was good—damn good, actually—and Lucius ordered them a few drinks, hoping to loosen Beverly back up. For a while it looked as though it was working until she spotted someone down in the crowd.

"Chloe!" She hopped up and took off.

Confused, Lucius set his drink down and went to find out exactly what was going on.

Beverly bumped and shouldered her way through the crowd. With her heart in her throat, she grabbed hold of Chloe's hand. Chloe glanced over her shoulder.

"I've got to talk to you," Beverly said urgently.

"But Kevin wants me…"

"I *really* need to talk to you. It's about tomorrow."

"Chloe!" Kevin Stayton shouted.

"I'm coming. I'll be right there," Chloe said. Then she retraced her steps back to Beverly.

Beverly moved away from the stairs and stood near the quiet corridor that led to the restrooms. There was no traffic for the moment. She gnawed on her lower lip, and shifted back and forth from one heeled foot to the other.

"Are you all right? What's wrong?"

"Chloe, I'm so sorry to do this, but I can't be in the parade tomorrow."

Chloe stared at her, openmouthed. "Wha—what did you say? You're not…"

"I can't. I know I said I'd do it, and I really hate to put you on the spot like this, but I can't."

"But why, Beverly? I mean, you don't even have to

do anything. You ride on the float and smile and wave. You don't have to *say* anything."

"I know that, but…I'm afraid I'm going to fall apart. I'll embarrass myself. I can't do it," she said, though it was sort of stretching the truth.

Behind them, Micah Ross took the stage again and talked to the crowd.

"Maybe you could think about it overnight? You can call me in the morning. But please don't say no right now," Chloe pleaded.

Beverly shook her head.

Kevin Stayton now took the mike. Chloe gasped. Her gaze went to the stairwell, and then back to Beverly.

Before Beverly could say anything else, Lucius grabbed her arm and pulled her back.

"What the hell is going on with you? You've been acting strange ever since we got here."

"Nothing. Everything is fine now." She smiled sweetly, feeling as if a load had been lifted from her shoulders.

Lucius frowned at her ability to run hot and then cold within the blink of an eye. "Are you sure?"

"Yeah." She eased past him to head back to their private balcony.

Still frowning, he followed her.

"And here she is!" Kevin proclaimed from the stage.

Beverly and Lucius returned to their love seat and stared down at the stage.

"I am delighted, thrilled, relieved and proud to introduce Chloe Jackson to everyone…"

The crowd went wild with applause.

"…as my future wife."

"Hot damn," Lucius laughed. "I *knew* something was going on with those two."

Chloe took the mike and waited until everyone had quieted down. "I know you're sick of hearing my name by now. I apologize for Kevin being such a bore about it...."

Someone laughed out loud. More laughter followed. Chloe looked momentarily confused and thrown by the tittering as she talked. "I appreciate Kevin's...his... uh..."

Chloe stopped and blinked. The laughter grew.

Beverly smiled as her eyes misted. "She didn't hear him."

Chloe's eyes widened as she turned toward Kevin. "Did you...what did you say?"

"Awww. This is so sweet," Beverly murmured to herself.

Kevin took the mike back, put his arm around Chloe's waist and pulled her close.

"I said, Chloe Jackson, will you marry me?"

The crowd went wild.

A chant began on one side of the stage. It picked up on the other, and suddenly began a wave around the room.

"Chlo-*e,* Chlo-*e,* Chlo-*e*..."

"Say yeessssss!" a woman yelled. Everyone laughed.

Chloe turned to Kevin. "Yes," she choked out, almost inaudible. "Yes, I will," she said a little louder, nodding.

"Ke-*vin,* Ke-*vin,* Ke-*vin!*"

Chloe reached for the mike and spoke clearly into it. "Yes, I'll marry you, Kevin Stayton."

The room erupted into wild cheers and whistling and applause. Beverly and Lucius jumped to their feet to applaud the couple. Beverly even wiped away a tear, which surprised her. She thought that all her romantic fairy-tale notions were long dead and buried. She personally knew what happened after the glittering ring and the "I dos." *Maybe it will be different for them,* she reasoned. At least she hoped so.

She smiled and watched the couple kiss and spin around on the stage. Yeah, she decided. It *will* be different.

When the newly engaged couple exited stage left, a local Atlanta band, Déjà, took to the stage and launched into a rendition of Notorious B.I.G.'s "Hypnotize." Lucius and Beverly took one look at each other and, like most of the attendees, bum-rushed the dance floor to get their groove on.

Shaking and gyrating bodies monopolized the floor and Lucius was determined to show that he knew how to pull up to her bumper just like the best of them. Beverly lost herself in the music as it shifted from East Coast driving bass to West Coast's hot beats like Dr. Dre's "The Chronic" and then polished off one set with R. Kelly's remix of "Bump and Grind."

Lucius was so all over her that it looked like he was glued on—and Beverly didn't mind at all. Shortly after that performance, they hurried out of the club just short of midnight. They were so hot for each other that they couldn't keep their hands off each other during the drive back to the hotel.

Beverly abandoned her seat belt so she could kiss and suckle his earlobe, while jamming her hand down in his crotch and stroking her new best friend. "Wait till I get you back to the room," she whispered and then slowly glided her tongue down the shell of his ear.

He shivered and reached a hand in between her legs. He slid her moist panties over and slid a finger deep into her wetness. "Looks like you're already ready for me," he said.

She sighed sexily against his ear and then moaned when a second finger joined the fray. To prove that she could keep up, Beverly unzipped his pants. "I hope you know how to concentrate," she said, then folded over into his lap and took him into her mouth.

Lucius nearly swerved out of his lane. He removed his hand from her body and then planted them at ten o'clock and two o'clock on his steering wheel. However, the feel of Beverly's warm mouth, coupled with the tightness of squeezing to the back of her throat, caused his toes to curl up off the accelerator to the point that he was driving a good twenty miles below the speed limit.

When Beverly's head began to bob at a faster pace, he could literally feel tears brim in his eyes, while his lungs felt as if they were on the verge of collapsing.

"Ooooh. Ssssssssh," he hissed repeatedly. Thank God the hotel finally came into view. But he had a hard time turning the wheel at the feeling of orgasm brewing at the base of his cock. Somehow he managed not to sideswipe a car that was leaving the hotel lot. Wanting to continue this groove that they were on, Lucius found a parking spot toward the back of the hotel and killed the engine.

Grinning, Beverly lifted her head and asked, "Condom?"

"Wallet. Back pocket," he panted and raised his hips.

She reached around and pulled out his wallet. After ripping the gold packet open and sliding on the condom, Beverly climbed onto his lap.

Lucius did his part by hitting the automatic button to slide his seat back so they could have a little more room to work. He didn't have long to wait as Beverly slid her panties to the side and eased down on him in one smooth motion.

"Aaaaaaahhhh," they both said as their bodies sighed in relief.

He hit another button and his seat reclined all the way to the back so he was practically lying down.

She leaned forward and drew his soft lips into a deep kiss while she began to ride him slowly and deliberately. Listening to his moans and groans filled Beverly with a power she hadn't felt in such a long time that she couldn't help but revel in it.

"You like this, baby?" she asked, squeezing her vaginal muscles.

Lucius sucked air through his gritted teeth and nodded.

"Let me hear you say it," she ordered.

He smiled wickedly, knowing the game they were about to play. "I love the way your body feels, baby. Especially when I do this." He surged his hip forward, rammed himself in all the way to the hilt.

She gasped, feeling like a tiny firecracker shot off toward the tip of her clit.

"Or when I do this." He surged forward twice in quick succession, making a hard smacking sound. To prove that he could take control at anytime, Lucius locked his hands around her waist and held her in place while his hips pounded away.

Beverly could barely breathe, let alone think, and she certainly couldn't be held accountable for whatever nonsense spilled out of her mouth while Lucius tried to drill his way to China.

As if their bodies were totally in sync, a violent tremor erupted and then surged through both of them like a bolt of lightning. When it passed, they were left hot, sweaty and panting.

"Damn. Has anybody told you that you're amazing?" Lucius asked once he was able to talk again.

"You might have mentioned it." She smiled and peppered his face with kisses.

"All right now. If you keep that up we're going to have to go another round."

"Promise?" She nibbled on the bottom of his lip and then grinned when she felt his cock quicken again.

Lucius gave her a hard smack on her ass. "Let's get you upstairs. There's a few more positions I'd like to try out."

"Good. I have a few of my own."

Chapter 9

The hotel suite was a wreck. Clothes were tossed everywhere, while chairs, desk tables and a nightstand were also overturned. Somehow the king-size mattress had gotten tossed off the box spring so that now half of it was on the floor. Coincidentally, it was the part they had fallen asleep on.

There was a phone ringing somewhere. Beverly half hoped that it was somehow a part of the wonderful dream that she was having where she and Lucius were laughing and playing with a most adorable little girl. The child looked so much like Lucius, with his beautiful brown skin and quarter-size hazel eyes, that Beverly's heart stirred and an old longing returned.

But the damn phone kept ringing.

Beverly opened one eye, looked around and was confused by the utter destruction around her. Had a hurricane hit the hotel? The phone rang again. She lifted her head, looked around. This time, she noted, Lucius snuggled up against her as if he'd fallen asleep suckling her breasts.

She felt around, her hand seeking for the ringing phone. After stretching a bit, she found it up near the wall and yanked up the handset. "Hello?"

"I know Ms. Thang ain't still sleeping?" Clarence said with a sarcastic chuckle. "Why didn't you answer your phone when I called? I know your butt turned in early."

Beverly turned her head back toward Lucius. "Um, not exactly."

Clarence emitted a small gasp. "Don't tell me you actually stayed out at that reunion dance and had a good time."

She giggled. "More like I've been having a *great* weekend."

"Whooooooooooo, Beverly girl!"

Beverly jerked the phone from her ear and then shook her head to stop it from ringing.

"C'mon. Spill it. Spill it," Clarence insisted.

She could actually picture him in his morning pink robe, with his heel propped up in a kitchen chair while sipping his morning coffee.

"Is he fine, girl? I know he's fine. Was it that freakum dress you had on Friday night? I know it was."

"Do you even need me for this conversation?" she asked.

"Hell, yeah," he drawled. "I need details. It's been so long since you got laid, I feared you were walking around with the Sahara Desert between your hips."

"Now you're just trying to be funny."

"And you're stalling."

Lucius stirred and then surprised Beverly when he latched onto one of her breasts like it was the most natural thing in the world to do first thing in the morning. With a few gentle strokes her nipples peaked and hardened.

Beverly closed her eyes and felt other parts of her body start to reawaken.

"Bev, do you hear me, girl?"

"Huh?" she said almost dreamily. Lucius's hands started roaming over her body, forcing her to spread her legs so he could test the wetness within. "Oooh."

"Awwww, hell naw," Clarence squealed. "I *know* that you're not still gettin' your freak on while I'm on the phone!"

"I'll have to call you…b-back," she panted and then slammed the phone down.

Lucius's head descended down her body. "I hope that wasn't important," he rasped, peeling open her legs like her body was a precious flower.

"No. This is more important," she said, guiding his head down and sighing when his mouth dipped inside to taste her body's fresh morning juice. At this point, Lucius knew her body like the back of his hand. He knew just how many licks it would take to make her come or how to tug gently on her clit to prolong the moment.

Right on time her clit started going through convulsions. Beverly closed her eyes as Lucius worked his fingers and his mouth faster and faster while her legs fluttered around his head like an erotic black butterfly.

At long last, she screamed out his name as her body imploded.

"How you feel, baby?" he asked, peppering kisses against her firm thighs.

Was he kidding? She felt amazing.

The suite's door swept open, the lovers jerked their heads to see the same Latina housekeeper from yesterday gasp with shock. "I'll come back later," she said *again* and then quickly backed out of the room.

Lucius looked up at Beverly's cranberry-red face. "I think she does that on purpose."

Beverly covered her face with her hands, embarrassed. "We should have put the Do Not Disturb sign on the door."

He nodded, realizing that was probably a good idea.

The phone rang again. Beverly had a sneaking suspicion that it was Clarence calling her back. She grabbed the phone, ready to have a little fun with her friend. "What is it, bitch?"

"*Excuse* you?"

The unmistakably feminine voice clearly was *not* Clarence. "Who's this?"

"Kyra. Who the hell do you think it is?" she said, offended.

Beverly bolted straight up. "Kyra, I'm sooooo sorry. I thought you were someone else."

"*Obviously.*" She cleared her throat.

Lucius snickered as he climbed onto his feet, his semihard dick swinging in between his legs as he headed toward the bathroom.

Beverly smacked her lips as she watched him.

"Bev!" Kyra shouted. "Are you still there?"

"Huh, what?"

"I was asking you why you're trying to back out on the parade at the last minute? You're about to give my girl Chloe a heart attack. What do you expect her to do at the last minute?"

Beverly was instantly irritated. "I don't know. Ask Darcy Knight to ride on the damn float."

"Is that what all this is about? Bitching Darcy? Forget her. She was a mean, evil girl and now she's a mean, evil woman."

Beverly sighed. "I know, but—"

"But nothing. You're riding that damn float even if I have to hog-tie you to it." Kyra then softened her words. "Besides, you don't want people mistaking Darcy for you, do you?"

Beverly grimaced. "God, no."

"Good. Then it's settled."

It was a statement, but it sounded more like a question.

Beverly knew that it was time to put on her big-girl panties and do the right thing. "All right. All right. I'll do it."

"Great. I'll see you at the brunch."

Disconnecting the call, Beverly stood and wrapped the bed's top sheet around her body. "What time is it?" She glanced around, trying to find the clock among the wreckage. When she finally found it, she saw that once again, she only had one hour to get ready for the school's brunch.

She raced to the bathroom, disappointed to see that Lucius had already climbed into the shower. "You couldn't wait for me?" she asked, dropping the sheet and then stepping in behind him.

"You were on the phone." He turned toward her and started soaping up her body, paying particular attention to some body parts more than others.

Beverly did the same.

When they stopped playing around and got out of the shower, it was clear that they were going to be late.

The brunch was taking place at Hollington's campus on the center lawn, known to students as the quad. There were large tents erected everywhere. It was a huge catered buffet affair with tables of mouthwatering breakfast food and sandwiches.

"I see some pancakes with my name written all over them," Lucius said as he toted their picnic blanket and searched for a good spot on the crowded lawn. There were a lot of children running around, being that the event was geared toward the alumni and their families.

"I wish I could've brought Ruby," Lucius said absently and then sighed.

Beverly had almost forgotten that he said he had a daughter. A surprising stab of jealousy hit her squarely in the heart. It was a strange reaction since she'd only known this man for a few days.

Days.

She shook her head. In some ways, this weekend felt as long as a lifetime and there were parts of her that felt as if she'd known Lucius all her life—that they had always had this amazing connection. A frown teased the corner of her lips. She needed to watch herself. The last thing she needed was to get caught up in something that would never be. She wanted nothing to do with love. This weekend was just about…fun.

"How about over there?" Lucius asked, pointing to a small spot a good hundred paces away.

"Looks good to me."

They quickly settled down and then Lucius took off after taking her brunch order.

"Beverly!"

Beverly turned around and saw Kyra rushing over toward her. She smiled. "Hey."

The women gave each other a brief hug.

"So are we still good?"

Still feeling a bit reluctant, Beverly nodded her head. The best way to get through this day was to just grin and bear it.

"I'm going to have to buy you an ankle bracelet," Terrence Franklin joked, coming up behind her, "because every time I turn around, you're gone!"

Beverly blinked in surprise. What were Kyra and Terrence doing together—again?

Kyra laughed. "Terrence, you remember Beverly Turner, don't you?"

"Of course. You were homecoming queen."

"Congratulations on all of your success, Terrence," she said, smiling.

"Are you enjoying the brunch?" he asked. "It's like one big ol' party out here, huh?"

"You can say that again. Chloe said that brunch would be open to the community, but I wasn't expecting such an enormous turnout."

"This is nothing," he told her. "Wait until the parade. The streets are going to be chock-full with—"

Kyra jabbed his side. "Beverly's a little nervous about being on the float," she explained, rubbing a hand along Beverly's back.

Nervous? Nerves had nothing to do with it.

"But she has nothing to worry about, right, Terrence?" Kyra asked.

"Just the thought of being on display in front of all these people is making me feel sick," she said, fingering the lace neckline of her cream-colored blouse. "I'm a fashion designer, Kyra, not a beauty contestant."

"You'll be fine." Kyra's voice was bright and full of cheer. "Would it help if we stayed with you until it's time to head over to the stadium?"

"Bev, you have nothing to worry about. It's a fun, family-filled event."

"Kyra's right," he agreed. "You're among friends, Beverly. So, go out there and make the class of '99 proud!"

She gave a low, shaky laugh. "Right, that's easy for you to say. You're not the one on top of that stupid float."

"Bev, you're gorgeous," Kyra told her. "With that pearly white smile and shapely figure, you're a force to be reckoned with, girl!"

"I second that," Lucius's familiar voice said, coming up behind Beverly.

"Hi, Lucius."

He kneeled and set their two plates down on the blanket.

"Well, knock me over with a feather, if it isn't the great Terrence Franklin!" Lucius chuckled. "I've been wanting to talk to you since Friday, but every time I turn around, you've got a crowd of people around you."

"Hey, man, what's up?"

"You don't remember me, do you?" Terrence shook his head. "I figured as much, but I'd hoped that you'd remember the offensive lineman who took all those hits for you in that state championship game."

"Lucius Gray?"

"Attorney at law," he added, with a laugh.

"Man, you were one hell of a tackle. How come you

didn't go all the way? With your competitive edge and strength, you could've had your pick of NFL teams."

Lucius pointed a finger at his chin. "I like this face far too much to let it get stomped on every Sunday afternoon!"

Everyone laughed.

"Beverly, can I steal you away for a second?" Lucius asked.

Terrence slipped a hand around Kyra's waist and squeezed affectionately. "We'll see you guys later," he said, nodding at Lucius.

"All right, man, have a good one." Terrence and Kyra strolled off.

Beverly blinked in surprise at the affection being displayed between the couple. Clearly the two had put their past behind them. But what had happened to Kyra's fiancé?

"Bev."

"Hmm?" She turned her attention back to Lucius. "So, what's up?"

"I just wanted to warn you that I ran into—"

"Hello, Beverly."

Beverly stiffened. She knew that voice anywhere. Slowly she turned around to see a face she'd spent the last few years hating—her ex-husband.

David flashed his toothy smile. "What—you're not happy to see me?"

Chapter 10

Lucius was torn.

He wanted to give Beverly her privacy, but there was something about this situation that didn't feel right to him. Not to mention, Lucius didn't like the way Beverly froze the moment her eyes landed on her ex-husband. There was a palpable tension that one needed a chainsaw to cut through. He glanced down at Beverly, waiting to see whether she would give him a signal to leave or not.

Instead, she moved closer to him so he eased an arm around her waist and then leveled a look at David Clark that made it clear that he had her back.

"What do you want, David?" Beverly asked, her voice razor-sharp.

David's smile remained in place. "What makes you think I want something?" he answered as if the question was ridiculous. "Why can't I just come over here to see how my ex-wife was doing?" His gaze finally shifted over to Lucius. "I would've done it last night, but, um, you looked...*a little busy* on the dance floor."

It was Lucius's turn to smile slyly.

Beverly sounded equally unfazed. "Well, in case you haven't noticed I'm still *a little busy.*"

"There you are, baby." Another woman joined the small circle, her arm sliding around David.

Lucius felt Beverly tense even more when her gaze landed on the *very* pregnant woman.

"Oh, hello, Beverly," the woman said.

Instead of answering, Beverly just turned out of Lucius's arms and walked away.

"That went well," David said.

Lucius blinked and then finally took off after Beverly, who had amazingly covered a great distance in a short period of time. When he caught up with her, she kept marching like a solider off to war. He followed while they threaded through men, women and children. It occurred to him that perhaps she didn't have a destination in mind and that she simply just needed to get away.

Needing to break the ice, he said, "You know we're walking away from the food, right?"

"Then go back and eat it if you're so damn hungry."

"Whoa, now." He grabbed her arm and forced her to stop. "Are you angry at me?"

She didn't snatch her arm back, but she did glare down at his offending hold until he released her on his own.

"Look, I'm not...I'm just trying to figure out what's going on."

"Nothing is going on," she snapped.

His brows jumped up. Did she really expect him to believe that? "So you just storm and stomp around for what…exercise?"

Beverly drew in a deep breath, warring with whether she should even bother to explain. But then she started shaking her head. Why bother? This man was only going to be in her life for what—a few more hours? "Just…" She blinked her eyes dry. "Just forget it. It's a long story and…" She sighed. "I don't feel like dealing with it right now."

One look at his face and she knew that he didn't like that answer. *Well, tough.*

She drew another breath, forced on a smile. "You know what? We made a deal, remember? We're supposed to leave whatever troubles we have at home."

"Neither one of us anticipated trouble following us here."

Beverly cocked her head, indicating to him that she was really trying here.

"All right." He held up his hands. "A deal is a deal." Lucius swung an arm around her shoulders. "So what do you say we get back to our blanket before an army of ants carries away our food?"

Beverly had a decision to make. Let David win and have her run home with her tail tucked between her legs or hold her head up high and enjoy this last day. She glanced back to where she'd left David standing. Him and his *pregnant* wife, Maureen.

Lucius read her mind. "I'm pretty sure they got the message to get lost."

She smiled and said, "You don't know my ex. He can be a little slow on the uptake."

"Then it makes even more sense why it didn't work

out between you two." When she laughed, he knew that
the day had been salvaged once again. "Come on. Let's
go eat before I douse *you* with ketchup."

"Hmm. Now that's something we haven't tried," Beverly said, brightening. Laughing, they crossed back over
to their blankets and tried again to enjoy the brunch. A
few more old college friends stopped by and everyone
reminisced about crazy teachers, crazy couples and
crazy parties.

Beverly laughed and cracked jokes but she couldn't
help scanning the area for David and Maureen. No matter what tricks she employed, she couldn't stop feeling a
lump of injustice in the pit of her stomach. The fact that
she'd spent most of her days—years—burying herself
in her work, trying to forget, trying to move on, while
David clearly had no trouble with it at all.

She pulled herself out of her malaise and flashed a
smile whenever she caught Lucius watching her. By
now, he probably thought she was emotionally unstable,
going from highs to lows within the blink of an eye.
Hell, right now she was thinking the same.

It was disappointing and distressing to know her
fragile emotions were still so very close to the surface. Perhaps all the work she'd put into herself was for
naught and she was no closer to healing than on that
first tragic day. Tears rushed forward but she blinked
them back and carried on.

The much-hyped parade was to start promptly at two
o'clock. Beverly made a quick change into one of her
personally designed gold-beaded gowns that she envisioned shimmering and reflecting the afternoon sunlight. Her reunion float was to roll from the college's

new stadium, wind around the small local streets and then end at the school's center lawn.

The moment she put on her white sash and checked the pins holding her crystal tiara in place, Darcy and her cackling crew popped up once again, giving her dirty looks and whispering behind their hands. Beverly had had enough and flipped the women the bird before storming by with her head held high.

As it turned out, the event was a lot more enjoyable than she'd anticipated. The cheers from the crowd as her float glided by performed an amazing job in lifting her spirits. Behind her, Hollington University's award-winning marching band got their jam on and clearly and easily elicited the loudest applause from the crowd.

By four o'clock it was all over and Beverly was pleased to say that she had survived. She stood taking pictures for a while and then changed back into her clothes and caught up with Lucius. He was engaged in an impromptu football game with a few of his old college buddies.

The moment he saw her, he called a time out and rushed to her side. "You looked beautiful up there today," he said, kissing her upturned face. "I was proud of you."

She beamed. "Thanks."

"Are we playing ball or what?" Kevin Stayton yelled.

"I'm coming!" Lucius shouted. Then he asked Beverly, "Do you mind killin' about an hour with these knuckleheads before we head back to the hotel?"

"Sure," she said, and then received another kiss before he raced off.

"It's almost like watching little kids," Chloe Jackson said, standing next to her.

Beverly hadn't even seen her standing there. "Yeah. I guess." She swallowed a lump in her throat. "About last night and my trying to back out of the parade…"

Chloe waved her off and said sweetly, "Don't worry about it. I'm just glad Kyra got you to change your mind."

Beverly chuckled. "No one can say no to Kyra."

The women laughed.

"By the way," Beverly said, "congratulations. That was a beautiful proposal last night."

Chloe's face darkened with embarrassment. "Thanks. I—I still can't believe it happened."

Smiling, Beverly turned her attention back to the men's game. It was clear to the average observer that the guys weren't as agile as they once were. It took many of them a considerable amount of time to get up once they were sacked. Beverly and Chloe were amused.

At dusk, the game was over, mainly because there were more injuries than touchdowns. Beverly helped a limping and laughing Lucius to his car.

"I don't think a man should be hit that hard after age thirty," he complained. "These bones aren't as strong as they used to be."

She laughed along with him as she tucked herself under his arm and supported most of his weight as they headed toward his car. But as luck would have it, David and his wife were also walking across the parking lot. She tensed, watching David hold open the passenger door of his Mercedes while Maureen struggled to get inside. When he closed the door, David's gaze scanned the lot and he found her staring at him.

He waved and she quickly dropped her head and kept moving.

Back at the hotel, Beverly and Lucius took another hot shower together. But it was all about getting clean instead of exciting each other. They devoured another meal from room service and then promptly fell into a deep, exhausted sleep in each other's arms.

When Lucius woke, the room was dark except for a small strip of moonlight. Yawning, he glanced at the clock and saw that it was well past one in the morning. The weekend was over. He would have to be at work in a few hours. He groaned at the thought of ninety-hour workweeks, endless negotiations and tedious court-room battles.

Truth be told, he had a love-hate relationship with his job. He loved being good at it, hated how it usu-ally destroyed his private life. He glanced down at the woman curled in the crook of his arm. Something about the way she clung to him touched his heart.

The question was whether that was a good thing or a bad thing.

Studying her sleeping face, he still saw the naked vulnerability she displayed when her ex-husband came onto the scene. Now, like before, he felt a fierce protec-tiveness toward her. He didn't know what David had done in their past to hurt her, but he definitely wanted to punch in the guy's face, all the same.

Was *that* a good or a bad thing?

As much as he had enjoyed this weekend, he had no time in his life for a relationship. Hell, he had a hard time trying to juggle weekend visitations with Ruby. Of course, that had more to do with his flaky and un-predictable ex-wife than anything.

We have a deal, he reminded himself. They had this

weekend and then they were to walk away. His heart squeezed.

Was *that* a good or a bad thing?

The questions kept coming and he found that he just didn't have any answers. He liked Beverly—a lot. But now this early Monday morning, he wasn't as sure as he was Friday night that he could have this one wild weekend and walk away, either. Maybe there was some middle ground. Would she be up for that—or was she an all-or-nothing kind of woman?

Beverly stirred in his arms and he automatically pressed a kiss against her forehead. She smiled, though he doubted that she was aware of it. She was so beautiful—but it was clear that there was more to her than what met the eye.

He pressed another kiss to her forehead.

Her nose.

Her lips.

Beverly's eyes fluttered open while she emitted a long kittenlike purr.

Their gazes locked and just like that their passions were reignited. Their light kisses deepened. Seconds later, their hands got into the mix. Roaming and touching and this time stirring emotions that were much stronger than lust. When he entered her, in a weird and erotic sense, it was like sliding into home.

So sweet.

So perfect.

So wonderful.

He started moving his hips; his strokes were slow, deep and languid. Unlike their wild weekend, he wanted to take his time making love to her. He wanted to see how deep he could go, how hard she would quiver and how often she would whisper his name. The intimate moment was heightened by the fact that they refused to break eye contact and it created an invisible bond that shook him to his very core.

Lucius sensed when Beverly's orgasm neared by her body's small tremors. Suddenly his name was being replaced by small gasps and high-octave sighs. As he watched her submit to the waves of ecstasy she looked even more beautiful…angelic.

I could make love to her forever. The rogue thought drifted across his mind at the precise moment his own orgasm hit. He cried out her name, shivered and shook before collapsing and pulling her close.

"Amazing," he panted, feeling a calm settle over him.

Beverly peppered kisses across his chest while he struggled to catch his breath. She was a good woman— a sweet woman. Lucius definitely wanted to see her again after this weekend. *Maybe we can work something out in the morning,* he thought as he drifted back off to sleep.

However, when he woke up again, Beverly was long gone.

Chapter 11

Two weeks later

It was near closing time at Hoops. Beverly felt her patience drawing near an end with a Buckhead socialite who kept griping about the dress Beverly designed to *her* specifications. Of course, it didn't help that every time Ms. Gerald came in for another fitting, ten or fifteen pounds had found its way onto the woman's large frame.

"Are you sure that you let this out?" Ms. Gerald snapped, frowning. "It shouldn't be this tight. If I sit down, it's gonna split straight up the back."

"Yes, ma'am." Beverly rolled her eyes and started removing pins...again.

The bell over the shop's door jingled and Beverly glanced back over her shoulder to see Clarence strolling in wearing a sharp tailored Boateng suit. Just the sight of her friend caused a smile to break across Beverly's face.

"There's my girl," Clarence said, switching his hips toward the back of the store. When his eyes swung to Ms. Gerald, he grimaced. "Now, Alicia, you *know* you need to start pushing back from the dinner table."

Beverly winced and then waited for the inevitable explosion, but to her surprise *Alicia* just smiled while her face reddened with embarrassment. "Maybe I have put on a couple of pounds."

"A couple?" Clarence said, jabbing a hand on his hips. "Giiirrrlll, you better come off that cloud of denial and deal with reality." He walked up to her and pinched her side. "This is definitely more than an inch. Oookaaay?"

Beverly bit and chewed at her bottom lip to keep herself from laughing aloud. Clarence could clearly get away with saying things that she couldn't and she loved him for it. By the time Clarence finished writing Ms. Gerald a reality check, the woman left Hoops with her dress and a vow to call Weight Watchers.

"I swear I should hire you on as a partner," Beverly said, locking the shop's door and flipping a sign to let people know that she was closed.

"Pleeeease. You couldn't afford me." He chuckled and brushed at invisible lint on his suit.

"So why are you so dressed up this evening?" she asked, marching to the back of the store while her evening employees finished cleaning up.

"It's Friday night. You know how I get down. I ain't interested in wasting my weekends with popcorn and Netflix like *someone* I know."

"I'm going to ignore that comment," she said, settling behind her office desk.

"Mmm-hmm." Clarence pushed tape measures, beads and strips of lace out of another chair and sat down. "You should join me tonight. Cassandra Wilson is playing over at Sambuca. You know that place packs in a higher grade of brothers on the regular."

Beverly blocked out everything he said after Sambuca. Instead she was transported back to the night she and Lucius danced cheek to cheek to "What a Diff'rence a Day Makes" and then, of course, what came afterward in her hotel suite. A soft smile touched her lips.

"Please tell me that smile means you'll come?"

She blinked and then frowned. "What?"

"Uh-uh, sister girl. Don't tell me that I'm up in here talking to myself," Clarence snapped.

"I'm sorry," she said, giving him puppy-dog eyes to sell the apology. "I was just thinking about...some business stuff."

"*Business?* Ha!" He made a dramatic show of rolling his eyes. "Now. I guess I have *stupid bitch* stamped across my forehead now, right? You're not sitting there twitching in your seat, twirling your hair and smiling because you're thinking about anything that has to do with business. I know what a sex trance looks like."

"A what?" she barked, trying to sound incredulous but instead sounding guilty as hell.

"Don't play me. You know what a sex trance is." Clarence leaned forward and propped his elbow up on the corner of the desk. "It's that distant look and goofy smile that hits a person's face when they're remembering some good nookie."

Beverly's face burned with embarrassment.

Clarence started snapping his fingers and then pointing at her. "Aha! I knew it! You're still thinking about
ol' boy!"

"I am not," she lied and then suddenly got busy shuf-
fling paper around.

"Why you lying?" He laughed. "Ain't no shame in
reminiscing, girl. I do it all the time." Clarence waved
her off and crossed his legs. "But *then* I pick up the
phone and make myself an old-time booty call. If it was
good once then it would be good again."

Beverly's body tingled at the suggestion, but she will-
fully shook her head. "I am not making a booty call."

"And why not? From what you told me, clearly this
Lucius guy knows how to tear up a G-spot. You keep
telling me that you don't want to be in a serious relationship so why not just have a *special* friend with certain benefits?"

"I thought *you* were my special friend?" she joked.

"If you had a few extra pieces and parts then maybe
we could talk," he quipped right back at her. "Until then
I think you need to call Luscious Lucius, saddle up and
get your rodeo on."

Even though there hadn't been a single day since her
school's reunion that she didn't think about her time
with Lucius, Beverly stubbornly shook her head. She
had made her decision the morning she'd walked out
of that hotel room with Lucius still fast asleep. It was
harder than she expected, which was the main reason
why she had to do it.

Falling in love was not an option. She'd been down
that rocky road before and she still had the bruises on
her heart to prove it. Who knows, maybe she was like
her mother. When she loved, she loved hard—and there

was a real dangerous possibility that she could fall in love with Lucius Gray.

"Well, since I'm up here talking to myself again, I'll just go on the prowl by my damn self again tonight," Clarence said, standing.

Beverly blinked out of her reverie again and flashed another apologetic smile. "I'm sorry. I'm just swamped," she said, electing to stick by her *thinking about business* story.

"Yeah, whatever." Clarence leaned down, gave her two quick kisses on each cheek and turned toward the door. "But you know once you blow the top off of that celibacy box it's harder to put it back on."

"Good night, Clarence."

"All right. Act like you don't know what I'm talking about if you want to. You'll see what I mean."

Beverly stared at the door long after he was gone, thinking.

Later that evening, Beverly arrived home. It was the same house she was rewarded in the divorce. She kept telling herself that she was going to sell it, but so far she couldn't bring herself to put it on the market. There were just too many memories—the same ones David ran away from.

She shook her head and entered the cold house. Dropping her keys and purse on the foyer table, she shuffled through the day's mail and then made a face when she saw the Netflix red envelope. "Damn you, Clarence." She tossed the mail on the table and then headed up the stairs.

Every night she tried her best to block out the cold chill, the stillness and the ghosts. Every night she failed. Upstairs, before entering her bedroom, Beverly stopped and then glanced at the room down at the other end of the hall—the same room that had always called out to her. It was the same room that made it impossible for her to ever be able to sell the house.

"Pancakes! Pancakes!" Ruby cheered, making little bunny hops around the kitchen in her footie pajamas.

"Then pancakes it is." Lucius winked and tugged a chunk of her morning bushy hair.

"And I want lots of syrup," she said, rushing over to the refrigerator.

"It's in the cabinet, baby," he told her as he grabbed all the necessary skillets. "But you can hand me a couple of eggs out of there."

Ruby hopped right to it, loving being her daddy's helper. Together they made big, fluffy golden pancakes smothered in maple syrup. Cooking was a ritual with them since Erica was never really known for her cooking…or cleaning.

However, Lucius was awkward with everything else. His patience was often stretched thin with endless episodes of *SpongeBob* and *iCarly* and his manhood was often challenged when his little princess insisted on his wearing fake pink boas and strawberry-tinted lip gloss.

Despite all that, Lucius was determined to show his little girl a good time. With his visitations becoming more and more erratic he had to make the precious few days that he did get with his daughter special. He was trying his best to make things work without dragging his ex to court. But if things kept going the way they were, he would have no choice but to get a judge to put Erica back in line. Plus, having Ruby over instantly filled his usually cold, lonely house with much-needed warmth and laughter. Not to mention it kept him from obsessively daydreaming about Beverly Turner.

That morning when he'd awoken to find the bed empty and all her belongings gone, he was at first confused and then angry. Sure they had made a previous agreement, but he was offended that Beverly couldn't even be bothered to stick around long enough to say goodbye. In a way, he felt used. The only thing that was missing was money being left on the nightstand.

It didn't stop there.

Thinking about Beverly had affected his work. He was making an unusual amount of mistakes and had almost cost Keith Johnson's widow from obtaining her much-deserved eight-figure settlement. It wasn't like him to be so easily distracted and at times he even wondered why he was so upset anyway. He got *exactly* what he wanted: a wild weekend with no strings attached.

Maybe it wouldn't have been so bad if he had requested at least *one* string. The thought of never seeing Beverly Turner again bothered him. To not hear her laugh, to not see her smile and not feel her incredible body trembling and quaking beneath him—

"Daddy, can we go to the zoo?" Ruby asked, tugging on his arm. "I want to see Yang Yang."

Lucius smiled. Yang Yang was one of the four panda bears at the Atlanta Zoo. Ruby loved pandas—always had.

"Sure, we can go to the zoo this afternoon. I just need to swing by the off—" She frowned and he caught himself. "You know what? Scratch that. No work today."

"Yay!" She bounced around in her chair.

After their late breakfast and a couple more episodes of *SpongeBob,* Lucius got ready for their day trip to the zoo. However, before they could leave, he had to conquer the near-impossible task of doing his daughter's hair. What made it even more difficult was the fact that Ruby was extremely tender-headed. She was whining and flinching long before the brush touched her head.

The end result was always a loose, messy ponytail that had quite a few wayward strands sticking every which way but loose. But she was clean and wearing clothes that matched. In his opinion that put him well ahead of the game.

During the ride out to the zoo, Ruby chatted about everything from her new best friend at school, Penny, to whether or not Papa Andrew was going to buy her a puppy for her birthday. Lucius's hands tightened on the steering wheel at hearing that Erica's fiancé had now been elevated to *Papa Andrew*.

It was the natural progression of things, he supposed, but it was hard for him to think of his daughter calling some other man daddy or *papa*.

"When are you going to get married, Daddy?"

The question was so out of the blue that Lucius was rendered speechless.

"You don't want to get married, Daddy?" she concluded when he hadn't answered her.

"Um. Well…" He cleared his throat. "I haven't really given it any thought, sweetheart."

"How come?"

Another cough. "Well, you know Daddy works a lot and—"

"How come?" She crossed her legs in her seat.

"So I can make a good living and uh, well, so I can support and buy you nice things."

"Oh," Ruby said, sounding disappointed. "I thought it was because you don't have a girlfriend."

Lucius laughed. "Well, there's that, too."

"How come you don't have a girlfriend?"

Another round of sputtering ensued and then he came up with the same answer as before. "Well, you know Daddy works a lot…and there's little time for, uh, Daddy to find a girlfriend."

Ruby's face twisted in a confused frown. "Papa Andrew works and he says that he's going to marry Momma."

Lucius's hands tightened on the steering wheel again. Now his daughter was comparing him to another man. This definitely wasn't good.

"Don't you get lonely, Daddy?"

He glanced at her, surprised. Were her questions based on curiosity or observation? After staring into her large hazel eyes, his heart tugged at her open and honest concern. "Daddy is never lonely when you're around," he assured her.

Her instant smile warmed his heart…until she said, "I still think you need a girlfriend."

"You do, do you?" He laughed.

"Yep. That way you *and* Mommy can get married."

"To different people," he clarified.

Ruby nodded. "That way neither one of you will be lonely—when I'm not around."

Lucius shook his head. "You're something else."

"I know!" She busted out into giggles. After Lucius found a parking spot at the zoo, they unbuckled their seat belts and started to scramble out of their seats. "What's this?"

Lucius glanced over to see his daughter holding up

a shimmering gold earring. Beverly's earring. A half smile sloped across his face as he held out his hand and Ruby plopped the gold jewel into it. "This…is an opportunity."

Chapter 12

Wednesdays were normally slow days at Hoops and it was then that Beverly and her employees would perform inventory calculations, rearrange the floor and/or do some intense cleaning. Basically, it was just busywork. Clarence, whose hair salon was just a few doors down, dipped into the shop around lunchtime, carrying two plastic containers of his and Beverly's favorite grilled salmon salad from Le Chez restaurant.

"I'm here to rescue you," he announced when he entered her office.

Beverly looked up from her endless amount of paperwork and smiled. "You're a lifesaver."

"That's what they all say." Clarence fluttered his long lashes and then set their food down on the corner of the desk while he removed his jacket. "You just make sure that you buy me a fabulous gift for Christmas next month. I got my eye on this *gorgeous* Louis Vuitton Bastille bag."

Beverly laughed. "Louis Vuitton? Girl, you better get your man to hook you up. I was thinking along the lines of a free manny and peddy."

"Hmmph. Cheap heifer."

"Whatever." She cleaned a spot on her desk and then reached for her salad.

"I come not only bearing good food, I got some gossip, girl." He pulled out a magazine. "Word is music mogul Micah Ross is getting hitched."

"Really?" Beverly said. "You know he came to my class reunion a couple of weeks ago?"

"I know. I'm still mad that you didn't get me an autograph—at least from that fine-ass Justice Kane."

"You're always mad." Beverly looked around. "What—nothing to drink?"

Clarence's gaze raked her up and down. "Oh, no you didn't."

Beverly turned toward the small personal refrigerator and pulled out two iced tea bottles. "Look at that. Bam! I got you," she said, laughing.

"Good thing or we would've just had to bust out some water up in here."

Beverly took the first bite of her food and moaned her approval.

"If you moan like that over some food then I just know how you—"

"Cut it out," she warned with a sharp look.

Clarence snickered. "Fine. I was just saying."

"So who is Micah Ross marrying?"

"Some writer chick...Tamara Hodges, I think."

Beverly dropped her fork. "Get out of here. Are you for real?"

Clarence frowned at her reaction. "What? You know her?"

Beverly nodded while recalling the brief conversation she had with Tamara at Cork's ladies' room and, more importantly, her admitting her pregnancy. It wasn't hard to draw a conclusion. "Wow. Micah and Tamara." She shook her head. "Seems like a lot of people were hooking up at the reunion."

"Oh? Maybe at your twentieth they'll just cut to the chase and call it an orgy party."

"My goodness. Don't you ever quit?"

"Well, one of us got to be scandalous. It's how we keep balance in the world."

At the knock on her door, Beverly glanced up to Leslie, one of her part-time employees.

"There's someone here asking for you."

She frowned. "Who is it?"

Leslie shrugged and walked away.

Beverly glanced over at Clarence.

"Good help is hard to find," Clarence joked.

She shook her head, took another bite of her salad and then went to go talk to the customer. However, the moment she walked into the front of the store, her eyes instantly zoomed in on Lucius, who was standing in the center of Hoops and scanning through a rack of clothes.

Beverly stopped short and blinked, as if it would somehow erase what had to be a mirage—that is, until Lucius turned and smiled at her. "Lucius."

"Well, I'm glad that you still remember my name."

Leslie and the other employees started shifting curious glances their way.

"What are you doing here?" she whispered, looking around and growing uncomfortable about what everyone might hear.

Unfazed by her less than enthusiastic response, Lucius strolled over to her with his sly grin firmly in place. "What if I told you that I missed you? Would that be so bad?"

She stepped back. "This is not a good time—or place."

Lucius looked around, caught the curious stares and then nodded as if he understood. "Well, what would be a good time—and place?"

Clarence rounded the corner from the back room. "Well, I guess I better get…" He stopped and with one glance at Beverly and Lucius, knew something was up.

"Hello," Lucius said, flashing his breathtaking smile.

"Weeelll, heeelllooo." Clarence sashayed his way to Beverly's side. "Now who do we have here?"

An image of two trains colliding flashed behind Beverly's closed eyelids.

When it was clear that she wasn't about to make the introductions, Lucius thrust out a hand to Clarence. "Hello, I'm Lucius Gray. I'm an old college friend of Beverly's."

"Lucius?" Clarence's perfectly groomed brows jumped, and then his eyes slowly drank in Lucius's profile while his own sly smile slid across his face. "Well, nice to meet you. I heard sooooo much about you."

Beverly groaned and wondered if it was too much to ask for someone to shoot her.

"Oh, really?" Lucius's gaze swung to Beverly, who didn't doubt that she was at least fifteen different shades of red. "I guess I should be flattered."

"Mmm-hmm," Clarence said, still checking him out. "And I'm jealous."

"Clarence!" Beverly snapped, finally finding her tongue again.

"What? I'm just telling the truth."

"Isn't it about time for you to go back to work?" she hissed, glaring at him.

"Actually, I…um, promised Leslie I'd help her clean up behind the counter," he lied and turned toward the counter, which wasn't far enough away, so he could eavesdrop.

"So you told him about me?" Lucius said.

Beverly turned back to Lucius, wanting to get him out of the shop fast. "Look, this *really* isn't a good time."

"Maybe *I'm* the one that needs to be embarrassed," he said, ignoring her protest. "After all, I thought what we shared was supposed to be private. You know, just between me and you."

She actually felt a prick of guilt.

Lucius leaned forward and whispered, "It's okay. I forgive you." When he stepped back, he winked.

Feeling as if she was just involved in some type of rope-a-dope, Beverly shook her head to clear her mind and then grabbed him by the arm and pulled him toward the door. "Thanks for stopping by to forgive me, but…"

Lucius didn't budge. In fact, he seemed content to remain standing right where he was. "I haven't said why I stopped by," he said, seemingly amused by her flustered state.

She pulled him again, but he still didn't move.

"I wanted to return something to you."

Beverly stopped, her eyes narrowed with mistrust. "Return what?" She swore to herself that if he whipped out a pair of panties or something she would go ballistic. She watched him carefully as he reached inside his pocket and...produced an earring.

"I found it in the car when I gave you a *ride* that Saturday night."

Clarence snickered and then coughed like he was choking on a gigantic chicken bone.

Beverly was now twenty different shades of red as she snatched the earring from his hand. "Thanks. *Now* will you go?"

Lucius realized that this whole thing was going terribly wrong and he needed to change up his approach or risk walking out of there and never seeing Beverly again. "Maybe we should start over," he suggested. "I get the impression that I've upset you."

Beverly crossed her arms and glared at him. "Now why on earth would you get that impression?"

Clarence popped up like a jack-in-a-box. "Don't mind her. She always acts like an old fuddy-duddy."

"Clarence!"

"Sorry," Clarence said, though he didn't look the slightest bit sorry as he slinked back toward the counter.

Beverly turned back toward Lucius. "We had a deal, remember?"

Lucius shrugged. "Deals can always be renegotiated." He slid his hands into his pants pockets and rocked on his heels. He was taking a big chance laying it all out like this. "I'd like to come back to the table."

She was shaking her head before he was finished talking. "I—I can't," she whispered. "I'm not ready to dive into any kind of relationship right now." Beverly glanced around, hoping she was talking low enough. "Please go."

He considered her words, and then stepped closer to her. "It doesn't have to be a traditional relationship," he whispered. "We can just continue on the same course that we were on. Sex with no strings attached."

Beverly blinked.

Hopeful since she didn't immediately reject the idea, Lucius moved even closer so that their bodies brushed lightly against one another. "I don't know about you but I haven't been able to forget about that weekend."

The mistrust in her eyes vanished and was replaced with remembrance and longing.

"You can't tell me that you haven't been thinking about it, too." He leaned down and whispered into her ear, "Surely, you remember how good we are together. I remember how deep and tight your body felt, and how much you quiver when you're about to come."

She closed her eyes as he continued.

"It's like tiny little earthquakes while you tighten around me, literally causing my toes to curl and my lungs to collapse as I struggle to breathe in your scent." For emphasis, he took a deep sniff of her floral-scented hair. "Say you'll go out with me again. I promise you, you won't regret it."

Beverly quivered as if experiencing a phantom orgasm just from the memory of their coupling. When she opened her eyes, she was staring into Lucius's hazel eyes, which were glazed with passion.

"Say yes," he whispered.

"I—I—"

"Say yes," Lucius insisted gently.

"I—I—"

"Yes!" Clarence shouted.

Beverly jumped and then sprang away from Lucius. How in the hell had she forgotten where she was?

Clarence rushed back to her side and took over the conversation. "Yes. She'll go out with you. What day is good for you?"

Lucius blinked. "Well, um, how about this Friday night?"

"She'll be there."

"Clarence!"

"Shut up, girl. You don't know what's good for you," he said, waving her off. "What time?" he asked Lucius.

"Uh—how about seven o'clock?"

Beverly tried to jump back in. "The store doesn't close until—"

"She'll be ready," Clarence said, wheeling and dealing. "Do you have her address?"

Lucius frowned. "Actually, no."

"Leslie," Clarence called.

Leslie popped up next to them and handed him a scrap of paper.

"She'll be ready promptly at seven o'clock. Don't be late," Clarence said.

"Clarence—"

"Don't pay her any mind," he insisted to Lucius. "I'll have her dressed, ready and possibly tied to a chair. Just leave the details to me."

"And me," Leslie chimed in.

"What is this—mutiny?" Beverly asked.

"Yes!" Clarence and the rest of her employees shouted.

Astonished, Beverly stood there with her mouth open.

Amusement lit Lucius's eyes. "Seven o'clock, it is."

But Clarence wasn't through. "Make sure you bring flowers, champagne and condoms."

"Clarence!" Beverly shouted, stomping on his foot.

"Ouch!" He hopped away from her. "All right. All right. Forget the *flowers*."

Laughing and stuffing her address into his pocket, Lucius finally turned toward the door. "See you Friday night."

Chapter 13

"I can't believe I let you two talk me into this," Beverly whined as she watched Clarence rummage through her walk-in closet for what seemed like the millionth time. He was in search of the perfect outfit for her date.

"I don't see what the big damn deal is," Clarence said, holding up another dress for Leslie's inspection. "It's not like you had anything to do."

Perched on one corner of Beverly's bed, Leslie chimed in, "I think I like that one the best."

Clarence's face lit up over the periwinkle blue one-shoulder gown. "I like this, too. She could rock it with a nice pair of silver hoops and those black pumps we saw a few minutes ago."

Leslie bounced and clapped her hands. "She'll need a little bling around her neck, too."

"See, girl. I like the way you think." Clarence winked.

Beverly rolled her eyes. "Does anybody care what I think—or want?" she complained.

"No!" Clarence and Leslie shouted.

Beverly flinched, astonished by their unrelenting bossiness.

"Besides," Clarence said, laying the dress out on the bed, "I highly doubt that you even know what you want—other than to be left alone in this gilded suburban prison that you cherish so much."

"Ouch." Beverly frowned from the sting of his words.

"Sorry, baby, but the truth hurts. The sooner you face it, the faster you can heal."

Instead of responding, Beverly sat on the edge of her bed and continued to pout with her bottom lip poked out.

Leslie took pity on her and went to her side. "Really. What's the big deal?" She shrugged. "He said there would be no strings attached."

"That's what he said the last time and yet he just pops up out the blue. Looks like a big, *long* string to me."

Leslie persisted. "He told you—to return your earring."

Beverly placed a hand against the young girl's cheek while she shook her head. "You poor, poor naive little girl."

"If you're so scared about strings, then don't whip it on him so hard," Clarence reasoned. "Girl, you need to stop treating men like they have the bubonic plague."

"I don't treat them like that. I treat them like they have the *cheating* plague. Men aren't designed to be faithful—especially when things get tough. I learned that the hard way."

Clarence wasn't falling for it. "Girl, will you exhale

already?" he asked, rolling his eyes. "I'm a man and I refuse to believe that nonsense."

"Me, too," Leslie said, frowning. "I believe that there is someone for everybody out there."

Beverly looked at the girl as if she had just dropped from the sky. "How old are you again?"

"Leave her alone." Clarence pulled Leslie to his side. "Ain't nobody talking about you two being faithful. This isn't that kind of relationship. Lucius made that perfectly clear. We are talking fucking...screwing... getting your groove on. Whatever the hell you want to call it. You can't tell me that the last time you two bumped uglies that you didn't come back to work mellow as hell. Damn, we couldn't get you to stop singing around the store." He looked at Leslie. "What the hell was the name of that song she was singing?"

"'I'm Every Woman,'" Leslie answered, smirking.

"Uh-huh." Clarence bobbed his head, grinning. "Came back looking and acting all brand-new. Now you've gone back to being a tense sourpuss."

"Am not." Beverly folded her arms and pushed her bottom lip out farther.

Clarence finally relented and went to sit next to her on the edge of the bed. "Look, all we're saying is that you need to look at this as every once in a while you need a little...*tune-up* to keep you in a good mood. And who better to do that with than that gorgeous hazel-eyed hunk? Girl, you were holding out on me. You didn't tell me that he was *that* fine. Don't think I didn't check out the dick imprint in those pants the other day. Mr. Lawyer Man is working with some serious equipment. Oookaaay?" He held up his hand and Leslie delivered a high five.

"Boy, you're a fool," Beverly said.

"No, girl. You're a fool if you don't stop looking a gift horse in the mouth. Now hop in the shower and wash your hair so I can blow you out, real quick."

With a final pout, Beverly stood and then shuffled her way toward the bathroom. Once she was in the shower, she faced her own insecurities about tonight. The real reason she was nervous about seeing Lucius again was that she didn't trust herself. She had just *barely* managed to walk away from him three weeks ago. The emotions that he so easily accessed scared the hell out her. Lucius was the kind of man any woman could fall in love with—herself included. It was really that simple and that scary. What if the next time she couldn't walk away? Would love and all its thorns scar up what was left of her heart?

The last time Lucius had been this nervous for a date, he had to think all the way back to his junior prom. That night he was convinced that he was going to throw up all over his sixteen-year-old date, mainly because her father was like the police chief of the Atlanta Police Department and he'd not only threatened to kill Lucius if anything happened—harmful or sexual—to his daughter, but he also promised that no one would ever find his body.

There was a lot of pressure riding on this date with Beverly. Mainly because it had been harder than he anticipated to convince her to go out with him again. Actually, he didn't convince her—her friends brokered the deal. If things went wrong tonight he had every reason to believe that she would kick him to the curb again and the door of possibilities would close forever.

It wasn't hard for him to put two and two together and conclude that Beverly's hesitance about dating had everything to do with her ex-husband, David Clark. Lucius would never forget how shaken up Beverly had been when David popped up at the reunion's Sunday brunch. There was a wound there still in need of healing. The crazy part was that lately he'd been thinking about him being the one to heal it. The train on which his thoughts were traveling was headed straight to the town of hypocrisy. What the hell did he know about healing old wounds? He had an ex-wife who couldn't stand him and a daughter she frequently used to emotionally blackmail him. The only way he dealt with his own issues was to bury himself in work.

Like Beverly did.

He frowned. Truth of the matter was that they had more in common than he thought.

Following the directions that were displayed on his GPS unit, Lucius turned on the long spiraling driveway leading to Beverly's house. "Nice," he said, as the stunning two-story brick home came into view.

Coming down the same driveway, Lucius rolled past a black Buick LaCrosse that suddenly blew its horn. He glanced over and saw Clarence and Leslie waving.

"Have a good time! Don't do anything I wouldn't do!" Clarence hollered and then sped past him.

Lucius laughed and shook his head. "Maybe I should put those two on my Christmas list."

However, when he climbed out of the car, there was no mistaking the eerie sadness that permeated the air. *Can a house be sad?* He shook his head, dismissing the crazy thought. He rang the doorbell and while he waited for Beverly to answer, again he glanced around the house and shivered when a strong gust of wind blew and caused a slew of fall leaves to stir and dance.

He heard footsteps approach and then a second later, the front door pulled open and revealed a different but even more stunning Beverly, compared to just a few days ago. "Wow."

She smiled. "That was just the reaction I was aiming for," she admitted.

Lucius's smile widened. "You changed your hair."

Beverly patted one side of her now-shoulder-length hair. "I just changed it back to its original color. You like it?"

"I love it," he said, staring at her golden locks. They matched her eyes perfectly.

As usual she wore a knockout dress that hugged her thick and dangerous curves. Lucius's erection started to tent his pants. Belatedly, he remembered the gifts in his hands. "Oh." He held up a bright bouquet of yellow roses and yellow Peruvian lilies. "I hope you like them."

Beverly beamed and took a good whiff of their fragrant scent. "Yellow for friendship."

Lucius tapped the side of his temples to indicate how much of a thinking man he was. "And—" he lifted the bottle in his other hand "—champagne."

Beverly's eyebrows arched with amusement. "Does that mean that I don't have to guess what's in your back pocket?"

"Well," he said, grinning, "an old Boy Scout always comes prepared."

She shook her head and then stepped back so that he could enter. "Come on in."

He crossed the threshold and stepped into a yawning stillness that felt a lot like a graveyard. Determined to put on his best face, he glanced around the immaculate and beautifully decorated home and said, "Nice place you have."

"Thanks. Come on in." She led him to the living room and gestured toward a full-length leather couch. "I'll be right back."

Lucius nodded and sat down, still taking in the place. The moment Beverly left him alone in the living room, he was uncomfortable about the house's silence. At his place, at least there were the annoying crickets chirping out in the yard. Here, there was nothing.

It was odd.

He continued looking around. The place was spotless and something told him that the room hadn't been used in a long time. He didn't know how he knew that, he just did. Plus—something was missing.

Lucius stood from the couch and slowly walked around the room. There were plenty of nice knick-knacks, an impressive mirror over the fireplace and an interesting silver art-deco clock on one wall and...

Then it hit him. The room lacked warmth, a sense of identity and character because there were no *pictures*. Women usually loved pictures and yet there wasn't a single frame on the fireplace mantel, tabletop or wall.

Beverly suddenly reappeared with the flowers in a vase. "Here we go. I'll just set these down over here," she said, placing them on the glass coffee table. "There, that looks nice."

"Beautiful," Lucius agreed, halfheartedly. He was ready to leave. "I guess we better get going. We have reservations."

"Oh. Okay." She smiled and they both walked back

to the foyer, where she retrieved a light black dress coat. "Where are we going?" she asked.

"How about we let that be a surprise?" He helped her slip into her coat and then escorted her out to his vehicle.

Beverly didn't doubt for a moment that Lucius had booked them at some fabulous restaurant for dinner. And he did: Nicholas, a stunning five-star restaurant that was a fixture on the Buckhead dining scene. However, instead of being escorted to a table inside of the restaurant, their host led them to a private table on the roof.

Beverly gasped at the stunning sight of the simple white linen tablecloth and an elaborate display of string white lights and candles. There was even a speaker where the music from the restaurant was being directed up there as well. "I don't believe it." She turned to him. "How?"

"Let's just say that I pulled a few strings." He winked and then led her to the table.

As Beverly walked, she felt as if somehow she was standing on top of the world. Below them was a mass of blinking lights, while above them hung a crystal-clear full moon. "This is so beautiful," she sighed. The little girl inside her felt like spinning around in a circle like a fairy-tale princess in a Disney movie.

"I'm glad that you like it." Lucius beamed from ear-to-ear.

"I *love* it."

"Madam." The waiter handed her and Lucius menus and then quickly told them about the night's special while simultaneously opening the bottle of champagne that Lucius had brought along. Once he took their orders, he bowed deeply and disappeared back down-stairs.

"Okay," Beverly said, "I have to admit that I'm very impressed."

"I do aim to impress and *please,*" he said.

"I can vouch that you can do both very well." She locked eyes with him and took a deep sip of her champagne. Beverly watched as his chest expanded with pride.

"You better watch out. You're gonna make a brother start blushing."

"Now that I would like to see."

His brows jumped. "Shall I tell you what *I* would like to see this evening as well?"

It was Beverly's turn to blush. "I think I might know what that might be," she said. "Who knows? Maybe if you play your cards right, you might just get what you want."

"Then expect me to be a good boy all night."

She exaggerated a frown. "I don't want a good boy."

Lust suddenly polished Lucius's hazel eyes. "Don't play with me. I'll have you spread out on this table in a hot minute."

"Promises, promises, promises," she teased just as the waiter and two servers waltzed out onto the roof, carrying their food.

Their eyes remained locked together as their plates were set before them. Their bodies were warming at the thought of what the night held for them.

"Will there be anything else?" the server asked.

"Yeah." Lucius pulled out a folded hundred-dollar bill. "We'd like to be alone for the rest of the night. If we need anything else, we'll call downstairs."

"Yes, sir." The waiter accepted the tip with a gracious smile and then gave them another deep bow before ushering the other servers back downstairs.

Beverly held her laughter in check until they were alone again. "Now you've given them the wrong impression. Lord only knows what he thinks we'll be doing up here."

"Whatever he's thinking I hope he's right," Lucius said.

"What—up here? I was joking earlier."

"I wasn't."

Beverly blushed again and took in her dreamlike surroundings.

"Have you ever made love outside before?"

"You *know* I have."

He waved that admission off. "A car doesn't count since technically you're inside of something."

"I'd like to have seen you tell that to a cop had we been caught."

"You're avoiding the question," he countered, smiling.

"I never really thought about it," she said, stalling.

Lucius chuckled. "So think about it now."

"Okay...so...maybe I haven't." She shrugged.

"Ahh. So I could be your first."

"I guess that's one way of looking at it."

Lucius wiggled his brows. "I will."

They continued to give each other teasing looks while they ate their meals. Though the food was wonderful, it was hard for Beverly to concentrate on anything other than the possibility of making love to Lucius on the rooftop.

"What's the matter? Are you not hungry?" he asked

after noting the small bites she was taking and how much food was left on her plate while his was almost clean. "If you don't finish your meal, you won't be able to have your dessert."

"Dessert?" Her heart started pounding.

"Mmm-hmm." He nodded. "Dessert is the best part of the meal. My favorite is something chocolate…with a creamy center."

Beverly twitched in her seat.

"Don't you like chocolate?" he pressed.

Beverly thought the altitude must be affecting her brain because suddenly she could barely think, but after a long pregnant silence she managed to whisper, "I love chocolate."

Lucius grinned. "That's what I remembered."

She grabbed her glass and tossed the champagne down her throat like it was water. This brother had all kinds of memories playing in her head. When she looked back over at him, she couldn't seem to get her gaze to rise above his luscious smile. The man had the sexiest pair of lips she had ever seen. Every few seconds she caught his pink tongue darting and gliding across his lips, and could feel her panties dampen a bit. Good Lord, how on earth had she been able to make it three whole weeks without that mouth caressing or kissing her body?

A new song began to play over the speaker and Beverly instantly recognized the first few bars of "What a Diff'rence a Day Makes."

Lucius recognized the music as well. "Would you care to dance?"

She smiled. "I would love to."

He stood from his chair and walked around to assist

her up. Standing from their table, Lucius took Beverly into his arms and they swayed together cheek to cheek. As before, Lucius hummed in tune to the music and Beverly's mind wandered.

How was it that being in his arms melted away all the stress and challenges in her life? If she allowed herself to be truthful with herself she felt completely and utterly safe in his arms. Nothing and no one could harm her while she was with him. Beverly closed her eyes and hummed along with him. She liked the way their voices blended together.

"Maybe we should take this act on the road," Lucius whispered in her ear.

"Celebrity couples rarely make it." Her eyes fluttered open when she realized what she had said.

Lucius pulled back so that he could stare directly into her face.

Beverly saw that there was a question in his eyes and for a few heart-pounding seconds she was afraid that he'd give voice to it. Instead, he smiled, kissed the tip of her nose and clearly decided to let it go. She placed her head back against his cheek and mentally said a prayer of gratitude because…what was she thinking? Was she secretly wishing for more than what he offered—more than she confessed to wanting?

Seconds later, she felt his soft lips pressing against the shell of her ear, then her cheek, and before she knew it they were sharing a gentle but soul-stirring kiss where their tongues danced and caressed one another. *Oh, God, he tastes so good.*

Lucius's hand crept down her back and then suggestively slid across and around her thick booty.

Beverly pushed herself up against his firm frame

and gasped when she felt his bulging erection press back against her pelvis. Without thinking she reached down, cupped him and then started stroking through the seams of his pants.

Lucius sucked in a long breath through his gritted teeth. "You know you shouldn't be starting anything you can't finish, right?"

"What? I thought your little friend just wanted to say hi to me."

"Little?"

She laughed at his inflated ego. "Hmm. Maybe I need some help with my memory."

"Maybe." He kissed her again, sucked on her bottom lip. "Come over here." He directed her back to the table and sat down in his chair. "Have a seat." He patted his lap.

Beverly hesitated.

"What—you scared?" he asked.

"Of course not," she said, accepting his challenge and taking a seat on his lap.

Lucius smiled and tipped her head toward him so he could reclaim her lips, but while he did so his free hand cupped and squeezed her breast.

Maybe it was the music, the night's air or even the full moon that emboldened Beverly, but she went back to cupping and stroking Lucius through his pants. As her hormones continued to spin and her body started to heat, she took it a step further by unzipping him and then caressing him through his black briefs.

"Don't stop there," he whispered.

Should she dare—out here in the open?

He pulled back from her lips to stare up into her eyes. "You don't have to if you don't want to."

At that moment, more than anything she wanted to please him *and* she wanted to do something that she had never done before. Summoning her courage, Beverly freed his erection from his briefs and exposed him to the sultry night air. She smiled, loving the feeling of holding him like this again.

Lucius moaned, "You have *wonderful* hands."

The praise only stroked her ego. "You like that, do you?"

He nodded. "You know what I'd like better?"

She waited.

"Stand up," he ordered.

Beverly did as she was told.

Lucius took a good long look at her. "I love that dress on you," he whispered, reaching out and slowly lifting it up. "It's a beautiful color against your skin," he added until he saw her sexy periwinkle-blue lace panties and garter belt. "I like it when a woman coordinates."

She laughed, more so she could get rid of some more nervous butterflies that fluttered in her belly.

"Hold your dress up," he said.

Again, she followed his orders while he reached into his back pocket and removed a condom. They were really going to do this out here on the restaurant's rooftop. Something wicked shivered down her spine and caused her clit to start pounding hard in time to her racing heartbeat.

"Now come back over here and climb back onto my lap," he said.

She glanced around, briefly wondering if anyone could see them from another roof or what would happen if their waiter came back upstairs. Beverly glanced back over at Lucius, her eyes locking with his. While watching the unmistakable passion flicker in his hazel eyes, she stepped closer and then straddled his hips.

Lucius slid the bottom of her panties over to the side and then sighed in ecstasy when she lowered onto his hard erection. It still amazed him how her body seemed to fit him like a glove, and when she began to move he was in serious danger of his eyes rolling out of his head.

Beverly didn't know how it was possible, but she was definitely having trouble getting air into her lungs. Lucius filled her thoroughly and completely.

"Oh, baby. I can't tell you how much I've missed you," Lucius panted, gripping her butt and helping her slam back down on his dick in a good even rhythm. "Pull your breasts out for me."

Still rocking her body, Beverly unhooked the pin that held the one strap on her dress together and allowed it to fall and pool at her waist.

Lucius's mouth watered at the sight of a strapless periwinkle bra. When she pulled her full breasts from their cups, he quickly leaned forward and sucked in her marble-sized nipples.

Beverly shuddered and quaked and before long, she felt her own eyes begin to roll to the back of her head. Nearing her first orgasm, her rhythm started to slow so Lucius found himself thrusting his hips up harder and faster. "That's it, baby," he panted. "You coming?"

"Y-yeeeesss. Please don't stop."

"I don't plan on stopping, baby." He hammered away while fighting for control himself. He didn't want to come before her, but it was looking like it was going to be a nail-biter to the finish line. Lucius could already feel his toes curling again—a dangerous sign.

"Ooooh, Lucius. Baaabbbeeeee."

"That's right, baby. Let yourself go," he urged. "Ahhh." He bit his lower lip.

Tiny sparks started shooting off in Beverly's head a second before her body started tingling and convulsing. "Oooh, baby. I'm coming."

Hell. So am I!

Beverly finally let herself go as she screamed out his name. Two seconds later, Lucius wrapped an arm around her body tightly and growled with his head planted in the valley between her breasts.

Collapsing against him, Beverly finally filled her lungs with the night's sweet oxygen. When she was finally able to speak, she said, "You're right. Dessert is the best part of the meal."

Luicus laughed and slapped her on the butt. "Let me get you out of here so I can really show you what you've been missing."

Chapter 14

Why did sex with Lucius Gray feel so much like making love?

This was the question that kept racing through Beverly's mind as her supposed *no-strings attached* lover continued to bump and grind in between her legs, all the while stirring up her emotions and eroding her sanity. Never in her life had a man expertly and consistently known when and how to work all of her G-buttons. It was as if he'd stolen her body's owner's manual and studied it inside and out.

Just like their rooftop extravaganza, the presidential suite at the Four Seasons Hotel turned out to be a hopeless romantic's dream: candles, music and red and yellow rose petals sprinkled everywhere. But the main attraction was the huge king-size bed with the leather-upholstered headboard. That was where they now continued to work out and exorcise their sex demons.

Sweat made their beautiful brown bodies feel like silk and it also made it easier for Lucius to glide so deep into her, it felt as if he was bumping up against her heart. Enraptured, Beverly was unaware that tears leaked from the slits of her closed eyes. All she knew was that she had never felt pleasure like this with anyone else in her entire life.

"What are you crying for, baby?" Lucius whispered and then kissed the tracks of her tears.

She shook her head instead of answering and by her hip movements urged him not to stop.

Still concerned, he asked, "Am I hurting you, baby?"

Was he crazy? Couldn't he see how good he was making her feel—how he'd easily abolished the concrete wall that she'd spent years building around her heart?

Lucius's hips stopped moving, causing Beverly to panic and claw at his back. "N-no. Don't stop!" she begged.

"All right, baby. I got you." He started his slow grind again while Beverly moaned her relief. "Is this what you wanted?"

No. This was what she needed, but she couldn't get the words out. The only thing she could do was squirm, whimper and cry.

"Don't you ever leave me like that again," he whispered hoarsely in her ear. "You hear me, baby?" For emphasis he buried himself balls-deep into her silky wetness, causing a baritone moan to resonate from within her soul. "There won't be any more of that creeping out while I'm sleeping nonsense. You got that, baby?"

She nodded vigorously.

"Let me hear you say it."

Beverly struggled to string words together for a complete sentence. "I—I won't…"

"Creep out in the middle of the night," Lucius aided her.

"C-creep out in the…m-middle of the n-night," she finished, just as her thighs began to shake and a wonderful pressure at the tip of her clit started pounding out of control.

"Look at me, baby," he ordered.

Her long lashes fluttered open and their eyes locked. The passion that stared back at her threatened to consume her. However, there was nothing that could make her turn away at that moment.

Lucius took her arms and stretched them over her head while he pounded in and out, his hips alternating from side to side without mercy. When her orgasm was just seconds from detonating, the moaning stopped while she held her breath in anticipation.

Then…it hit and her voice came back to full power, screaming his name and not giving a damn if the people in the next room heard her or not. Lucius quickly followed her over the edge of sanity, exploding so hard he shook from his very foundation. He collapsed, panting and raining tiny kisses across her fevered brow.

How on earth does this woman keep doing this to me? He slid down next to her and pulled her close. To his amazement, she was already knocked out fast asleep. He smiled, his male ego expanding. As he stared down at her from his lofty cloud of pride, he drank in her glowing and angelic profile. *She's so beautiful,* he marveled, feeling his heart muscles squeeze.

Lucius thought about his pledge for them to have a no-strings-attached nonrelationship and recognized the joke it was. He was already attached; he had been from the first moment he saw her stroll into that bar wearing that knockout red dress. If he was really truthful with himself, he would admit that he had fallen hard for Beverly Turner and that he was tangled in so many strings that he could barely breathe.

He leaned down and brushed a butterfly kiss against the tip of her nose. This was peace and serenity like he'd never known and now that he had her back in his life he knew at that moment that he would move hell and high water to keep her in it.

Beverly stirred in his arms and once again her eyes fluttered open.

"Hello, sleepyhead."

She smiled sheepishly. "Did I pass out?"

He nodded and tweaked her cheek. "Maybe you overexerted yourself."

Beverly laughed.

"What?"

"You're fishing for a compliment," she accused.

"Who, me?" Lucius pressed a hand against his chest in mock innocence. "I was just making an observation. You know, judging by the amount of sweat and hollering you were doing, I said to myself, 'Self, if Beverly don't slow down, she's going to overexert herself.'"

She popped him on the shoulder. "You're not funny."

"No?" He frowned. "Maybe there's something wrong with your funny bone. I should take a look at it." Lucius pulled back the top sheet and pretended to look under her breasts.

"What are you doing? My funny bone isn't under there."

"Shhh. I'm in charge of the inspection here." He tickled her side and giggled. "Oooh. Maybe your funny bone is over here." Lucius moved over and placed a kiss against the curve of her hip.

Beverly sighed.

"Nope. That's not it." He slipped down farther and could tell by the way her stomach muscles tightened that she was holding her breath, waiting for his next move. Smiling, he dipped two fingers inside the fat folds of her pussy. Her wet walls quivered around his fingers. "Maybe it's here." He kissed those same fat lips. "Should I check inside here, baby?"

Beverly managed a weak, whispered reply. "Y—yes."

Without missing a beat, Lucius scooped her firm thighs into his hands and then began to lick each side of her throbbing clit.

Beverly shook and moaned.

"Oh, this is some good candy here," he praised. "You can give a brother a sugar high."

She smiled as she squeezed her big breasts together and pinched her nipples.

Lucius's long tongue slithered and snaked its way inside her, lapping up her sweet juices until her thick, chocolate thighs began quaking again around his head.

"Oooh, Lucius. You're going to make me come again," she moaned.

He licked harder, faster.

"Aaaaaaaah." She swirled her hips, grinding her wetness against his open mouth.

Lucius waited until he knew that she was hot and ready, then slipped two fingers inside her moist cave.

Beverly's nails clawed at the soft sheets. New tears surfaced and rolled from her eyes as bliss blossomed and enfolded her. Before she knew it, she was crying— *really* crying.

Lucius glided up her tall body, gathered her in his arms and rained more kisses across her face. "Shhh, baby. Don't cry, it's going to be all right," he promised.

Would it? She didn't know anymore. Beverly curled under his shoulder and washed his chest with her tears. Why was she crying? She wished she knew. Maybe it was nothing or maybe it was everything. Tomorrow she would probably hate herself for this—to allow herself to be this vulnerable with Lucius, but for right now, she didn't care. She just wanted him to hold her.

It was a long time before her tears subsided. When they did, she was both surprised and relieved that there didn't seem to be any awkwardness hanging in the air between them. However, something did change—something small and invisible that was growing stronger by the second.

The question was whether or not she could handle it. She closed her eyes and tried to block it out, but love nipped at her heart, determined that it would not be denied. *No strings. No strings,* she chanted inside her head. But she imagined that there was another voice, laughing at her futile attempt.

Beverly vowed that she would hang on, by the tips of her nails, if need be.

I won't fall in love. I won't fall in love. Her tears started up again.

"Awww, sweetheart. Don't do that." He started kissing away her tears again.

She clung to him and said without thinking, "Make love to me." *What? What did I just say?*

"Yes, baby. Anything you want." Lucius maneuvered around, slid on a new condom and entered her so deftly and smoothly that she came on the spot. When she caught her breath again, she locked gazes with him. She was getting accustomed to seeing that same hunger and passion in his eyes and she was loving it as much as she was afraid that she was falling in love with him.

Beverly pushed and then rolled him over to take the top position.

Lucius licked his fat, juicy lips as he watched her wind her hips. Her first strokes were so slow and deep that even though he didn't say anything, his twisting facial expressions said it all. She picked up speed, causing her round butt to slap hard against his legs and hips. Suddenly, he wasn't so quiet, sucking and hissing through his gritted teeth.

Beverly knew he was on the brink of exploding, but was also struggling to prolong the moment. She smiled and pounded down on him without mercy. As far as she was concerned, she was in control of this groove and she wanted him to come when she wanted him to come.

Lucius was swept away by how good Beverly looked gliding up and down, and then grinding every other stroke. Her full breasts jiggled and bounced and were causing a brother to get dizzy. But he knew that he had to give up the ghost when he felt that familiar tingle in his toes. He reached around and filled his hand with her bouncing booty. Soon he was moaning and groaning so loud, he wouldn't be surprised if people thought there was a wounded animal in the room.

Beverly's wet walls started to contract and before he knew it, they were both crying out to the heavens and then floating somewhere in the clouds.

Chapter 15

For two bliss-filled weeks, Lucius and Beverly continued with their farce of a *no-strings-attached* relationship and everyone working at Hoops took notice of Beverly's remarkable change. Not only would she sing "I'm Every Woman" but she had added "Tell Me Something Good" and "Sexual Healing" to her musical repertoire. Bottom line, she felt good—damn good—and there was no point in pretending otherwise. Of course, now her good mood brought out the green monster in her friends.

"Now I'm just flat-out jealous," Clarence admitted after watching Beverly flit around the store, smiling grandly to all the customers that flowed through her door. "I know I said I wanted you to relax, but I don't know if I can handle all this saccharine, bubble-gum B.S."

"I guess that means you still haven't found yourself a new man?" Beverly asked, ignoring his attempt to rain on her parade.

"Don't worry about me, sweetheart. I'm just sitting on the bench for a couple innings. I'll be back in the game before the seventh-inning stretch. You can believe that."

"Well, I think it's wonderful," Leslie said, refolding a stack of sweaters at one of the display tables. "Life is too short to be miserable. If your man is giving you what you need, then more power to you."

Beverly held up her hands. "Well, I wouldn't exactly call him *my* man. More like my very good friend with fringe benefits."

"Don't you mean French benefits?" Clarence started making annoying kissing noises.

Beverly didn't break her stride, but flashed him the bird for his heckling. "I don't know how many times I've told you that green is *not* your color."

Clarence rolled his eyes. "Whateva. My next man is gonna be fine and is going to put your big-dick play-boy to shame."

"Clarence!" Beverly stomped her foot. "Boy, I have customers in here," she hissed.

He glanced around the store. "Please, we all grown folks up in here."

Leslie snickered.

"Don't you have customers today?" Beverly asked.

"Not until two o'clock—and don't change the subject," he warned. "We're in the middle of stirring your fruit punch right now. Are you and Mr. Lover-Lover spending Thanksgiving together tomorrow or are you going to your parents'?"

Beverly's cheeks flushed guiltily. "Well, Lucius has mentioned that since his ex-wife was taking his daughter to Boston that he would be alone for the holiday."

Clarence and Leslie shot a look at each other.

"What?" Beverly asked.

"You know when you start spending the holidays together it means you taking things to another level."

Beverly glanced away. It felt as if she and Lucius were advancing to another level, despite her having a few conflicting emotions.

Clarence crept over to her, his eyes narrowing with suspicion. "Do you *want* things to move to a new level?"

She shrugged. "I don't know. I'm just going with the flow right now."

"Oh, my God," he gasped, pressing a hand to his chest. "You're really feeling this brother." Suddenly, Clarence threw his arms around Beverly. "I was just playing before, but, girl, I'm so proud of you taking this huge step."

"Whoa. Whoa. Whoa." She tossed up her arms and wiggled out of his embrace. "I didn't say all of that. I'm just taking baby steps."

Clarence's neck swiveled back. "Baby steps? Girl, you slept with him on your first date—well, I don't even know if you can call it a date."

"Will you please keep your voice down?" Beverly hissed. After another glance around, she said, "Contrary to what you might believe, I don't want everybody to know my business."

"Please. You just scared that everybody is going to think that you're a ho. Screw 'em. Hos need love, too."

Beverly pressed two fingers against the center of

Clarence's head and pushed him away from her. "Boy, you're too much."

"All right. All right. I'm happy for you. I think it's great that you're diving back into the pool of love." He held up a hand before she could protest. "I know. I know. You didn't say anything about being in love, but—" he locked gazes with her "—it's written all over your face whether you want to admit it or not."

The bell above the shop's door jingled. Beverly turned and then immediately her face lit up. "Kyra!" She rushed over and embraced her friend. "What are you doing here?"

"I came by to see you, silly. And to show you this— *bam!*" She threw out her hand where a white diamond solitaire sparkled back at them. "Your girl is engaged."

Beverly's eyes bulged. "Oh, my God."

Clarence literally hip-bumped Beverly out of the way. "Ooooh, girl. Who the hell are you marrying— Michael Jordan or some damn body? Leslie, come look at this chick's rock."

"Isn't it gorgeous?" Kyra giggled.

Beverly stood with her mouth hanging open. "You and…"

"Terrence," Kyra supplied. "He popped the question. Can you believe it? After all these years, we're actually going to get married. Bev, it was sooo sweet, he proposed to me at the same exact spot where we met ten years ago at Hollington." Her bubbling excitement was infectious.

"That's wonderful," Beverly finally said, opening her arms and embracing her friend. "I'm so happy for you."

"Thanks. My other good news is that Terrence accepted the coaching and teaching job at Hollington. So we'll be staying right here in Atlanta." Kyra stepped back and smiled at her. "I keep pinching myself every ten minutes to make sure I'm not dreaming."

Knowing the history between Kyra and Terrence caused Beverly's heart to overflow with joy for her friend.

Clarence beamed. "Sounds like love was all up in the air at that college reunion shindig. What—this makes the third engagement?" he asked, looking to Beverly for confirmation. "I wonder if my hair college throws reunion parties. Maybe I'm missing out on something."

"Speaking of which," Kyra said, beaming. "Did you hear about Tamara Hodges and Micah Ross?"

Beverly folded her arms. "Yeah. We read about it in *Luster* magazine."

"Stunning, huh?" Kyra giggled. "No doubt Micah is going to throw her some fabulous wedding out in La La Land, but I tossed in a good word for Hoops to Tamara. So don't be surprised if she drops in."

Beverly blinked. "I don't do wedding gowns."

"Not the gown, silly. But for her engagement party dress. The dress will get a lot of attention since Micah is a big-time mover and shaker in the music industry."

Beverly lit up. "Thanks, girl."

"C'mon. You know I'll always have your back. Plus, I was hoping by hooking you up it will mean I'll get a little discount on my own engagement party dress?"

"I'll do better than that. Your dress will be my wedding gift to you."

"Aww. Thank you."

They shared another hug and then Beverly led Kyra to the alteration room, where she could take down her friend's measurements and discuss her vision for what type of dress she'd like for a quaint engagement party. Leslie brought back a couple of flutes of champagne and before Beverly knew it, two hours had passed and Kyra had to go.

"'Bye, I'll see you in a couple of weeks," Beverly said, waving.

As Kyra was leaving Clarence was returning to the store.

"Finished with your afternoon appointment?" Beverly asked.

"Mmm-hmm," he said, following her to her office with a slick smile.

She stopped, not liking his calculating smile. "What?"

"What-what?" He played dumb.

Beverly folded her arms beneath her chest and waited him out.

Clarence finally relented. "I just keep thinking that with so much reunion love in the air that *possibly* it's infected one more couple."

She quickly caught his meaning. "I'm *not* in love."

He folded his arms to match her stance. "Methinks thou protest too much."

"Mr. Gray, I have a Kevin Stayton on line one," Maggie chirped over Lucius's speakerphone.

Surprised, Lucius pulled his nose out of the piles of legal briefs and picked up the phone. "Kevin! How the hell are you?"

"I'm doing good, man. I'm doing good," Kevin said. "I know it's been a minute since the reunion and when we talked about the CHRIS Kids Foundation."

Lucius eased back in his chair. He had forgotten

about Kevin's request about helping the charity foundation.

"I'm sorry about taking so long getting back to you, but things have been a little hectic dealing with wedding preparations."

"Hey, it's cool. I completely understand. I've been meaning to congratulate on your pending nuptials. That was really cool taking the stage at the reunion dance party. I kept telling Beverly that something was going on between you two."

Kevin's deep laughter rumbled over the line. "Yeah. I don't think I'll forget Chloe's stunned face when my proposal finally sunk in. Priceless."

"I'm happy for you, man." Lucius was unprepared for a sudden stream of fantasy images of him dropping on one knee before Beverly. Only problem was he suspected her response wouldn't be anything like Chloe Jackson's at the reunion dance party, but more like a screaming heroine in a horror movie. For now, he had to settle for the pretense of a *no-strings-attached* relationship, despite the fact that they practically saw each other every day now. In fact, she spent more nights at his place than hers. A lot of times, she used the excuse that his house was a lot closer to her shop than her own, but he knew the truth. She was starting to care for him—maybe even love him—but she was nowhere near ready to admit it.

Lucius forced himself to concentrate on Kevin's phone call. He was more than happy to agree to do pro bono work for the CHRIS Kids Foundation. He'd heard a lot of good things about the charity based here in Atlanta and was extremely impressed at Kevin's passion and dedication to the group. After the call, he glanced at his watch and smiled when he saw that it was exactly five o'clock.

"Time to go." He quickly tossed a few case files into his briefcase and grabbed his suit jacket.

Maggie entered the office, carrying a new stack of legal briefs, but then stopped and stared at him. "Leaving?"

"Yep. I'm calling it a day," he said, wondering whether he should stop by the store and surprise Beverly with a home-cooked meal tonight.

His secretary set the briefs down on his desk and then crossed her arms. "All right. What gives?" she asked cautiously. "I've never known you to just work forty hours a week."

"And if I recall, you always said that I worked too much."

"And since when do you take my advice?"

He walked from behind his desk. "Heeey, better late than never, right?"

Maggie shook her head as she followed him out of the office. "*Something* is going on with you—I'm inclined to believe that it may be a woman."

"Are you now?" he said, refusing to sate her curiosity.

"It's that or you jumped the fence and are seeing a man," she goaded.

"Hmmm." Lucius refused to take the bait, and pressed a button for the elevator.

"Oh, you're good," she said.

Lucius chuckled as the elevator's door slid open. "Good night, Maggie."

"This isn't over," she warned, laughing.

In the parking deck, Lucius hopped into his Crossover and turned over the engine. Lauryn Hill's CD was still in his CD player, which only boosted his good mood. Unfortunately, that all ended when his cell phone rang five minutes later. "Hello, Erica," he said flatly.

"What time are you going to be home?" she asked without preamble.

He frowned, recognizing an Erica trap when he heard one. "Why?"

"Because I'm bringing *your* daughter over. Is that a problem?"

"Of course not," he said, insulted.

"Good—because you're keeping her through the Thanksgiving holiday."

"All right." Lucius waited for an explanation, but when clearly there wasn't one forthcoming, he asked, "I thought you were taking her to Boston?"

"Well, I'm not. *Okay?* There's no reason why she can't stay with you. You're her father, remember?"

Lucius drew a deep breath and counted to ten. "I'm not complaining about keeping her, Erica. I just wanted to know why there was a change in plans. I'd love to have her for the holidays. I just wanted to know—"

"Great. It's settled," she snapped. "Now what time will you be home?"

"I—I guess in about ten minutes. Why?"

"I'll see you in ten minutes." She hung up.

Lucius pulled the phone from his ear and stared at it. "What the hell was all that about?" He didn't have to wait long to find out, because Erica and Ruby were standing on his doorstep waiting when he pulled into his driveway.

"Daddy!" Beaming, Ruby raced over to him as he climbed out of his vehicle.

"Hey, baby." He swept his arm around her and gave her a big hug. "How are you doing?" He kissed her on the cheek and then carried her on his hip as he walked to the door, where he nodded to his ex-wife. "Erica."

She didn't respond to the greeting. "I'll be back Monday to pick her up."

"All right." Lucius nodded but found it strange that it seemed like she was going out of her way not to look at him.

"Goodbye, baby." Erica leaned over and kissed Ruby's cheek and then raced to her car.

Lucius stared, trying to figure out what had just happened. He and Erica weren't always on the best of terms but he couldn't think of a reason for her just treating him like he was something stuck on the bottom of her shoe all of a sudden. He watched as she started her car and jetted out of the driveway like a bat out of hell.

"Daddy, are we going to have turkey or ham for Thanksgiving?"

He smiled and winked at his daughter. "We can have whatever you like."

"I want ham!"

"Then ham it is!" Lucius turned around and stuck his key into the front door when he remembered something. "I hope you don't mind, but Daddy is also going to have a friend over as well."

"A girlfriend?" she inquired, perking up.

"I guess you could say that."

Chapter 16

Beverly spent Wednesday night at her house, doing something she hadn't done in a long time: baking. It was the least she could do since Lucius had insisted on doing all the major cooking for their Thanksgiving meal and her mother had always taught her to never show up to such things empty-handed. For the occasion she made one pumpkin pie and one pecan pie.

Now that it was getting close to the time for her to head out to Lucius's place, she found herself getting nervous about this *surprise* that Lucius had hinted about last night on the phone. Mainly because Clarence had also spent the last twenty-four hours popping all this nonsense about their spending time together on a major holiday meant that her and Lucius's relationship was moving to the next level. Was this what Lucius was thinking, too—and did this *surprise* have something to do with that?

Lord, she hoped not.

If Beverly had her way their relationship would remain on this level—cruise control. She didn't ask too much from him and he didn't ask too much from her. Just sex.

Of course they had been spending an awful lot of time together lately, but that was normal for new lovers. Eventually that would dial back and they would just see each other whenever the need or mood arose.

So you wouldn't mind if he started seeing other women?

Beverly's heart squeezed when the unbidden question floated across her head as she wrapped her pies in aluminum foil. *Of course not,* she lied to herself. *Why should I care if he decides to see other women?* She clenched her jaw as her blood pressure surely climbed while thinking about Lucius holding another woman the same way he held her—or kissed her.

Turning, Beverly crossed her arms and leaned back against the counter while her emotions churned like a tornado inside of her. What the hell was going on with her? Why was she getting upset about a fictional woman?

"Get it together, Beverly," she whispered and shook her head. "You're getting ahead of yourself."

After a few deep breaths, she felt her nerves settle down. Surely she was blowing things out of proportion. For all she knew Lucius wanted to surprise her with some special dish he made and nothing more. He hadn't given her any hint that he was thinking their relationship was anything more than what he declared.

That's not true.

Beverly was suddenly flooded with memories of

words exchanged in bed. How many times had he asked her whom she belonged to or hold out giving her the orgasm she craved until she admitted that they were more than friends? *That was just sex talk,* she told herself, but suddenly she wasn't so sure.

The phone rang, startling her. Grateful for a reprieve from her own troubled thoughts, Beverly rushed to answer it.

"Happy Thanksgiving."

Lucius's deep baritone put an instant smile on Beverly's face. "Happy Thanksgiving."

"What time can I expect you to come over?" he asked.

"Oh, probably about an hour," she estimated.

"Good. I should have everything done by then."

"Sooo, hmmm…can I get a hint about this surprise now?" Beverly asked.

Lucius chuckled. "Nope. You're going to have to wait."

"Ugh!"

"Patience is a virtue," he said, laughing. "Now hurry up and get your butt over here. I think I fixed enough food to feed half of Georgia."

"All right. See you in a few." She hung up the phone and then raced upstairs to finish getting ready. But when she reached the top of the stairs, her feet slowed when her gaze skittered to the closed door at the other end of the hallway. For the past few weeks, she had been flying high between work and her new love affair, and for the first time in years, she'd almost forgotten… *No. I'll never forget,* she vowed, as she walked toward that closed door.

When she reached out and her hand wrapped around

the cold brass knob, a renewed wave of sadness engulfed her—so much that she resisted pushing the door open. What was the point? Her eyes glossed as she released the doorknob and stepped back.

"Get it together," she whispered brokenly. Why was she insisting on punishing herself? Beverly turned away from the door just as a few tears skipped down her face. Why was she so determined to keep punishing herself? Why couldn't she just move on?

She closed her eyes, drew in a deep breath and focused on something that made her feel good. It didn't take long for Lucius's image to surface and a wonderful calm to settle over her. When she opened her eyes, she knew beyond a shadow of a doubt that she was in trouble.

Lucius tried and tried but finally had to give up on his daughter's hair. He just couldn't seem to get it to do what he wanted it to do. "How about we just wear it down today?" he asked.

"Okay," Ruby said, excited and anxious for him to stop pulling on her head. She grabbed the brush from his hand and quickly started to repair the damage he'd caused. In a couple of strokes, she returned to looking normal. "We need to curl the ends. Do you have a curling iron?"

He blinked. "Can't say that I do."

She pouted her lips.

"But it looks fine the way that it is," he assured her. The last thing he wanted to do was try to work something hot and electrical in her hair. With his luck, he would burn half her face and head and people at the hospital emergency room would be looking upside his head like he was a child abuser or something.

"But I want to look nice when I meet your girl-friend," Ruby whined.

"What are you talking about?" Lucius said, aston-ished. "You look gorgeous. Look at you in that dress." He turned her around to face the bathroom mirror. "Beverly is going to take one look at you and think that you're some fairy-tale princess."

Ruby giggled. "She will not."

"Sure she will. Look at those adorable cheeks." Lu-cius pinched and wiggled them around. "And that nose." He tweaked it using two knuckles. "I don't think there's a cuter nose in the whole wide world."

Laughing heartily, Ruby tried to get away from her dad, but he was now in a tickling mood and he started attacking her waist and belly. His daughter squealed in a tone that nearly burst his eardrums. A while later during the melee, they became aware of the doorbell ringing.

"I'll get it," they shouted in unison and then took off running through the house.

Lucius could have easily overtaken his daughter, but he shortened his strides and allowed her to beat him down the stairs and to the front door. By the time he caught up with her, she'd opened the door and a stunned Beverly blinked down at his daughter.

"Um, well, hello!" Beverly said after finally finding her voice. "And who might you be?" she asked, smiling.

"I'm Ruby. My dad's daughter."

Beverly laughed. "Ahh. I should have known. You have his eyes."

"Daddy said that you'd like my cheeks and nose."

Lucius smacked a hand against his forehead—but it got worse.

"Are you my dad's girlfriend?" Ruby asked, curious.

Beverly stuttered. "I—I—"

"Why don't we invite her inside the house?" Lucius said, coming to her rescue.

Ruby jumped out of the way and hand-combed her hair back down.

A nervous Beverly crossed the threshold, holding two aluminum-wrapped pies.

"Those smell good," Lucius said, hoping to put her at ease since she looked like a scared rabbit. "Don't they smell wonderful, Ruby?"

"Mmm-hmm." Ruby bobbed her head and slammed the door. As everyone walked toward the kitchen, she tugged her father's hand and said in a loud whisper, "She's pretty, Daddy."

Lucius's chest expanded with pride. "I know," he whispered back.

Beverly blushed as she set her desserts on the kitchen counter. "So I take it that you are my surprise today," Beverly said, beaming.

"Yep." Lucius wrapped an arm around her. "Today I'm sharing this holiday with my two favorite ladies. So let's make this official. Beverly, this is Ruby and Ruby, this is Ms. Beverly."

"Hi!" Ruby enthusiastically waved. "Are you going to marry my dad?"

Beverly tensed.

"Ruby." Lucius tried to hint to his daughter to cut it out.

However, she only frowned and asked, "What's wrong with your eyes, Daddy?"

Beverly giggled. "It's okay, Lucius." She walked over to stand next to Ruby. "Me and your daddy are just good friends."

Technically this was the truth, but Lucius still felt slighted—stung. Apparently his daughter felt the same way, judging by the way her face twisted in a frown.

"Enough of this, ladies," Lucius proclaimed, clapping his hands together. "Why don't you two help me get dinner out on the table?"

Beverly looked relieved. "Sounds good to me."

"Okay," Ruby agreed and then proceeded to follow Beverly around like she was her small shadow. And of course, she chatted away nonstop about everything from the class pet turtle at her school to how her mother and her fiancé had chosen to go to Boston for Thanksgiving without her.

To Lucius's great surprise and relief, Beverly seemed to be a pro when it came to dealing with children. She listened attentively and asked questions that Ruby was only too eager to answer. A casual observer would have thought that the two were lifelong friends the way that they carried on. Once dinner was on the table, everyone took their seats, held hands and said their prayers.

After that, Ruby attacked the ham as if she hadn't eaten in a week.

Beverly was amused.

"She *really* likes ham," Lucius tried to explain.

"So I see." She smiled lovingly at Ruby.

Lucius watched the two of them and his chest expanded with pride. It was the first time in a long while that this table had hummed with laughter and joy. The three of them looked like a real family. He liked the way they looked together and how they interacted with one another and as time rolled on, he found himself wishing that the day wouldn't end. When the football game got started, they piled into the living room with cans of root beer, Ruby's favorite, and got ready to cheer on the Dallas Cowboys against the Pittsburgh Steelers.

When the Cowboys made their first touchdown, Beverly hopped up and taught Ruby a cheer from her old cheerleading days. Ruby loved anything that involved her shaking her butt and acting semi-grown. On the second touchdown, his girls forced him off the couch and jostled him to participate.

Up and down, our team don't mess around,
Because we're the best from the east to the west.
And when our team is up, you're down.
Go Cowboys!

There were a couple of snaps and pops in there Lucius couldn't quite pull off, which sent Ruby and Beverly into hysterical laughter.

It was a great day—one Lucius knew that he would never forget.

Promptly at 9:30 p.m., Ruby finally reached the point of exhaustion and passed out curled up on Beverly's lap. While she slept, Beverly couldn't stop smiling and stroking the girl's long and tousled hair. The child was such an angel that she'd easily won Beverly's heart the moment she introduced herself as her father's daughter.

"You two look good together," Lucius whispered, strolling into the living room. "I think Ruby really likes you," he observed.

"I think I really like her, too," Beverly admitted softly. "You have a beautiful child."

"Thanks." He walked over and gently scooped Ruby out of Beverly's lap. "I better go put her to bed." Ruby rolled up against her father's chest without stirring and he quickly strolled out of the living room and headed up the stairs.

Beverly continued smiling in his wake, thinking how this holiday was the best one she'd had in a long while. But then she remembered the mess in the dining room and kitchen and decided that she should help Lucius clean up.

When he returned downstairs a few minutes later, he found her in the kitchen loading up the dishwasher. "You don't have to do that," he said, walking in with a few more plates. "You're company."

"I don't mind," Beverly admitted. "Besides, this will go by faster if we both do it."

Lucius apparently wasn't going to look a gift horse in the mouth and didn't protest any further. Together they busted suds, loaded the dishes, wrapped leftovers, took out the garbage and cleaned all of the countertops. Two hours later, the place was spotless and they congratulated each other on a job well done.

"It's late. I better be heading home," Beverly said, stretching and rubbing the muscles on the side of her neck.

"Go?" He frowned and eased behind her so he could take over massaging her neck and shoulders. "I don't want you to go."

Beverly tried to respond, but Lucius's strong hands were performing some kind of voodoo magic, causing her to become as limp as a wet noodle. "Oooh, goodness, that feels good."

"You like that, baby?" He leaned down and brushed his lips just below her right earlobe.

Despite her exhaustion, Beverly's body tingled in response.

"It's too late for you to be out on the road," Lucius whispered. "You know there's a spike in crazy people on the roads during these long holiday weekends."

"But what about Ruby?" she asked weakly.

"She's asleep." His hands slid down her shoulders, changed directions, then roamed up her flat belly and cupped her large breasts.

Beverly moaned; her panties dampened. "What if she wakes up?"

"She won't."

"She could."

Lucius chuckled. "Then we'll have to make sure that we're extra quiet." He squeezed her breasts; his fingers rotated her hard nipples through her blouse and bra.

Beverly's knees buckled, forcing her to lean back against Lucius and bump up against his hard erection. Suddenly, she couldn't remember what the hell they were talking about. Her hips took over as she grinded back against his dick, loving the cheap thrill that it gave her.

"Go ahead, baby. Work it out," he panted, letting her do what it took to get off.

It wasn't long before she worked herself up into such a frenzy that she wanted more than this sexual appetizer.

Lucius easily read her mind and whispered, "Let's

go upstairs. In the morning you can just sneak to one of the guest bedrooms before Ruby wakes up."

Problem solved, Beverly took his hand and damn near dragged him up the stairs. He chuckled softly at her impatience. On the top floor, they held their breath and crept on the tips of their toes past Ruby's room. Of course it seemed like every sound was super magnified, especially when Lucius turned the knob to his bedroom and the door hinges screeched like nails down a blackboard.

They both gritted their teeth and waited expectantly for Ruby to stir.

Nothing.

Beverly and Lucius glanced at each other, relieved, and then continued their tiptoe adventure into the bedroom. Once inside, they braced themselves again when he had to close the door behind them. After that was done, they waited a few more seconds before turning around, grinning like two thieves getting away with the crime of the century.

"Come here, baby," he whispered and wrapped an arm around her thick waist.

Beverly glided into his arms and welcomed his hungry kiss. She drank in his heady, sweet taste. She moaned softly as his hands worked quickly to unbutton her blouse, which he then slid off her shoulders. With a snap of his wrist, her bra popped open and joined her top that pooled around her feet.

"Oh, let me taste these titties," Lucius said, dropping his head lower and sucking a fat nipple into his mouth.

Instantly, her eyes rolled to the back of her head. She struggled to keep the noise down as he squeezed, licked and sucked her to paradise. The rest of their clothes were removed in a blurred fury and the next thing she knew, she was being pressed into the center of his firm, king-size mattress.

In the six weeks they'd known each other, Lucius had learned all of Beverly's hot buttons and he now took his time pushing each and every one of them while she writhed and moaned as softly as she could. When that started to become too hard for her, Lucius flipped her onto her back and instructed her to bite into the pillow—which she readily did when he entered her from behind.

Lucius rained kisses on the back of her shoulders and down the center of her spine, all the while slapping his hips against her firm, round ass. As much as his body felt like home to her, Beverly remained amazed how much he filled her up. To drive her even crazier, he reached around her hip and ran the pads of his fingers along the tip of her throbbing clit.

She nearly screamed out loud.

"Shhhh," he urged as he continued to pound away. "We don't want to have to stop this groove now, do we, baby?"

"N—no," she moaned.

"Does this feel good, Bev? Huh? You like how I work your body, baby?"

"Y—yeeessss."

"That's what I thought. Down there talking about going home. You knew I wasn't going to let you go without my dessert." He started to swing his hips from side to side. "Now, didn't you?"

"Ooooooh."

"Didn't you, baby?" he insisted. "You know you belong to me, right? I can have you anytime I want, can't I?"

"Ooooh."

Lucius stopped. "What—I can't get this anytime I want?"

Beverly's eyes flew wide in panic. "Baby," she whined, thrusting her hips back, trying to get him to continue.

He made one long stroke. Stopped. "Can I have this anytime I want?"

"Yes, yes," she panted, climbing on her knees and gliding back on his long dick. She wanted more—needed more.

"Look at you," Lucius murmured. "Work it, baby." He smacked and squeezed her ass cheeks as she continued to ride him hard and deep. "Oooh, yeah. That's my girl."

Beverly glanced back over her shoulder, watched him as his face twisted and contorted with ecstasy. To turn up the heat, she started rotating her hips.

Lucius growled.

"Shhh," she whispered, smiling. "You don't want to stop this groove now, do you?"

"Come here." He chuckled and forced her to stand up on her knees though they still grinded together. "You play too much," he moaned in her ear, still working her clit and thrusting into her warm wetness.

A low heat simmered in Beverly's belly as stars started to blink behind her eyes. Lucius stroked with all he had, causing a glorious friction to tip her over the edge. Her thighs trembled, her breath thinned.

"You coming, baby?"

She wanted to answer but only managed to nod while her gasping started to heighten.

Mindful of who was sleeping just across the hall,

Lucius was forced to place his hands over her mouth. However, Beverly responded by sucking on his fingers, while he continued to knock the air from her lungs. Two more pumps and Beverly quivered and convulsed, her orgasm causing a kaleidoscope of colors to spin behind her eyes.

Lucius followed, his explosion marrying their souls together to the point that neither could tell where one of them started and where the other ended. Hot and sweaty, they collapsed back onto the bed. "God, I love you," he whispered raggedly, peppering more kisses against her back.

No answer.

"Beverly?" He leaned over and saw that she had once again fallen fast asleep. Lucius smiled, kissed her shoulder and snuggled up against the curve of her back, and allowed sleep to claim him.

Once his breathing settled and evened out, Beverly's eyes fluttered open as tears streamed from the corners of her eyes and soaked her pillow.

Chapter 17

The four-day holiday weekend turned into a minivacation for Lucius, Beverly and Ruby. First thing Friday morning, after Beverly snuck down to the guest bedroom before Ruby woke, they all gathered for a big breakfast and then got ready to hit the malls for the first shopping day of Christmas.

When Beverly saw the wild concoction Lucius had created on his poor daughter's head, she quickly marched the child back up the stairs and performed an emergency hair makeover with all the pretty bows and ties her mother had packed in her overnight bag. When they reemerged, Ruby strutted like the princess she was in front of her dad.

Lucius gave a thunderous applause and whistled mightily before offering his little girl his arm and escorting her and Beverly out to their vehicle.

Beverly's heart melted at the way Lucius doted on his daughter. It was there for the world to see how much he loved her. This was the kind of man she should've married the first time. As soon as the thought crossed her mind, she had to shake the troubled direction of her thoughts. This was the sort of thinking that could land her in trouble.

All the stores were teeming with anxious and over-zealous shoppers. Lucius kept trying to pull them into every electronics store they passed, while Ruby and Beverly sought out toys and clothes stores. Before long, Lucius was reduced to holding bags while his girls kept disappearing behind changing-room doors and then coming out to model different outfits.

Of course he loved every one of them and ended up dropping a fortune before lunchtime.

Saturday and Sunday entailed more shopping with a Disney movie tossed into the mix. But nothing was more adorable to Lucius than watching his daughter attempt to mimic the way Beverly walked or talked— sometimes even the way she laughed or gestured with her hands.

When Beverly caught wind of what Ruby was doing, she appeared flattered and rained a lot of hugs and kisses on her. This was the kind of woman he should have married the first time. She was beautiful, strong and independent. Yet, at the same time, caring, loving and willing to give and share her time.

During the weekend, Lucius kept feeling as if they were already like a small family, and the more he thought about it, the more he liked the idea. The truth of the matter was that he loved waking up every morning curled up with Beverly. When she wasn't around, he couldn't stop thinking about her. And when she *was* around, he couldn't keep his hands off of her.

They were a perfect fit in every way—but he was still sensing her trying to resist the inevitable. Every time he would mention the word *love,* she would either pretend not to hear him or conveniently fall asleep. Frankly, he was on to her, but he was willing to let it slide—for now.

"Well, well. Look who decided to come back to work," Clarence said when Beverly finally strolled into Hoops Monday afternoon.

"What? I knew the girls had everything under control," Beverly said, flashing a smile at Leslie as she sauntered toward the back of the store.

Clarence followed, switching his hips and carrying on his arm a gorgeous Fendi B Bag. "Clearly you've forgotten that usually *we* have a standing date every Black Friday," he said, folding his arms and leaning against the door frame of her office.

Beverly's mouth dropped open as her eyes widened to the size of half dollars. "Oh. My. God," she gasped. "Oh, Clarence, I'm so sorry." She blinked and shook her head. "I don't know how on earth I'd forgotten about—"

"I do," he drawled. "I know you're not going to sit up in here and tell me that you weren't over at Mr. Lover-Lover's with your legs wrapped around his waist."

"Clarence, behave."

"I am behaving. You ought to be glad I'm not cussing you out for having me up at four o'clock in the morning freezing my butt off. I was trying to do my patriotic duty in wrecking the hell out of my credit cards and I got stood up." He pressed a hand against his chest.

"Nobody stands me up. Then I'm blowing up your cell phone and you don't answer that."

Beverly winced. "I left it charging on my charger at home."

"Hmmph."

"Okay. I'm sorry. I was wrong. I did sort of get caught up with Lucius and Ruby."

"Ruby-who?"

"Ruby. Lucius's daughter."

Clarence moved over to the chair next to her desk. "He introduced you to his daughter?"

"Yeah. Her mother changed her plans at the last minute so he had her this weekend." She smiled. "You should have seen her. She's the most adorable thing. Looks so much like her father."

Clarence said nothing, but eyed her up and down.

"What?" she asked defensively.

"Nothing." He shrugged.

Beverly's eyes narrowed. It was obvious that her friend was lying. "Spit it out."

"It's nothing."

Silence.

"I just find it interesting that you seem comfortable about being around his child. You know...since you've had a hard time dealing—"

"It's not the same thing," she said, cutting him off.

Clarence tossed up his hands, signaling that he was backing off.

Beverly shifted in her chair, annoyed and irritated. But when she thought about Ruby's adorable face, she couldn't help but soften up a little bit. She really did enjoy the time she'd spent with the little girl. In fact, she was flattered by how the child attached herself to her like they were lifelong best friends.

She loved that.

"Well," Clarence said, breaking the silence, "I think it's great. There. I said it. I'm not going to say anything else." He popped out of his seat and headed toward the door. "Wait. I lied." He turned and faced her. "All jokes aside, I really hope you don't try to mess this up. It's well past time that you move on and embrace whatever happiness you can find in this life. And there's no denying that Lucius Gray makes you very happy."

Lucius had planned on at least working a half day the Monday after Thanksgiving, but Erica never showed to pick up Ruby and he had to revamp his day and take his daughter to school. Finally he hopped up and dialed Erica's number to see what the holdup was, but was further frustrated when she didn't answer at any of her contact numbers.

Still he put up a bright front for Ruby, but secretly started worrying about the court case he'd planned to start preparing for today. Lucius had promised himself that he wouldn't do any office work during his father-daughter time. He had done it once years ago and Erica had made him feel guilty for doing so. Since then, he'd promised that when Ruby was around, those rare times, he would give her his full attention. Today challenged that promise.

"Daddy, you're missing the show!" Ruby shouted from the living room.

"All right. Here I come." He hung up the phone and returned to the great adventures of SpongeBob and Patrick. That's where they remained until five o'clock, when he finally stood and went to make dinner from their Thanksgiving leftovers.

Ruby seemed unfazed by the fact that her mother never showed and just simply returned her pink overnight bag up to her room. "Is Beverly coming home for dinner?" she asked, settling into her chair at the dining-room table.

He smiled into her eager eyes. "Um…I don't know," he answered truthfully. After the extensive time Beverly had spent with them over the weekend, he didn't want to pressure or make her feel obligated to spend more time with Ruby simply because she liked her.

"I like your girlfriend," Ruby said simply. "You should marry her."

Lucius laughed at the way his daughter just cut to the chase. "Why are you so determined to get me hitched?"

She shrugged. "Because I want you to be happy."

Their identical hazel-eyed gazes locked and Lucius's heart overflowed at seeing Ruby's open sincerity. "Thank you, baby." He leaned over and pressed a kiss against her forehead.

His daughter beamed. "So are you going to call her and tell her to come over?"

"How about I call her and *invite* her over?" he amended with a wink.

"Goodie!" She hopped up from the table and raced to retrieve the cordless phone like a future Olympian. "Here you go, Daddy. Call her."

Lucius laughed as he took the phone. "All right. All right. Calm down."

Instead of returning to her chair, Ruby danced and hopped around while chanting, "Call her. Call her."

Relenting to peer pressure, Lucius dialed Beverly's

cell phone. "Hello," he said, when she finally picked up, but before he could issue the invitation, Ruby snatched the phone and brokered the offer.

"Hey, Beverly. Do you want to come over?"

Pause.

Ruby's gaze shot up to her father, and he feared that Beverly was politely turning down the offer.

"Pleeeease?"

Lucius reached for the phone.

"Oh, goodie!" Ruby resumed bouncing around. "See you when you get here!" She handed her father the phone back.

"Hello." He checked to see if Beverly was still on the line.

"She's so adorable," Beverly said softly.

"And clearly crazy about you," he said, standing from the table and moving toward the kitchen so that his little girl wouldn't overhear him. "Look, I hope you don't feel pressured to—"

"Don't be silly. I'd love to join you guys for dinner. It'll save me from having to cook something myself."

"So you're just using me for my cooking?"

"For your cooking in the kitchen *and* the bedroom," she teased.

"Awww. I get it." He glanced around and then lowered his voice. "You're just using me for my body."

"You didn't know?"

He sniffed and pretended to be offended. "I was hoping that I'd finally found a woman who loved me for me—for my *mind,* as well as my body."

Beverly laughed.

"I have *feelings,*" Lucius continued dramatically.

"Does that mean that you don't want me to come over?"

"Now I didn't say *that* exactly."

"That's what I thought," she said.

Lucius laughed. "So what time can we expect you here?"

"I'm leaving the shop now. Give me about twenty minutes."

"All right. We'll see you then." He disconnected the call and started back to the table, where Ruby still bounced around in her chair. When the phone rang, Lucius snatched it up, thinking it was Beverly again. "Forget something, baby?"

Pause.

"Hello?"

"Lucius?" Erica questioned.

"Oh, there you are." Once again, he turned his back to the dining-room table. "Where in the hell are you? I thought you said that you were coming back today. I missed a whole day at the office."

"Oooh. Poor baby. Did the law office implode without you?"

He took a deep, calming breath. It wasn't going to do any good to try to explain anything to Erica. "Okay. Fine. When are you coming to pick up Ruby?"

Silence.

"Erica?"

"Look, Lucius. Things are complicated right now. Andrew and I didn't go to Boston this past weekend."

Not sure where this was heading, Lucius folded his arms and leaned against the kitchen door. "Okay. So where did you go?"

"Las Vegas," she said. "We eloped."

Silence.

"Lucius?"

"I guess that means that congratulations are in order," he said.

"Th—thank you."

He drew in a deep breath. "Soooo, when do you think you'll be coming back?"

Silence.

An icy fear dripped down the center of Lucius's spine. "You *are* coming back, aren't you?"

"Look, Lucius. Andrew isn't ready to be a father right now. And it really bothers him that Ruby looks sooo much like you."

"What?!"

"Hey, don't yell at me," she snapped. "It's not like this is easy for me. I'm not completely turning my back on Ruby. I'm just…*we* need some time alone right now. Sometime down the line, Andrew may adapt to the idea of being a full-fledged stepfather."

"What—she's going to miraculously stop looking like me?" he hissed. "I don't believe this. I can't believe that *you* are just dumping your daughter."

"I am not *dumping* her. I'm leaving her with her father. You are that, you know."

"Stop it, Erica. You're not going to guilt-trip me. This is about you and the cowardly way you are handling this. I'm more than happy to keep Ruby, especially now that I know how her *stepfather* feels."

"It's not that Andrew *hates* her."

"Save it," Lucius snapped. "Just go off and enjoy your new marriage. It sounds like you two deserve each other." He disconnected the call, wanting to scream and throw the phone against the wall.

"Daddy, your food is getting cold," Ruby yelled.

Lucius drew a couple of deep breaths. He couldn't believe this was happening. As of this moment, he was a full-time single father. That meant new schools, day care—and how would this affect his erratic hours at the job?

"Daddy!"

Exhaling a long breath, he forced a smile to his face. "Here I come, baby."

Chapter 18

When Beverly heard about Erica abandoning her child so she could be free to start a new life with her new husband she was just stunned. She couldn't imagine a *mother* deciding to do such a thing. It even forced her to reevaluate some of the things that had gone on in her marriage.

The unfairness.

The injustice.

And poor Lucius was just stunned and tried his best to shield Ruby from all the real drama that was going on between her parents. It was also clear in the next two weeks that Lucius was overwhelmed. Choosing new schools and day care centers were monumental decisions and it pulled at Beverly to see Lucius wrestle with so many tough choices. Ruby on the other hand seemed pleased about the whole arrangement, especially the continued time she spent with Beverly.

In the beginning, Beverly kept telling herself to not get too close. This situation had nothing to do with her. But Ruby, like her father, had crept under her defenses and stolen a piece of her heart whether she liked it or not. By the second week in December, Beverly had gone from the no-strings-attached sex partner to acting and behaving like a member of this small family who laughed at the dinner table and cheered on their favorite football teams on Monday nights. And it was a complete madhouse in the mornings when everyone was trying to get to school and work on time.

As Clarence joked, Beverly was part of the family all but in name. The idea of that both thrilled and frightened her. How did she get here—and so fast? When she questioned herself on why she hadn't just walked away, the answer was so obvious it smacked her in face. She was in this situation because, despite her precautions, she had fallen in love with Lucius Gray.

She loved everything about him. From the way he loved and supported her to the way he sat his daughter on a pedestal. And though he struggled with the toll of suddenly becoming a single full-time father, he went out of his way to hide his distress from his daughter. Although she sometimes missed her mother, Ruby Gray just knew that her father loved and adored her—and that's all that Lucius wanted her to know.

Clarence kept eyeing his friend warily, constantly warning her not to be her own worst enemy. Still there were parts of her that were panicking. She doubted her ability to be able to travel this road to its natural conclusion. And there was no doubt what that conclusion was. Every night, Lucius whispered words of love and now those same words were seeping into their daily phone conversations. The situation both thrilled and terrified her.

What was so wonderful about Lucius was that he seemed to sense her inability to say the words back, even though she went out of her way to make sure that she showed him how she felt every time they fell into each other's arms. But she couldn't get herself to say the words. Saying them would change everything.

She just wasn't ready for that.

At precisely five o'clock, Maggie looked up from her desk to see Lucius calling it a night. "I don't know what's come over you these past couple of months, but I have to admit, I like it."

"Because when I work forty hours that means you do, too?" he asked.

"There is that," she admitted. "Plus, it gives me a complete thrill to know that I was right. A woman is responsible for all of this."

"Only if by woman you mean a certain eight-year-old," Lucius countered, grinning.

"Nuh-uh." Maggie waved a long manicured nail at him. "My husband and I went to the movies yesterday and you'll never guess who we saw sitting just a couple of rows in front of us."

Lucius coughed and pretended to clear his throat.

"Ringing any bells?" she taunted.

"You shouldn't be spying on your boss," he warned playfully and then headed to the elevator bay.

"For what it's worth," she called after him, "I think she's beautiful."

It was a superficial comment, but it still caused Lucius's chest to expand with pride. "Yeah," he acknowledged, "she is."

Lucius picked up his chattering daughter at precisely 5:30 p.m. from a private day care center. While buckled in the backseat, Ruby decided it was her duty to reeducate her father on his multiplication times tables by using her huge flash cards. When they were getting ready to pass by the Shane Diamond Company, Lucius's foot eased up off of the accelerator. "Baby, do you mind if we take a little detour?"

"Okay," she said absently as she continued to flip through her cards.

After parking and walking hand in hand with his daughter into the large building, Lucius's heart began to flutter.

"Can I help you, sir?" an attractive saleswoman inquired.

Lucius drew in a deep breath. "I'm looking for the perfect engagement ring."

Ruby's head jerked up at her father. "Daddy, are we going to propose to Beverly?"

A large smile spread across Lucius's face. "Yes, we are, baby. Yes, we are."

Beverly was torn.

She'd told herself that she was going to spend some quiet time alone at home. Give her the chance to step back and clear her mind. But after she'd closed the shop, she started wondering what Ruby and Lucius would be doing that night. So when Lucius called to see if she'd like to join them for dinner at Ruth's Chris Steak

House for dinner, she accepted the invitation without missing a beat.

After hanging up, Beverly chastised herself for caving so easily. She wanted her space but she couldn't stay away. What sense did that make?

"That's what love does to you," Clarence said when she explained the situation to him. "Have you thinking you're coming when you're going. You should know this. You've been here before."

That was the wrong thing to say because she had been here before—though it was a little different, she reasoned. David Clark was never as caring and giving as Lucius. Everything was about supporting him and encouraging him with his schooling and then career. And when...

"You're doing it again," Clarence warned.

She looked up. "What?"

"You're thinking about things...people you couldn't change."

She shrugged and started to deny it, but what was the use? Clarence knew her better than anyone. He could smell B.S. a mile away.

"Why can't you just admit that you love him?"

"What does that have to do with anything?"

"Who needs a heart when a heart can be broken?" he inquired.

"Exactly."

Clarence rolled his eyes and chuckled. "Face it, girl. You can't run from love the rest of your life. The past is the past and it's time for you to bury it and move on."

Beverly heard what he was saying and she waited for his message to sink in, but the bottom line still remained: she was scared.

* * *

"How's my tie?" Lucius asked his daughter after nervously tying and retying the damn thing about a thousand times.

"Here, let me help." Ruby hopped up onto the edge of his bed and told him to kneel down so she could wiggle his tie around. "There," she announced. "That's better."

Lucius turned toward the full-length mirror on the back of the closet door and was stunned that indeed his tie was now ramrod-straight. "Weeelll, thanks, sweetheart." He delivered a quick peck against her cheek. "Wish me luck."

"Good luck, Daddy!"

He walked downstairs and thanked Maggie for agreeing to babysit Ruby on such short notice.

"Not a problem. It gives my husband ample opportunity to try to find a good place to stash my Christmas gift." She shrugged. "It won't do him any good. I'm a hound dog when it comes to sniffing out gifts."

"Now why don't I have any trouble believing that?"

They laughed and before Lucius walked out of the door, he gave Ruby explicit directions to be a good girl and to mind Maggie while he was gone. After another kiss good-night, he was out the door, the weight of the ring heavy in his pocket and on his mind.

Beverly was glad that she'd insisted on meeting Lucius at the restaurant instead of having him pick her up. At least she would have one last out. Of course if Lucius started playing footsies or looked at her a certain way, she could still end up at his place scratching up his back and climbing the walls. When it came to Lucius she was a sex addict.

When she entered the glass doors of Ruth's Chris Steak House, Lucius was already there standing near the hostess stand. When he turned and flashed his beautiful smile at her, her knees weakened and her heart fluttered. *I'm fighting a losing battle with this man.*

He walked over to her and she slid easily into his arms. "Hey, baby. You look beautiful."

"Thank you." She glanced around. "Where's Ruby?"

"Home with a babysitter. It's just you and me tonight. I hope you don't mind."

Beverly smiled. "I guess I'll just have to suffer through."

"Mr. Gray, your table is waiting," the hostess informed him.

Lucius turned while still holding Beverly on his arm. "Shall we?"

"We shall." She allowed him to escort her to their waiting table, smiled when he held out her chair and blushed when he kissed her cheek before walking to his own chair. It was then that she noticed there was something different about his demeanor, something about the way he smiled at her.

Suddenly it felt like a vat of butterflies had broken from their cocoons and started fluttering like mad in the pit of her stomach. Without explanation her palms started to itch and she could hardly sit still in her seat.

Lucius either ignored or didn't notice her fidgeting, but he smiled at their waiter when he appeared with the menus and ran through the night's special.

Beverly hardly heard a word that was said; she just wanted a glass of wine to try to settle her nerves.

"Are you all right?" Lucius asked.

She glanced up and noticed that he and the waiter

were staring at her expectantly. "Oh, yes. I was just thinking about all those choices," she lied. Glancing down at the menu, she just randomly picked an entrée number and then smiled tightly when she handed the menu back over to his waiting hand.

Lucius cocked a brow at her. "Are you sure you're all right?"

"Fine," she squeaked and then coughed to clear the growing lump from her throat. Thank God their bottle of wine arrived. She watched almost impatiently as the waiter showed the label to both her and Lucius before uncorking and pouring the damn thing. At the first taste of the heady liquid, she sighed and nearly melted with relief.

Lucius smiled, obviously thinking whatever was troubling her was now over with. "Better?"

"Much." She took another long gulp and drained the rest of her glass.

"You must have been thirsty," he joked.

"Something like that." Beverly averted her eyes. She still had the sneaking suspicion that Lucius was up to something tonight—and she feared that she knew what it was. *Please, God, let me be wrong.*

Lucius didn't know what to make of Beverly's behavior. It was actually setting him on edge, causing him to reevaluate what he wanted to do tonight. First, she had insisted on driving herself to the restaurant and now she seemed to be going out of her way not to meet his gaze. It all made for an uncomfortable start to what he wanted to be a romantic evening.

By the time their meals were delivered to the table, they had already suffered through strained bouts of silence, stiff smiles and sporadic, awkward and choppy conversations.

"Hmmm. This is good," Beverly said.

"Yeah. This place serves the best steaks in town," he offered and then they fell silent again.

It wasn't until Beverly started in on her third glass of wine that she truly began to loosen up and started relating a few funny incidents that had happened in her shop that day. Lucius listened intently, finding her work fascinating, mainly because it was so different from his own profession. He even challenged her by asking whether she'd ever thought about stepping outside of the box and starting her own label.

Beverly loved the fact that Lucius was so interested in her work. It was just another example, in a long list of examples, of how different he was from her ex-husband. *Why can't you stop fighting this?* she asked herself while battling an unexplainable rush of tears. As much as she had shared with him in such a short amount of time, there was still a lot she hadn't—especially the part that haunted her soul.

"Let's make a toast," Lucius said, suddenly lifting his wineglass.

Beverly forced on a smile and followed suit.

"To the past few months. May they only be the beginning of something wonderful."

Was tonight their two-month anniversary? Beverly's hand started to tremble, but she clinked her glass to his in solidarity and added, "Hear, hear."

The rest of their dinner passed by in a blur. Lucius never quite felt the right moment had approached for him to whip out the diamond ring in his pocket. Another idea popped into his mind—something that would perhaps help to relax Beverly. "You know what's just a couple of blocks from here?"

Beverly's gaze shifted up to his in curiosity.

"The downtown Hilton," he supplied. "The place where we met just two months ago tonight." He leaned forward and carefully placed his elbows on the white linen tablecloth. "What do you say that we revisit where the magic started?"

A sparkle finally glittered in Beverly's eyes. The idea definitely had appeal.

"Remember how big and soft their beds were?"

Beverly's brows hiked as she gently bit her lower lip.

He smiled, his voice dropping even lower. "Remember how I had you bend over and grab your ankles?"

She nodded, squirmed in her chair.

"Maybe this time I'll tie you up," he suggested slyly.

From the corner of Beverly's eyes, she saw their server across the way. She literally jumped up from her seat and yelled, "Check, please."

As luck would have it, Lucius and Beverly were able to check into the same room number at the Hilton in downtown Atlanta. And as before, they stumbled into the room pulling and tugging at each other's clothes as if the fate of the world depended on them merging as fast as possible. Yet, the moment Lucius entered her, it seemed as if everything in the universe instantly went into slow motion. It wasn't about who could outfreak the other by bending and twisting in new and innovative ways, but about making love and touching each other's souls.

Lucius's long and deep strokes had tears surfacing and leaking from Beverly's eyes as if she had truly reached the heavens. *What is he doing to me?* Beverly gasped when Lucius's hips dipped and rotated in a hypnotic groove.

"I want to make love like this with you forever," he whispered against her ear. "I want to feel you every morning and taste you just like this every night." Lucius's lips brushed against her shoulders. "Wouldn't you like that?"

Beverly sighed and moaned.

"Hmmm?" His kisses moved to her sensitive neck. "Don't you know how much I've fallen for you, baby? You know how much I love holding you like this. Look at you. You like how I make you feel, don't you?"

"Aaaah," Beverly moaned.

Lucius's strokes slowed even further, causing her to claw impatiently at his back. "You don't love me, Beverly? Is that what you're trying to say?"

"N—no."

As a reward, his hips returned to their previous rhythm. "Do you love me?"

She bit her lips, trying to prevent the truth from spilling.

"I want to hear you say it," he urged. "I know you do. I can feel it." He captured her lips in a long, deep kiss, determined to coax her confession out of her. When he finally came up for air, he asked, "Do you feel it, Beverly?"

A familiar tremble started in her thighs and moved up to the tip of her clit and lower belly. Her breathing became choppy, her defenses lowered.

Lucius dipped his head low, licked at her breasts. "Feel that, Beverly?"

"Y—yes."

His toes tingled. "Damn, I love you, woman." He pulled her legs up and hung them over his shoulders so he could get as deep as he possibly could.

As bliss unfolded from every pore of Beverly's body, she chanted Lucius's name and finally told him what he'd been longing to hear. "I love you, baby."

In what was becoming a habit, after Beverly's third orgasm, she curled up to Lucius and fell asleep. Unfazed, Lucius just smiled and pressed a kiss against her forehead and then gently climbed out of bed and tiptoed to his jacket, which was lying with the rest of his clothes on the floor.

When he crept back to the bed, he held in his hand the diamond ring he'd hoped to have given her during dinner. He carefully climbed back into bed, opened the jeweler's burgundy velvet box and plucked out the two-carat, princess-cut diamond ring and prayed like he'd never prayed before that he'd guessed the right size. Quietly, he reached for her left hand, lifted it and slid the platinum band up her ring finger.

Perfect.

Lucius kissed her temple again and curled up against her. He couldn't wait until she woke up and saw the diamond twinkling on her finger. With one more kiss to the back of her head, he closed his eyes and drifted off to sleep.

When he woke up, the bed was empty, but the engagement ring sat gleaming on the pillow next to him. Stunned and heartbroken, he reached for it and belatedly noticed a folded note. Lucius opened it and read the one word scrawled across it. *Sorry.*

Chapter 19

"You did what?" Clarence asked, cupping his ear toward her. "I know I didn't hear you right."

Beverly huffed and rolled her eyes. "I knew that I shouldn't have told you." She stood from her desk and marched out of her office, but she knew good and damn well that it was going to take more than that to get her best friend off her back once she fed him a juicy story.

"Hold up, Bev. Why did you break up with Lucius? You're crazy about the guy."

At the front cash register, Leslie tried to pretend that she wasn't listening to her boss's private conversation.

"C'mon, Clarence. You know why. I promised myself years ago that I didn't want to marry again. And what happened to his promise about a no-strings-attached relationship?" Beverly tossed her hands up in the air. "There are so many strings I feel like I'm choking."

"You don't think that you're exaggerating a bit?"

"No." She wiped at a tear before anyone could see it fall. "And mighty funny Lucius suddenly wants to get married just weeks after he becomes a full-time single father."

"What are you saying?"

Beverly shrugged and said words she didn't believe. "I'm just wondering whether he's really looking for a wife or a new mother for his eight-year-old daughter."

Clarence shoved a hand against his hip. "I ought to wash your mouth out with soap for that."

"What?" she asked defensively. "It's a legitimate question."

"It would be if I didn't see how that man had to practically beg you to go out with him *before* his ex-wife abandoned her daughter with him. You had that boy whipped from day one and you know it. All this other stuff you're saying is extraneous B.S. and you know it." He turned abruptly toward Leslie. "Ain't I right, girl?"

"Well, if you ask me—"

"I'm not asking you," Beverly snapped. "Get back to work."

Clarence jumped to Leslie's defense. "Hey, don't take out all your frustrations on Leslie. You're wrong and you know you're wrong."

"Fine. Maybe I'm just scared then," she said, laying it all out on the line. "What's wrong with that? This whole thing is going at warp speed. A shoe has to drop sooner or later."

"So why not throw your shoe in first?"

"Stop pretending that you don't know what I'm talking about. I can't be a wife again. I can't be that precious little girl's...mother." She choked over that last word. "I just can't."

The shop's doorbell jingled.

Beverly mopped at her eyes, put on a smile and turned to see Tamara Hodges stroll through the door. She blinked. "Oh, my God, Tamara." Her eyes then fell to the small but noticeable bulge of her belly. "You look…wonderful," she announced with amazement and then embraced her for a quick hug.

"You're sweet," Tamara gushed, pulling out of Beverly's arms and glancing around. "What a lovely shop. It's hip and beautiful—so totally you."

"Now who's being sweet?" Beverly winked. "So Kyra told me a couple of weeks ago that you needed an engagement dress?"

Tamara blushed. "Yes. Can you believe it? I'm about to be Mrs. Micah Ross."

"Oooh." Once again, Clarence hip-bumped his way into the small circle. "*You're* the one marrying that gorgeous music mogul?"

Smiling, Tamara blinked at Beverly's overzealous friend. "I take it you've heard of him."

"Who hasn't? Giirrll, let me see the ring!" He didn't wait for her to do it on her own. Instead, he grabbed her hand and then faked a heart attack when he saw it. "Chile, is that a ring or a small planet?"

Delighted with his theatrics, Tamara laughed. "It is beautiful, isn't it?"

"I'd say." He glanced over at Beverly. "'Tis the season for brothers to be passing out diamond rings."

"What?" Tamara asked, confused.

"Don't mind him." Beverly moved around Clarence and gently directed Tamara away. "Why don't you just tell me what kind of dress you had in mind…?"

* * *

Lucius was angry.

Despite this, he put on a brave face so his daughter could enjoy the Christmas holidays. The last three days were particularly hard with Ruby constantly asking when Beverly was coming back over—which was remarkable since she hardly mentioned her own mother.

Balancing work, home and the approaching holiday had Lucius feeling like he was burning the candle at both ends. However, at night he relished the exhaustion. It was the only thing to help him sleep through the night. Yet, it was the first few minutes upon waking that really got to him. He missed the mornings when he'd awakened curled like a spoon against Beverly's curvy bottle shape. If he concentrated, he could still recall the coconut scent in her hair.

Lucius's heart ached while he waited for his alarm clock to tell him to get out of bed. Until then, he easily pulled up Beverly's angelic face from memory and recounted everything he loved about it. At exactly 5:30 a.m., he flung out an arm and shut off the alarm's loud and annoying buzz. However, he didn't climb out of bed. Instead he remained nestled in his white cotton sheets, staring up at the ceiling.

Lucius huffed, rolled over onto his side and stared at the clock. Its loud ticking sounded as if it was hooked up into an amplifier. In no time his heart and the muscles along his temples thumped in precise harmony.

Maybe he should just stay in bed today.

"Daddy! Daddy!" Ruby bolted into his room, hopped

up onto the bed and started shaking his shoulders. "Daddy, it's time to get up."

He groaned. Why did he have the child that sprang out of bed in the mornings? He rolled over and couldn't help but laugh at the sight of her hair sticking up all over the place. "I'm getting up, sweetheart." He reached out and mussed her hair up even more. "What do you want for breakfast?"

"Waffles!"

He rolled his eyes because her answer came as no surprise. "All righty," he said, peeling back the top sheet and climbing out of bed. "Waffles, it is!"

In the kitchen, Lucius endured another long line of hard-hitting questions about Beverly's whereabouts and whether he thought that she was mad at them.

"Maybe you should just call her and apologize," Ruby said.

"What makes you think that *I* did something wrong?"

This time his little girl made eyes at him as though he'd asked a dumb question. "C'mon, Daddy. You're a boy."

It was on the tip of his tongue to ask what the heck that meant, but Lucius feared she would actually have an answer. "Let's just say it's a little more complicated than that, sweetie."

The toaster popped up their waffles and Lucius quickly placed them on their plates and grabbed a bottle of syrup.

"Daddy, can we go shopping tomorrow?" Ruby asked, cutting into her food. "I want to buy Beverly a Christmas present."

Once again Lucius weighed whether he should go ahead and tell her that Beverly was likely never coming around again, but when he looked into her eager hazel eyes, he just couldn't get himself to say the words. "We'll see, sweetie. We'll see."

Beverly played with her cereal while allowing the house's silence to cloak her. She had long ago lost count of how many times she'd looked at her finger and recalled how that beautiful ring Lucius gave her had sparkled on her hand. Then, like now, tears had rushed to her eyes and her heart ached for something she'd long told herself that she didn't want.

Yet after three days that fear was being replaced by another. The fear of living the rest of her life in this house...alone.

She pushed her bowl away and marched out of her kitchen to go get dressed. As she shuffled up the stairs, a familiar icy cold lifted an army of goose bumps along her arms and caused her hackles to rise. At the top of the stairs, Beverly's gaze immediately went to that closed door at the end of the hallway.

I really should get ready for work, she told herself, but her feet were already carrying her toward the forbidden door. The knob was cold, as usual, but today, she opened the door anyway. From the moment she saw the blue walls, her vision blurred and tears snaked from her eyes.

The room hadn't changed in five years. Her gaze shifted from the Spider-Man sheets on the twin-size bed to the mass of action figures crammed in a clear plastic tub next to the window. That familiar sense of injustice bubbled up inside of her. She walked over to the bed and eased down onto the edge, but it wasn't long before she was blinded by the seemingly endless stream of tears of a mother who'd lost her child.

Chapter 20

With it being Christmas Eve, Lucius planned only to put in a couple of hours at work. There was another major litigation case coming around the bend and he was already worried about how he was going to juggle it all given his new responsibilities at home. "Where there's a will, there's a way," he muttered under his breath.

However, his butt had hardly hit his chair a full minute before Maggie was buzzing in over the speakerphone. "Mr. Gray, I have Mitch Paulson here to see you."

He frowned at the phone and then punched in a few keystrokes on his computer.

"He doesn't have an appointment," she said, answering his unspoken question.

Annoyed but knowing how valuable the boisterous

businessman was to his company, Lucius instructed Maggie to send him on in.

Paulson strolled through the door; his bulky six-six frame shrank the room around him. It was just eight o'clock in the morning and the large cowboy was already puffing on a thick cigar and looking like he was ready for his morning brandy. "I knew that you'd be in the office today," he said, cocking his hand like a gun and firing an invisible shot.

"Just for a couple of hours," Lucius assured him and then gestured to the chair in front of his desk. "Have a seat."

"Don't mind if I do." Paulson chuckled and folded into the chair with a slight grunt.

"Now what can I do you for?" Lucius asked, returning to his own chair.

"Well, I want to sue the government," the Texan announced.

"Again?" Lucius asked with a wry smile.

"Well, they're always pissing me off," he said simply.

Lucius chuckled. "Well, what did the government do this time?"

"I'm suing for their abuse of eminent domain," Paulson huffed.

Braiding his fingers together, he listened patiently to his lawsuit-addicted client. His case this time sounded no more convincing than the legion of others that Kendall, Hendrix and Gray, LLC had worked on for the brash Texan. For the most part, they were willing to kill as many trees as Paulson wanted as long as Paulson was willing to write checks.

"Well, I'll certainly jump right on it," Lucius assured Paulson when he finished his long spiel. He stood and offered the man his hand. "I should have some preliminary paperwork for you to review by next week."

Paulson winked. "I knew I could count on you." He accepted Lucius's handshake. "By the way, whatever happened with you and that hot tamale at the bar a couple of months ago?"

Lucius stiffened as his hand fell away, but he quickly recovered and tried to shrug off the question. "Aww. Well. You know. You win some, you lose some."

"Is that right?" Paulson's thick salt-and-pepper brows crashed together as his gaze seemed to look at Lucius as if he was made of glass. "Hmmm. When I saw you two at Ruth's Chris Steak House a few nights ago, I thought you'd struck a love connection—judging by the way you were looking at her." His statement shaved a few inches off Lucius's plastic smile.

Instead of remaining evasive, Lucius came clean. "I thought so, too."

"She dumped you?"

"I guess you can say that," Lucius answered, despite being uncomfortable by the line of questioning.

"Aww. Damn. That's too bad." Paulson chomped on his cigar. "I was sort of hoping that at least one of us could get a second chance at something a little more meaningful than..." He glanced around the room. "Than the spoils of success. You know my motto—A Career Is Great, But a Woman Is Better."

"I remember you saying something like that."

Paulson continued to read him. "It was the hours—"

"No. No." Lucius shook his head, amazed that he *wanted* to talk about this. "Believe it or not, my job had nothing to do with it. I guess we should have just remained two ships passing in the middle of the night."

"I hear what you're saying but you sound like a man barely held together with tape. Do you love this girl?"

Lucius hesitated. "I thought I did."

Paulson cocked his head and waited a little longer for the truth. "I do. Madly. Deeply."

"Then what the hell are you doing here?"

Lucius dropped back into his chair and exhaled a long, frustrated sigh. "Because our love apparently is a one-way street."

"You sure about that?"

"Pretty sure. I call myself being romantic by sliding an engagement ring on her finger while she was sleeping, thinking I'd wake to smiles and kisses. Instead I woke to an empty bed—except for the ring and a note."

Paulson grimaced. "Ouch."

"That's putting it mildly."

"What'd the note say?"

Lucius shrugged. "Sorry."

"I mean you don't have to tell me if you don't want to."

"No. I mean that's what the note said. 'Sorry.'"

"A woman of few words."

Lucius nodded and then reflected over the events from the past several months. "Maybe I rushed her. I know she still has a few scars left from her first marriage. The whole time, she tried to keep me at arm's length, but I thought I was breaking down her defenses. In fact, I would have staked my life on it."

"Maybe you did." Paulson removed the cigar from his mouth. "What did she say when you talked to her?"

Lucius pulled out of his reverie. "I haven't seen her since."

"You're kidding me, right?"

Lucius looked up. Shrugged.

"I thought you said you loved this girl? You're going to just go down without a fight?"

Frowning, Lucius shifted uncomfortably in his seat. "What do you mean?"

Paulson started laughing. "C'mon. You're a man of the world. Surely you know anything worth having is worth fighting for. You love the woman, you fight for her. Assure her that you're nothing like the creep that broke her heart. You keep at it until you convince her—that or until she issues a restraining order—whichever comes first."

"What are you, Dr. Phil now?"

"He's not the only Texan that knows how to dole out common sense."

Lucius laughed.

"Okay. All jokes aside, son. If you really want her, you're going to have to fight for her."

Hoops was crowded with last-minute Christmas shoppers. Lucius took a deep breath to try to calm his nerves, but there was nothing he could do about the large lump bobbing in the center of his throat. After talking to Paulson, he'd felt like a complete idiot for not realizing what he needed to do sooner. Of course, Beverly was still gun-shy about walking down the aisle again. How many times had he seen that fear up close and personal, especially at Hollington's class reunion?

Looking back, he knew that his proposal was all wrong. He needed to look Beverly in the eye and assure her that he was nothing like David Clark. He needed to address her fears one by one and then make it clear that he was willing to wait for as long as she wanted him.

Instead, he had allowed his pride to prevent him from seeing what was perfectly obvious.

"Excuse me," he repeated to one woman after another as he threaded his way toward the front cash register. Behind the counter there was only one face he recognized. "Um, Leslie, right?"

The young lady's eyes rounded wide with surprise. "Lucius...I mean, Mr. Gray. You finally came."

He frowned. "Were you expecting me?"

"Sort of." She quickly scooped a cell phone out her pants pocket.

Lucius frowned. "Um, is Beverly here?"

Leslie held up a slender finger and punched in a few numbers. "Clarence, he's here." Pause. "Okay." She disconnected the call. "He's on his way over."

"Clarence?" Why on earth would she think he wanted to speak to him? "Is Beverly here?" he asked again.

"No. Sorry. She never made it in this morning."

He frowned, wondering whether there was a problem. He turned to leave, but was surprised when he ran smack into Clarence. *How in the hell did he get here so fast?*

"Good. I caught you," Clarence said, panting. "It certainly took you long enough to show up."

"Is there a problem?"

"The only problem I see is that my best friend is trying to throw away her best chance for happiness." He folded his arms. "You do intend to try and make her happy, don't you?"

"If she'll let me."

Clarence eyeballed him a little longer and then finally said, "Come with me."

Lucius frowned, but followed the strutting man to the back of the store. At the small employee break table, Clarence told him to take a seat. Curious, he did what he was told and then waited.

"Beverly is at home," Clarence started.

Lucius jumped to his feet.

"But before you go flying over there I think I need to arm you with a little information."

Now Clarence had his undivided attention. He sat back down and leaned back in the small metal chair and crossed his arms. "I'm listening."

It rarely snowed in Atlanta and to have that rare phenomenon occur on Christmas Eve had to be something like a billion-to-one odds. Still, it gave Lucius the feeling that he was driving through a magical snow globe. When he pulled into the driveway leading toward Beverly's house, he was once again hit by how lonely and sad the house appeared—and now he knew why.

He parked the car and climbed out of the vehicle. For a few seconds he stood outside, just staring at the house. The cold and sadness permeated his bones and chilled his soul. Finally, he strolled up to the door, rang the doorbell and waited. Around him, the snow thickened, transforming the place to look like a whimsical painting.

After a few minutes, it was clear that Beverly wasn't coming to the door. He turned toward a large potted plant, tilted it over and retrieved the key that Clarence told him Beverly kept there for emergencies.

Lucius slipped the key into the lock and then slowly entered the house. "Beverly?" he called out, closing the door behind him.

The house roared with silence. He started to check downstairs, but something told him that she was more likely to be upstairs. "Beverly, sweetheart?" he called again as he ascended.

It wasn't until he reached the top stair that he heard the soft whimpers. His eyes immediately zoomed to the cracked door at the end of the hallway. On autopilot, he moved toward the heart-wrenching sobs, trying to prepare himself for what he might find on the other side. Placing his hand on the door, he gently pushed it open farther.

Beverly sat hunched over on the small twin-size bed, holding a large picture frame and rocking back and forth. It took a second, but she stopped and slowly lifted her tear-filled eyes. "It's not that I don't love you," she said in a quivering voice as if they were picking up on an unfinished conversation. "I do. Lord knows I do, despite my trying to fight it. But…"

Lucius walked over to the bed while she struggled to collect herself. He knelt down in front of her and reached for the picture she held in her arms. "May I see him?"

Beverly released the frame and then watched Lucius's face when he looked down at Gregory William Clark.

"He was a handsome boy. How old was he in this picture?"

"Five," she said with a nostalgic smile. "It was taken maybe three months before he was diagnosed with cancer. He had acute lymphoblastic leukemia. We spent a full year fighting that disease and then…it was just over. His little body couldn't take it." She feverishly wiped at her tears. "At first, I was so glad that he no longer had to endure all of that pain and suffering. But then I started missing all those smiles and hugs that he was always trying to give out."

Lucius stared at the handsome boy that looked more like his mother than his father and his heart broke for what the world had lost.

"For a year, I lived in Egleston Children's Hospital, reading him stories, mopping his fevered brow. David…" Beverly sniffed and then shook her head. "Let's just say our marriage was on life support after Gregory passed away. David seemed to think I could just snap my fingers and be over it—apparently, it worked for him." She shrugged. "Two years later he had an affair and then we got a divorce." She sighed. "It was all a pathetic tragedy—one I vowed that I would never repeat."

Lucius looked up and met her steady gaze.

Beverly continued. "I did everything—medication, therapy. The only thing that worked was when I convinced myself to build a wall around my heart and just bury myself in my work." She smiled tenderly as she reached out and stroked his face. "And then you came along…and then your beautiful daughter. Suddenly I was part of a family again…and I loved it."

Lucius grabbed hold of her hand and kissed it. "Ruby and I both love having you as a part of our lives," he said. "And we want you back."

"I'm sorry I ran out on you. I know I promised never to do that again, but…" She broke eye contact to glance around the room. "I should have told you about Gregory sooner."

"You needed more time," he said, understanding.

"A little," she agreed. "But now I know it's way past

time for me to let go—time for me to sell this place and move on." Beverly's gaze found his again. She searched through the windows of his soul and saw nothing but love.

"I'm not David," he said. "I'll never let you go through anything by yourself. I promise to love and support you through thick and thin. I give you my word."

She leaned forward and brushed a feathery light kiss against his lips. Suddenly, in this gloomy room, hope had penetrated. "I know you will. And I promise you that I'll love and support you through thick and thin, too. And I promise I'll be a good stepmother to your little girl."

Lucius's smile widened before he leaned closer for a stronger, deeper kiss. "I love you."

"I love you, too."

Reaching into his pocket, Lucius pulled out the burgundy velvet box and popped open the lid. To his surprise his hand trembled as he removed the platinum ring nestled in the center. "Beverly Turner, will you do me the great honor of becoming my wife?"

"Yes." She bobbed her head while tears streamed down her face. She watched as Lucius slid the engagement ring back onto her finger—where it belonged.

Smiling, he swept Beverly up into his arms and carried her out of her son's old room. "Where's your bedroom?"

"Down the hall, last door on your right," she whispered.

As he walked, their gazes remained locked, and without words their eyes said so much. In her bedroom, Lucius laid her gently onto the bed and kissed her so tenderly that a new wave of tears crested and slid from the corners of her eyes. From his lips she tasted true love. What few doubts she had about walking down the aisle again melted away. In her head, she could already see what their forever entailed: their businesses growing, their family expanding and their love never-ending.

Lucius took his time peeling away her clothes. His eyes, as well as his touch, made love to her in ways that were just mind-blowing. When their bodies joined, Beverly realized that everything that she'd ever gone through, good and bad, was meant to lead her to this perfect moment.

As their bodies moved in time to a rhythm only their hearts could hear, Beverly made sure that she reciprocated all that she was feeling. After her orgasm hit and left her panting, she had a hard time discerning exactly where her body ended and where his began. Then again, it didn't matter. From this day on, they would live and breathe as one.

Watching as love and pleasure ebbed and flowed across Beverly's beautiful face, Lucius felt his heart swell. He looked forward to making love to this woman for the rest of his life. As sure as he breathed, he knew that there was nothing he wouldn't do to keep Beverly at his side—forever and always.

Ruby woke up Christmas morning to what she declared was the best Christmas surprise ever: Beverly sitting next to the large Christmas tree in the living room. "Beverly, you're back!" Ruby actually bypassed the large, pretty decorative boxes and launched herself into Beverly's arms, overwhelming her with hugs and kisses.

"Of course I'm back. I couldn't stay away from my favorite girl for long."

Lucius entered the room, carrying a tray of hot chocolate and beaming at his two favorite girls. Just then Ruby noticed the sparkling diamond on Beverly's hand. "You're wearing Daddy's ring!" Her head jerked from Beverly to her father. "Does that mean she's going to marry us, Daddy?"

Lucius set the tray down on the coffee table, folded one arm across his chest while his free hand stroked his chin as he contemplated the question. "Hmmm. That's a very good question." His sparkling gaze at long last settled on his daughter. "Why don't you ask her?"

Ruby was only too happy to comply. "Beverly, are you going to marry us?"

Beverly laughed as tears rose and skipped over her lashes. "I most certainly am."

"Yay!" Ruby's arms flew back around Beverly's neck, almost choking her.

"All right. All right," Lucius said, coming to Beverly's rescue when he saw how her eyes bugged out. "Time to dig into these Christmas gifts."

As if finally remembering what day it was, Ruby released her death grip and sprang out of Beverly's lap to jet over to the tree. For the next three hours Beverly and Lucius sat curled up on the sofa, watching Ruby tear through the boxes like a Tasmanian devil, squealing at every large *and* small gift.

The whole scene felt like a special Christmas fairy tale to Beverly, but she only had to look to the man sitting beside her to know that it was all so very real. It was hard to believe that just a couple of months ago she didn't know this wonderful man, and now she couldn't imagine a life without him. Who would have ever thought that a simple college reunion would have changed her life? And she wasn't the only one. Chloe and Kevin, Tamara and Micah, and even Kyra and Terrence had all found or rediscovered love.

Lucius looked up from the beautiful watch she'd given him, then narrowed his gaze in suspicion. "What are you thinking so hard about?"

"Hollington," Beverly answered. "I think this year we owe them a *big* donation."

He leaned over and kissed her. "I couldn't agree with you more."

Epilogue

Six months later

There's a reason June is the perfect time for weddings in Georgia. And on this midsummer evening the sun was setting, the air was moist and a light breeze carried the wonderful sweet scent of magnolias. With everything being so perfect, Beverly was sure that at any moment someone was going to wake her up and tell her that the past eight months had been nothing but a dream. Yet after giving herself several pinches on the arm, she finally accepted that this day was very much real.

Her three smiling bridesmaids—Chloe, Tamara and Kyra—had gushed over her first handmade white-and-silver beaded wedding dress and even managed to fill her head with ideas of perhaps starting her own wedding-gown line. Beverly appreciated the praise, but knew her friends were working overtime in trying to soothe her nervousness about taking her second trip down the aisle.

It was a big step…and one that she was wholeheart-edly committed to making.

Her nervousness didn't stem from any questions of her love for Lucius. Far from it. In fact, she didn't even think it was possible to love him any more than she did right now. He was her knight in shining armor who had most assuredly rescued her from a future of bitter lone-liness. And he had confessed that she had rescued him from the same fate. Nowadays, most of their friends and family had teased them about not being able to keep their hands off each other or how effortlessly they fin-ished each other's thoughts and sentences.

Her nervous jitters came solely from her fierce de-sire to be the best wife and mother Lucius wanted and needed her to be.

"Stop worrying," Beverly's mother whispered in her ear, mere minutes before she needed to rush out to her seat. "You picked a winner this time."

Beverly's cherry-red smile stretched across her face. It absolutely warmed her heart that this time around, her parents approved of her choice for a husband. And of course they simply adored Ruby, but who didn't? Ruby, with her warm smile and infectious laughter had taken to Beverly becoming her stepmother like a fish to water.

But Ruby had her melancholy days—especially when Erica reappeared shortly after New Year's with a change of heart, wanting Ruby back. Lucius's patience with his ex had finally snapped. He'd had enough of the games and had hauled Erica's butt into court for full custody. Enough was enough. As a result, Ruby had her good days and her bad days, but Beverly and Lucius worked overtime to make sure Ruby knew without a doubt that she was wanted and very much loved.

When the wedding planner signaled for everyone to take their places, Beverly's heart kicked up a couple of notches.

"You look faint," Clarence said, alarmed. "I'm going to get you some water." Without waiting for a response, he raced out of the room while Chloe, Tamara and Kyra aided her in taking a seat.

Chloe grabbed a leaflet from a nearby nightstand and began fanning it profusely in Beverly's face. "Honey, are you sure you're all right?"

The cool breeze was just what Beverly needed. "Yes. Yes. I'll be fine."

Tamara's perceptive gaze narrowed into a squint. "I hope I'm not being too nosy, but…are you pregnant?"

Beverly blushed.

Her bridesmaids gasped, then squealed with delight.

"I can't believe you didn't tell me!" Kyra admonished with a dramatic stomp of her foot, but in the next second swept her friend into her arms while still being careful not to muss her up too much.

"When did you find out?" Chloe asked, her own pregnancy clearly evident. No one doubted that Chloe and Kevin were extremely happy. The three-month newlyweds couldn't keep their hands off each other either. And there was no wonder. Chloe's pregnancy had transformed her from a subtle beauty to a dynamic one. Everyone noticed her now whenever she walked into a room. Her black hair shone, her flawless skin glowed. It was a wonder to all who knew her now how she could ever have been a silent wallflower.

Tamara had had a similar transformation. Still a new-lywed herself, her body had gone through a few minor changes, too. Bigger breasts equaled a happier husband. That is, whenever Micah junior felt like sharing. So far, Tamara and her husband split their time between Los Angeles and Atlanta, but it was looking more and more as if the small family would settle down out west.

Beverly continued to blush like a prepubescent teen-ager as she finally answered Chloe's question. "Three days ago."

There was more gasping and squealing.

"Does Lucius know?" Chloe asked, wide-eyed.

"No." Beverly shook her head. "I'm planning to make the announcement at the reception."

"Oh, my God." Tamara clasped Beverly's hand. "He's going to be thrilled!"

"I know." Beverly bubbled.

"Who's going to be thrilled about what?" Clarence asked, returning to the bridal suite with a pitcher of ice water.

Chloe opened her mouth to fill Clarence in on Bev-erly's surprise, but Beverly quickly grabbed her friend by the wrist to catch her attention, then silently shook her head.

"What's this?" Clarence set the pitcher down on a table and folded his arms. "Why do I smell a secret in the air?"

"No offense, Clarence," Beverly said, flashing him a kind smile. "But if we tell you, then it won't be a se-cret anymore."

Clarence gasped and spread a hand across his heart. "What? Girl, you know I can keep a secret. Okay...so I've dropped dime on a few things from time to time."

He shrugged. "But I promise—whatever it is, I'll keep my mouth shut."

Beverly shook her head. "Sorry."

Clarence poked out his bottom lip and hit her with his huge puppy-dog eyes.

"Not going to work."

The wedding planner slipped her head back into the suite. "What are you all still doing in here? Places! We're on in *two* minutes."

The bridal party scrambled.

Clarence sputtered after Beverly, "But—but—"

Lucius waited at the outdoor altar next to the preacher, with his heart lodged in the middle of his throat. A few more guests hurried to their seats. Lucius smiled, then his attention shifted when the music started. Ruby, the flower girl in an adorable white-and-silver dress, strolled down the aisle next to her four-year-old cousin Alan, the official ring bearer.

Halfway down the aisle Alan decided he wanted to go and sit next to his parents and had to be coaxed back to finish his walk to Lucius's side. The whole episode was adorable and had the guests laughing. However, minutes later the bridesmaids walked arm in arm with the groomsmen—who in this case were their new husbands.

Mr. and Mrs. Kevin and Chloe Stayton.

Mr. and Mrs. Micah and Tamara Ross.

Mr. and Mrs. Terrence and Kyra Franklin.

And then Clarence, the man of honor, and the best man, Mitch Paulson, made their way down the aisle—an unlikely duo, to say the least. But the broad-shouldered Texan seemed to take it all in stride. Clarence worked the aisle like a mini two-step fashion runway. But he reeled it in at the last moment and took his place next to the bridesmaids.

At last the music changed. Lucius straightened his back as the moment he'd been waiting for finally arrived. Beverly made her grand entrance while hooked on the arm of her father.

She was a stunning vision and completely stole his breath away. Lucius was overwhelmed by his love toward his approaching bride—a love so strong that it both frightened and awed him at the same time. When she stopped before him and smiled, it felt as if his heart was literally melting and pooling at her feet.

Together they turned toward the preacher. Lucius could barely pay attention to what was being said once Beverly stopped beside him. All that kept flooding through his mind were all the possibilities that their future held. When it came time for the wedding vows, Ruby moved to stand next to him and together they recited the words they had written together. Perfect pearl-shaped tears glided down Beverly's beautiful face as she said her own memorized vows to Lucius. At long last, their love was proclaimed and sealed with a kiss.

"Ladies and gentlemen," the preacher said. "May I present to you Mr. and Mrs. Lucius and Beverly Gray."

Their guests cheered as they tossed out a mixed shower of rose petals and confetti at the beautiful couple. Minutes later, everyone milled over to the reception hall. Beverly and Lucius kept their hands and lips locked together for most of the time. After the speeches from the man of honor and the best man, Beverly knew that it was time to make her big announcement. A vat of butterflies filled her belly as she took the microphone from Clarence and stood from the table.

"I have an announcement I'd like to make."

Curious, Lucius looked up and watched his nervous wife. *Wife.* He loved the sound of that.

Beverly took a deep breath. "First I'd like to say that Lucius and I are very grateful that all of you could come today and be a part of this beautiful wedding." She smiled broadly, then took another breath.

Sensing that she needed a little encouragement, Lucius reached for her hand again and squeezed.

Beverly's smile grew brighter as she turned toward him and met his loving gaze with her own. "What I have to announce will even be news to my adoring husband."

Lucius's brows rose in surprise.

"Honey," Beverly began, while her eyes misted, "we're pregnant."

Lucius's jaw dropped while the wedding party once again cheered enthusiastically. In the next second Lucius jumped to his feet and swept Beverly into his arms. "Oh, my God, baby. Are you sure? This in incredible."

Beverly bobbed her head as tears streamed from her eyes.

Moments later Clarence announced that it was time for the couple's first dance. Lucius offered his wife his arm, then led her to the floor, just as Lauryn Hill's "Sweetest Thing" began to play. Beverly and Lucius smiled into each other's eyes. They were the happiest people on earth.

The wedding party remained an adoring, captive audience throughout the dance and when the song ended the crowd rewarded them with applause. Clarence stood with the microphone while wiping tears from his eyes.

"Y'all just don't know what my girl Leslie and I went through to get these two together."

Leslie waved from one of the tables.

"Now," Clarence continued, "we want to invite the following newlyweds to join our loving couple on the dance floor. Chloe and Kevin Stayton, Tamara and Micah Ross and Kyra and Terrence Franklin."

The crowd applauded again while Clarence continued, "For those who don't know, all four couples you see on the floor now, met or reunited at their college reunion last year."

Another round of applause.

"So let that be a lesson for you all to show up when you get those pesky invitations in the mail."

The crowd laughed.

"For the next song we invited R & B sensation Justice Kane to transport you all back to that fateful reunion weekend," Clarence boasted. "Enjoy."

Justice Kane took the microphone and launched into his hit song "Tender to His Touch."

Lucius's arm tightened around Beverly. "In case I haven't told you today, I love you, Mrs. Gray."

"And I love you, Mr. Gray. Forever and ever."

He leaned in for a long, tender kiss. "I'm going to hold you to that, my love."

Her smile ballooned. "That's what I was hoping for, my love."

Lucius's smile matched her own. "Say that again."

"My love," she whispered and delivered another kiss. "My love. My love. My love."

* * * * *

SPECIAL EXCERPT FROM

HARLEQUIN®

Desire

A sneak peek at

STERN, *a Westmoreland novel*

by New York Times *and* USA TODAY *bestselling author*

Brenda Jackson

Available September 2013.
Only from Harlequin® Desire!

As far as Stern was concerned, his best friend had lost her ever-loving mind. But he didn't say that. Instead, he asked, "What's his name?"

"You don't need to know that. Do you tell me the name of every woman you want?"

"This is different."

"Really? In what way?"

He wasn't sure, but he just knew that it was. "For you to even ask me, that means you're not ready for the kind of relationship you're going after."

JoJo threw her head back and laughed. "Stern, I'll be thirty next year. I'm beginning to think that most of the men in town wonder if I'm really a girl."

He studied her. There had never been any doubt in his mind that she was a girl. She had long lashes and eyes so dark they were the color of midnight. She had gorgeous legs, long and endless. But he knew he was one of the few men who'd ever seen them.

"You hide what a nice body you have," he finally said. He suddenly sat up straight in the rocker. "I have an idea.

What you need is a makeover."

"A makeover?"

"Yes, and then you need to go where your guy hangs out. In a dress that shows your legs, in a style that shows off your hair." He reached over and took the cap off her head. Lustrous dark brown hair tumbled to her shoulders. He smiled. "See, I like it already."

And he did. He was tempted to run his hands through it to feel the silky texture.

He leaned back and took another sip of his beer, wondering where such a tempting thought had come from. This was JoJo, for heaven's sake. His best friend. He should not be thinking about how silky her hair was.

He should not be bothered by the thought of men checking out JoJo, of men calling her for a date.

Suddenly, he was thinking that maybe a makeover wasn't such a great idea after all.

Will Stern help JoJo win her dream man?

STERN

by New York Times *and* USA TODAY
bestselling author Brenda Jackson

*Available September 2013
Only from Harlequin® Desire!*

REQUEST YOUR FREE BOOKS!

2 FREE NOVELS
PLUS 2 FREE GIFTS!

KIMANI™
ROMANCE

Love's ultimate destination!

KROM13R

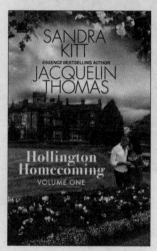